KELLY ORAM

BLUEFIELDS

Published by Bluefields Creative

Copyright © 2014

Edition 3.0, 2016

Edited by Jennifer Henkes (www.literallyjen.com)

ISBN 978-0-9914579-5-3

Also by Kelly Oram

Serial Hottie

Joni, Underway

If We Were a Movie

Sixteen Kisses

The Jamie Baker Series:

Being Jamie Baker

More Than Jamie Baker

Remember Jamie Baker

The Science Squad Series:

The Avery Shaw Experiment

The Libby Garrett Intervention

The V is for Virgin Series:

V is for Virgin

A is for Abstinence

The Supernaturals Series:

Chameleon

Ungifted

Scion

For my daughter, Jackie.
Because every girl deserves her own fairy tale.

Prologue

THE PROBLEM WITH FAIRY TALES IS THAT MOST OF THEM BEGIN with tragedy. I understand the reasoning behind it. No one likes a pampered heroine. A great character needs trials to overcome—experiences to give them depth, to make them vulnerable, relatable, and likable. Good characters need hardships to make them strong. The idea makes sense, but it still sucks if you're the heroine.

My life had never been much like a fairy tale. I'd had no magical wishes come true, but no real tragedy, either. My dad had an affair and left Mama and me when I was eight, but other than that, I'd had it pretty good.

I'm sort of pretty—long, wavy black hair and smooth golden-brown skin, thanks to the Chilean heritage on my mother's side. But I have my dad's big, bright-blue eyes. I'm sort of smart—mostly A's without ever having to study much. And I'm sort of popular—not exactly the prom queen, but never without my friends or a date on Saturday night, either.

I may have grown up without a father, but my mom was my best friend and that was good enough for me. Life, in general, was good enough. Then, last November my mom decided to surprise me with a weekend ski trip to Vermont for my birthday, and I got my first real dose of character-building tragedy.

"I booked us the full spa package so we can thaw in the Jacuzzi and get massages when we're sore from skiing all day," Mama confessed as we left the city of Boston behind us for the next four days.

"Wow, Mama! Not that I'm not grateful, but can we afford that?"

Mama laughed at me. I loved the sound of her laugh. It was a light, fluttery sound that made me feel as if I could float away on it. She always laughed. She was the most exuberant person I'd ever known. For her, life just couldn't be any better.

"Listen to you, Ella. You're turning eighteen, not forty."

I grinned. "Like you are next month?"

"*Cállate!* That is our secret. If anyone asks, I will be thirty-nine for the rest of my life."

"Sure, you will. Wait…are those…*crow's-feet?*"

"Ellamara Valentina Rodriguez!" my mother gasped. "These are *smile lines*, and I am extremely proud of them." She looked at me, and her bright eyes crinkled into *smile lines* around the edges. "With you as a daughter, I have had to work very hard to get these instead of gray hair."

Snorting, I picked up my phone, which was dinging instant messages at me.

"You be nice to your mama, or I will embarrass you horribly in front of all the cute boys this weekend."

I'd had a witty retort ready, but forgot it when I saw the message on my phone.

Cinder458: Your blogaversary is coming up, right?

Cinder458, or just Cinder to me, is my best friend in the whole world besides my mom, even though I've never met him. I've never even spoken to him on the phone. We've been e-mailing nonstop since he stumbled across my blog, *Ellamara's Words Of Wisdom*, about two years ago.

My blog is a book and movie review blog. I started it when I was fifteen, and my third blogaversary was indeed coming up soon.

The name *Ellamara* is in honor of my favorite character in my favorite book series, *The Cinder Chronicles*. It's a fantasy series written in the seventies and has become one of the most cherished stories in modern literature. Hollywood is *finally* making the first book, *The Druid Prince*, into a movie.

Ellamara is also my name. My mother read the books when she was a girl and loved them so much that she named me after the mysterious druid priestess. I was proud of the name, and of my mom for loving Ellamara best instead of liking the warrior princess Ratana like everyone else. Ellamara was a much better character.

Cinder is obviously a fan of the series, too. It was the name Ellamara, and my post on why she was the most underappreciated character in the book, that drew Cinder to my blog in the first place. He loves the books as much as I do, so I liked him instantly—even if he was writing to argue that Princess Ratana was better suited for Prince Cinder. He's disagreed with most of my reviews ever since.

EllaTheRealHero: Do all those Hollywood friends of yours know you use words like blogaversary?
Cinder458: Of course not. I need your address. Got you a blogaversary present.

Cinder got me a gift?

My heart flipped.

Not that I was in love with my Internet best friend or anything. That would be utterly ridiculous. The boy was cocky and stubborn and argued with everything I said just to be infuriating. He also had lots of money, dated models—which meant he had to be hot—and was a closet book nerd.

Funny, rich, hot, confident, book lover. Definitely *not* my type. Nope. Not at all.

Yeah, okay, fine, so he wasn't my type by default because he lived in California and I live in Massachusetts. Whatever.

Cinder458: Hello? Ella?? Address??
EllaTheRealHero: I don't give out my address to creepy Internet stalkers.
Cinder458: I guess you don't want this autographed first-edition hardback of *The Druid Prince*, then. Shame. I had it signed it to Ellamara when I met L.P. Morgan at FantasyCon last week, so I can't try to impress any other girls with it.

I didn't realize I was squealing until the car swerved.

"*Por el amor de todo lo sagrado, Ellamara!* Do not scare your poor mama like that. We're in the middle of a snowstorm. The roads are dangerous enough without you screaming like a banshee."

"Sorry, Mama. But Cinder said—"

"*Híjole muñeca*, not that boy again." I recognized the tired voice. I was about to get one of my mom's favorite lectures. "You do realize he is a complete stranger, right?"

I shook my head. "He's not. I know him better than I know anyone."

"You've never met him in person. For all you know, everything that he says could be lies."

I'll be the first to admit I'd wondered that before because Cinder's life sounded a bit like a rockstar's, but I'd known him long enough now that I believed he wasn't a liar. "I really don't think so, Mama. It's possible he embellishes a little, but who doesn't?

And what does it matter? He's just an Internet friend. He lives in California."

"Exactly. So why do you waste so much time with him?"

"Because I like him. I can talk to him. He's my best friend."

Mama sighed again, but she smiled at me and her voice softened. "I just worry that you'll fall for him, *muñeca*, and then what?"

That was a good question. Which was exactly why Cinder was *not* my type.

Not my type.

Not. My. Type.

Cinder458: Address. Noun. The location at which a particular organization or person may be found or reached. (Or mailed amazing presents.)

EllaTheRealHero: Did your car tell you that?

Cinder drives a Ferrari 458. He told me that once when I asked what the numbers in his screen name meant. I looked the car up. It costs more than my mom makes in five years. I like to give him a hard time about his overindulgent ways. And yes, the car actually does talk to him.

Cinder458: Not driving, so my phone did. Address, woman. Now! Or I won't tell you who signed on to play Cinder in the movie.

I almost shrieked again. The movie was green lighted, but the cast hadn't been announced. Cinder's dad is some big shot in the movie industry, so Cinder always knows stuff beforehand.

EllaTheRealHero: No way! Tell me! I'm dying!!!

I never got to find out which actor was going to immortalize one of the most beloved characters of all time because a logging truck hit a patch of black ice and slid across the two-lane highway straight into Mama and me. I'd been looking down at my phone when it happened and never saw it coming. I just remember hearing my mother's scream and being thrown against my seat belt as an air bag exploded in my face. There was a quick moment of pain so intense it literally took my breath away, and then there was nothing else.

I woke up three weeks later in a burn center in Boston when the doctors brought me out of a medically-induced coma. I had second and third-degree burns covering seventy percent of my body.

My mother was dead.

 1

I can't remember many specific details of the accident, but the fear I felt that day is still crystal clear in my memory. I have nightmares all the time. They're always the same—a few blurry images and a mesh of chaotic sounds, but I'm paralyzed with terror so strong I can't breathe until I wake up screaming. The dread itself is the main focus of the dream.

If the sun weren't blaring so rudely into my face, and my body didn't ache from the five-and-a-half hour flight from Boston, I'd have thought I was back in my dream. I was *that* terrified as I sat in the driveway looking at what was to be my new home.

So far, I'd only seen the view from the car between the airport and my father's house up in the winding hills above Los Angeles. It was enough to know that LA was nothing like Boston—despite what the traffic on the freeway would have me believe.

I wished it were only the change of scenery that I was scared of. I spent eight weeks in intensive care and was then in a rehab center for another six months. Eight months of hospitalization total, and now I was being released into the care of the man who'd walked out of my life ten years ago—him and the woman he'd left me for, along with the two daughters he'd replaced me with.

"I should warn you that Jennifer has probably cooked up some sort of welcome home surprise."

"Not a party?" I gasped, my terror exploding into something that might finally kill me. I never thought I'd live through a hell most people couldn't even imagine, only to be offed on my first day out of the hospital by a group of random strangers wanting to welcome me home.

"No, of course not," my father assured me. "It's nothing like that. Your new rehabilitation team stopped by last week and prepped the whole family. Jennifer knows meeting a lot of new people will be too overwhelming at first. I'm sure it will be just her and the girls, but there's probably a nice dinner waiting for you along with welcoming gifts, and possibly decorations. She's very excited to meet you."

I couldn't say the same.

When I didn't respond, my dad glanced at me with that look of helplessness he'd been watching me with since I came out of my coma and found him sitting beside my hospital bed. It's a look that is seventy percent pity, twenty percent fear, and ten percent awkwardness. It's as if he has no clue what to say or how to act with me—probably because he hasn't seen or talked to me since I was eight.

He cleared his throat and said, "You ready, kiddo?"

I would never be ready.

"Please don't call me that," I whispered, working hard to speak around the lump suddenly clogging up my throat.

He blew out a long puff of air and tried to smile. "Too old for that now?"

"Something like that."

In truth, I hated the nickname because it reminded me of Mama. She always called me her little *muñeca*, or baby doll. When I was about six, Dad started calling me *kiddo*. He said it was because I needed an American nickname too, but I think it was because he'd been jealous of the relationship I had with Mama even back then.

"Sorry," Dad said.

"It's fine."

I opened the car door before the awkwardness choked us to death. Dad came around the car to help me get out, but I brushed him off. "I'm supposed to do it."

"Right, sorry. Here."

As I moved my legs out one at a time, he handed me my cane and waited as I slowly pulled myself to a stand.

It took effort, and it wasn't pretty, but I could finally walk on my own again. I was proud of that. The doctors hadn't always thought it would be possible, but I pushed through the pain and regained a lot of my range of movement. The scars were bad enough. I didn't want to be confined to a wheelchair for the rest of my life, too.

I was glad for the slow walk up the driveway. It gave me the time I needed to brace myself for what waited inside.

Dad waved a hand at the house in front of us. "I know it doesn't look like much from the front but it's bigger than it appears, and the view from the back is spectacular."

Didn't look like much? What did he expect me to think of the two-story postmodern multi-million dollar house in front of me? He'd seen the small two-bedroom apartment Mama and I lived in back in Boston. He'd been the one to clear it out after Mama's funeral.

Not knowing what to say, I just shrugged.

"We had your room set up on the ground floor so that you won't have to use the stairs except to get to the main family room, which is only down a short flight of steps. You also have your own bathroom and we've had it converted so that it's now handicap accessible. Everything should be all ready for you, but if it proves that the house doesn't work, Jennifer and I have already talked about finding something new, maybe down the hill in Bel-Air where we can get a nice ranch-style."

I closed my eyes and took a deep breath in an attempt to not glare or say something rude. He spoke as if I would be here forever, but I was so gone as soon as I was allowed.

I had a moment of weakness during a low point in my rehabilitation, and I tried to take my own life. I'd been in the hospital for three months at the time, with no end in sight. I could still hardly move, I'd just had my seventeenth surgery, I was told I'd never walk again, I missed my mother, and I was in so much physical pain that I just wanted it all to end.

Nobody blamed me for my actions, but now nobody believed that I wasn't a threat to myself anymore. I planned to stay in Boston, finish the school I'd missed online, and then go to Boston University when I was ready. I was eighteen and had the money saved, but when my father realized what I was planning, he had me legally declared mentally incompetent and forced me to come to California with him.

It wasn't easy for me to be civil with the man. "I'm sure the house is fine," I grumbled. "Can we please just get this over with so I can go to bed? I'm exhausted and I really hurt after traveling all day."

I felt bad for being short with him when I saw disappointment flash in his eyes. I think he'd been hoping to impress me, but he didn't understand that I'd never had a lot of money, and I'd never needed it. I was content with the humble lifestyle I had with Mama. I never even used the checks he sent every month. Mama had been putting them in a bank account for years. I had enough in there to pay for college—another reason I would have been fine on my own.

"Sure, honey—" He paused and winced. "Sorry. I suppose that name is off the approved nicknames list, too, huh?"

I grimaced. "How about we just stick with Ella?"

Inside, the house was as immaculate as the burn center. It probably had alarms that went off if a speck of dust landed anywhere. My rehab team would be thrilled. The place was posh and the furniture all looked highly uncomfortable. There was no way this house would ever feel like home.

The new Mrs. Coleman stood in an enormous kitchen,

setting a silver platter of fruit and dip on a granite countertop when we came around the corner. I think the tray might have been actual silver. When she noticed us, her entire face lit up into the hugest, brightest smile I'd ever seen on anyone. "Ellamara! Welcome to our home, sweetie!"

Jennifer Coleman had to be the most beautiful woman in all of Los Angeles. Hair as golden as the sun, eyes as blue as the sky, and lashes that reached all the way to the moon. Her legs were long, her waist was tiny, and her giant boobs were perfectly round and perky. *Bombshell* was the only word that came to mind.

I don't know why I found her beauty surprising. I knew she was a professional model—print and commercials, not fashion. She did things like shampoo and skin cream commercials, so she actually looked healthy and not skinnier than a crack addict.

Judging from the size of her house, she must have done pretty well for herself because my dad may have been a big shot lawyer, but U.S. attorneys didn't have outrageous salaries. Back when he lived with us, we had a moderate house in the suburbs, but we certainly weren't driving a Mercedes and living up on a hill in a house with its own gate.

Jennifer stepped forward and gave me a careful hug, kissing the air next to my cheek. "We're so excited that we finally get to have you here with us. Rich has been telling us so much about you for so long I feel like you're already part of the family. It must be a relief to be in a real home again."

Actually, leaving the rehab center was one of the scariest things I'd ever had to do, and being here was the opposite of relief. But, of course I didn't say that. I tried to think of something that was true and not too insulting. "It's a relief to be off the plane."

Jennifer's smile turned sympathetic. "You must be so tired, you poor thing."

I swallowed back annoyance and forced a smile. I hated people's pity as much as I hated their stares, if not more. Before I had to figure out something to say, my two new stepsisters came bursting through the front door.

"Girls, you're late." Jennifer sounded irritated, but she'd plastered that big, phony smile back on her face. "Look who's home!"

The two sisters slammed into each other as they came to an abrupt halt. They were twins. Not identical, I didn't think, but they looked so similar that if not for the haircuts, I bet I'd still mix them up. I knew from pictures Dad had showed me that Juliette was the one with long blonde locks that fell in silky waves halfway down her back, while Anastasia had a sleek, angled bob that swept across her face and came to a sharp stop at her chin. It was so perfectly coiffed that she looked as if she'd stepped straight out of a hairstyle magazine.

Both girls were as gorgeous as their mother—same blonde hair, blue eyes, and perfect figures. And they were both so tall! I'm a modest five foot six, and they both towered over me. Of course, they were both wearing heels that gave them at least four extra inches, but I bet they were still both pushing five-ten without the shoes. They were over a year younger than me, but could easily pass for twenty-one.

Not bothering with any kind of hello, Anastasia lifted a hand to her chest. "Oh man, I'm so glad your face isn't messed up."

Juliette nodded, eyes wide. "Totally. We looked up pictures online of burn victims, and, like, *all* of them had these hideous scars on their faces. It was so gross."

My dad and Jennifer let out matching nervous laughs and went to stand by the twins. "Girls," Jennifer admonished mildly, "it's not polite to talk about people's deformities."

I flinched at the term. Was that what she thought of me? That I was *deformed*? My face may have been lucky, but my shoulder down the right half of my body and everything from my waist down was covered with thick, raised pink scars that popped in contrast to my naturally-tanned skin.

My dad pulled both girls close to his sides, tucking one into each arm. In their heels they stood at almost the same height as his six feet one inches. I remembered him being a decent-looking man, but he was really quite handsome standing next to his picture-perfect family. He still had a full head of thick brown hair, and, of course, my bright blue eyes. "Honey, these are my daughters, Anastasia and Juliette. Girls, this is your new stepsister, Ellamara."

He grinned proudly, flashing his perfect lawyer smile as he squeezed both girls. The creases around his eyes hurt my heart. Smile lines. He'd obviously spent his life laughing a lot. I also noticed the fact that he'd called the twins his daughters. Not stepdaughters.

Ignoring my desire to curl up into a ball and cry, I lifted a hand out in greeting. "It's just Ella. Ella Rodriguez."

Neither girl took my hand. "Rodriguez?" Juliette scoffed. "Shouldn't it be Coleman?"

Letting my hand fall back to my side, I shrugged. "I changed it to my mother's maiden name when I was twelve."

"Why?"

"Because I *am* a Rodriguez."

Both my stepsisters looked as though I'd somehow offended them. I had to clench my jaw to keep from spouting obscenities at them in Spanish. My glare slid to my father. "Where's my bag? I need to take my medicine, and then I need to rest. My legs feel swollen."

Jennifer argued with her girls in heated whispers as my dad led me across the main floor of the house to my room. I didn't care that they were fighting about me. I was just glad to have the introductions over. Hopefully now I could avoid them as much as possible.

I sat down on my hospital-style bed that would elevate at both the head and feet, and swallowed a couple of pills before I looked around my new room. The walls were a soft yellow—no doubt intentionally so, because some doctor had told my father that yellow was a soothing, cheerful color. Honestly, it wasn't that bad, but the furniture was this awful frilly white set that made me feel like I was six years old again. It was hideous.

"Do you like it?" Jennifer asked hopefully. She'd come into the room and taken her place at my dad's side. He wrapped his arm around her waist and kissed her cheek. It took some serious effort not to cringe at them.

Again, I chose my words carefully. "I've never had stuff this nice before."

Dad picked up some kind of touch-screen remote. "You've got to see the best part." He grinned as he began pushing buttons. "I can show you how to use this later. It controls the TV, stereo, lights, fan, and windows."

"The *windows?*" My windows were controlled by remote?

Dad puffed his chest out and with one last tap on the screen, the floor-to-ceiling sheer white curtains along the far wall slid open, revealing an entire wall of windows with a sliding door in the middle. Then, with another touch of a button, the sunshades on each window rose up, letting a flood of light engulf the room.

Dad opened the door and stepped out into the sunset onto a wooden balcony that overlooked the whole city of Los Angeles as far as the eye could see. Beyond the balcony, the ground dropped off out of sight. Apparently, the house was on the side of a cliff.

"You have the best view in the house. You'll have to come out here and look at all the lights after dark. It's really something to see."

Given California's reputation for earthquakes, I found the prospect of standing on that balcony a bit disturbing.

Dad came back in and once the sunshades and curtains were all back in place, he turned to me with a hopeful expression. He caught me eyeing the laptop on the desk with trepidation. It was silver and looked as thin as a pancake. I'd always wanted one of those, but somehow it didn't seem so appealing anymore.

Dad walked over and flipped the laptop open. "I hope you

don't mind the change. The computer you had in your apartment was so ancient. I thought you'd like this better. I had someone back up the hard drive before I got rid of it. I also got you a new phone since yours burned." He picked up what looked like an iPhone in a hot pink case and handed it to me. "We added you to the family plan—unlimited everything, so don't worry about calling your friends in Massachusetts. It's not a problem at all."

I cringed. I hadn't contacted any of my friends since the accident. By the time I was capable of calling people, so much time had passed that I figured everyone had already moved on. I was going home with my dad and wouldn't be going back, so I never saw the point of trying to keep in touch. Now that I was thousands of miles away, I *really* didn't see the point.

My dad must have realized this too because he forced a brittle smile and rubbed the back of his neck as if he was suddenly extremely uncomfortable.

"Thanks," I said. "So, um, where are all *my* things?"

Dad's face relaxed, as if I'd just asked an easy question on a much safer topic. "Everything from your bedroom, except for the furniture, obviously, is packed in boxes in your closet."

In my *closet?* "How big is the closet?"

Jennifer found this funny. "Not as big as mine, but I doubt you have the shoe problem that I do."

I didn't want to tell her that my mother and I both had a shoe problem. We had the same size feet and must have had a truckload of shoes between us. Not that I'd be wearing any of them ever again. No open-toe sandals or heels of any kind for me now—only special shoes that therapeutically support my burned feet and scream "grandma." They'd fixed my hand, giving me enough movement back that I was able to write again—sort of. I was still working on making my handwriting legible, but they couldn't entirely save my toes.

"We left everything in boxes because we thought you'd want to unpack and arrange things yourself," Dad said. "But if you'd like help, we'll be happy to do whatever you need."

"No. I can manage. What about Mom's stuff, and the rest of the apartment?"

"I packed everything that looked significant—pictures and things, and some of your mom's belongings that I thought you might want. There wasn't much, just a couple of boxes worth. They're with your things. Everything else I got rid of."

"What about the books?" My heart started pounding in my chest. My bookshelves were not in this room, and I seriously doubted they were in my closet. "What did you do with all of my books?"

"All those books in the living room? I donated them."

"You *what?*"

My dad flinched when I yelled and got that panicked expression back in his eyes. "I'm sorry, sweetheart. I didn't realize—"

"You *gave away* all of my books?"

Maybe it was a stupid thing to lose it over after all the emotional stress I'd been through that day, but I simply couldn't handle the thought of my books being gone. I'd been collecting them for years.

Ever since I'd learned to read, it'd been my favorite thing to do. Mama had been giving me books for my birthday and Christmas—and sometimes simply because she felt like it—for so long it'd become a tradition.

I'd gone to book signings and conventions all over the northeast and had dozens of books signed by all of my favorite authors. Every time I'd go to Mama with that look in my eye she'd laugh and say, "Where to this time?" At each signing, I had someone take a picture of Mama and me with the author and taped the picture to the inside cover of the book it went with.

Now, the books, the pictures, and the memories...they were all gone. Just like Mama was gone. I'd never get them back, and I could never replace what I'd lost. It was like losing her all over again.

My heart broke into a million tiny pieces, shattered beyond repair. I burst into uncontrollable sobs, rolled over on my bed, and curled up into a tight ball, wishing I could somehow block out the pain.

"I'm sorry, Ellamara. I had no idea. You weren't awake to ask. I can get you new books, though. We'll go this week and you can get whatever you'd like."

The thought of him trying to replace that collection revolted me to my core. "You don't understand!" I screamed. "Please, just go away."

I never heard the door click shut, but no one bothered me after that until the next morning. I cried for hours until I passed out from exhaustion.

 2

THE ONE THING I WILL SAY FOR CALIFORNIA IS THAT EVERYONE here is so good-looking. On the one side, it sucks because it will only make my scars stand out more when everyone around me looks so perfect all the time. On the other hand, though, I enjoy spending time with cute guys just as much as the next girl, and my entire new rehabilitation team is gorgeous. This is nice because it makes all the time I have to spend with each of them so much more pleasant.

My dietician and my nurse are both hot guys in their thirties. My dietician is also a part-time personal trainer. I've never been much of an exerciser, but the guy makes me want to join a gym. My physical therapist is only twenty-eight and is downright mouthwatering. He seriously looks like he belongs on TV and not in my living room, forcing me to exercise until I feel like crying. Physical therapy these past two weeks has been something I almost look forward to. Almost.

I gasped at an unexpected surge of pain and held my breath so that I wouldn't cry out.

"Come on, Ella, just one more. I know you can do it. All the way to your shoes this time."

I wanted to cry, but I did one more toe touch because Daniel smiled at me with so much confidence that I couldn't let him down. And I swear he batted his eyelashes. I pushed my fingers toward the floor, stretching my new skin in some of the tightest places. I knew physical therapy was supposed to be hard—it takes the phrase "no pain, no gain" literally—but I just couldn't make my fingers reach my shoes. My whole body was burning. Tears pricked my eyes and I stood back up. "I'm sorry. I can't. I feel like my body is going to rip open any second."

Daniel frowned—not in frustration or disappointment, but out of concern for me. The action was swoonworthy. "You reached your shoes once on Monday. Are you doing your exercises every day like we talked about?"

"Yes, but I think my skin hates the California air. It's been irritating me all week."

"Let me see," Daniel demanded. I pulled up my shirt a little so he could inspect my back, and lifted my pant legs for him to get a good look behind my knees. "Why didn't you say something sooner? I shouldn't have been pushing you so hard. You're not scratching, right?"

"I'm trying not to."

"And sun exposure? No sunbathing on the back patio? No trips to the beach?"

"Yeah," I scoffed. "Parading around in public in a swimsuit is on the top of my to-do list. I haven't even left the house once since I got here. I'm practically a vampire now."

Daniel stopped inspecting my skin and frowned again. This time I was in trouble. "First of all, the beach is amazing and you'd love it. Next summer when your skin is stronger, I'll take you there myself." Delicious Daniel, in nothing but a pair of swim shorts? That would almost be worth the stares. "And second, when is your nurse coming?"

"Not until Monday."

"That's not soon enough. You're way too dry. Your skin's still adjusting to the climate change. Cali's a lot drier than the East

Coast."

"My hair would agree with you."

Daniel laughed and began rummaging through his backpack, seemingly on a mission. "Aha! I do have some with me." He pulled out a bottle of mineral oil and grinned. "Go change and I'll give you a rub down. Your mom has a massage table, right? I thought she said that last time I was here."

I didn't realize I'd frozen until the playful smile on Daniel's face fell.

"She's not my mom," I said, though that wasn't what had my stomach suddenly tied in knots. "And yes, she has one, but you don't have to do that. I'm sure I'll be fine until Monday."

He'd seen my scars already, but an arm or a leg here and there was different than witnessing the whole picture at once.

Daniel looked me straight in the eye, as if he knew exactly what my hesitation was. "Ella." His voice was gentle but stern. "You'll be cracked and bleeding by Monday. We can't risk tearing your grafts. You don't want another surgery, do you?"

"No." My voice shook as I wrestled with my emotions.

"If you're that uncomfortable with me, I can call Cody or you can have one of your parents do it, but it has to get done today."

As if I'd have my dad or Jennifer do it.

I hated when my nurse had to see me just as much as I'd hate for Daniel to see, so there was no sense in asking him to call Cody. I took a deep breath and nodded. "Sorry. You're right. It's fine. I'll go change."

"Good girl." Daniel smiled at me so sincerely full of pride that it tugged at my insides. "You're one of my bravest patients, you know that?"

I managed to laugh. "I bet you say that to all your patients."

Daniel grinned. "I do, but I really mean it with you."

"I bet you say that to all of them, too." With a roll of my eyes, I headed for my bedroom to put on a dreaded bikini.

When I finally built up the courage to walk out of my bedroom, Daniel had already set up the massage table in the living room. I held my breath, but when he looked up, he smiled as if nothing were different. There wasn't a second's hesitation. Not even a flinch. He simply patted the table.

That's why I loved doctors. The staff in the burn center in Boston was all exactly the same as Daniel. To them, I was just another person. During my stay there, I'd even fooled myself into thinking life wouldn't be so bad.

On my trip from Boston to LA, I'd had on shoes, pants, and a long-sleeve shirt. The only scars that had been visible were on my right hand, and of course I walked with a limp. People stared as if I were an alien with three heads. They whispered and pointed and flinched. I couldn't imagine what it would be like to leave the house in a tank top and shorts.

Building up a little courage, I headed toward him, but when I came into the room Jennifer saw me. She'd been carrying a couple of glasses full of lemonade and when she caught sight of me with all my scars exposed, she gasped and her eyes glossed over with tears. She had to set the glasses down and sit. "I'm sorry," she whispered. "Rich said it was bad, but I had no idea...I'm so sorry, Ella." She looked up at me and flinched again. "Excuse me," she said, and then all but ran upstairs to her room.

I closed my eyes and took a deep breath. Daniel gave me a minute to compose myself and then gently took my hand. "Do you need help up?"

Normally I would have tried to do it myself, but this time I let him lift me onto the table. I lay down on my stomach first because I wasn't ready to look at him. I couldn't after I'd just made my stepmother run from the room.

"I don't know why my dad paid for in-home care," I grumbled as Daniel began to soak my sensitive skin in mineral oil. "The burn center's not that far away. I would have much rather gone there to do all this stuff."

Daniel was quiet for a moment and then he said, "I wish I could tell you that it's going to get better. It's never going to be easy, Ella. People are always going to react—some worse than others."

"At least the stepwitches aren't home. Jennifer may be tactless, but at least she tries to be nice. Witch One and Witch Two make the devil sound tame."

Daniel sighed. "Look at the bright side. You'll always be able to tell who your real friends are. Someday when you decide to settle down and get married, you're only going to get the absolute best cream of the crop for a husband."

I snorted. As if there were any chance that someone would date me now, much less choose to be stuck with me for the rest of his life.

"Don't you dare laugh at the idea that someone would love you, Ella. Flip," he demanded. When I rolled onto my back, he tried to make a mad face at me. He wasn't very good at it. "You are smart, witty, and strong. And you're beautiful."

"Again, you're my doctor. You have to say that."

Daniel didn't laugh. He looked straight down at me, as serious as I'd ever seen him. "Breathtakingly beautiful," he insisted. "You have eyes that could haunt a man's dreams."

I wanted to make a joke, but something in Daniel's face made it impossible, so I just whispered "Thanks" as my face turned bright red.

"There are people out there that will be able to see past your scars to the girl inside," Daniel said, "but you're not going to find them if you hide away in this house all day. Don't think I forgot about that, missy. I'm warning you now that I am totally going to rat you out to Dr. Parish."

I groaned. My sessions with my psychiatrist were almost more painful than my physical therapy.

"Don't give me that face. It's for your own good. Sitting around this house all day is not what you should be doing, and you know it. You can regress, Ella. You don't want all your past months of hard work to go to waste."

"But I'm doing my exercises every day. I promise I am."

"It's not the same. You need to be active. You need the variety in your movements. You need to be doing all those things that you used to do without ever thinking about it. Besides, you'll get depressed, and then you'll stop working so hard. Then I'll look bad and your dad will fire me. You might want to get rid of me, but I promise you any replacement he finds will torture you just as much—only they won't be as cool as me."

The man had a point. If only everyone were half as cool as Daniel.

My father came into the room then and silently examined my skin as Daniel finished moisturizing it. His brows fell low over his eyes and he pointed at my skin. "Why is she like this?" He'd been there to witness many a rub downs when I was in the hospital in Boston, so he could see the difference.

My father was looking at Daniel, so I let Daniel answer the question. "She's used to the humidity in Boston. You might want to have her nurse check on her more frequently until her body has time to adjust to the California weather."

Dad nodded. "I'll call Cody today. Is she okay to leave the house like this? I need to take her to register for school."

Ugh. Physical therapy, horrifying my stepmother to tears, dry skin, extra visits from my nurse, and still, my day just miraculously got a lot worse. Amazing.

Daniel—who was self-aware enough to realize that talking about people as if they weren't in the room when they were actually standing right there was beyond rude—spoke to me when he answered my father. He winked and said, "The fresh air will be good for you."

MY FATHER ENROLLED ME IN THE SAME FANCY PRIVATE SCHOOL the twins went to. The closest I'd ever been to private school was watching teen dramas on TV. The school claimed a 98% success rate for their college placement program. My high school in Boston sported metal detectors and boasted a 63% graduation rate.

As if that wasn't bad enough, the school required uniforms. They went with the traditional white polo shirts, or turtlenecks in the winter, and navy blue pleated skirts. I'd spent the summer locked up in the house, and the few occasions my dad and Jennifer had forced me out in public I'd covered myself head to toe. Now they expected me to go to school wearing short sleeves and a knee-length skirt? Didn't they understand how mean teenagers were?

My father was all smiles as we got back in the car after our meeting with the principal. "So?" he asked. "What do you think? Are you excited? It's nice, isn't it?"

It was *too* nice. The school was caged in behind enormous iron gates and a guard shack, and was perched on a giant sprawling lawn. It was made up of a number of smaller buildings that were connected by covered archways, reminding me of an old mission. I could hardly believe the place was a high school.

As Dad navigated us out of the parking lot, my heart started fluttering in that familiar way I've come to recognize as a panic attack. I turned fully sideways in my seat and grasped his arm. "Dad, please don't make me go there."

He was startled by my sudden intensity. "Why, what's wrong?"

"School is going to be hard enough as it is. Please, please, please don't make it worse for me. That place is crazy. At least in public school I'll know what I'm getting into—same crap, different school. The doctors said I needed 'familiar.' That"—I waved my hand toward the school behind us—"is *not* familiar. I can't do it. Don't make me go there."

My panic was one hundred percent sincere, but my dad had the nerve to laugh at me. He brushed my anxiety off as if it were nothing. "Don't be ridiculous. You'll be fine there, you'll see."

"Why can't I do online school? I could probably make up the time I missed and get my diploma in a few weeks instead of repeating my whole senior year."

"You know why you can't do online school. Your doctors have all told you the importance of getting you back into a normal routine as soon as possible. The longer you stay a shut-in, the harder it will be for you to ever live a normal life."

I scoffed at that. "You think I'll ever live a normal life again?"

"What do you want me to do, Ella? I'm just trying to follow the doctors' orders. I'm trying to do what's best for you."

I wanted to scream. He didn't have any idea what was best for me. "Fine. Can I at least go to a public school, then?"

My dad looked appalled by the suggestion. "Why on Earth would you want to do that?"

"Uh, no uniforms, for starters, and because kids are allowed to express themselves there and be individuals. There will be a lot more freaks. I'd have a much better chance at blending in."

"You're not a freak."

I shot my dad a disbelieving look, daring him to say that again. He didn't.

"Even if I weren't crippled and scarred, I wouldn't want to go to that school. I'm not like Jennifer's daughters. I don't belong at some snooty, over-privileged, fancy rich-kid school."

"You're being very judgmental, Ella. At least give it a chance before you decide you hate it."

"But—"

"Besides, no daughter of mine is going to go to public school when I can provide her with a better education."

I found that completely offensive, considering my entire education thus far had been from public school. "It didn't seem to bother you last year," I snapped. "But then, I guess I wasn't really your daughter last year, was I? Or all the years I attended public school before that."

My dad froze, his expression sliding into a serious poker face. I could only take that to mean I'd really pissed him off or hurt his feelings. Probably both, but it didn't matter at that point. I was too angry, too scared, and I missed my mom too much to care what the man who'd left us thought.

"You're already enrolled. I'm not sending you to public school. End of discussion."

I shut my mouth and flopped back in my seat, opting to stay silent and glare out the window the rest of the way home. End of discussion? Fine. I didn't care if that was the last discussion we ever had.

 3

Brian

I slumped back in my chair and plugged my earbuds into my phone. Maybe Katy Perry's newest album would keep me from dying of boredom. I hated these meetings.

Once the music filled my ears, I breathed a small sigh. Much better. Nothing calmed my soul like Katy's sexy voice. And she was so beautiful. I let my eyes drift shut and imagined her roaring for me in my own private serenade. Maybe she'd go out with me. One of the idiots in this room had to know how to get in touch with her people. As soon as they stopped talking—if they *ever* stopped—I'd ask. Hopefully they could do something useful for once.

A finger tapped me on the shoulder, but I ignored it.

"Brian!"

Sighing, I yanked the headphones out of my ears. Those moments of reprieve never lasted long enough. I opened my eyes to find the majority of my management team glaring at me. My father, popular film director Max Oliver, sat directly across the large conference table from me, looking as though he wanted to strangle me. Good.

This would be the last time I ever worked with my father. If it hadn't been *The Cinder Chronicles*, I would never have taken the job in the first place. Family and business should never mix—especially not when it was *my* screwed-up family.

My new assistant, Scott, set a paper in front of me and then reached around me to pass the stack on to my co-star, Kaylee Summers. I groaned at the list of dates printed on the paper. Crumpling the schedule into a small ball, I leaned far back in my chair, aimed, and tossed. The makeshift basketball dropped into the wastebasket across the room without touching a single side—*swish*. "Ha! Two points!"

Holding up a hand for a high five, I turned to Kaylee. "Did you see that? Maybe I found my calling too early in life. I think I'll try out for the Lakers next season."

Kaylee gave me her usual disdainful look and left me hanging. Whatever. Scott would be good for one. I turned to him next. He glanced nervously around the room, but was ultimately too chicken to ignore my request and slapped my hand.

I laughed at the guy's nerves. "Relax, Scotty. I'm the only one in this room that can fire you, so when in doubt, indulge me, not them. They won't blame you."

"Are you finished wasting all of our time?" my dad snapped.

Rage swept through me, as it often did when my father was around. I swiped Scott's copy of the schedule and waved it around. "This stupid meeting is a waste of everyone's time."

My entire management team took great offense to my statement, but it was my agent, Joseph, who spoke up. "That is the outline for *The Druid Prince* publicity tour. You need to pay attention to it."

"Why? That's what Scotty's for." I threw my arm over my assistant's shoulder. "This guy has mad scheduling skills—that's why I hired him. He's probably already got eight different backups of this list printed out and stashed away for emergencies. There's no way he'd ever let me miss a meeting. Believe me, I tried my hardest to miss this one."

Joseph sighed. "You're here because your assistant can't approve the schedule for you."

"You need my approval?" I scoffed. "As if I have some kind of say in any of this?"

"Of course you do."

I wanted to laugh, except it really wasn't funny. I hadn't had a say about anything since my first teen movie hit number one in the box office. Agents, managers, publicists, lawyers, image consultants, personal trainers, a million others... They controlled my life now—what I could and couldn't wear, what I could and couldn't eat, what functions I could and couldn't attend, what I could and couldn't say. Hell, they'd scheduled this entire publicity tour without once consulting me. What they'd handed me just now was an itinerary that was already set in stone.

Scanning the list, I saw that there were weeks of interviews, photo shoots, public appearances, movie premieres, guest appearances on both radio and TV talk shows. LA, New York, Chicago...

I met Joseph's eyes and raised a brow into a challenging arch. "I'm sure you already have the flights and hotel rooms booked, so what the hell does it matter if I approve of any of this or not? What if I don't approve of any of it? *The Kenneth Long Show?* That guy's a total douche. I definitely don't approve of that."

Joseph grimaced, but his face settled into a look of grim determination. "*The Kenneth Long Show* is primetime network television. It's the most popular talk show in existence. He has *millions* of viewers. You can't pass up an interview with him because you don't like him."

"Fine, but what's this *Celebrity Gossip* crap? They're a damn tabloid."

My publicist—also a total douche—cleared his throat and jumped in to defend the schedule. "They're the largest tabloid in the world. If they like you, they can make you the most famous person in world, and if they don't, they can turn you into the biggest joke to ever come out of Hollywood."

"They're already watching you, Brian," my manager, Gary, added, scowling at me. "It's better to work with them and get on their good side than have them plastering stories like *this* all over the media every week."

Gary threw the latest copy of *Celebrity Gossip* down on the table and slid it to me. I read the caption and smirked. Getting Adrianna Pascal to come home with me last weekend had been the most worthwhile thing I'd done all year.

"You made out with world-famous rock star Kyle Hamilton's girlfriend at his own birthday party."

Heh. We did a lot more than make out that night. I looked around the room with big, innocent eyes. "Were they still together?"

"You broke off their damn wedding."

I shrugged. "The guy's an egotistical prick. Besides, if she really loved him, she wouldn't have been all over *me* all night."

My father finally lost it. "This is not the kind of press you need right now!" he roared. "You think you're the first hot shot teen star to try and run with the big boys? You're not! Hollywood sees new assholes like you every year. If you can't get your shit together, your next big gig is going to be some where-are-they-now reality TV show twenty years from now."

I glared at my father with more loathing than I'd thought physically possible. My dad had never respected me, never had faith in me. He made fun of every movie I ever did. He constantly said I couldn't handle "playing with the big boys" ever since I told him I wanted to make my own way in the movie industry rather than just let him cast me in his movies. Now he was just waiting for me to fail so that he could throw it in my face.

"I've had enough of this bullshit." I pushed my chair back from the conference table, crumpling the second schedule into another ball. This time I was too angry to concentrate, and my shot missed the trash can.

Before I could storm out of the meeting, Lisa, the executive producer of the film, and the only person in the room besides Scott I could actually stand, met me at the door and blocked my way.

"Brian," she said, taking my hand. Her smile was completely patronizing, but I still softened to it. "We know you're frustrated. You've had some bad luck with the paparazzi over the last year, but this press tour is important."

Some bad luck? Ever since I was cast to play Cinder, I'd become the paparazzi's new golden boy for the entire female market. They'd stuck to me constantly in order to sell millions of magazines to every woman in the country between the ages of twelve and sixty. They followed me everywhere. I couldn't wipe my ass anymore without having it plastered on every magazine cover in America. I hadn't had a moment's peace in over a year.

"It's important for all of us, Brian, but especially for you," Lisa said. "You've been handed a gift with this part. Cinder is the role of a lifetime and you *nailed* it. Everyone, critics and the average moviegoers alike, is going to fall in love with your performance. If you play your cards right, you could have a shot at an Academy Award nomination."

That made me pause. Joseph jumped on my hesitation. "She's right, Brian. There's been some buzz."

Heads bobbed in agreement all around the conference table. Everyone smiled except for Kaylee, who probably couldn't stand that I'd completely outshone her in this movie. There was definitely no Oscar buzz around her name.

Unable to help myself, I glanced at my father. The guy was one of the biggest names in Hollywood. As much as I hated the man, I could never help trying to earn his approval.

Dad met my gaze with a serious expression. "You did really well."

The praise shocked me so much that I returned to my seat. "Thanks."

My dad nodded. "This movie could earn you a lot of respect around town. It could transition you out of teen idol status and make you a serious A-list player." He picked up the magazine off the table and added, "But Hollywood's elite don't like to let in people who bring this kind of drama with them. It doesn't matter how good of an actor you are—if they don't respect you or they think you're going to cause them trouble, they're not going to keep working with you."

Unfortunately, he was right. If my team was serious about the amount of buzz I was getting for this performance, then I was going to have to step up my game a little. I was going to have to find a way to make people take me seriously. That wasn't easy to do when the world considered me nothing but a yummy piece of eye candy.

"What am I supposed to do?" The antagonism was gone from my voice, but not the bitterness. "I can't help it if all people want to talk about when they interview me is my abs and whether or not I'd ever consider dating a fan. It's not my fault that I'm too damn good-looking to be taken seriously."

"What if we get him involved in a charity?" someone asked.

"Too gimmicky," someone else responded. "It's been done too much. People would see right through it."

"How about enrolling him in college?" another person suggested.

Yes! I could get on board with that. I'd always wanted to go to college. I'd been homeschooled with a private tutor my whole life. The closest thing I'd ever gotten to a real school was playing a high school student in the movies.

"Hey, yeah, I could do that. I could go to UCLA—go Bruins! I'd like to study English Literature."

Joseph shook his head, sending me a sympathetic smile. "That's a really good idea, but you wouldn't have the time."

"But we've wrapped on *The Druid Prince*," I argued. "I don't have anything going on right now. I could totally do it. I can take a couple years off and go to school. It'd keep me out of trouble."

Everyone in the room collectively shook their heads.

"Why not?" It pissed me off that they were so quickly

dismissing the idea. "What would prove that I'm responsible more than getting a college degree? I'm plenty smart enough. I'd get good grades."

Lisa smiled, but it was full of pity. "Of course you would, but there are five books in *The Cinder Chronicles* series. When *The Druid Prince* hits theaters and breaks box-office records—which it will—the studio will green light the other four movies. They're already working on the next script. You'll be filming again by spring."

My heart sank. I should have known I wouldn't be allowed to do something as normal as go to college. I reached for my earbuds again. My opinion clearly wasn't needed in this conversation, and whatever scheme they came up with, I was sure I'd need Katy to cheer me up.

"What if he got engaged?"

I dropped my phone before the music had a chance to play. *"Excuse me?"* I gaped in horror at my publicist and waited for the idea to be laughed out of the room, but no one objected. "You can't be serious. *Engaged?"*

"Actually, it's brilliant!" Joseph said. "This nation lives for a great romance. It satisfies the teeny boppers *and* it shows the world that Brian Oliver is growing up. That he's ready to settle down from his bad-boy ways and start taking life seriously."

I tried not to take offense to that. I'd always been serious about my career. I'd been working since I was a kid, and never had a chance to be a normal teenager because I'd been too busy *taking life seriously.*

"I'm too young."

"It's more romantic that way, and no one will blame you when you break it off later."

"Who the hell do you suggest I get engaged to? Am I just supposed to go pluck some random girl off the street and give her a ring?"

"I'll do it."

The whole room went silent. Kaylee was texting on her

phone and didn't look up to meet anyone's gaze, but she shrugged, knowing that she had the whole room's attention. "This is my first movie. I could use the publicity."

Fighting back my gag reflex, I cringed. If ever genetics had let down the human race, it was in the creation of Kaylee Summers. She was like those chocolate bunnies they sell at Easter—delicious on the outside, completely hollow on the inside, and too much of her was bound to make you sick to your stomach. It was bad enough I had to play nice with her at work. No way in hell could I keep up the pretense off set.

"I love it!" Joseph declared.

"Genius!" Gary agreed.

Even my father smiled enthusiastically and said, "It's perfect."

"Hell no! If I have to get engaged, it's Katy Perry or no one."

Kaylee looked up from her phone long enough to laugh. "You wish."

"The only one dreaming here, babe, is *you*."

Anger flashed in Kaylee's eyes, but her smile turned predatory. "What's the matter, baby? We hooked up once before, and I don't remember you having any complaints then. Come on, do this with me. We could have some fun with it."

I shuddered. "No way."

Several people in the room sighed, and again it was left up to Lisa to coax me back into compliance. "Brian, think about it," she urged. "A real-life romance between the two of you would generate millions in free publicity. Your fans would eat it up. It would be great for the film, and your career."

"A real-life romance with *her?*" I repeated. "I think you're overestimating my acting abilities, Lisa."

That wiped the smug smile off Kaylee's face. "Asshole."

I returned the sentiment without shame. "Bitch."

"Man up, Brian," my dad interrupted. "This isn't just about you. We *all* need this. This is my first dive into more serious films. If my lead actor could earn an Academy Award nomination, I could get any kind of job I wanted after this and not just action flicks."

"It's not like it has to be real," Gary added. "And it won't last forever. Just a couple of months being seen together in public, and then after the movie releases you guys can break it off. No harm done. You could get engaged fairly quickly and just tell people you dated in secret during the filming. Secret love affairs are exciting. The world will go crazy over it."

Looking around the room, I felt the need to punch something. There was no way I was getting out of this meeting a single man. Kaylee smirked at the defeat in my eyes. "I'll make us a reservation somewhere nice. Oh, and my ring better be platinum and at least three karats."

4

THE ONLY WOMAN ON MY REHABILITATION TEAM WAS MY PSYCHO-logical therapist, but even she was still young and attractive. Her being a girl was really for the best, though, because I was actually required to put together coherent sentences in our sessions, and that seems pretty impossible for me to do around Delicious Daniel.

Dr. Parish started with the inquisition before I'd even settled myself into the big leather wingback chair in her office. "How was your week, Ella? Any progress to report?"

I loved the chair, but I hated my weekly therapy sessions. They were awkward at best and I always left them feeling awful. "I finally caught up on all the episodes I missed of *Once Upon A Time*." That was the only progress I could think of. It was basically the only thing I'd done all week.

"You know I was talking about your family."

"Those people are not my family."

Dr. Parish smiled at me. "I understand why you feel that way. However, they *are* your family and you need to accept that. You need to find a way to build a relationship with them."

"I can't build a relationship with people who don't like me

and don't want me around. The only time I ever talk to the twins is when they call me to make sure I'm hiding in my room before they bring their friends home, and they tell me they'll text me when it's safe for me to come out."

The thing about Dr. Parish is that she never loses her cool. I know that she must get frustrated, but somehow she always looks and sounds genuinely sympathetic. "I'm sure you're misinterpreting their intentions. Perhaps when they call to tell you they're bringing friends home, it's their way of trying to include you."

I snorted at this. Dr. Parish is a smart woman, but she has way too much optimism. "Anastasia's exact words when she called me yesterday were 'Hey, Stepfreak, I'm bringing some of my friends home, and they all have this, like, really bad fear of dogs, so make sure you lock yourself in your room this evening. I'll text you when it's safe to come out.' Call me pessimistic, but I don't think I misinterpreted that."

Dr. Parish's eyes narrowed, but she said nothing.

"The best part about it," I continued on, "was all the laughter in the background. She was with her friends when she called to tell me this. She waited until she had an audience on purpose."

"Did you talk to your parents about your stepsister's behavior?"

Again, I laughed without humor. "She's said worse to my face with both my dad and Jennifer standing right there. They always just force these nervous laughs like 'Oh, how sweet, the girls are joking around with each other.' They never say anything. They're in total denial. They give those girls whatever they want and let them do whatever they want. Juliette at least has the decency to just pretend I don't exist if I stay out of her way, but Ana is a vicious, rotten, spoiled princess. I wouldn't be friends with her even if she did give me the chance. She's not the kind of person who is healthy for *anyone* to be friends with. She's a quintessential Mean Girl—like the kind they make movies about."

Dr. Parish sighed. She set down her pen that she's always taking notes with during our sessions and took her glasses off to rub at her eyes. Obviously tired of going around in circles, she changed the subject. "Let's talk more about your attempted suicide."

I groaned, but I still tugged at the sleeves of my shirt. I had scars all over my body, but the ones on my wrists were different. Those scars were my own fault. That moment in my life was a decision I truly regretted. Something I was ashamed of. "That was a mistake," I whispered. "I wasn't even that serious."

"I've read the reports, Ella, and I've seen a number of attempted suicide cases. Had you had more than a steak knife available to you, you'd have succeeded. You almost did. You weren't messing around."

"Fine, maybe I was serious about it, *then*, but I wasn't thinking clearly. That was a really bad time for me, but I've gotten a lot better."

Dr. Parish didn't believe me.

"I can walk again! I'm learning how to write with my bad hand again! The doctors in Boston told me that wasn't supposed to be possible. Do you think I would have worked so hard and put myself through so much more pain trying to accomplish those things if I still thought about ending my own life? I got overwhelmed after my accident and lost my head for a while, but I'm not suicidal anymore! Why won't anyone believe me?"

Dr. Parish got up from her desk and walked a box of tissues to me. After I grudgingly took one, she sat down on the other chair next to mine. "I do believe you, Ella," she said. "You have a lot of roadwork ahead of you still, but I know you've come a long way from that dark place. What you don't understand is that until your life is a lot more stable, it would be very easy for you to find yourself back there. At least living in your father's home, whether you feel comfortable yet or not, there is someone looking after you who loves you and has your best interests in mind."

That made me so angry I started to shake. "You think that man loves me? You think he has my best interests in mind? He doesn't even *know* me! The other day he enrolled me in the same school his daughters go to. It's this fancy private school like you see on TV shows about rich kids with messed up lives."

"It's probably a great school, Ella."

"Maybe, but that doesn't mean it's the right one for *me*. He took me to see the place when he registered me, and I felt like I'd gone to some alien planet. I grew up going to a public school in inner city Boston. We had metal detectors, not a sushi bar. I am not going to fit in there. I'm not even going to know how to interact with the kids there. We'll have nothing in common. Everyone there will be just like Anastasia and Juliette. Plus, we have to wear uniforms—short skirts and polo T-shirts! It's going to be hell for me."

When Dr. Parish sighed, I tried to defend myself in a way that didn't just sound as if I was whining. "Public school would be a lot more familiar to me. It would be a lot more diverse. I would be able to wear whatever I wanted so I wouldn't have to always have my scars on display like some kind of freak show. I would be able to blend in more. Plus, there might even be a few other kids on a five-year plan there. You think kids go to a school like Beverly Hills Prep Academy and get held back? As if I don't have enough to deal with already, I'm going to be a full year older than all the other seniors. Plus, I already have an arch enemy who doesn't want me to go there and has promised to make my life hell if I get in her way."

I waited for Dr. Parish to tell me I was misinterpreting Anastasia's threats again, but she didn't. She went back to her desk and started taking more notes. "Have you voiced any of these concerns with your father?"

I gave her another humorless laugh. "I had a massive panic attack when I saw the place. I understand why you don't want me to do homeschool, so I asked if he would at least send me to public school. I gave him all the reasons I just gave you. I told him I thought it would help me adjust better if I was on more familiar ground and less anxious. I begged him. And do you know what he did? He laughed at me! I was in the middle of a legitimate panic attack. I was begging for his understanding. I was in tears, and he laughed. He told me I was being ridiculous and that I was going to love it there. He told me no daughter of his was going to go to public school when he could provide them with a better education."

As was pretty common during my therapy sessions, I started crying again and had to get another tissue. "The man can't have my best interests at heart, because he has no clue what my best interests are. He doesn't know a thing about me, or what I need. He's just a snob who's now stuck with a freakish girl from a part of his past he tried to bury. I'm his deep, dark, disgraceful secret. He's more concerned about saving face with his friends than he is with me."

I blew my nose and got my tears under control. Once I could talk again in a rational manner, I said, "Look, I know you're trying to help me and all, but the fact is my dad's house is just not a healthy environment. It's awkward and stressful, and it's only making everything that much harder for me. My whole rehabilitation process would be so much easier if I could just move out on my own."

Dr. Parish sat there for a minute, silently contemplating what I said. "If you could leave on your own," she finally asked, "where would you go? Back to Boston?"

Finally, a topic that wasn't depressing. "I don't know," I said honestly. "I lost my spot at Boston U, and all my friends have moved on. Things wouldn't be the same if I tried to go back, so I'd probably pick somewhere else."

"So where would you go?" Dr. Parish asked again. "What would you do with your life?"

"First, I'd finish high school in some online program. If I did that, I could start now and be done in a couple of months instead of having to repeat my entire senior year. Then, I'd still go to college. I know I want to study journalism. I guess I'd just have to decide where I wanted to go. I could go anywhere now, but I want to be an entertainment writer/reviewer, so it'd probably be here or New York. Probably New York because I'm partial to the

East Coast."

I knew I'd said the wrong thing when Dr. Parish's eyes narrowed. "You would leave, just like that? Go off to some college all by yourself in some town where you didn't know anybody? Had no friends?"

"Lots of kids do that." I kicked myself for sounding defensive. I knew that would work against me, but I couldn't help it. I hated how people were always pointing out that I had no one left.

"Lots of kids aren't recovering from such a traumatic experience as you, and even then, most of those kids have a strong support system back home."

I scoffed. "And you think I have that here? You think my dad and his family are a support system?"

"No, I don't," she said simply.

I was shocked by her answer. Everyone I'd met since the moment I woke up from my accident had tried to push my dad and his family on me as if the fact that my father and I shared the same blood meant that we were all going to automatically love each other and be insta-BFFs.

"Perhaps you're right that living with your father and his family isn't the best thing for you," she said slowly.

My heart perked up at this tiny ray of hope, but I tried to squash it. There had to be a catch somewhere. She wasn't going to sign off on my mental health, which is what I needed if I wanted to be free of my dad's supervision and living on my own.

Dr. Parish put her notepad down and leaned back in her chair. "Ella, I know you see me as your prison warden, but I hope you understand that I really do want what's best for you. It's my job to help you figure out what that is, and help you get to a place mentally where you can accomplish it. I want to see you succeed. I want to be able to sign your release papers for you, but you have to prove to me that you're ready for that."

So, she wasn't going to get me out of my father's house. My hope was appropriately extinguished. "What does that mean?" I grumbled.

"It means that if getting you a place of your own is really what's best for you, then that's what we're going to work toward. But I'm not going to let you do that until you can prove to me you won't be completely alone. I don't believe you're ready to be by yourself. I think that would put you in danger of falling into another severe depression. You need friends. You need a solid support system. If you don't believe your family will be that for you, then find others. Make some friends. Join a support group. Try to get back in touch with some of your old friends in Boston. Even if they have moved on and you don't live near them, you still need people you can talk to. If you can build yourself a real support system, Ella, then I'll take you apartment shopping myself."

Dr. Parish's promise stuck with me through the rest of the day. I needed a support system, and there was only one place I could think to start.

5

Brian

I TUGGED ON THE COLLAR OF MY SHIRT AS I PULLED UP TO THE restaurant. Of course Kaylee picked The Ivy for our first "date." It was only one of the most well-known celebrity haunts in Los Angeles. Photographers camped out front on the sidewalk every night of the week, and tonight was no exception. The flashes started going off when we were still half a block away because the paparazzi all recognized my car. They were going to freak out when they realized I was dining with Kaylee Summers tonight.

"You ready to do this, baby?" Kaylee taunted from the passenger seat.

My stomach churned. Kaylee had been a little too eager for this whole charade from the get go. She'd thrown herself at me when we first met and I made the mistake of bringing her home. It only took me a couple of days to realize how stupid that had been. She couldn't seem to understand that one night of fun to get the tension out of the way when filming was just that—one night of fun. It took me weeks to convince her I wasn't interested in anything more, and I'd had to parade dozens of other girls in front of her to get her to understand.

I glanced at her again. She covered her lips in some glossy stuff and then laughed. "You look like you've been asked to carry out a prison sentence."

I almost smiled. That statement was amazingly accurate.

"I don't know why you're being so grumpy about this. Most men would kill to be in a relationship with me."

Even if Kaylee weren't a conniving, high maintenance, self-centered bitch that was dumber than a goldfish, I wouldn't date her for real. I didn't date anyone—at least not more than once. "I don't do relationships."

"Why not? I think they're fun."

In order to be in an actual relationship, one was required to use their heart, and my heart didn't work anymore. It hadn't for over eight months now, but I wasn't about to explain that to Kaylee. "I just don't."

Kaylee stopped primping and turned in her seat to look me over with scrutinizing eyes. After a moment her lips curled up into a smug smirk. "How ironic. Hollywood's favorite heartbreaker doesn't date because he got burned by a girl."

Clenching my jaw, I cut my glance back out the front window. I didn't talk about Ella with anyone, least of all Kaylee.

Kaylee laughed again. "Wow. Whoever she was, she certainly did a number on you."

I glared at her. "This topic is off limits. Drop it, or I dump your ass on the curb and find someone hotter to amuse me for the night."

Kaylee's smile disappeared and her eyes glinted with malice. "This relationship is going to skyrocket my popularity. I'm not going to let you ruin it for me because someone dumped you. If you mess this up, I will ruin your career. By the time I'm done with you, you'll have to move to the North Pole in order to escape the drama I will bring to your life."

As much as I hated to admit it, Kaylee's threat was real. This may have been her first film, but her parents were some of the most powerful people in town and she had even more powerful friends—hence the reason she landed a part she wasn't good enough for in the first place. Her father was the head of the studio that had green-lighted *The Druid Prince.*

I had some star power behind me and acting skills that couldn't be ignored, so I had a little breathing room to stand up to Kaylee here and there, but if I ever pissed her off badly enough, I had no doubt that she could do some serious damage to my career. I was really stuck in this nightmare—at least through award-voting season. If I could just get my nomination and show the Hollywood A-listers that I was worthy of being one of them, then I could dump Kaylee and they'd probably congratulate me for making such a smart choice.

I leaned back against my headrest, closed my eyes, and sighed. "You amaze me sometimes, Kay. I've never met anyone who can pull off bitchy as naturally as you do."

"I don't have to be a bitch, Brian."

I cracked a wary eye open, and Kaylee gave me a sultry smile. "You may not like relationships, baby, but you're in one now." She leaned over and spoke softly into my ear. "I can make these next few months a living hell for you, or I can make them very, very pleasant."

She went to work trailing sensual kisses down the side of my neck while her hand fell to a dangerous place on my inner thigh. Her long nails scratched through my jeans with just enough pressure to drive me crazy.

I sucked in a breath. I didn't want to give in to her, but *this* Kaylee was definitely more pleasant than the whiny, cruel version I would be stuck with if I didn't play along. Carefully, so as not to piss her off further, I pulled her hand away from my lap. "In two more seconds I won't be able to get out of this car. Unless you want to skip dinner and get straight to dessert, I suggest you keep your hands to yourself."

Kaylee chuckled as she moved back to her side of the car and reapplied her lip gloss, yet again. "Tempting. But we need to be seen together before we can get to the fun stuff. Plus, I'm hungry."

"Right." As if she was going to have anything more than bottled water and a few bites of lettuce. "Whatever."

I let out another breath and finally opened my door, immediately finding my "public" smile, when people started shouting for my attention. All thoughts and feelings turned off. The numbness that helped me survive the last year took over. I welcomed it, *embraced* it.

The chaos faded out as I smiled for the crowd. Acting was a skill I did well, a game I loved. This date with Kaylee was just another act, so I would perform, and I would do a damn good job of it.

I walked around the car, and, like the perfect gentleman, opened the door for Kaylee. Once I helped her from the car, I slipped my arm around her waist. "Smile for the cameras, *princess*," I teased loud enough for our audience to hear and then placed a soft kiss on the sensitive spot of skin behind Kaylee's ear.

Kaylee shivered with pleasure. As we walked into the restaurant, she murmured into my neck. "Mm, maybe you do deserve an award. I almost believe you want me right now." See? I totally deserve an Oscar.

Twenty minutes later I was so bored stiff that I nearly cried tears of joy when my phone dinged, informing me I had an e-mail. It was probably just Scott sending some change in my schedule, but even that was more appealing than listening to Kaylee drone on about the details of our upcoming engagement. She had the proposal all planned out from the time and place I was going to do it down to the very last line I was supposed to say to her. *Shoot me now,* I thought when she mentioned needing to plan an engagement party.

I reached for my drink at the same time as I pulled my phone out of my pocket and then froze when I opened my e-mail.

You have 1 unread message.
From: Ellamara
Subject: Cinder?

"Holy shit!"

My glass slipped from my fingers and fell to my plate, sloshing red wine all over both Kaylee and me. Restaurant staff came flying from all directions when Kaylee shrieked, but I hardly noticed. I couldn't take my eyes off of my phone.

"Holy effing shit!"

"Brian!" Kaylee screeched. "What the hell is the matter with you?"

I ignored her, and, with a shaking hand, opened the e-mail, praying this wasn't some kind of sick joke.

To: Cinder458@gmail.com
From: EllaTheRealHero@yahoo.com
Subject: Cinder?

Dear Cinder,

It's taken me weeks to build up the courage to write this e-mail. I've just had no idea how to say hello after so much time passed. I never messaged you back that day because I was in a car accident. I was in a coma for a while and then stayed in the hospital for a long time after that.

I couldn't hold back my gasp. I always figured it was something like that, but having it confirmed made the nightmare real in a way it hadn't been before.

Ellamara and I had always been just anonymous e-mail friends, but the last time I spoke to her, I asked for her address so that I could mail her something. It was a huge step in our relationship, but I was to the point where I was willing to chance it. I needed more from her. Wanted to *be* more to her.

I took a risk, got her a gift I hoped would win her heart, and asked for her address. She called me a creepy Internet stalker, but I was sure she was kidding—until she never messaged me back. At first I figured her phone died, and then when she didn't get back to me that day I briefly worried that I had scared her away. But then she missed her First Sentence Friday post on her blog the next day and I *knew* something was wrong.

I wrote her e-mail after e-mail, and waited day after day for her to write back, or at least post on her blog again, but after a few weeks I gave up hope. I knew that even if I completely freaked her out that day and made her never want to talk to my creepy Internet-stalking ass again, Ella would never have given up on her blog. Ever. Not unless she was dead. Which was the conclusion I finally resigned myself to when an entire month went by without word from her. For months, I mourned the loss of my best friend and the girl I'd fallen in love with—was still mourning her loss up until five seconds ago.

Swallowing a lump that had suddenly risen in my throat, I read the rest of the e-mail.

My mother died in the accident, so I had to move in with my dad and his family. He packed up my apartment and it was rented out again long before I got out of the hospital. I never got to go home. I never got to see any of my old friends. I never got to say good-bye to anyone. Not even my mother. I missed her funeral.

I'm sorry it's taken me so long to write this e-mail, and I still don't know if I'll be able to click SEND. It's just everything is so different now, and thinking about the past hurt so much that I couldn't face it. I haven't contacted anyone from my old life. I thought about starting my blog again, but my dad got rid of all my books while I was in a coma and now I don't have the heart to do it anymore.

I'm so sorry that I just disappeared. I'm sorry if I hurt you. I didn't mean to. I hope you can forgive me. I just want you to know that your friendship always meant a lot to me. (It still does.) I think about you all the time.
Miss you,
Ella

I sat in my chair, staring at the e-mail while the room spun around me. Ella was alive. Ella had e-mailed me. And she *missed* me. It was almost too miraculous to believe.

I swallowed again, but this time I was fighting off nausea as well as emotions. I was reeling over the fact that she was alive, but to hear that she'd been through something so awful, too? She lost her mother and had to move in with a father that had abandoned her years ago. The thought of Ella going through all of that was agony.

The emotions spiraling out of control inside me were almost impossible to contain. I couldn't help the elation I felt, the relief and joy in knowing that she was alive, but at the same time, my heart was breaking all over again. I was sick with worry for her. She must have felt so alone all this time.

"Brian!"

Kaylee's shrill voice snapped me out of my shock. Blinking a few times, I met her questioning glare over the table.

Someone else interrupted, saying, "Mr. Oliver? Are you all right?"

I shook my head, trying to clear away the last of my daze, and looked up at the restaurant manager hovering over our table. The woman was holding out a cloth to me. It wasn't until she urged me to take it that I noticed I'd spilled my wine. I accepted the cloth and dabbed at myself. "I'm sorry about the mess."

"Don't worry about that," the woman said. "I'm more concerned about you. You look so pale. Are you unwell? Do you need some sort of assistance? Should we call a paramedic?"

"What? Oh! No. I'm all right. I was just startled. I'm so sorry." I pulled the valet slip out of my breast pocket and handed it to the restaurant manager. "Could you have the valet bring my car around? I'm afraid I need to leave. And it's urgent, so…"

The manager nodded, but the look of concern in her eyes intensified and she frowned. "Of course, Mr. Oliver, but are you sure you're all right?"

Was I all right? If this woman only knew. I was better than I'd been in over eight months. The missing piece of my heart had just come back to me. Ella had e-mailed me! And I hadn't responded yet…

"Mr. Oliver?"

Waving the woman's concern off, I hit the reply button.

To: EllaTheRealHero@yahoo.com
From: Cinder458@gmail.com
Subject: RE: Cinder?
Ella!!!!! I AM FREAKING OUT RIGHT NOW! Out to dinner with a friend. Give me ten minutes. Do NOT go anywhere!!!!!!!

As soon as I hit SEND, I jumped to my feet and slipped the manager some cash and a card. "This is my personal assistant's number. Would you please contact him about the bill—for dinner and for whatever mess I've caused? Thank you for everything, and again I'm sorry for the trouble."

I didn't wait for a reply. I made my way out of the restaurant as fast as I could and was already climbing into my car when Kaylee came scrambling out of the restaurant behind me.

"Brian!" she hissed. She forced a smile at all the curious paparazzi and softened her voice. "Baby, are you sure you're feeling okay? Do you need me to drive?"

Oh, yeah. That.

I'd forgotten all about Kaylee, but the look she gave me over the top of the Ferrari made me remember the act I was supposed to be putting on for the public. Truthfully, I didn't care anymore if Kaylee had a tantrum and tried to destroy me. The only thing that mattered was that Ella was alive and she was waiting for me to talk to her. But starting a fight would take longer than keeping Kaylee happy, so I flashed her a panty-dropping smile. "I'm fine, *baby*. I just feel terrible for ruining such a sexy dress, and I think it's important that I get it off of you as quickly as possible."

Surprise flashed in Kaylee's eyes, but her whole face lit up and she beamed at me. "You're so naughty."

She giggled and then turned to say something to the men with their cameras, but I didn't wait around to hear what it was. I climbed in the car, buckled my seat belt, and rolled down the passenger window. "Babe, stop flirting with the cameras and get your sexy ass in the car now. I can't wait any longer!"

Kaylee shot another smile at the paparazzi and climbed into the car. As I sped away from the restaurant, she unleashed the tirade she'd been holding back while in public. "Have you lost your mind? What the hell was all that? You made us both look completely stupid, and you *ruined* my dress! Those photographers just got pictures of me with *wine* down my front!"

"I don't give a shit about your stupid dress. Ella e-mailed me and I need to get home so I can talk to her."

Kaylee gasped.

I was driving too fast to take my eyes off the road, but I felt the heat of her stare. It was hot enough that I feared she might spontaneously combust. If she burst into flames and ruined my leather seats, I was going to be pissed.

"This is all because some girl e-mailed you?"

"Ella's not just *some* girl. She's *the* girl. The *only* girl."

"*WHAT?*"

"This is a damn publicity stunt, Kaylee. Our relationship is *fake*. Don't forget that."

"Maybe, but if you think I'm going to let you sneak around

with some skeezy bitch while you're supposed to be dating me—"

"This isn't about *you!*" I snapped. "I just found out that the most important person in my life *didn't* die eight months ago. She's been in a freaking coma and she just e-mailed me to tell me that she's still alive! I'm a little freaked out right now, so don't give me any more shit! I *need* to talk to her."

Miracle of miracles—I managed to stun Kaylee speechless.

Five minutes later, I pulled through the security gate of my Hollywood Hills home. When I turned the car off and started to get out, Kaylee gaped at me. "You're just going to go inside and call this *Ella* person?" She spat the name with loathing. "What am *I* supposed to do?"

As if I cared? I shrugged. "Call a cab."

"A *cab?*" Kaylee shrieked in horror. "You expect me to take a *cab* home? This was our first public outing together. You know we were followed after we left the restaurant. There is no way in hell I'm going to be photographed leaving your place right after we got here, alone and in a damn *cab*."

Kaylee was fuming and clearly looking for a fight, but I didn't want to take the time to get into it with her. "Then come in. Stay the night for all I care, and I'll take you home in the morning."

Kaylee followed me in the house, still raging. "You're damn right you'll take me home in the morning. After you take me out to a nice breakfast to make up for this bullshit, and you'll even give me a shirt to wear like a *real* boyfriend would."

Irritation swept through me. All I wanted to do was talk to Ella, and Kaylee was worried about some stupid publicity stunt. I took off my blazer and ripped the shirt I was wearing underneath over my head. "Enjoy it, *princess*," I grumbled as I threw it at her. "It's the closest you're going to get to me tonight. The guest room's down the hall on the right."

I stormed off to my bedroom, slamming and locking the door behind me.

I DID IT. I E-MAILED CINDER. AND LESS THAN FIVE MINUTES LATER, I got a reply. The second I read his e-mail, my entire body relaxed. I was just so relieved. It was Cinder! I'd spoken to Cinder! He sounded the same as he always had, and he seemed eager to talk to me. Maybe I did have one friend left in the world.

A small piece of my dead heart came back to life, and I took what felt like my first real breath since the accident. My hands shook with anticipation as I logged into my instant messenger and waited. My stomach was a mixture of all kinds of butterflies—nervous, excited, fearful, happy...

The minutes ticked on. Ten minutes passed, then fifteen, and finally twenty. I thought I would go insane. I thought I would reach through the computer and strangle him for taking too long if he made me wait another minute. And then he was there.

Cinder458: So sorry. It took me longer to get home than I thought it would.
EllaTheRealHero: Home? You left your friend? You didn't have to do that.

Cinder458: Are you kidding? Ella, I thought you were *dead*.
EllaTheRealHero: Are you serious?

My heart dropped into my stomach. He thought I was *dead?* I wondered if all my friends back home thought that, too. I wondered if I should let them know I wasn't. I didn't think I could handle the questions.

Cinder458: What was I supposed to think? You disappeared mid-conversation! I wrote you a million e-mails. I checked your blog and your Twitter every day for months. I couldn't think of any other reason that you would just suddenly stop blogging.

I know you can't actually hear emotion in an e-mail, but Cinder sounded so upset. I felt awful that he had to go through all that. I know if the shoe had been on the other foot, I'd have been crazy with worry.

EllaTheRealHero: I'm so sorry. I shouldn't have let you worry like that for so long.
Cinder458: Don't apologize to me, Ellamara. You have nothing to be sorry for. I'm just glad you're okay. I still can't believe I'm talking to you. I nearly fell out of my chair when I got your e-mail.
Cinder458: My date thought I was insane, by the way. Definitely not getting any from her now, and she's really hot. Totally your fault.

For a second, I burst into laughter. He was the same old Cinder. Then I realized what he said, and my heart skipped another beat.

EllaTheRealHero: You were on a *date????* Cinder! I can't believe you ditched her. What a jerk.

Cinder458: Eh, she was too high maintenance, anyway.

EllaTheRealHero: *Cinder!!!*

Cinder458: Get over it, woman. It was a stupid date. You were more important. That e-mail almost made me cry. Effing *tears*, Ella! Why are we even talking about me? I can't imagine what you've been through. I know how close you were with your mom. And you had to move in with your dad? You haven't seen him in years!!! How are you? Is there anything I can do? You want me to fly out there and steal you away from him? Or at least punch him in the face? I can't believe he got rid of your books.

Already the world seemed brighter. Life wasn't nearly as bad as it had been half an hour ago. My overwhelming loneliness was gone. There wasn't really a light at the end of the tunnel yet, but at least I wasn't in the dark by myself anymore.

I should have known Cinder wouldn't have changed. I should have e-mailed him months ago in the rehab center once I could move again. Oh, well. No use dwelling on the past. I had him back now, and that was all that mattered.

EllaTheRealHero: No punching. My dad is a big, bad U.S. attorney. He would bury you in court, get you thrown in jail, and probably even take your fancy talking car.

Cinder458: Whoa, whoa, whoa, not my precious! Okay, okay, so no punching him or kidnapping you. But seriously, Ella, what can I do? I feel helpless here *chica*. Talk to me.

EllaTheRealHero: I don't want to talk. I am so sick of

talking. The only people I talk to anymore are doctors, and all they do is make me *talk*. I don't need another doctor. I need a friend. I need someone to make me laugh and help me take my mind off everything. Don't treat me like I'm going to break. Yell at me and don't let me get away with anything when I start acting like a brat.

Cinder458: Would I ever miss an opportunity to call you a brat?

EllaTheRealHero: No. That's why I need you. My life is upside down right now, and I really need something familiar. I need normal.

Cinder458: I can do normal.

I laughed a genuine, happy, lighthearted laugh. It was the first *real* laugh I'd managed since my accident. There was nothing forced or awkward about it. I hadn't done it because I was nervous about anything or trying to hide my real feelings. I just laughed because I was in a good mood (and because what Cinder said was ridiculous).

Dr. Parish was going to be happy. Maybe, if I was lucky, she'd stop hounding me about spending time with my dad and the step-witches, but I doubted it.

EllaTheRealHero: Sure you can, rock star. You wouldn't know normal if it bit you on your ridiculously good-looking face.

Cinder458: You've never seen my face. How do you know it's good-looking?

EllaTheRealHero: Because no ugly person could have an ego as big as yours.

Cinder458: You're right. I'm gorgeous. I'm also probably way too amazing to accomplish normal, but I can definitely handle familiar. You've seen the cast for *The Druid Prince*, right? I've been going crazy not being able to talk to you about it.

I laughed again. This *was* familiar. My mind drifted back to the early months in the hospital. The doctors kept me in a medically-induced coma for three weeks because my pain was too much and I was having so many surgeries. After they brought me out of it, there were still a number of weeks where I was groggy and incoherent—in and out of consciousness. The hospital staff told me that for weeks I would call out for my mom and Cinder.

One day, one of my nurses recognized the name Cinder and brought me an entertainment magazine. The cover boasted an article about Hollywood's leading It Boy landing the role of fantasy's most cherished prince. I guess the thought of teen sensation Brian Oliver playing Prince Cinder was so horrifying it brought me right out of my stupor and sent me into a *tizzy*, as my nurse called it. And that was *before* I learned who was directing.

EllaTheRealHero: Ugh! Don't remind me!

Cinder458: ?

EllaTheRealHero: Why does Hollywood always have to ruin everything?

Cinder458: You think it's going to suck?

EllaTheRealHero: Kaylee Summers as the Princess Ratana? She's not even an actress! She's a supermodel!

Cinder458: Who knows, maybe acting is her calling.

EllaTheRealHero: And maybe Max Oliver just thought she was really hot. They don't even have her in a dress in the movie. She's decked out in some slutty, tight, leather getup like Xena: Warrior Princess. It's disgraceful. And forget any chance of them following the story. With Max Oliver directing, you know it's going to be nothing but a bunch of over-the-top mindless action.

Cinder458: Wow. So you're really not a fan of Max Oliver, then. I thought you were joking all those times you wrote scathing reviews of his movies on your blog.

EllaTheRealHero: I thought *you* were joking every time you defended him. Max Oliver is your go-to director if you want flashy car chases, big explosions, and half-naked women—which I know is your favorite kind of movie—but even you have to admit he is so wrong for *The Druid Prince*. And of course he just *had* to go and bring his son on to play Cinder! Why??? Why are they doing this to me???

Cinder458: What!!! I thought you'd be happy about that. Brian Oliver will make an excellent Cinder. That dude is awesome.

EllaTheRealHero: LOL! I never knew you had some big, gay celebrity crush on Brian Oliver.

Cinder458: Remember what we said about you being a BRAT?? It's not a crush. I just think he's perfect for the part.

EllaTheRealHero: Sure, he *looks* the part, but he's only ever done cheesy teen movies. Who knows if he can pull off the drama? Not that there will be any with his father directing.

Cinder458: I will admit that Max Oliver is wrong for the movie, and Kaylee Summers definitely has air for brains, but I don't think the movie will suck. They got Academy Award Winner Jason Cohen to adapt the script, and you're wrong about Brian. He can do it. There's even some Oscar buzz in town right now.

EllaTheRealHero: Teen Choice Award buzz, maybe. Best Kiss and Hottest Abs, definitely, but Best Actor? I'll believe it when I see it.

Cinder458: Whatever, brat. He'll at least be nominated. I'm calling it now. He did this one indie drama, *The Long Road Home*. Watch it, and I promise I'll let you grovel for forgiveness once you realize how wrong you are about him.

EllaTheRealHero: Ha! Okay. I'll check it out. I should go now, though.

Cinder458: Don't go yet.
EllaTheRealHero: Why?
Cinder458: I don't know. I just don't want you to.

Cinder could be so sweet when he wanted, but that's not why that little confession caused my chest to constrict. Nobody had wanted me around since my accident. My father brought me home, and he and Jennifer tried to be nice, but it was obvious I wasn't really a part of the family.

Sometimes I'd come out of my room and it would take Jennifer a second too long to force a smile on her face. And why wouldn't it? I was my dad's forgotten past. I was a disruption in her perfect, beautiful world, and I came with a lot of baggage. She put up with me, and I didn't think she hated me, but she didn't like me, either. The stepwitches definitely didn't want me around. I'd been so sure that nobody would ever want me again.

EllaTheRealHero: Afraid I'm going to disappear again?
Cinder458: That's not funny. You scared the crap out of me, woman!!! I thought I lost you forever. Are you sure you're okay?

Okay was a relative term.

EllaTheRealHero: I'm much better now that I'm talking to you. I really missed you.
Cinder458: I missed you more. You can't ever disappear on me again. I need you, Ellamara, oh wise and beautiful mystic priestess of the Realm. I need your guidance and council.
EllaTheRealHero: As if you ever listen to a word I say.
Cinder458: I always listen. I just rarely agree.

EllaTheRealHero: That is because you are foolish and shallow, young druid prince.

Cinder458: You forgot handsome.

EllaTheRealHero: And conceited.

Cinder458: Oh, how I've missed you constantly cutting down my ego.

EllaTheRealHero: It's a nearly impossible task because it's so inflated, but I try my best.

Cinder458: I suppose I should let you go now. If it's late here, it must be almost morning for you.

I hesitated to respond. Part of me was desperate to tell him the truth, to tell him I lived in LA now, and ask to meet in person. I wanted so much to have a face to put with his name. I wanted to hear the laugh behind all the LOLs he typed. I wanted to know how his voice sounded when he called me *woman* every time he was frustrated with me.

The problem was I knew once I met him I'd want so much more than that. Mama had been scared I'd fall for him someday, but I'd already fallen for him. In fact, I was certain that I was hopelessly in love with him. I always had been.

Cinder wouldn't want me. What guy would when he could have any beautiful girl he wanted? I was pretty sure Cinder would still be my friend if he saw my scars, but to what extent? Would he be embarrassed of me? Would he be like my stepsisters and not want to introduce me to his perfect-looking friends? Would he be like Jennifer and be afraid to look at me? Or like my father, stuck with an awkward acquaintance because he felt obligated?

If we met, we could never go back from that. It would undoubtedly change everything. I couldn't take that risk when he was all I had, so I said nothing.

EllaTheRealHero: Thanks for ditching your date to talk to me tonight.

Cinder458: Anytime. Talk again soon? You're not going to disappear on me again?

EllaTheRealHero: Not if I can help it. I'll watch that movie and get back to you. Goodnight, Cinder.

Cinder458: Goodnight, Ella. Thanks for writing me. I'm really glad you're okay.

He signed off and guilt swelled in me. Not telling him felt like a lie. "Maybe someday," I whispered to myself as I shut the laptop. I hoped it was true. I hoped someday I'd find the courage to face him.

My first day of school went pretty much as I'd expected it would. Everyone stared. I wore my winter uniform even though it was still so hot out because it covered my skin, but it didn't matter that people couldn't see my scars. They watched me limp around on my cane and stared at my long-sleeves and tights, knowing exactly who I was and what I was hiding beneath my clothes.

Some people tried to be discreet, or tried not to look, but their eyes drifted back to me anyway. Those were the kids who would force a smile my direction or speak to me out of politeness when they had to. Other kids stared openly, laughed, pointed, and teased me in an attempt to make the kids around them laugh.

No one made an effort to befriend me. No one stuck up for me when I was being teased. Some looked as if they felt bad for me, but were too afraid to intervene. I figured they were probably the kids who had been the target of the bullies until I came to school and took their places. Not even those kids invited me to sit with them at lunch. They were too afraid to be nice to me.

I did my best to ignore it all, but it was going to take time for me to get to the point where it wouldn't hurt me—if that was even possible.

My stepsisters were absolutely no help to me. I had both of them in at least one class and we all had the same lunch, but as I'd suspected would happen, they'd assumed the pretend-Ella-doesn't-exist tactic. The only time we spoke the entire day was in the parking lot after school. Anastasia greeted me with a nasty glare as she opened the passenger door of their tiny two-door convertible. "Parking in the handicapped section is so embarrassing."

Juliette dumped her backpack on the backseat and climbed behind the wheel. "Whatever. It's the best space in the entire parking lot. It's so close we'll be out of here before the real traffic."

Anastasia scoffed at her sister and pulled the passenger seat forward, gesturing for me to climb into the backseat. Was she kidding? "You know I can't climb in there, right?"

Anastasia shrugged. "Then walk home. I'm not riding in the back the whole year."

I closed my eyes against the sudden sting of frustrated tears. This had been an awful day and I just wanted to get home. "I'm not trying to be difficult. I physically can't climb back there."

"Ana!" Juliette hissed. "Would you just get in?"

"No. This is *our* car. We shouldn't have to be punished because the freak can't use her legs."

She'd raised her voice enough to gain the attention of half the kids in the parking lot. If she was truly embarrassed of me, she was definitely handling the situation the wrong way. Juliette obviously thought so, too. She glared at her sister and walked around the car to drop the keys in Anastasia's hand.

"Thanks," I mumbled when Juliette climbed into the back and pulled the seat back so that I could sit down.

"Whatever."

Anastasia looked at us both, then shook her head in disgust. After slipping into the driver's seat, she gave her hair a flip and glanced at her sister in the rearview mirror. "I can't believe you just gave her what she wants. Are you going to sit back there every day for the rest of the year?"

"Would you just go, already?" Juliette snapped. "People are

staring."

The ride home was silent, save for the Top 40 pop on the radio. Jennifer was home and waiting to greet us with huge smiles and a million questions. I wanted to go straight to my room and stay there until tomorrow, but my stomach won the battle against my willpower. I hadn't eaten breakfast or lunch, and I was going to be sick if I didn't get some food in me.

"How was your first day?" Jennifer asked the three of us as we all wandered into the kitchen.

Deciding she really only cared about her daughters, I let them field the questions and headed straight for the fridge. "It was a nightmare," Anastasia grumbled behind me. "Mom, she just walked around like a zombie, even though people kept laughing and pointing at her and stuff. It was like she had some nasty disease. She sat down in the cafeteria at lunch, and the kids at her table scattered like cockroaches. The place was packed—like, every seat was taken—but nobody would sit by her. She had the whole table all to herself. It was so embarrassing."

Unable to hold my temper in anymore, I slammed the fridge shut and turned around. "It was embarrassing for *you?*"

"Um, duh," Anastasia sneered. "Everyone knows you live with us. They kept asking us why our stepsister was such a freak all day. It takes you a hundred years to get anywhere, and you wore long-sleeves and tights even though it's, like, eighty-five degrees outside."

Juliette scoffed. "What else was she supposed to do? You've seen her legs."

I couldn't tell if she was defending me or insulting me, but Jennifer seemed to think it was the former because she nodded as if she agreed. "Ana, show a little compassion. How would you feel if you had to walk around school with a limp and look the way she does?"

My jaw dropped. If this was her idea of sticking up for me, I'd rather she didn't. But she was so clueless I couldn't even say anything or get angry at her. What would be the point?

Jennifer flashed me her most sympathetic smile. "It's fine to wear the long-sleeves and tights if they make you more comfortable, Ella."

Gee, I felt so much better now that I had her approval.

"Oh! That reminds me." Jennifer's face lit up with excitement and she pointed a finger at me. "I got something for you while I was out shopping today."

Both Anastasia and Juliette threw me startled, questioning looks as Jennifer disappeared upstairs to her bedroom, but I just shrugged them off. I had no idea what she was talking about. I grabbed a V8 juice and a string cheese from the fridge and sat down at the counter.

Jennifer was back before I finished my snack, and she had several small bags in her hands. "I've been thinking a lot about your scars," she said as she plopped an ocean of cosmetic products in front of me. "I'm in the modeling business, you know, so beauty and skin care are kind of my forte. I talked to a bunch of my friends, and I got you some creams, oils, and moisturizers that are supposed to really help reduce scarring."

I wasn't sure how to react. The gesture was thoughtful in a weird Jennifer way. It was almost sweet, even, until Ana scoffed. "I hate to break it to you, Mom, but no cream is going to fix her."

I thought the same thing, but it still didn't feel good to have it pointed out.

Jennifer frowned at Anastasia, and then down at my scarred hand. "Well, obviously it's not a cure or anything. You have so much scarring that it's not going to ever really go away, but some of these might help with all the weird blotchy patches and maybe smooth out a lot of the raised bumps. Those are really what stick out so badly. If we could smooth you over and even out the skin tone, your scars might not look so startling."

Oh my gosh, she thought I was hideous.

"There's always plastic surgery, too."

"Plastic surgery?" Did she really think I looked so terrible I needed surgery?

Jennifer, completely missing the horror in my voice, nodded enthusiastically. "Oh, totally. I talked to a doctor friend of mine about you. I showed him some of your medical photos and he said—"

"You talked to someone without asking me?" I gasped. "You showed him my *pictures?*"

Jennifer flinched, startled by my outburst. "I didn't want to say anything until I knew if he could help you. I didn't want to get your hopes up. But, Ella, he said there are definitely things he can do to help you. You won't always have to look as bad as you do now."

And that was it. I couldn't take one more second of this conversation. "I can't *believe* you did that."

"I was just trying to help."

"By telling me that I'm so ugly it's *startling*, and that I need plastic surgery?"

Anastasia choked on a laugh and muttered, "Well, it's the truth."

"Anastasia!" Jennifer snapped, horrified. "Don't you *ever* say something that rude again." After glaring at her daughter, she set her frustrated gaze on me. "That's not fair, Ella. You know that wasn't what I meant. I just want to help you look better, and if there are things we can do—"

"I've had enough surgeries, thanks."

Jennifer closed her eyes and reached up to rub her temple. It made me feel like a jerk. She was so tactless, but in her own twisted, insensitive way she really was trying to help me. Too exhausted after my nightmarish day to fight with her, I tried to settle down. I slipped off my stool and grabbed the bag of products she'd given me. "I'll ask my rehab team about this stuff, okay? I have to get permission before I put anything on my skin."

Jennifer calmed down too, and nodded. As I walked away, she called out to me in a smaller voice. "I really was just trying to help, Ella."

Ugh. And now I had to feel guilty on top of everything else.

I stopped walking and turned to face her. "I know. I'm sorry. I've just had a horrible day and I need a break. I'm going to go soak in a bath for a while."

"Try a little lavender oil in the tub. There's some in that bag. It's very soothing for nerves."

I STAYED IN THE BATH UNTIL THE WATER TURNED COLD AND HAD a good cry. It wasn't so much the stares from the other kids or being treated like a pariah that reduced me to tears once I was finally alone—it was more knowing that this was going to be my life from now on. Ana was right; nothing was ever going to fix my limp or my scars. The horrible day I'd had today was going to be on repeat forever.

Eventually, my father knocked on my bedroom door and then poked his head in the room after I answered. "Ella. We're going out to dinner in fifteen minutes. Can you get ready to—" My eyes must have still shown the evidence of my breakdown, because he blanched and came to sit on the edge of my bed. "Are you okay, honey?"

I didn't feel like rehashing my day with him, so I shrugged. "Fine. I just don't really feel up to going to dinner."

"Of course not, Ella," Jennifer said, joining us. "You can stay home if you need to."

My dad glanced back and forth between Jennifer and me a couple of times, and his frown deepened. "No, you can't," he said to me. "Sitting here alone tonight isn't going to make you feel any better. You need to come with us."

Before I could snap at him, Jennifer placed her hand on his arm and said, "It might be best to let her stay. School didn't go well. The girls had a tough day, and they're all a bit emotional right now."

As if this were the most shocking news ever, my father threw me a startled glance. "Was it really that bad?"

I glared at him. "Of course it was! What did you think it was going to be like?"

While I reached for a tissue, Jennifer leaned closer to my dad and lowered her voice. "It sounded awful, from what Juliette and Anastasia told me. Rich, maybe we *should* let her stay home and do online school."

"Yes, *please*," Anastasia begged, coming into my room with Juliette, as if I'd called some sort of family powwow.

Juliette nodded in agreement. "I think that would be best for all of us."

Dad took in all of our expressions and then surprised us all with a furious outburst. "No!"

"But, Rich—"

"No, Jennifer. You know why we can't do that. This is how her life is going to be from now on. She has to get used to it."

My empty stomach flopped in my gut. Not that I wanted to be coddled, but there was absolutely no empathy. No acknowledgement of how hard my day must have been for me. No attempt to comfort me in any way.

"You heard what her doctor told us. She has to learn how to interact with people. She can't isolate herself, or she'll only get worse."

"But she's never going to make any friends," Jennifer argued. "She'll be scarred for life." Jennifer, realizing that I already was scarred for life, cringed. "Emotionally, I mean."

Her faith in me was astounding. She thought I was every bit the freak her daughters did. That I was so bad I needed surgery, and I'd never have any friends. I can't say I didn't worry about the same thing, but as the parental figure she was supposed to at least pretend it was possible. A little optimism from anyone would have been nice.

"Maybe we could find her a special school, for other kids like her," Jennifer suggested. "They have schools for kids with disabilities. Maybe she'd be happier if she was with her equals."

My jaw hit the floor. My *equals?* As if being crippled and scarred somehow made me, and other handicapped kids, lesser people? My lawyer father should have been all over that ignorant, discriminatory comment, but instead he looked at her with interest. "Maybe you're right. I'll ask her team about the possibility."

I was crushed. I knew he'd left me for these people a long time ago, but I still felt betrayed right then. He was my *father*. He should have been defending me. He should have at least been concerned for my feelings. "Hello!" I screamed. "I'm right here! If you're going to discuss me like I don't have a mind or feelings of my own, could you at least do it behind my back?"

Jennifer paled and my father brought his hand up over his eyes, rubbing his temples with his finger and thumb as if his head hurt. "You're right, Ella. I'm sorry. Why don't you and I go to dinner tonight and we can discuss this alone?"

"What?" Juliette shouted. "Dad! That's not fair! We have reservations tonight!"

"I know, sweetheart, but Ella's had a really bad day. I think we could both use the one-on-one time."

"We've *all* had a bad day! What about us? Everything's always about her now! Back-to-school dinner is a family tradition. You can't forget about your real family just because her life sucks."

I couldn't handle one more second of this. "Relax, Juliette. I don't want to steal your evening." I was too tired to keep up my anger at my dad. "You don't have to break tradition for me. Go have your family dinner, or whatever. I'm fine."

"Ella." Dad sighed. "You're coming, too. You're part of the family."

I was wrong about being too tired to be mad. Rage bubbled up in me, giving me a second wind. "No. I *was* part of your family. You left me for this one."

"Honey, that's not—"

"Don't, Dad," I interrupted before he could start giving me excuses. "We both know that if Mama hadn't died I'd still be nothing but a distant memory to you, so don't pretend you care about me."

For a moment my father looked as though I'd slapped him, and then he lost his patience. "I can't change the past, Ella! I'm doing the best I can now, and that will just have to be good enough. You had better figure out a way to get over your anger because, like it or not, we *are* your family now. You're stuck with us, so suck it up and get in the car."

I wanted to say no. I wanted to put my foot down and make him have to drag me, kicking and screaming. He'd hurt me for ten years. He didn't get to walk back into my life and expect to just have my forgiveness. He hadn't even apologized. But the less fuss I made, the sooner I'd be able to get out of this house.

"Fine, whatever."

My dad took another deep breath and forced himself to calm down. "Thank you. Hurry and change. We have to leave in ten minutes."

I frowned down at my jeans and long-sleeve T-shirt. I looked normal enough. "Why do I need to change?"

"Providence is only one of the nicest restaurants in Los Angeles," Anastasia bragged. "They won't let you in if you look like a Walmart ad."

It wasn't until that moment that I noticed the twins were both dressed to kill. My dad and Jennifer were dressed up, too. Great. My father's very presence commanded respect, and Jennifer belonged on his arm like the perfect trophy wife. Anastasia and Juliette completed the picture, looking like a couple of pampered heiresses. This family deserved their own reality show.

After Dad ushered everyone out of my room so I could change, I stared into my closet for an eternity, knowing I'd never find anything that would make me fit in with the Colemans. As I slid the hanging clothes from one end of the rack to the other, I came across my mother's little canary-yellow cocktail dress. Mama and I didn't get the chance to dress up that often. We were never poor exactly, but we had to watch what we spent, and we had to save up if we wanted to do anything extravagant. One time, though, when I was about thirteen, she'd dated this professional salsa dancer for a few months, and he loved taking her out dancing, so she'd splurged and bought the dress.

I hugged the dress to my face and took a deep breath. It didn't smell like her anymore, but that didn't matter. It was my favorite thing of hers that she ever wore. She always looked so beautiful in it. I'd cried with relief when I went though the boxes my dad packed and saw that he'd saved it.

"I miss you so much, Mama," I whispered. "It's not fair that I have to do this alone. I *need* you."

Before I realized what I was doing, I'd slipped the dress over my head. It fit me so well, it felt like fate. The dress had spaghetti straps and stopped at the knee. The thought of leaving the house with my scars showing made me physically ill, but people were going to stare at me no matter what, so why not take a piece of my mother with me? I was going to need her if I wanted to survive this dinner.

I put on the string of pearls she always wore with the dress and twisted my hair up the same way she used to, then stared at myself in the mirror for a long time. If I ignored the scars, I almost felt like a human being again. I could see my mother staring back at me out of the glass. I looked just like her, except for the eyes.

"I love you, Mama," I whispered as I grabbed my cane and headed out to face the firing squad.

Slowly, I made my way to the front entryway where everyone was waiting for me. When I came around the corner, they all took one look at me and froze.

"Oh, no. You are *not* wearing that!" Anastasia cried.

I couldn't help feeling defensive. I loved this dress. "What's wrong with it? You're all wearing dresses."

"Mom!" Anastasia sent Jennifer a pleading look.

"It's a beautiful dress, Ella," Jennifer said quickly. Her voice was so patronizing I may as well have been five years old. "But are you sure you want to wear it?"

"Why wouldn't I?"

Jennifer froze for a moment and then forced a pained smile on her face. "Well, honey, it's just that it's…a little revealing."

That was another slap in the face. I glanced at Anastasia and Juliette and folded my arms across my chest. "It's longer than either of their dresses, and *my* cleavage isn't hanging out for the whole world to see."

"No, no, I didn't mean that," Jennifer backtracked. "I know the dress isn't inappropriate. That's not what I meant."

I was an idiot. I couldn't believe it took me that long to understand what everyone's problem was. "You meant you don't want me to wear the dress because it shows my scars. You're as embarrassed of me as they are."

Jennifer shook her head frantically until her eyes filled with tears. She turned her head into my dad's shoulder, weeping. He threw his arms around her and glared at me over her head. "That is enough, Ellamara. Just because you're having a hard time doesn't mean you can walk all over this family's feelings. You've proved your point. Now stop being difficult and just go change your clothes."

I hadn't known my heart could break any more than it already had. Even my dad, my own flesh and blood, didn't want to be seen with me if my scars were showing. "I didn't put it on to prove some kind of point! This was my mother's dress. I just wanted to have *my* family present at this *family* dinner. I shouldn't have to change just because you're too embarrassed to be seen with me. It's not my fault I disgust all of you."

My dad cursed under his breath when he realized his mistake. All the blood drained from his face, leaving him pale as a ghost. His voice cracked as he whispered, "Ellamara, I'm sorry. I thought…"

"I know what you thought!" His apology was too little, too late. "You keep telling me that you guys are my family, but you're not. If my mother had seen me in this dress, she would have hugged me and told me she was proud of me for trying to be brave—not ask me to change my clothes. That's just sick. She wouldn't be embarrassed of my scars. She wouldn't care about them at all because she loved me. *She* was my family."

I turned around and headed for my room, wishing more than anything that I could have run there. I wasn't going anywhere with any of them now. My father really would have to throw me over his shoulder and carry me if he wanted me to leave the house.

Brian

I KNEW I SHOULD NEVER HAVE GIVEN SCOTT KEYS TO MY PLACE. How the hell was I supposed to avoid people when I couldn't lock out the one person determined not to let me skip my meetings?

"Brian?" Scott called out as he entered the house. He found me sitting on the living room sofa three seconds later. "You were supposed to be there over an hour ago. Kaylee threatened to remove my man parts if I don't have you there in twenty minutes."

I looked down at the IM box on my laptop and sighed.

Cinder458: As much as I am enjoying this groveling session, I have to go.
EllaTheRealHero: Yeah, yeah, your Friday night awaits you, Mr. Popular. Go have fun.

I smiled. I supposed I could enjoy myself now.

Ella had finally watched my movie *The Long Road Home* like I'd asked her to. She'd been so surprised that she wrote a hilarious review entitled "My Sincerest Apologies to Mr. Brian Oliver." It was a movie review like the ones she used to write for her blog before her accident, except it was written in the form of a personal letter to me, apologizing for thinking I was going to ruin Cinder. It was brilliant.

After she sent me her review of *The Long Road Home*, I immediately wrote her back and insisted she start blogging again. I knew how much Ella loved her blog, and it had killed me when she said she wasn't going to do it anymore. It may have taken weeks of begging, but Ella had finally posted her review today. She gave a brief explanation that she'd been in an accident and unable to keep up with her blog, but thanks to an argument with a certain "obsessed fan" of hers, she was back and had to start with her thoughts on the cast of *The Druid Prince*. She'd started with her apology letter to Brian Oliver.

When I found the post this afternoon, I signed on to welcome her back to the blogosphere, and we ended up getting into an argument in the comments section of her post about Princess Ratana's costume. Quite a few of Ella's readers had already found her post and were jumping into the debate as well. I was pleased to see that my side was winning, despite the welcome-back lovefest Ella was getting from her fans.

Cinder458: It shall be as my wise priestess asks. I wasn't really looking forward to this evening, but now I promise I will have lots of fun in honor of your return to the blogging world.
EllaTheRealHero: You're a weirdo.
Cinder458: I am not. You love me.
EllaTheRealHero: Yes, you are, and yes, I do. Goodnight, Cinder.

A violent longing filled me as I stared in shock at Ella's reply. I expected her to come back with something about my overinflated ego, and instead she admitted she loved me. She'd never said something like that before. I knew it couldn't possibly be the same way that I cared for her, because only I was crazy enough to fall for a random stranger on the Internet, but at least she loved me in *some* way.

Cinder458: Goodnight, Ella.

I hesitated and then typed one last message.

Cinder458: I love you, too.

I let out a breath as I hit ENTER. Maybe it was on instant messenger, and maybe I'd never met Ella in person, and probably she thought I was joking, but I'd never said those words to a woman before. For me, this moment was huge.

A long whistle startled me out of my epiphany. I looked up to see Scott standing behind me, reading over my shoulder with wide eyes.

Ugh. Time to get back to reality.

After a long stretch, I closed my laptop. Before Scott could ask about Ella and what I'd just written to her, I said, "You win. I'm coming. We can't have you losing your man parts on my account."

. . . . .

"CAREFUL," SCOTT WARNED AS WE ENTERED THE CLUB. "KAYLEE IS pissed that you didn't show up on time tonight."

I smirked. Of course she was pissed. Tonight was her twenty-first birthday, and according to her, it was the night we were supposed to get engaged. She rented out the most exclusive club in LA for her party and invited every VIP she knew. And, from the looks of it, every paparazzi in the state of California, too.

If Scott thought Kaylee was pissed now, he should just wait until I broke off the fake relationship instead of giving her the ring I was supposed to buy—and hadn't. "A word to the wise, Scotty: run while you still can."

Scott wasn't fast enough. Kaylee pounced on us both the second we came through the door. "Baby!" she squealed, plastering herself against me. "What took you guys so long?"

Her voice was happy, but the fire in her eyes explained exactly how pissed she was. She'd brought an entourage of friends and birthday well-wishers with her, and after politely saying hello to them all, I took Kaylee by the hand and said, "Can we talk privately for a minute?"

Kaylee's whole face lit up. "Sure!"

She made a face at the crowd that suggested she thought she was getting a birthday surprise, then let me drag her off to a private table.

I didn't waste any time. As soon as I was sure no one could overhear us, I said, "I don't want to do this."

Kaylee rolled her eyes. "Yeah, you've made that quite clear since the moment it was suggested in that meeting."

"Let me rephrase." My patience was already wearing thin. "I'm not *going* to do this."

Kaylee's eyes narrowed into thin slits. "The hell you're not."

"Kaylee." I rubbed my temples and took a breath. I wasn't going to fight with her if I could help it. "Give me a break, okay? Things have changed for me since that meeting."

If Kaylee were a cat, she'd have arched her back and puffed up her tail. As it was, she stiffened and folded her arms across her chest. "You mean that girl?"

That girl? Ella was so much more than *that* girl. "Yes, I mean Ella. If I'd known she was alive, I never would have let anyone talk me into this stupid plan in the first place. Now that I have her back, I'm not going to ruin things with her by getting pretend-engaged to you."

Kaylee began to tremble slightly from the rage building up inside her. She was going to explode any minute. "So you're just going to dump me for her? Are you going to ask her to be your fake fiancée instead?"

I was so horrified by that thought that I lost my temper. "I'm not doing this fake shit with you anymore! We have to break it off right now. I'm going to go to Boston to meet Ella. I'm going to tell her who I am, and I don't want her to think I have a girlfriend when I do. I want to date her, and I refuse to keep it secret or make her wait for me while I prance around LA with my fake fiancée in front of cameras."

I hadn't thought Kaylee's eyes could open any wider, but I was wrong. They grew so big they nearly popped out of her head. Her mouth fell open, too, and she leaned forward over the table that separated us. "Wait a minute." She threw a hand up, as if she were going to shake a finger at me. "She doesn't know who you are? You've never *met* her?"

My cheeks grew warm with embarrassment. I knew it sounded crazy, but I also knew what I felt. "My relationship with Ella is…complicated."

"Define 'complicated.'"

I didn't want to talk about Ella with Kaylee. Kaylee would never understand. Ella was the best thing in my life, and Kaylee would only want to tear that apart. Kaylee was like poison. I wasn't going to let her taint what I had with Ella. "I don't have to explain myself to you."

"Yes, you do!" Kaylee hissed. "You're breaking up with me. I deserve an explanation."

I clenched my jaw and once again tried to keep my temper in

check. "We aren't really breaking up. We aren't actually together."

"We may as well be. It's what everyone thinks. What about the publicity? What about our careers? What about proving you're not just some arrogant player? What about our *plan*, Brian?"

"If we make it amicable, say it was mutual and that we're just better as friends, it won't be so bad. You'll still get plenty of publicity when the movie comes out, and I'll just stay out of trouble. We'll be fine."

"Sure, we'd be *fine*," Kaylee agreed, spitting out the word *fine* as though it left a bad taste in her mouth. "But think of how much more we could be if we stick to the plan. We could become the next Kanye and Kim, the next Brad and Angelina! Between your father and mine, and the way the entire nation loves us, we could own this town. Fame is just a popularity contest, and we're the prom king and queen. We're *supposed* to be together."

Her anger died just a tad and her voice softened. "We could be great together. If you would just stop fighting this and do it for real, you'd see. I could make you happy, Brian."

There was no way in hell Kaylee could ever make me happy, but I managed to keep that thought to myself. "I can't do that. I'm in *love* with Ella."

The force of my statement shocked us both. I sucked in a breath and blew it all out of my lungs after that admission, but it felt so good to admit it out loud that I said it again. "I love her, Kay. I can't be with you—I can't even pretend anymore—when all I want is her."

Kaylee sat back in her seat and stayed quiet, surprising me with the amount of pain in her eyes. I expected her to be pissed off that she wasn't getting her way, but I never dreamed she'd be hurt by my rejection.

I reached across the table and placed a hand over hers. "I'm sorry."

After a minute, Kaylee looked up as if she were contemplating a new approach. She pulled something small out of her purse—an engagement ring—and held it out for me to see. She slipped it on her finger, as if she just wanted to see what it looked like, and sighed wistfully. "It's beautiful, isn't it?"

Oh shit. I was the one who was supposed to get the ring. What the hell was she doing with it? "Why do you have that?"

Kaylee pulled her eyes away from the diamond. The look she gave me caused a bad feeling in my stomach. "I'm not an idiot, Brian. I knew you were going to try and weasel out of this tonight."

In a flash, her entire countenance changed and she became the evil woman I had just pictured devouring my assistant. "I don't give a shit who you love. I'm not going to let you ruin this for me. I will, however, ruin *you* if you don't step up your game right now. I'll ruin your father, too. There are going to be four more *Cinder Chronicles* movies, and directors can easily be replaced. My father *owns* the two of you, and Daddy gives me whatever I want. I'll make sure neither of you ever work a real job in this town again. And then, when you're finished in Hollywood and you finally run crying to your precious little Ella, I'll destroy her worst of all."

My heart stopped beating at the threat, and all my blood turned to ice. Kaylee could definitely do some major damage to both my father's and my career, though I doubted she could ruin them entirely. But she could destroy Ella. It didn't matter that she didn't know who Ella was; the second I met Ella, the world would know—the world always knew everything I did. Once I moved beyond anonymous Internet friend status with her, I'd never be able to keep her secret.

Kaylee was cruel, and Ella had been through so much. If Kaylee wanted to, she could find every crack in Ella's armor and use her tragedies to break her to pieces without ever even meeting her. There was no doubt in my mind that if I scorned Kaylee now, she would do exactly that.

"Ah," Kaylee said with satisfaction. "I see we finally understand each other, don't we?"

"If you even think of dragging Ella into this—"

"Oh, no, you've already dragged her into this, and if you want me to stay away from her, then you go all in. No more half-assed appearances and bad attitudes. You take all that sappy, pathetic puppy love in your heart and you make the world believe it's all for me. Make *me* believe it, Brian."

Kaylee jumped to her feet without warning, squealing loudly and hopping up and down with crazy, giddy excitement. "Yes!" she cried. "Yes, yes, with all my heart, yes! Of course, I'll marry you!"

She bounded around the small table and jumped on me before I even realized what was happening. She planted a kiss on my mouth while everyone in the entire room gathered around, clapping and cheering.

As soon as I could break free of the kiss, I took a few deep breaths and pulled Kaylee close so that I could whisper in her ear. "You have no heart, you bitch."

"Sure I do, baby, and it only beats for you." She thrust her newly blinged-out hand out to the crowd for everyone to see and cried, "We're getting married! Best birthday present ever!"

Kaylee gave me another evil smile and fluttered her eyelids, saying, "I love you so much."

She waited for me to say it back, but I wouldn't do it. I would never say those words to her, whether I meant them or not. "Good" was what I replied instead, earning a hearty laugh from the crowd.

Rage flashed in Kaylee's eyes, but she couldn't say anything with everyone watching. She forced her smile a little brighter and kissed me again. I hated it, but I had absolutely no choice other than to kiss her back. I couldn't let her hurt Ella. I wouldn't even let her figure out how I knew Ella. I'd just have to wait to tell Ella the truth until after Kaylee was finished with me. I could only pray Kaylee's plans didn't include a trip to Las Vegas and a legitimate marriage certificate.

THE WEEKS STARTED TO PASS. EACH DAY BLENDED INTO THE NEXT, and nothing ever changed. I hated it, but I learned to deal with it. For the most part, I left people alone and they left me alone. When the kids at school did tease me, they were never too outwardly aggressive. They mocked me from a distance. I ignored it as best I could. I kept my head down, I did my work, and I never cried. At least, not in school.

I always managed to save my tears until I was locked in my bedroom. I'd get it out of my system, and then I would e-mail Cinder. He'd tell me some ridiculous story, or say something completely moronic about a book or a movie, and I'd be compelled to argue. Either way, he always made everything okay.

Cinder asked about my accident, and my mom, and living with my new family occasionally. I knew he was worried about me, but I just couldn't talk about it with him. He was my ray of sunshine. He was the only thing that kept me sane. I couldn't do anything to change that. When he asked, I told him I was doing okay, and that was it. He never pushed for more. When I said I didn't want to talk about sad topics, he said okay and then distracted me with things he knew would make me laugh.

He also talked me into blogging again. I'd watched that Brian Oliver movie he told me about and was pleasantly surprised. Cinder had been right. There was more to Brian Oliver than a pretty face. He had some depth, and there was a possibility—a *slight* possibility—that he might be able to save *The Druid Price* from being total Hollywood crap. When I sent Cinder my review, he'd liked it so much he insisted I post it. It took some coaxing, but eventually I did. After that, writing other reviews was easy. My followers welcomed me back with open arms, and another tiny piece of my broken heart fused back together.

The first time a box of books arrived at my house from a publisher, I was forced to explain myself to my father. He'd been relieved that I had a hobby besides hiding in my room. He went straight out and got me a set of bookshelves filled with books, and a new e-reader. He even got me on some kind of press list so that I could go to media screenings of movies for free. I still didn't like the guy, but even I could admit that was cool of him.

Between my blog and Cinder, life had become somewhat bearable. Time passed this way until Halloween, and then my world took another spin. I was in my second class of the day and my teacher, Mrs. Teague, gave us the last ten minutes of class as free time. It wasn't a minute after I pulled out a book that I felt someone looming over my shoulder.

Jason Malone, one of Anastasia's on-again off-again playthings, was smiling down at me. "What's up, Ella?" he asked when I'd finally given in and looked at him.

"Nothing." I knew this wasn't a friendly gesture. Jason had been one of my most obnoxious torturers this year. "What do you want?"

He laughed and stepped up to the side of my desk. "I was just wondering what you were doing for Halloween tonight. Are you planning on going to the dance?"

"No."

I turned my attention back to my book, hoping he would leave. He, of course, didn't. "Bummer," he said. "They're having this contest to see who can come as the most horrifying monster. Your sister thinks you could win."

I knew where this was going, so I didn't play into his game. I simply said, "She's not my sister."

"She said you wouldn't even need a costume. She said you could come in shorts and a tank top and they would just hand you the crown. She said people would run screaming at the sight of you."

"Yeah, that sounds like her."

I scanned the room to check the time and saw Juliette sitting a few seats over, watching Jason and me with a scowl on her face. I met her eyes and she quickly looked away, trying her best to pretend I didn't exist.

I wasn't surprised that she wouldn't make Jason stop, even though she was the only girl in the class that probably could have. She and I had two different classes together, and she'd watched me take this kind of harassment all year without ever saying anything. But at least she wasn't standing over Jason's shoulder, giggling and egging him on the way Anastasia would have if she were here.

Class was almost over now, thankfully, so I reached for my backpack. I guess Jason didn't like the fact that he hadn't upset me, because he took the book out of my hands before I could slip it in my bag.

"I'm curious, Ella. Are you really as hideous as she says you are?"

"Give me my book back."

"You want it? Show me your scars."

I'd become a pro at not reacting to the things people say, but that was so shocking that I gasped. "Excuse me?"

Jason smirked, excited to see that he'd finally hit a nerve. "You always wear those long-sleeve shirts and tights. The whole school knows what you're trying to cover up. Just let me see. I promise not to run screaming." He laughed. "Unless it's true."

I chose to get angry because when I was mad it was a lot easier to control my tears, and I would *not* cry in front of this jerk.

"Go to hell." My voice quivered, but it didn't break.

"Is that where you went to get those burns? Why'd they send you back? Are you such a freak that even hell didn't want you?"

My whole body started to shake. I had to lay my bad hand flat on my desk to keep from balling it into a fist and hurting myself. Jason watched the action and then said, "Come on, Ella, let's see it."

He reached out, quick as a flash, and yanked my arm up, reaching to push up my sleeve. He didn't pull that hard. It never would have hurt a normal person, but I'd never regained full movement in my right arm. I wasn't capable of fully extending it. When Jason jerked it, I felt the skin tear near my elbow.

I screamed as fire shot up my arm and through my whole body. Jason dropped me as if he'd caught fire from me. I clamped my good hand over my arm, but it didn't stop the pain. For the first time since I started school, I cried in front of my classmates.

Juliette reached Jason and me at the same time as Mrs. Teague did. I saw the rage in Juliette's eyes, but was in too much pain to be shocked when she pulled Jason away from me and screamed at him. "You stupid asshole!"

"What is going on here?" Mrs. Teague demanded.

Juliette shoved Jason and Mrs. Teague out of the way and knelt down beside my desk. "Are you all right?"

"No." I lifted my hand off my arm and showed her the bright red stains seeping through my white turtleneck. "He tore the skin graft."

Juliette swore.

Jason looked as if he were about to faint, and the rest of the class was freaking out. Even Mrs. Teague gaped down at me with wide, panicked eyes. Only Juliette never lost her cool. "We need to call your nurse. Where's your phone?"

"Backpack," I gasped. "School nurse should have pain meds. It really hurts."

Juliette nodded. "Come on." She helped me out of my chair. Instead of handing me my cane, she pulled my good arm over her shoulders.

Mrs. Teague picked up our backpacks and my cane. "I'll take this stuff to the office," she said, and then snapped her fingers at Jason. "You, come with me now!"

My father was on a rampage. The guy was a prosecuting attorney, after all. He lived to deliver threats. He was in the principal's office with the door closed, and I was down the hall in the nurse's office, but I could still hear his muffled, angry shouts. So far he'd threatened to get Jason thrown in jail, sue his family, sue the school, and get Mrs. Teague fired.

After yet another roar, I cringed. "If I have to have another surgery, he's going to bring this institution to utter ruins."

My nurse, Cody, gave me a sad smile as he finished taping the bandage around my arm. "I wouldn't be surprised if you do need one. Your arm shouldn't have torn so easily. The scar is too thick inside your elbow. I want you to schedule an appointment with your surgeon when you get home today, and you need to take it easy for a while during your PT."

When Juliette called my dad and explained what happened, he'd called both my nurse and my psychiatrist and asked them to come to the school. I couldn't decide if it was a paranoid move, or if he just wanted to make more of a show for the poor staff he was terrorizing.

I felt enough like an idiot for being hurt so easily in the first place. Then there was the spectacle my dad was making. Add the special doctors coming to the school just for me, and I was even more of a freak than ever. But at least Cody was cool. It was nice to have one friendly face amidst this chaos.

"You'll have to give Daniel that message about taking it easy in physical therapy yourself," I told Cody. "He'll never believe me. He loves to torture me."

"I know," Cody teased. "I've seen a few of your sessions together. The guy is a sick, twisted harbinger of pain."

Cody and I were both laughing when my dad came in the room with Dr. Parish. "She's *laughing?*" Dad asked, surprised. A smile crossed his face. "You're a miracle worker, Cody."

"Nah, I just gave her a lot of good pain medication."

"So that's your secret?" Dr. Parish asked. "I can't ever get a smile out of her."

"That's because you suck all the fun out of everything," I grumbled. Dr. Parish was a nice enough woman, but I hated our sessions. "You're always so serious."

"Your mental well-being *is* serious, Ella. I wish you would take our sessions *more* seriously."

"Is she all right?" my dad asked Cody, then looked at me. "Are you?"

"I'm fine."

"I'll need to come by every day to check on her until the wound is closed, but she should be fine in a week or so. She needs to have it looked at by her surgeon, just to be safe."

"I'll schedule it this afternoon. Is she okay to talk now? Her principal and the police would like to speak with her."

"She's on some pretty heavy pain medication, but her judgment shouldn't be too impaired."

"I wish it were," I muttered as I followed my dad down the hall.

"In here." Dad held open the door to a small conference room. "Juliette, you too!"

I looked back as Juliette scrambled from a chair in front of the reception desk. I still couldn't believe she'd helped me. I met her eyes as she walked past me into the room, but she quickly looked away. Obviously, helping me out in an emergency didn't make us friends.

Before I walked into the conference room, the door to the principal's office opened. Two police officers escorted a dejected Jason out in handcuffs. A pair of highly pissed-off parents followed them. I tried to hurry inside the conference room, but Jason's mom saw me and stopped me. "Miss Coleman?"

I suppressed a sigh and turned around. "My name is Rodriguez, not Coleman."

Jason's mom frowned, but didn't ask. "My son has something he'd like to say to you."

She glared at Jason until he muttered an apology. His "I'm sorry" was about as sincere as my "It's fine."

He couldn't take his eyes off my bandaged arm. Cody had had to cut off my sleeve above my elbow in order to examine the wound, so my scars were now on full display. The fact that Jason was seeing them made me feel violated. "Looks like you got what you wanted after all," I said. I held out my arm so he could get a really good look. "So is it true? Am I really horrifying enough to win a crown?"

I was so angry that I'd forgotten about the other scars on my wrist until Jason gasped. I followed his wide-eyed gaze to the marks left by my suicide attempt, and so did his parents. We all echoed his gasp.

I wanted to disappear. I wanted to run and hide and cry until I shriveled up and ceased to exist, but I couldn't. I couldn't show even more weakness now that he knew this secret about me. Instead of shrinking away in horror, I pulled up the sleeve on my other arm and let Jason see the full extent of my shame.

"Make sure you get a good look so you have lots of details to tell all your friends tomorrow. I can't wait to hear all the witty things you guys will come up with for this."

I shoved my wrists a little closer to him, and he flinched away from me. "Shit, Ella. I'm sorry, okay?"

This apology seemed a little more sincere, but it didn't really make me feel any better. "You want to know why you've never been able to make me cry?" I asked. "Because you're trying to tear down someone who's already hit rock bottom. You can't make me feel any worse about myself than I already do. You're pathetic, Jason—you and all the other jerks in this school who have nothing better to do with your lives than pick on a cripple."

I realized I might have gone too far when Jason's mom gasped again and burst into tears. I was surprised that my father hadn't tried to stop me, but when I glanced up at him he was glaring so hard at Jason that I guessed he didn't care how rude I was. He met my eyes and placed his hand gently on my shoulder. "Ellamara, come on, honey."

My dad steered me into the conference room as the cops nudged Jason toward the exit. There was another set of cops sitting at the conference table with Principal Johnson and Mrs. Teague. Dr. Parish and Cody were both there too, along with Jennifer and Juliette.

Once I sat down, the questions started flying. These people were all supposed to be on my side—my "support system," as Dr. Parish liked to call them—but it felt like the Spanish Inquisition. Eventually they dragged every detail of my encounter with Jason out of me. I'd left Anastasia's name out of the conversation, but when my father heard the bit about the costume contest he was on his feet spouting more threats.

"I thought there was a zero-tolerance bullying policy at this school! I thought the students had to sign a personal conduct code to come here! I should have this entire institution put under investigation!"

My dad whirled around and leaned over my chair, invading my personal space as if I were one of his criminals. "I want the names of everyone who's been hassling you."

I accidentally snorted a laugh, and my dad's eyes flashed. "This isn't a joke!" He pushed a paper and pencil at me. "I want their names, Ella! All of them!"

"I can't possibly list everyone who's been mean to me since I got here. That's half the school. I don't even know most of them."

"Half the school?" His face turned a scary shade of red. "Then just give me the ringleaders. I'll have them all expelled."

I sighed. "If you do that, you're only going to make things worse for me."

"She's right," Juliette said, speaking up for the first time. "If you get people in trouble for teasing Ella, they'll hate her for being a narc."

"These kids have to be held accountable, or they will never stop!" Dad roared.

"Fine, you want a name?" Juliette snapped. "Anastasia Coleman."

The entire room froze. Slowly, Dad stood up to his full height and turned to face Juliette. *"What?"*

She shrugged defiantly. "You asked who the ringleader was. Anastasia beats out anybody in this school, hands down."

My dad's voice was eerily calm when he said, "Is this true, Ella?"

I glared at my lap and said nothing.

"You want to know why Jason really did what he did today?" Juliette asked.

"Juliette, don't. She'll only start making my life hell at home, too."

Juliette sat back and shut her mouth, but it was too late. Dad glared back and forth between us, making it very clear that we would tell him everything he wanted to know, and we would tell him *now.* "What did your sister have to do with what happened today?"

Juliette broke first. "You know how she dumped Jason last week? Well, he asked her if they could get back together and go to the Halloween dance as a couple, and she said she'd only do it if he got Ella to show everyone her scars."

I sucked in a breath. I hadn't known that.

Dad looked as if he was counting to ten in his mind so that he wouldn't explode. After a minute he asked, "How long has this kind of thing been going on?"

Again, the question was directed at me, but it was Juliette who responded. "Since she got here, but it's been getting worse the last few weeks."

Everyone in the room was quiet. It felt as if we were all waiting for the axe to drop, only I had no idea whose head was going to get lobbed off. It was one of the police officers who finally broke the silence. "Well." He cleared his throat and rose to his feet. "I believe we have all the information we need for now."

His partner followed his cue and added, "We'll be in touch, Mr. Coleman."

"I don't want to press charges against Jason," I blurted before the cops could leave the room.

They turned around and waited for me to say more.

"What do you mean you don't want to press charges?" Dad asked. "That boy *assaulted* you." He looked at the waiting policemen and said, "We're not dropping the charges."

"Sir, your daughter is over eighteen. If she chooses not to—"

"I have court-ordered custody of Ellamara right now," my dad interrupted. "I have every right to make that decision, and I damn well want to press charges."

Both cops threw startled looks in my direction, and the room fell into its most awkward silence yet. The nicer of the two cops tried to give me a sympathetic smile as he said, "If he has legal custody, then I have to go with his decision. I'm sorry."

They started to leave and I panicked. I lost my temper and screamed at my father. "Damn it, Dad! Stop worrying about your own damn pride for two seconds, and please just trust me for once! *Please!*"

My dad's anger vanished and he stared at me, dumbstruck.

"Jason grabbed my arm—that's all," I continued desperately. "I know it was crappy of him, and I know you're pissed about it, but he didn't know what could happen to me. He didn't *mean* to hurt me. I'm sure he got suspended, or whatever. That's punishment enough. If you send him to jail or sue his family, you really will just make things worse for me. *Please* don't cause me any more trouble."

My dad recovered from his shock and pulled his face into a frown. He cast a withering glance at Juliette and she nodded vigorously. "She's right. It'll make things worse."

It stung a little that Dad still needed Juliette's confirmation and couldn't just take my word for it, but I was glad Juliette stuck up for me.

My dad clenched his jaw and sucked in a harsh breath through his nose. "Fine," he grunted. "We'll drop the charges. But you had better tell me if he ever gives you any trouble, Ellamara." He looked at Juliette and said, "That goes for you, too."

We both nodded.

"We'll need you to sign some paperwork," one of the cops said.

"We'll stop by the station after we're done here."

My dad shook the guys' hands, and after they left Principal Johnson looked at me. "And so the question left to answer now is what do we do with *you*, Ellamara?"

"What do you mean?"

"I'm not sure that this school is the best place for you," Principal Johnson said slowly.

My defenses jumped into high gear. I hated this school with a passion, but it pissed me off that they wanted to throw me out of it. "You want to kick me out? But I didn't do anything. It's not like I egg people on. I don't even fight back."

"We know that, Ella," Dr. Parish said quickly. "You're not in trouble. I think Principal Johnson is just concerned about you. Obviously something isn't working here, and we need to figure out what's best for you."

Principal Johnson nodded in agreement. "Your parents and I believe a school for physically disabled children might be more suitable for you."

"A *special* school?" Juliette cried, as horrified by the thought as I was.

Jennifer had suggested this to my dad once before. Apparently they'd discussed it more seriously than I thought. I hated the idea then, and I hated it now. "How would locking me away in a school like that help me?"

"I don't believe it would," Dr. Parish said. "I disagree with your parents and your principal on this matter."

"We just want you to be more comfortable," Jennifer insisted. "You wouldn't be teased in a school like that. You wouldn't be the only one with disabilities. You'd have some time to get used to your body, and maybe even make some friends."

Dr. Parish shook her head. "That won't help her." She met my eyes and said, "You manage well enough physically, and mentally there's not a thing wrong with you. Sending you to a specialized school would only be indulging your social anxiety and self-deprecation. You might find a year of reprieve, but it wouldn't do a thing to help you in the long run. If anything, you'll only have a harder time adjusting after you graduate."

"But she can't just keep going on like she is, either," my dad argued. "You said making her go to school would help her get better, but she's not getting any better."

"I agree with Mr. Coleman," Principal Johnson added. "Ella is not adapting here. She makes no effort to assimilate. She doesn't speak to her peers. She doesn't participate in any school clubs or extracurricular activities. In the two months she's been here, she has only become more withdrawn."

Dr. Parish sighed. "Would you both please address Ella directly, and stop verbally attacking her? I understand that you're frustrated, but what happened today was in no way her fault. Remember that she is a *victim* here. She needs your support, not your anger."

My eyes snapped wide open. Go, Doc! I've never seen anyone talk down to my father like that. I smirked at the abashed looks on both men's faces as they felt the wrath of Dr. Parish for the first time. The woman was formidable. Maybe my dad would understand a little more now why I hated my sessions so much.

She was tough, but effective. Both my dad and Principal Johnson apologized to me, and Principal Johnson gave me a pleading look. "I know you've been harassed by some, but you can't be getting it from *every* student here. Have you tried talking to anyone? Have you reached out to anyone at all?"

I hadn't, and everyone knew it. I gritted my teeth, hating that he had a point. "Fine. I haven't been making enough effort, but that's not a reason to kick me out of school."

"Ella, you promised me you would try to build a support system, and you're not doing it," Dr. Parish said. "You're not recovering socially."

"You wouldn't either, if you had to deal with the crap I put up with here."

Like always, Dr. Parish was unfazed by my snark. "If you're so unhappy here, then maybe we should transfer you somewhere else. I think you were right about public school being a more suitable environment."

Too bad Dr. Parish hadn't been there at registration. "It's too late for that now. I don't want to transfer again. I hate it here, but at least I know it now. What if I switch schools and the curriculum is different? I'm already a year behind."

"Then how can we help you? Your depression is getting worse. You've said as much in your sessions many times."

Everyone in the room frowned. They looked disappointed in me, as if I were letting them all down on purpose. It made me so angry. "Of course I'm depressed!" I shouted. "You would be too if you had to live my sucky life! It's hard enough just to get out of bed every morning!"

That was the wrong thing to say. The adults in the room exchanged so many knowing glances, it was as if they had an entire conversation in their minds. "Richard," Jennifer pleaded quietly, "it's time."

"Time for what?" Principal Johnson asked. I was glad he did

because I wanted to know what she was talking about, but I was too scared to ask myself.

My dad looked at me with a beaten expression. "Ella, sweetheart, we've been worried about you for a while. You're not getting better, not adjusting, and I don't know what else I can do for you. I think maybe it's best if we send you to a place where you can get the help you need."

I stared at him, bewildered. I didn't think it was possible that this man could hurt me any more than he already had, but his words lanced my heart with a pain so sharp it took a minute to feel it. "You want to send me away?"

"I just want to help you."

I glanced from him to Jennifer. She'd been the one to suggest it. Her voice had sounded desperate. I shook my head. "You want to get rid of me. You both do. You've never wanted me."

My dad swallowed. "You're sick, honey. You need help before you do something to hurt yourself again."

I sighed. It always came back to this. No one was ever going to let me live that down. "I'm not going to hurt myself. And I don't want to go to a hospital. I won't. You can't make me."

My dad's face filled with pity. "I can make you, Ella, and I will if it's best."

"But I'm not suicidal! I swear!" I sent an accusing glare at Dr. Parish. "You know I'm not! Tell him I'm not going to kill myself!"

"I know you're not," Dr. Parish said, and then repeated it to my father. "I don't believe Ella is in danger of hurting herself." I breathed a sigh of relief, thankful she'd backed me up, but then she pinned me with a serious look. "I know you're not suicidal, but I agree that some time in a hospital might be a good idea for you."

"*What?*"

"Ella, it's not a negative thing. You'd be surprised what a little time in a controlled environment could do for you. Wouldn't you like the help? Don't you *want* to feel better?"

To my horror, I started crying. "I don't want to go to a mental hospital and have one more thing for people to make fun of me about. I don't want to be cut off from the world again. I don't want to fall even more behind in school. Please don't make me."

The room was quiet except for the sound of my sniffles. Principal Johnson handed me a box of tissues. I didn't expect anyone to give me a chance—my hope had already been smothered—but my father spoke up. "All right, honey. If you don't think it's a good idea, then I trust you."

I pulled the Kleenex away from my eyes and blinked at my dad. "Y-you do?" He was the last person I would have expected to come to my defense.

My dad met my gaze with a silent apology. "Yes, I do." He turned his attention to Dr. Parish and Principal Johnson. "A lot of this is my fault. I need to trust her judgment more. If I had just listened to her in the first place about attending public school, we probably wouldn't be having this trouble." My dad turned his attention back to the others. "Is there anything we can do to keep her in school and out of the hospital?"

I took a deep breath, but my lungs refused to release it as I waited for my fate to be decided.

"I would feel better if Ella agrees to start meeting with me every other day instead of once a week, for now," Dr. Parish said. She gave me a stern look and added, "And we don't want your depression getting any worse, so for the time being you shouldn't be alone. Your bedroom has to be off limits except for sleeping, and even then you have to keep the door open at all times. You also have to make an attempt to integrate more with your step-family and the kids here at school. No more keeping to yourself. Find someone to eat lunch with. Make friends."

"You could join a club," Principal Johnson added hopefully. "The other students need to see you making an effort to be social. You might be surprised how many kids are simply intimidated by the situation. I'm sure there are some who would be friendly if you broke the ice first."

"Maybe if Ana would let them," Juliette grumbled under her breath.

I doubted it, but if joining a club would keep me out of a depression clinic, then I'd figure something out. Maybe they had a book club or something, or I could write for the school paper. That wouldn't be so bad. The no-bedroom thing was going to suck, though. After a few weeks of that, I might just be begging them to lock me away.

"Do we have a deal, Ella?" Dr. Parish asked.

"What if I can't? What happens if nothing changes?"

I jumped when a hand reached for mine. I looked up to find my dad smiling at me. "It will," he promised. "We'll get through this together, okay?"

He sounded so warm and full of confidence that I didn't know how to respond. I stared at him like an idiot.

"I know you don't believe me, Ellamara," he said, speaking softly now, "but I *do* love you. I want you to be happy. I want you to feel comfortable in my home and with my family. I'm sorry my daughter has been making that difficult for you. We'll make sure that stops, and maybe for now you could just start spending some time with me before you worry about Jennifer and the girls. You're my daughter, honey. I'd like the chance to get to know you a little."

He smiled at me again, and it was the first time since our reunion that I felt he was looking at me like a father. I could see worry, but also pride. He was looking at me as if he knew me, as if I wasn't a stranger or someone he was afraid of, but someone he really cared about.

I pulled my hand out of his grip and grabbed another tissue.

I'd always wanted my dad to look at me like that, but now that he'd done it, it scared me. Of course part of me wanted to build a relationship with my father, but the heartbroken half wasn't sure I was ready to trust him. I wasn't sure I could forgive him for abandoning me.

"I wasn't there for you when I should have been," my dad

said, "but I'd like to be there for you now. If you'll let me."

"Okay," I croaked. I felt my cheeks heat up, so I quickly looked at Principal Johnson and then Dr. Parish. "I'll try, okay?"

I DIDN'T HAVE TO GO BACK TO CLASS THAT DAY, BUT JULIETTE AND Anastasia still beat me home. I went to the police station to officially drop the charges against Jason, and then my dad took me over to the burn center to meet with my surgeon. By the time we got home, it was after four.

I'd had a horrible day, and I was exhausted. I headed straight for my room when we walked in the door, but apparently my dad intended to follow through with Dr. Parish's orders to keep an eye on me at all times. "Honey, remember what Dr. Parish said today." His voice was strained with awkwardness.

"I was just going to change and get my computer."

Letting the lie slide, he glanced down into the main family room where the soft sounds of the TV were bouncing up the stairs. "Do you want me to ask Jennifer and the girls to come hang out up here?"

I shook my head. "I can make it down the stairs."

I took my time exchanging my uniform for a soft pair of yoga pants and a loose long-sleeve T-shirt, but my dad was still waiting for me when I emerged from my room. If he was going to hover like that all the time now, I wasn't going to last a week before I found myself in a center for suicidal teens. At least he made himself useful and carried my laptop and backpack down the stairs for me.

The twins were lounging on the long sectional sofa doing homework while watching *Access Hollywood*, and Jennifer was in the corner of the room killing herself on an elliptical. Red-faced and dripping with sweat in a sports bra and short shorts, she looked like a magazine ad for exercise equipment. Her face lit up as Dad entered the room. "So?" she asked hopefully. "Good news?"

Her voice gained the twins' attention. Juliette glanced up briefly and then went back to her math book, but the look I got from Anastasia told me she'd already gotten a lecture. Judging by the severity of her glare, some serious punishment had been handed down.

"Good news is, the tear wasn't that bad," Dad said. "Bad news is, she's still going to have to have surgery on her inner elbow. They said we could wait until after the holidays."

Jennifer sent me a sympathetic look that I ignored as I sat down at the small desk in the far corner of the room.

"There's room on the couch, Ella," my dad said, setting the laptop down for me.

"I'm fine here."

When Jennifer cleared her throat, I looked over, but her gaze was directed at Anastasia. Ana rolled her eyes and released a dramatic sigh as she glanced over her shoulder at me. "Sorry."

Yeah, sure she was.

I wasn't the only one unconvinced. "Ana," Jennifer warned.

Another eye roll. Another sigh. "I'm sorry, Ella."

Yeah, still not convincing, but Jennifer didn't push it. Instead, she changed the subject. "Ella, would you like to go to the Halloween dance tonight? You can have Ana's ticket since she will *not* be going this evening."

Not that I didn't relish the fact that Anastasia was grounded, but going to the dance sounded about as fun as spending another six months in rehab. "No, that's okay. I wasn't planning on going anyway. I've never really been a fan of dances." Not exactly true—I used to love going to dances, but considering I couldn't dance anymore, the appeal was sort of gone for me now.

"It's not a problem," Jennifer insisted. "We've still got a couple of hours to find you a costume, and I'm sure Juliette wouldn't mind taking you."

Well, if she wasn't going to take the hint... "Look, I appreciate the gesture, Jennifer, but what would I do there? I couldn't dance with anyone. Couldn't be on my feet very long. I don't have a date, or any friends to keep me company, and I wouldn't want to ruin Juliette's night by making her sit it out with me. I'm afraid dances are just not in my future anymore. It's okay, though. I got to go to junior prom and senior homecoming before my accident. I was a royal court princess, even, so I'm not missing out."

"You were a homecoming princess?" my dad asked. I'd have been more offended by his surprise if there wasn't also a hint of pride in his voice.

Ana, Juliette, and Jennifer all looked just as stunned. Jerks. "Shocking, I know, but I did, in fact, used to be normal. I had friends, went out on dates, had a life... Some people actually liked me."

I officially killed the conversation and we all fell into awkward silence. The only sound in the room was Billy Bush droning on about Brian Oliver and Kaylee Summers getting engaged at her birthday party last weekend. Of course they did.

I had a whole day's worth of missed schoolwork on top of my homework, but I noticed that Cinder was signed into his messenger and couldn't resist shooting him a quick message.

EllaTheRealHero: And fiction becomes reality...
Cinder458: Do I dare ask?
EllaTheRealHero: Brian Oliver and Kaylee Summers got engaged. Once again the prince falls for the warrior princess,

only this is worse. At least Princess Ratana could fight. What's Kaylee Summers good for?

Cinder458: Sex?

I snorted, but quickly stifled my smile when I earned the attention of everyone in the room.

"Something funny?" my dad asked curiously.

I looked at my IM and rolled my eyes. "More like tragic and typical."

EllaTheRealHero: That's probably all Brian Oliver dates her for. I take back what I said about him having depth. He's obviously as much of a shallow moron as every other guy on the planet.

Cinder458: Not including me, right?

EllaTheRealHero: Are you kidding? You're the worst of them all.

Cinder458: Ouch. Someone's in a mood today.

I let out a sigh. He was right. I shouldn't be taking my anger out on him. It wasn't his fault he was powerless to Kaylee Summers' perfect, swimsuit-model body any more than it was Brian Oliver's. I mean, if I had the chance to make out with someone as hot as Brian Oliver, I doubt I'd turn it down.

EllaTheRealHero: I'm sorry. You're right. I've just had the worst day ever and now I'm grumpy. I got grounded from my room and am being forced to live amongst the step-people.

Cinder458: Don't you mean you got grounded *to* your room?

EllaTheReal Hero: Nope. From. I'm not allowed to be alone

right now, which means no hiding from the stepwitches in my room. The Powers That Be have conspired against me and are forcing me to "integrate" with my family OR ELSE.
Cinder458: What does that mean, exactly?

I sat there, staring at the cursor on my computer. For the first time ever, I felt like telling Cinder what was going on with me. I didn't know why. I was never the type who needed to cry for attention, but my fingers were hovering over the keys, itching to unload my problems. The thing is, I was really upset, and I knew Cinder would listen.

All of a sudden, I just started typing.

EllaTheRealHero: If I can't start getting along with my dad's family and make friends at school, they're going stick me in a mental institution.

It was the keyboard equivalent of randomly blurting something out.

Cinder458: What? That's ridiculous! Why would they do that?
EllaTheRealHero: Long story.
Cinder458: I'm waiting…

I stifled a groan, already regretting my moment of weakness. Cinder was always subtly trying to get me to talk. Of course he was going to jump on this tiny nugget of information I'd just given him. It had been just enough to give him the excuse to push me the way I knew he wanted to.

EllaTheRealHero: There was this guy hassling me at school today and it got a little out of hand.

Cinder458: What happened??? I'LL KILL HIM!!!!

EllaTheRealHero: Nothing. It was an accident. But my dad and the principal found out that I've been getting bullied and they called my therapist. Now they're all worried that I'm going to try to kill myself again, but really, it was nothing I haven't been dealing with since school started. The only difference is that now they know about it.

Cinder458: What do you mean try to kill yourself *again*????

I let out a curse and slapped my hand over my face. How had I let that slip?

I couldn't believe I'd admitted all that to him. I'd just told the world's most confident guy—who was beautiful and popular and had the perfect life—that I was a suicidal loser who got picked on at school. He was never going to talk to me again.

I made a lame attempt at damage control, but it was probably too late.

EllaTheRealHero: After my accident, things were really bad for a while. But I learned my lesson. It's okay, really. I'm a lot better now. Everyone's just paranoid, and they're all overreacting.

Cinder458: Are they? You're not really having those kinds of thoughts, are you?

EllaTheRealHero: No!!!

Cinder458: I'm serious. I know you never want to talk about all your family stuff, but promise me you're not thinking about that. Swear it!

EllaTheRealHero: I promise, Cinder. I swear to you it's not that bad anymore. My life's no picnic, but how could I ever want to end it when I have you to talk to every day?

Cinder458: This isn't a joke, Ella.

EllaTheRealHero: I'm not joking. You are seriously the best part of my day every day. I'm so glad I have you to talk to.

Cinder458: Then how about we actually *talk* for once? Call me? (310) 555-4992

I sucked in a breath. *Call me.* Those two little words practically stopped my heart. I read the ten-digit number over and over again. The sight of it terrified and exhilarated me at the same time. Before the accident I'd often fantasized about talking on the phone with him into all hours of the night, but I'd never had the guts to ask for his number, and he'd never asked for mine. Now here I was, staring at the key to finally hearing his voice.

Could I do it? Could I talk to Cinder on the phone?

Cinder458: Ella?

EllaTheRealHero: I don't know...

Cinder458: We've known each other for almost three years. I think it's safe to move to the phone call stage of our relationship.

A simple phone call didn't seem like much, but it was actually huge. There was a certain level of intimacy that came with talking to someone on the phone—of hearing their voice. It would make Cinder so much more than just a faceless Internet friend.

EllaTheRealHero: It just seems different somehow. More intimate or something.

I knew he couldn't see me, but I blushed as I typed that last sentence.

Cinder458: It is. That's why you have to call me. I need to know that you're really okay, or I'm going to go crazy. I need to hear your voice. Call me right now, woman. Please???

He seemed desperate. He *needed* to hear my voice? Could he really mean that?

"Ella?" Jennifer startled me so badly I let out a tiny squeak and jumped in my chair. "Are you okay? You look like you've seen a ghost."

I was so caught up in my conversation that I forgot I was in the same room as everyone. They were all staring at me now. The twins clearly thought I was a freak, and Dad and Jennifer both watched me as if they were afraid I was going to make a run for the kitchen knives any second. "It's nothing," I muttered, blushing under their scrutiny.

Cinder458: Ella, my phone isn't ringing. Why isn't my phone ringing?

I looked back up at my father, who was watching me closely. He had that same sincerity about him that he'd had at the school this morning, as if he was truly concerned for me. I'd promised him I would try harder. I promised I'd make more effort to be social. I was pretty sure calling Cinder would qualify.

Deciding to be brave, I waited until my family stopped paying attention to me, then picked up my phone and dialed his number with shaking hands. He answered on the first ring. "Hello?"

His voice was deeper than I expected. Just that one word sent chills through me. But it sounded...confused. Why did he sound confused? He was literally waiting for my call.

"Cinder?" I wanted to kick myself for how small my voice sounded.

"Ellamara! That *is* you. My beautiful and wise mystic priestess of the Realm, we speak at last."

"Holy crap, your voice is sexy!"

I slapped my hand over my mouth. I did not mean for that to come out of it. It's just that he sounded like he could melt butter—or women's hearts—simply by speaking. His voice was deep, rumbly and hypnotic. The guy didn't talk, he *purred*.

"So I've been told," he teased, laughing—a low, rich sound ten times more dangerous than his speaking voice.

To my utter mortification, I'd once again gained the attention of everyone in the room. They were all gaping at me, and who could blame them after what I'd just blurted? Each of their startled expressions was slightly different. My father looked horrified, while Jennifer had something akin to an excited gleam in her wide eyes. Juliette was smirking, and Anastasia was looking at me the way she always did—with barely concealed loathing and contempt.

I blushed and shut my laptop as I said, "Uh, hey, Cinder, can you hold on a sec?" I gave my dad a pleading look. "Can I take this in my room?"

Before my dad could answer, Juliette frowned at me. "What kind of a name is *Cinder?*"

"Oh my gosh, that's that guy who always leaves comments on her blog!" Anastasia cried suddenly. "Ella has an Internet boyfriend! What a freak!"

She was so loud I was sure that Cinder heard her.

"Ana!" Dad growled.

"What? Online dating is so gross!" She turned to me and added, "I hope you know Internet creepers don't count as real boyfriends, even if you talk to them on the phone."

"Anastasia, that is *enough!*" my dad roared. "You've just added another week to your grounding! Go to your room! Now!"

"With pleasure!" she shouted back. "I was only down here because you were forcing me to babysit the suicidal freak, anyway!"

I wanted to die as I watched Anastasia stomp up the stairs.

Cinder, no doubt, heard all of that. He couldn't see it, but my face was so red it hurt. How could I possibly talk to him now? I was so nervous I was on the verge of throwing up.

"Ella?" Cinder asked when things got quiet. "Are you there?" He sounded hesitant.

"Welcome to my life," I said with a sigh of defeat. "Sorry about that."

"It's okay."

It was definitely not okay. I was so humiliated. It was a miracle I wasn't crying. I think that was only because I was still in so much shock. "Look, thanks for giving me your phone number, but maybe this is a bad time."

My dad scrambled to his feet, waving his hands at me. "No! You don't have to end your call. We'll give you some privacy." He glanced at both Jennifer and Juliette. "Won't we, ladies?"

His blatant desperation for me to talk to someone—even a stranger from the Internet—was as embarrassing as Anastasia's outburst. Even worse, Jennifer was just as bad. "Of course! You go ahead and talk to your boyfriend, Ella," she squealed. "We can keep an eye on you from the kitchen. I have to get dinner started anyway."

While I was busy dying from her use of the word *boyfriend*, she hopped off the elliptical. She hurried to catch up to my dad, seeming more than happy to finish her workout early. As they started up the steps, they both turned back to Juliette, who had sprawled out on the couch instead of getting up.

"I was here first," Juliette said in response to their expectant looks. "There's no way I'm going anywhere near the upstairs with Ana in the mood she's in, and I really don't care about Ella's love life. Besides, she's not supposed to be alone, anyway. What if she tries to throw herself off the balcony or something?"

Was there anyone in the world that didn't feel the need to humiliate me? I glared at Juliette, and she just waved a pair of ear-buds at me and shoved them in her ears. "I'll turn the volume up."

My dad and Jennifer both gave me such hopeful looks that I

couldn't argue anymore. I rolled my eyes and made my way over to the armchair my father had been lounging in.

Once Dad and Jennifer were gone, I glanced over at the couch. Juliette was already doing what she did best—ignoring me. She was bobbing her head along with her music as she read out of a textbook. I doubted she could hear me, but I spoke softly anyway, just in case.

"Cinder? Are you still there?"

"I didn't realize upping our relationship to phone buddies would come with a boyfriend title. Does that mean if we ever meet in person, we'll have to get married?"

Surprised, I burst into laughter. Juliette glanced at me with one raised eyebrow, but went back to her textbook without saying anything.

"Sorry, I don't do polygamy, and I'm pretty sure you're already married to your car."

"Funny."

The flat tone in his voice set me off giggling again, and then I sighed. "Man, it feels good to laugh. I really have had the worst day ever. Thank you for making me call you. I can't believe we're finally talking, though. I've always wondered what you sound like."

"Me too. I even googled videos of people with Boston accents once."

I laughed again. "Shut up. You did not."

"I did, and you don't disappoint. Say *car* for me again."

"You're such a dork," I replied, but then I gave in and said, "car."

It came out *cah*, and Cinder laughed. "I love it," he said. "Speaking of Boston… You did not call me from there."

I managed not to gasp, but my stomach dropped. I'd completely forgotten about caller ID. How was I supposed to explain why we had the same area code? "Um yeah…no. I know. That's because my dad lives in LA. I've been here since I got out of the hospital."

I waited for him to freak out on me and demand we meet, but the line was silent for a minute, and then he quietly asked, "Why didn't you ever say anything?"

I was surprised at how cautious he sounded. Maybe I'd hurt his feelings by not telling him I moved. Hopefully I could explain it without having to tell him what my accident did to me. "I don't know. It took me a while before I was brave enough to e-mail you at all. Then everything went right back to normal between us so fast that I never really thought about it. You've always just been an Internet friend, you know? I think I might have been afraid to ruin that."

He let out a breath that sounded suspiciously of relief. Maybe he was just as afraid of meeting in person as I was. The thought was as disappointing as it was relieving. "Yeah, I know what you mean. The fact that we've never met has always been my favorite thing about our relationship."

"Why?"

"I guess in person it's hard for people to see past the outer me—the looks, the money, the car, the connections—but since you can't see those things, you only see the real me. It's nice."

"Wow, Cinder." I snorted. I knew he was being serious, but that's what made it so funny. "That was so incredibly profound of you. I'm impressed."

"You see?" Cinder laughed. "You're giving me a hard time right now. Nobody who knows me in person would ever do that. Most people act so fake toward me. They say whatever they think I want to hear, and they do whatever I want them to."

"Well, it's no wonder you're so egotistical. Maybe you're right about the anonymity. I don't know that I'd be able to tell you how stubborn, argumentative, and shallow you are to your face. Or that you have horrible taste in movies. Especially not if you're as swoonworthy as you say you are. Then who would be left to keep you from turning into a true self-absorbed jerk?"

Cinder laughed again—a huge, deep, bellowing laugh. I could picture him throwing his head back, his entire gut convulsing from the action. Not that I imagined he had a gut, of course. Anything less than a six-pack didn't seem like his style.

Cinder sighed his way down from his laughing fit. "Oh, Ellamara. You are the only girl in the world that ever says things like that to me. That's why—infuriating, self-righteous, opinionated, and obnoxious as you are—you are my favorite person in the whole world."

My lungs seized up, making it impossible for me to breathe. But somehow the burning sensation in my chest was the best feeling in the whole world—like turning your face to the sunshine or drinking hot chocolate after being out in the snow.

I prayed Cinder wouldn't be able to tell I was crying, but luck seemed to have left me forever when my mom died. "Ella?" His voice went from lazy and relaxed to high alert. "What's the matter? Why are you crying?"

"I'm fine." I'm not sure he believed me with all my sniffling. "It's just, it's nice to have someone who cares. You're my favorite person, too. You're my best friend."

Cinder was quiet for a moment. When he spoke again, he dropped all hints of the confident, sexy, funny guy I knew so well. "Are you sure you're really okay? I mean, you would tell me if you weren't, right?" There was true vulnerability in his voice. "I had a friend commit suicide once. Ella, the thought of losing you like that—"

He cut off so abruptly that I would have thought the line went dead except that I heard him clear his throat as if trying to get his voice back under control. "You do have someone who cares," he said softly. "No matter how bad things are at home or at school or whatever, you have me. You're my best friend, too. You have my number now. Save it in your phone and call it anytime—day, night, the witching hour—it doesn't matter. Okay?"

It took me a moment—and a series of deep breaths—before I could respond. "Okay."

"Promise?"

"I promise. As long as I always have you, I'll be fine." I kicked myself internally and laughed. "Wow, that sounded really cheesy. You see? That's why I didn't want to call you. I can filter my stupid mouth so much better when I have to type out my thoughts."

Cinder laughed again. "Ah, but then you would miss out on all the sweet nothings I plan to whisper in your ear now that I know how much you like my ultra-sexy voice."

I blushed but refused to let him know that his flirting rattled me. "I never said ultra, you egomaniac. But you should definitely consider recording audiobooks for a living."

"Hmm. That's not a bad idea." Cinder's voice dropped to that slow, seductive purr again as he asked, "Would you like me to read to you, Ellamara?"

I thrilled at the thought and couldn't quite mask my excitement. "Seriously?"

"Why not? Before you called, I was getting ready to have a *Top Gear* marathon all by my lonesome."

"You are such a liar. Tonight is Friday night, and it's Halloween. There is no way you don't have plans."

"I don't have important ones. It's just a stupid party that my sort-of girlfriend wants me to go to."

"Your 'sort-of' girlfriend?"

"Yeah." Cinder stretched the word out in a long breath. "It's a long story, but I'm not that into her. I'd much rather stay home and read with you. Besides, I can't hang up on you when you've had the *worst day ever*. What kind of best friend would that make me?"

I almost cried again. The offer was so sweet. And thoughtful. Reading was a passion Cinder and I shared. We read and discussed books all the time. We'd even decided to read the same book at the same time before, but we'd never read one together. Cinder had to know how much that would mean to me.

"It has to be *The Druid Prince*," I said.

Cinder laughed. "It's already in my hands."

WHEN I WENT BACK TO SCHOOL ON MONDAY, THE WHISPERS AND stares were as bad as they'd been on my first day. It was nothing new. I kept my head down as I always did, and prayed things wouldn't be worse because people blamed me for Jason getting suspended.

So far nothing traumatic had happened, but as I sat down at lunch in my normal seat at a small table in the corner of the cafeteria, a hush fell over the whole room. I'd just noticed the unnatural stillness when I felt someone standing behind me.

Slowly, bracing myself for whatever torture was about to ensue, I turned around to face whoever was behind me. I was shocked to see Juliette standing there. Next to her was a girl I'd seen around school, but who wasn't in any of my classes. She had violet eyes—obviously colored contacts—and bright red hair with platinum blonde streaks in it. It was a combination I'd never seen before, but it actually suited her very well.

Her hair was twisted up on her head and clipped into place with hair clips made of brightly-colored feathers. Her shoes, backpack, and fingernails were all works of art, the same way her hair was. I imagined she would be something to behold if she weren't constricted to the limitations of our school uniform.

She was pretty, but not the same gorgeous knockout type that Juliette was. She was wild in a way that demanded respect. She was the kind of girl you couldn't help but follow down the hall with your eyes. The girl that guys feared, yet secretly wanted at the same time.

And she was smiling down at me.

"Ella, this is Vivian Euling," Juliette said in a bored voice. "Vivian, my stepsister, Ella."

I still had no idea what was going on, but I was pretty sure Juliette wasn't masterminding some vicious scheme, and Vivian was holding out her hand to me, so I took it. As we said hello to one another, Juliette reapplied her lip gloss and said, "My work here is done." She walked away without another glance.

I turned my eyes back up to Vivian and she gave me another warm smile as she sat down next to me and took a sack lunch from her backpack. "I hope you don't mind." I shook my head and Vivian smiled again. "I think Juliette is playing matchmaker with us."

"She what?"

I turned around and saw Juliette sitting at her normal table with all of the most popular people in school. She was laughing and joking around with them, not paying the slightest attention to me, just like always. You'd never know something out of the ordinary had occurred if it weren't for the way Anastasia was still gaping at her in shock.

"I have dance with Juliette," Vivian said. "We're not friends or anything, so I was surprised when she came up to me this morning and asked if she could introduce us."

"She did?"

I knew how incredulous I sounded. I could feel my face contorted in confusion, so I wasn't surprised when Vivian laughed. "She said she thought we would have a lot in common," she explained while rolling her eyes. "Considering she knows nothing about me, and I doubt she's made any effort to get to know you, either, even though you're stepsisters, I can only assume she was pairing one outcast with another."

That surprised me. Not Juliette's thinking that being outcasts would make two people automatic friends, but I couldn't imagine why a girl like Vivian would have no friends. "You don't strike me as the loner type. You seem so confident and nice, and you're so pretty."

"I also was raised by two dads."

I was still confused. "What does that matter?"

Vivian did a double take.

Figuring she was the type who could take a joke, I smirked. "Massachusetts was the first state to allow same-sex marriages, so, no offense, but that makes you totally old news to me. I hope you weren't expecting special treatment or anything."

Vivian's eyes flashed, surprised, and a wide grin spread across her face. "I like you."

I laughed, but it died quickly as I glanced around the cafeteria. "Picking on me I understand, considering this is the town where image is everything, but you'd think people would be more open-minded about your situation."

"You'd think," Vivian agreed. "I'm sure at Hollywood High I'd fit right in, but at a pretentious private school like this one I'm an easy target. It also doesn't help that I'm here on scholarship. My dads are humble costume designers. They make enough to afford our two-bedroom apartment in West Hollywood, but that's about it."

Now *that* made perfect sense. "And the picture becomes even clearer. I was raised by a single mother."

Vivian rolled her eyes again. "So you're saying not only are we both social outcasts, we're both poor, too."

"Exactly." I joined her with an eye roll of my own, but then sighed and glanced at Juliette. "It may have been a shallow and judgmental perception, but it was still thoughtful of her to try to help."

"True." Vivian followed my gaze to my stepsisters' table. Juliette was laughing with a girlfriend, while Anastasia was sitting in some guy's lap—some guy who was decidedly not Jason. "But then, Juliette's always been the lesser of two evils."

I nodded in agreement. "Sometimes I think she might not be so bad if she didn't have her sister poisoning her mind, and a completely clueless mother teaching her what's truly important in life."

At Vivian's questioning look, I said, "Designer clothes and an eight-hundred calorie a day diet."

Vivian laughed again. "I think Juliette was on to something. You might just be a kindred spirit."

THE RIDE HOME FROM SCHOOL WAS A TENSE ONE, THANKS TO THE rage bubbling just beneath the surface of Anastasia's Marc Jacobs Daisy-scented skin. When we got home she stomped inside, slamming the door in Juliette's face. By the time I managed to climb out of the car and get in the house, the two of them were laying into each other.

"...*humiliated* us like that!" Anastasia was screaming.

"All I was doing was cleaning up the mess *you* made. You're the one who embarrassed us."

"It's bad enough we have to be associated with her. Now she's BFFs with *Charity?*"

"So what? Let them be freaks together. They aren't hurting anything."

"Not hurting anything? What if they start making out in the cafeteria and stuff? We'll be sisters of the lesbian crippled freak!"

"Um, her name's Vivian, not Charity," I said, setting my backpack on the counter as I headed past the two of them into the kitchen.

Juliette rolled her eyes. "People call her that because she's the school charity case."

"Nice." I scoffed. "You know, Anastasia, just because her dads are gay doesn't mean she is. Even if she were, why should you care? It has nothing to do with you."

Anastasia glared at me so hard her eyes became bloodshot. "Stay away from me," she hissed, storming off to her room.

Once we heard the door slam, Juliette shook her head as if disgusted with her sister. "She'll cool off in a few weeks."

I stared after her as she headed down into the family room to get started on her homework. It had been such a strange day. I didn't understand Juliette at all. In the few months I'd lived here, she'd gone from being rude to simply ignoring the fact that I existed, to actually coming to my rescue on Friday. Then, this morning she risked the wrath of her sister to help me find a friend. It was a really sweet thing to do. I couldn't figure out why she'd done it—especially because, while she wasn't outright hostile toward me anymore, she clearly still didn't like me.

After raiding the fridge and not finding anything appetizing, I grabbed a couple of my usual V8 fruit juices and made my way down to the family room. Instead of heading for the desk in the corner, I sat down on the couch and held out one of the drinks to Juliette. "Want one?"

She frowned at me, but warily accepted the juice. "Thanks."

We did our homework in silence with the TV once again muted on some entertainment news show. Eventually, Juliette sighed. "Some girls have all the luck. Can you imagine being *engaged* to that perfection?"

Startled from my work, I looked at the TV just in time to see Brian Oliver on the screen, heading into some club with a scantily-clad Kaylee Summers hanging all over him.

There was another dreamy sigh from Juliette. "He has got to be the hottest guy ever to roam the Earth."

I couldn't disagree. He was six foot one, had dark hair, milk chocolate eyes, and a body so perfect it hurt to look at it. He was one of those actors who could play either the pretty boy, or the sexy bad boy—depending on how they dressed him up. At the moment, he was sporting a leather jacket and a five o'clock shadow that made you want to defy your parents, jump on the back of his motorcycle, and let him drive you off into the sunset after having had his name tattooed somewhere on your body.

He always smiled as if the world were his oyster, and yet he had that smoldering thing down, too. Countless girls had fallen victim to that gaze. The thing that I liked best about him, though, was how he seemed so sharp. In every interview I'd ever seen him do, he was playful and cocky, but witty. He bantered with those talk-show hosts as if *they* were the ones in the hot seat. The guy had some major intelligence hiding behind that pretty face.

I matched Juliette's wistfulness and said, "I'd definitely have his babies if he gave me the chance." Clearly, I'd spent too much time talking to Cinder lately.

Juliette snorted but stopped laughing when she realized it was *me* she was joking around with. Things got awkward again fast. We both went back to our work, but this time I couldn't keep quiet. "Thanks for helping me yesterday in class and for talking to Vivian."

Juliette shrugged as if she didn't think it was worth talking about, but I couldn't let it drop. "Why did you do it?"

Juliette considered not answering my question, but then said, "Mostly because Ana's being such a jerk. I was mad about having you here too at first, but it's really not that bad. You stay out of our way and keep a low profile at school. She's the one making it worse by constantly trying to turn the whole school against you, or at least making them too afraid to be nice to you. I'm sick of the drama. All of our lives would be easier if you weren't such a freakish loner, and you'd have a lot more friends if Ana would just back off."

Once again she turned back to her work. I went back to mine too, but after another ten minutes or so I had another question I needed an answer to. "What exactly did I do? Why do you both hate me so much?"

I knew Juliette wouldn't deny the implication that she hated me. She was a very direct person. Most of the time the stuff she said was shallow, judgmental, or just plain ignorant, but at least she always told you what she really thought. She wasn't afraid to say what was on her mind, and I had to admire that about her. "Different reasons," she said. "Ana feels threatened by you."

"What?" I laughed incredulously. "That's ridiculous."

"Not really. First of all, you're Dad's *real* daughter. She's worried that he's going to start playing favorites." After a short pause, she said, "I'd be lying if I weren't jealous about that, too."

I was shocked. Juliette and Anastasia were jealous that Rich was my dad? As if that made some kind of difference? It'd never stopped him from loving them more than me before.

"Second, you have scars and you limp, but you're actually really pretty aside from that. Some of our friends have said as much. Plus, everyone thinks you're really funny."

"What? How can people think that? Nobody knows anything about me."

"When we learned about your blog, Ana told everyone at school about it, trying to show them what a nerd you are." Juliette smirked. "Her plan totally backfired because everyone loved it. Half of our friends follow you now."

The kids at school followed my blog? I didn't know what to say to that. It seemed impossible. Juliette saw the look on my face and shook her head. "You're not nearly as hated as you think. Yeah, there are a few people who've been really mean to you, but everyone else respects you."

"They *respect* me?" There was no way she'd get me to believe that.

"You're tortured at school, but you never let it get to you. You never complain, and you never get anyone in trouble. All anyone could talk about today was how cool it was of you to drop the charges against Jason.

"Plus, you keep to yourself so much that you're, like, mysterious. People are intrigued by you. They're starting to like you. Rob Loxley even has a crush on you. That's why Ana got so mad and made Jason do what he did. She thought Rob was going to ask her to the dance, and instead he asked her if she thought *you* would go to the dance with him."

I was shocked. I didn't see how what she was saying could be possible, but she wouldn't make up a story like this just to be cruel. Anastasia would, but not Juliette. Juliette was a lot of things, but she wasn't a liar.

Juliette went back to her homework, giving me the chance to process everything she'd just told me. After a minute she didn't look up from her work, but she said, "If you want me to give Rob your number, I will. He's a pretty decent guy. Kind of quiet for my taste, but you guys might hit it off."

I didn't respond right away, and Juliette didn't seem to care if I answered her or not. I didn't know how to feel about someone having a crush on me. I wasn't ready to be in a relationship. I couldn't go outside in short-sleeve shirts, much less have some guy wanting to see me or touch me. A boyfriend couldn't even hold my hand when I walked because I have to use my cane in my good hand, and I didn't think I could let someone hold my scarred hand.

"I don't know," I finally answered. "I'll think about it."

"Whatever."

That was the end of our conversation until Jennifer called us up for dinner later. Juliette turned off the TV and started to pack up her stuff. I didn't want to risk annoying her, but as long as she was somewhat talking to me, I needed one last answer.

"Hey, Juliette? I know we'll never be like actual sisters or anything, but I don't want to be enemies forever, either. You told me why Anastasia hates me, but what's *your* problem with me?"

Juliette stopped shoving books in her backpack and looked at me. All of her usual indifference was gone, and I could see anger in her eyes. "I wouldn't have a problem with you if you weren't always so mean to Mom and Dad. They're good parents. They've gone out of their way to do everything they can for you. Dad almost lost his job because he spent so much time in Boston while you were in the hospital. They renovated your room. They give you everything you need. They always do nice things for you, hoping it might make you happy. They try so hard to help you, and you throw it back in their faces all the time."

Her words iced me over like a bucket of freezing water splashed in my face. Of all the things I could have imagined, I never would have thought she was just being protective of my dad and Jennifer. And the thing is, after she'd said that, I realized that there wasn't just anger in her eyes, but hurt.

"You treat our parents as bad as Ana treats you," she said. "Especially Dad, and he doesn't deserve that. He's a good man. He may not be my biological father, but he's my dad. He's raised me since I was seven years old, and he's never treated me like I wasn't his real daughter. He's loved me like I was his own."

All the conflicting emotions in me were so confusing. I was shocked, for one thing. I never realized I was acting so horribly. I wasn't even sure if I really had, or if Juliette was just being defensive and exaggerating. But if I had...I wasn't that person. I didn't treat people like that. I'd always considered myself to be kind. I didn't like being compared to someone like Anastasia.

At the same time, I was also angry. Part of me thought Juliette had no right to think anything at all about my relationship with my father. It was none of her business. But more than anything, I was hurt because she had the relationship with him that I should have had, and she acted as if there were nothing wrong with that.

"That's not true," I whispered. "He's loved you much more than if you were his own child, because I *am* his child and he didn't love me at all. Did you know he didn't even say good-bye to me when he left? I was eight years old. I came home from school one day, and he was just gone. There was no note, no phone call, no anything. I just never saw him again.

"I grew up without any father at all because *my* dad was out here giving *you* hugs, and tucking *you* into bed at night, and loving *you* like a real daughter instead of me. Talk about having something thrown in your face all the time. How do you think it makes me feel to have to live here and see how happy you all are together?

Do you have any idea how much it hurts every time I hear you and Anastasia call him Dad? To know that he loves you—really, truly loves you? I'm his *daughter*, and he only took me in because he had to."

I took a breath and put my books back in my backpack. I couldn't handle this conversation any longer.

"I'm not saying you don't have a reason to be angry," Juliette said, "but you asked what my problem is with you, and that's it. We were happy before you came here. Now my parents fight a lot more, and Ana and I barely speak except to yell at each other. I get that you have problems, and I understand that this sucks for you, but it doesn't change the fact that you're making everyone in this house miserable. You're ruining my family."

I apologized as I shouldered my backpack and stood up. "I'm sorry." I tried not to sound bitter, because I really was sorry. "If I had any idea how to change that, I would."

I turned to leave and saw Jennifer standing on the stairs, watching Juliette and me with a stricken expression. From the puffiness of her eyes, I was sure she'd heard that entire conversation. "I'm sorry," I mumbled again as I made my way past her.

Brian

WHEN THE PATRIOTS SCORED YET ANOTHER TOUCHDOWN, I decided I needed another drink. As I wandered into the kitchen and cracked open another beer, I thought of Ella. Ella was from New England. She was more of a baseball fan—apparently being from Boston means you're born with Red Sox pride in your blood—but if she followed football at all, she was probably laughing right now. I took a long, refreshing swallow of ice-cold Corona and sent her a quick text.

If you're a Patriots fan, I might have to disown you.

Her reply was almost instant.

LOL! You're safe. Not a big football fan. But if I ever learn you root for the Dodgers, we can't be friends anymore.

A second text followed that one, saying, **Why? Who are they beating right now?**

I smiled at the question. Ella didn't care about football, but she was still willing to talk about it with me. I started to type a reply, but then realized that after three years I finally had her number and could talk to her now. "The Packers are down three touchdowns and a field goal," I said when she answered my call. "It's very demoralizing."

"Green Bay? Are you seriously a cheesehead?"

She laughed and I smiled again. Her laugh was my new favorite sound in the whole world. "I have never had—nor will I ever have—the urge to wear a foam cheese hat, but yes, I am a Green Bay fan."

"Why?" Ella asked. "Are you *from* Wisconsin? Oh my gosh, please say yes. That would be too funny. Please tell me the California playboy act is all a ruse and you're secretly the son of a dairy farmer."

I laughed. "I'm sorry to disappoint you, but I really am Los Angeles born and bred. My mother lives in Green Bay, though. She married a very enthusiastic Packers fan so, over the years, since LA doesn't have a football team, I've adopted Green Bay as my own."

"That is a little disappointing. I'm sorry your team is losing, though. I'll send you some good-luck vibes."

"Appreciated."

I smiled again and took another sip of my beer. A loud cheer erupted from the living room where a bunch of my buddies were watching the game. Hopefully that meant Green Bay finally scored, but now I wasn't that interested in going back to find out.

I slipped outside onto the back patio and shut the door behind me. Ella was quiet on the other end of the line, and suddenly I had no idea what to say to her.

I'd never been in a girl's "friend" zone before—the thought of a girl not wanting me that way was absurd—but I was worried that's where I fell on Ella's radar. She had no problem telling me she cared about me, and she teased me all the time, but she never flirted with me, even when I would flirt first.

I was shocked when I found out she'd moved to Los Angeles and hadn't told me, and she'd been so hesitant to call when I gave her my number. It was almost as if she didn't want to be anything more than Internet friends. Three years and she'd never even asked for my real name. Granted, I'd never asked for hers, either, but that was only because I had no idea how I was going to handle the "I'm Brian Oliver" conversation when it finally came up.

Talking on the phone changed our relationship a little, and I wasn't sure quite how to tread the water now. I felt nervous and a little stupid. The feelings were so foreign to me that I almost didn't recognize them as self-consciousness. I'd never been self-conscious with a girl before.

"So…" I had to clear my throat when my voice didn't want to produce sound correctly. "What are you up to? Is it okay that I called? It's not weird or anything?"

"No, it's not weird. I like it. You can call me whenever you want. Even if it's just to complain about the Packers losing Monday Night Football."

The teasing in her voice melted away my nerves. I wasn't going to miss them. "How are things? Better than Friday? Are you surviving the stepfamily?"

"I guess. Things are kind of strange, but not in a bad way. My one stepsister is still Freddy Krueger, but I had a talk with the other one and she really isn't as horrible as I thought. We came to an understanding, at least. I think. Anyway, happier subjects. Make me laugh. You're the only one who ever does."

My heart sank a little at the request. Why did Ella refuse to let me in? All her talk about mental institutions and suicide the other day really freaked me out. I knew she was having a hard time adjusting to her new life with her dad, but I had no idea her depression was so serious. I couldn't stop worrying about her.

I wished there were something more I could do to help than make her laugh, but if that was what she said she needed, then I couldn't let her down. I racked my brain for something she'd find amusing, but it wasn't easy because I wasn't really in a laughing mood anymore. Not when she was out there in need of someone to love her, and the only person I was allowed to be with right now was the freaking spawn of Satan.

And I was suddenly inspired. "Have you ever read *The Taming of the Shrew?*"

"I haven't read the play, but I've seen the old Elizabeth Taylor movie."

"My girlfriend is the shrew, only there's no taming her."

Ella laughed. I was glad to have successfully cheered her up, but I wished I were joking. "I'm serious. I think she might actually be the devil reincarnate."

"She sounds a lot like my stepsister."

"Worse. I promise. Much, much worse."

"Then why are you dating her?"

"Because she's really hot and the sex is good?"

I knew that would work. Ella's disgusted groan made my smile come back. "Nice, Cinder. How completely shallow of you."

Ella was teasing, but she also believed me. She really did think I was nothing but a shallow, egotistical playboy. Yeah, I sort of was, but that was only because the girls I knew were all like Kaylee and not worth giving my heart to.

I hated that my reputation might disappoint Ella. She wasn't interested in players like me. I was proud of her for that, but it rankled me at the same time because that was probably the reason I was just a friend to her. I couldn't tell her everything, but I was suddenly desperate to make her understand that there was more to me than the guy she believed I was. "Honestly, it's not her looks. It's more complicated than that. She's kind of this high-profile girl."

"Celebrity or supermodel?"

I smirked.

"Heiress?"

If she only knew how right she was. Kaylee was all three of those things, but I couldn't tell Ella that. Kaylee and I were in the media too much right now, and I didn't want Ella to figure out who I was on her own. That wasn't going to be easy for her to swallow. I wanted to be there face to face when I explained. "No comment," I said, and she burst into laughter.

"Ha!" she shouted. "I knew it! Mr. VIP with his fancy women. You should try dating a nice, quiet librarian or something. Then you might not have to call your girlfriend a shrew."

"Actually, that could be hot—hair in a bun just screaming to be let down, some nice, thick glasses, a tight skirt, and a silky blouse with lots of buttons for me to rip open? I would totally make love to her up against the stacks in the classic literature section."

There was a choking sound and then Ella said, "Um, okay, that was definitely an over share."

I grinned at her bewilderment and dropped my voice to that low, soothing tone I knew she liked. "Are you blushing right now, Ellamara?"

"I'm pretty sure even my grandmother is blushing in her grave after that visual, Cinder."

That *visual?* My smile widened even further. Had she just pictured *herself* as my fantasy librarian? *Friend zone, my ass. Brian Oliver is no woman's friend.* I had to take advantage of this opportunity.

"Have you ever thought of becoming a librarian, Ella? You'd probably make a really good one, what with your love of reading and all your haughty indignation. Or I could totally picture you teaching in a boarding school, handing out detention slips and spanking all the naughty boys with a ruler."

"Spanking naughty boys with a ruler?" Her voice was so flat that I burst out laughing. "You are hopeless, Cinder. How about we get away from the cheesy porno dialogue and go back to the complicated 'no comment' shrew you mentioned. Tell me why you're really dating her, if it's not just the sex."

"You're no fun." I pouted, but then sighed for real. Kaylee was such a mood killer. "All right, fine. So she's basically The Boss's Daughter, right? And, of course, she's totally in to me."

"Oh, of *course.*"

"Yes, of course. Stop interrupting me, woman."

"Stop making me."

Infuriating girl! I had the sudden urge to shake my phone. "Anyway… She's got a lot of clout, so my dad and a bunch of other people are really putting the pressure on me to keep her happy."

"That's awful!" Ella's voice sounded equally amused and appalled. "How can you let them tell you who to date?"

"It's complicated."

Grimacing, I chugged the last of my beer. I knew I sounded ridiculous, but how could I make her understand? "My *life* is complicated. There are a lot of people who think they own it. Especially my dad. I don't really have a lot of control over anything."

"Do you ever stand up for yourself?"

"When I can."

"And you don't think the choice of who you date is one of those times?"

"Not this time. This chick is really important. If I broke it off and she had a tantrum—which she definitely would—she could really screw up a lot of things for a lot of people. Me, more than anyone. I'm stuck for now. I'm hoping that if I can just be a big enough jerk, she'll get tired of me and dump my sorry ass."

"That is seriously crazy, Cinder. You know that, right?"

"I know." Shaking away all depressing thoughts, I headed back into the house and tossed my empty beer can in the trash. "But it's not the most horrible thing in the world." It was only temporary, after all, and I had Ella to keep me sane until it was over.

"Because at least she's super hot and the sex is great?"

I chuckled at Ella's sarcasm. "Right. Although, maybe it's not as great as I thought. You've really got me stuck on this librarian idea. I bet I could—"

"Okay, this is where I hang up," Ella interrupted.

Laughing again, I opened the fridge. All this talk of hot librarians—*Ella* as a hot librarian—gave me the munchies. "Why?" I asked as I spotted some fresh strawberries. My brain immediately went to feeding them to Ella, and then I thought of other things I could do with Ella. "You don't want to work out any dirty fantasies with me? It's your fault I'm having them. What are you wearing right now, anyway?"

"HA!" Ella laughed. "No! We are not going there. Not ever, Cinder."

"Why not?"

"Just, no, you perv!"

Ella was trying to hide it, but I had her completely flustered and I loved it. Asking her to call me was the best decision I'd ever made. "Your loss," I teased. "I could have rocked your world, baby."

"What the hell are you doing?" Kaylee suddenly shrieked, startling me so badly I dropped the strawberries all over the floor.

Shutting the fridge, I turned around to find Kaylee so red-faced I was sure she'd heard a lot more of that conversation than just my last statement. For some reason, that made me want to laugh. I had to bite down on the inside of my cheek to keep from doing so. "I gotta go," I said into the phone. "I totally just got busted by the shrew."

"The *what?*" Kaylee screamed.

On the other end of the line, Ella giggled. "Congratulations. I'll keep my fingers crossed that you get dumped."

At hearing that, I couldn't hold back my laughter any longer. "You're the best. I'll call you later."

I hung up the phone and met Kaylee's glare with big, innocent eyes. "Problem?" I didn't wait for her answer before I bent down to clean up the mess of spilled fruit.

Kaylee's heels clacked across the tile floor as she crossed the kitchen. They came to a stop in front of my face, and the right one began tapping obnoxiously. "What do you think?" she spat.

"I think we're not in public, Kay, so I can do whatever the hell I want."

"There is a whole room full of people out there. Any one of them could have heard you."

"But they didn't."

"I did."

I pulled the last AWOL strawberry from beneath the fridge and stood up. After chucking the container in the garbage, I noticed Kaylee was still standing there, waiting for an answer. The only one I could think of was "Good." She'd hated that response so much when I gave it to her at the club in front of all her friends that I'd adopted it as my number-one reply lately.

"Why do you insist on being difficult?"

Snorting, I pinned her with an obstinate look. "Maybe because I'm being blackmailed into a fake engagement with the Wicked Witch of Hollywood?"

Kaylee glared again and then stomped her foot as she huffed in annoyance. "Your father's here, and he brought Zachary Goldberg with him," she said, storming out of the room.

No way. I followed her out of the kitchen and, sure enough, there was my father and one of the most prestigious film directors in LA standing behind the sofa with beers in their hands, cheering on the Green Bay Packers.

"Hey, Dad. What are you doing here?"

Even more shocking than my father's presence was the huge, happy smile he greeted me with. "There's the man of the hour!" I tried to hide my shock as he jovially clasped his arm around my shoulders. "Son, you know Zachary Goldberg, don't you?"

Still stunned, I shook hands with my idol. "We've never met, but it's an honor. I've followed your work since I was a kid."

A hand slipped around my waist and forced my smile to stay up as I introduced Kaylee. "Ah, yes," Zachary said, leaning in to kiss Kaylee's cheek—the customary LA greeting for someone of the opposite sex. "My congratulations to the happy couple. Between the surprise engagement and your upcoming movie together, the two of you are the talk of the town right now."

Kaylee subtly squeezed the arm she had around me in a very "I told you so" manner. "All good, I hope," she said, as if she were the first person to ever come up with that oh-so-clever response.

I tried not to roll my eyes at the cliché. If Kaylee could be half as smart as she was evil, she'd be a genius.

Zachary was polite enough to laugh with her. "It's all very good," he promised, shifting his eyes to me. "Especially in regards to you, Brian. I've heard all sorts of buzz about your performance in *The Druid Price*. Your father was just showing me some of the footage this afternoon. Very impressive."

I tried to contain my surprise, but my head was spinning. Zachary Goldberg was one of my all-time favorite directors. He had a true talent for drama and had been nominated for more Academy Awards than Steven Spielberg. Praise from him was hard earned. "Thank you, sir."

"Call me Zachary, Brian. Please."

"Okay, Zachary. Well, welcome. Make yourself at home. I hope you like the Packers, because any Patriots fans have to watch the game from outside, and they only get the cheap beer."

Zachary laughed heartily as he shook his head. "I wish I could stay, but I've got the wife at home waiting for me. You know how it is." Zachary glanced between Kaylee and me, grinning. "Well, maybe not yet, but you'll find out soon enough."

Forcing a laugh, I pushed my acting skills to the limit. "I'm looking forward to it."

Zachary believed the lie. "I just wanted to stop by and meet you in person. I'd love to set up a meeting with you sometime soon. I've got my hands on a brilliant adaptation of *The Scarlet Pimpernel*, and I think if I had you attached, I could get the green light."

My jaw nearly dropped to the ground, but this time I didn't bother to try to hide my excitement. "You're doing *The Scarlet Pimpernel?*"

Zachary's eyebrows climbed up his forehead. "You're familiar with the story?"

Was I *familiar* with it? "I *love* the story. I've read all the books. I would kill to play the part of Sir Percy."

Zachary chuckled. "I knew you were the man I wanted to talk to. Are you available to meet sometime this week?"

"I—hold on." I turned to where my friends were all still engrossed in the game. "Hey, Scotty!"

I'd invited my assistant, and the poor guy was so Boy Scout that the few Playmates present kept mauling him. He hadn't stopped blushing since he arrived, and he looked really relieved to be needed at the moment. "What's up, Brian?"

"Do we have time to meet with Mr. Goldberg this week?"

"We'll make time."

"I'll come, too!" Kaylee jumped in. "I can bring my father," she told Zachary. "He's a big fan of Brian's, you know. I'll bet the three of us could talk him into signing on."

Zachary licked his lips and gave Kaylee the biggest smile I'd ever seen on a grown man. "That would be fantastic, Kaylee."

From the way Zachary's eyes lit up, I wondered if that hadn't been part of his intent all along. Everything in Hollywood was always a power play. Getting the millions upon millions of dollars needed to fund a major motion picture was never easy no matter who you were, and getting the green light for a classic period piece like *The Scarlet Pimpernel* was damn near impossible.

"I'm not familiar with the story," Kaylee said, "but it sounds pretty exciting."

"Oh, it is. And you would look stunning in an eighteenth-century costume. I'm sure we could find a place for you in the film somewhere, if you were interested."

"What a generous offer, Zachary. Thank you."

I watched the two of them schmooze each other with a sense of astonishment. I may have hated Kaylee, but even I had to admit the power that I, as Hollywood's hottest up-and-coming actor, and Kaylee, the heiress of the city's largest motion picture studio, had together.

Kaylee was right. We could own this town together if we really wanted to. The problem was: I didn't want to. Not if Kaylee and I had to be a couple to do it. As flattered and excited as I was about possibly working with my favorite director playing another of my favorite characters, I was worried that Kaylee was going to like the power we had a little too much and not want to let me go after the awards season was over. Somehow, I was just getting sucked in deeper and deeper.

My little heart-to-heart with Juliette didn't change anything between us, but I was eternally grateful to her for introducing me to Vivian. Vivian and I didn't have a lot in common—she was a prima ballerina and obsessed with anything fashion related, while I was content reading books and hadn't been to a mall in over a year—but we still got along like sisters who'd been suddenly reunited after being separated at birth.

She ate lunch with me again the next day and insisted I come home with her after school and do my homework at her house. Knowing what was waiting for me at home, I was grateful for the offer.

She lived in a smallish apartment in West Hollywood. It was old, cramped, a little disorganized—actually, it looked like Jo-Ann Fabric had exploded inside—but it felt more like home after being there for three seconds than my dad's house probably ever would.

"Ignore the chaos," Vivian said as she picked up a pile of hot pink tools out of the entryway and hung it over the back of a chair. "I've tried to explain to my dads that gay men are supposed to be neat freaks, but they refuse to listen."

Her dads were in the dining room, lost in a sea of

brightly-colored fabrics, sequins, lace, and feathers. One was sitting behind a sewing machine while the other was standing, pinning a sleeve to a gorgeous dress on a sewing mannequin. They both looked up and grinned when we walked in, their smiles as bright as the dress they were working on.

The one standing pulled a pin out of his mouth and said, "Honey, if we wanted to be stereotypes, we would have become hairdressers."

"Says the man wearing a teal boa." Vivian laughed and, waving a hand at the man, said, "Stefan Euling—aka Dad. Dad, this is Ella." Next, she gestured to the man at the sewing machine. "And that's Glen Euling. He also answers to Dad."

After saying hello, I watched Stefan work for a moment. The strand of feathers around his neck matched the sequins on the dress. "It's for the hem of the dress, right?" I asked. "You're making a ballroom dancing dress?"

The man grinned at me as though he'd never been prouder of anyone in his life. "Good eye!"

"My mother dated a professional salsa dancer once. I was never graceful enough for the sport, but I *loved* the dresses."

"They're the main costume designers for that reality TV show *Celebrity Dance Off*," Vivian explained. "As you can see, they like to bring their work home with them."

"No way!" I squealed. "I *love* you guys! The dresses are the only reason I watch that show! Is that dress for one of the dancers? Is it for Aria? It looks like an Aria dress."

Vivian rolled her eyes at me. "You've just made two new friends for life."

"It is for Aria," Stefan said. "You really are a fan, aren't you?" His eyes roamed over me from head to toe with a critical eye, and then he said, "Dress size 1-2, right?"

I looked down at my school uniform, a little startled that he'd guessed right. The outfit wasn't really form-fitting to begin with, and I'd untucked the shirt the minute I climbed in Vivian's car. "To my dietician's dismay," I answered, nodding. "He's always trying to get me to gain more weight. How did you know?"

Glen laughed. "He always knows. The man has a gift for sizing people up. If the majority of our clientele weren't women, I'd be insane with jealousy."

"A little jealousy is healthy for a man," Stefan teased. "Keeps you in line." Before Glen had the chance to argue, Stefan smiled at me and said, "Would you like to try the dress on? I need to make a few adjustments, and you're almost exactly Aria's size. You'd be the perfect stand-in."

A surge of excitement rushed through me at the thought of putting on the dress, but it was soon replaced with horror as I pictured myself in the sleeveless, backless gown.

"I promise not to poke you," Stefan urged.

"Oh, it's not that." I gulped and it felt as if I'd swallowed one of the pins he promised not to stick me with. "It's just, um, I was in a car accident and I...um..."

"Ella, nobody here is going to care about your scars, I promise," Vivian interrupted. She sounded firm but kind, and the look in her eyes said she wasn't going to let me say no.

"But it's such a beautiful dress. I'd just spoil the effect."

"Hogwash!" Glen looked up from his stitching with a disapproving frown. "You have the face of an angel. Those eyes are stunning. If anything, that dress doesn't deserve to wear *you*."

I blushed at the smile he flashed me.

"Ella," Vivian said softly, "true beauty comes from inside a person. If you feel beautiful, then you'll look beautiful to others no matter what's on the surface." She pointed at the dress hanging on the mannequin. "That dress would make *anyone* feel beautiful. Just try it on, please? For me? Because if you don't stand in for them, they're going to make me do it, and I have a much more important task to deal with right now."

"What task?" I asked, distracted from my panic attack.

She held up a handful of fabric scraps and something that looked suspiciously like a bejeweling gun, a wicked gleam in her eyes. "I'm going to give your cane a little cosmetic surgery."

Ten minutes later, I stepped out from behind a changing screen in a dress made for a queen. The skirt flowed to the floor, covering my legs, but my entire back, shoulder, and right arm were exposed. I cleared my throat to get everyone's attention, then held my breath and tried not to shake too much as they appraised me.

They all took in the sight of my scars—I couldn't blame them; it would have been impossible for anyone not to look—but none of them stared too long before moving their eyes to the rest of me.

Glen rose from his seat at the dining-slash-sewing table and came to stand in front of me with his arms folded across his chest. Stefan joined him, and the two of them began slowly circling me like a couple of lions stalking a gazelle.

"Oh, we are *good*," Glen finally said, breaking into a wide grin.

Glen twirled his finger as if he wanted me to turn around. I did, and came face to face with a full-length mirror. I gasped at what I saw in the reflection. Glen scooped my hair up and twisted it up on my head, pulling a few of my curly black ringlets down around my face. "What did I tell you?" he asked. "An angel."

He was right. I looked amazing, and I wasn't even wearing any makeup. The dress, along with the way Glen and Stefan stood behind me, smiling almost reverently at the girl in the mirror, made me feel beautiful for the first time since my accident.

My eyes glistened and I turned around, grinning at Vivian for all I was worth. "I *love* your dads."

"You won't be saying that hours from now when your feet are aching and you have to pee and can't because you're covered in pins," she teased, but the smile on her face betrayed how much she loved and was proud of her parents.

"Hours?" I asked as Stefan helped me up onto a stool.

Stefan waved us off as if we were being ridiculous. "A small price to pay for such a work of art," he said, shoving a handful of pins in his mouth.

He and Glen both got down on their knees at my feet. While

Glen held out the bottom of the dress and pulled the material tight, Stefan unwrapped the strand of teal feathers from his neck and reached for a pin. He took particular care in finding just the right placement before carefully attaching the feathers to the hem of the dress. They were like a couple of surgeons operating on a patient. I really could be standing here for hours.

"You're not related to my physical therapist, are you?" I asked. "He likes to find unique ways to torture me, too."

That set all three of them into peals of laughter. Glen looked up at me with sparkling eyes and pointed at Stefan. "I wouldn't get him laughing like that, if I were you. He was lying about his ability to not poke you."

We all laughed again, but despite Glen's warning I felt no stabs of pain. After that, Stefan and Glen went to work on the dress while Vivian began hot-gluing pieces of fabric to the metal shaft of my cane. It was either going to look like a beautiful patch-work quilt or something out of a Tim Burton film. After a minute of comfortable silence, Vivian said, "So, I sit next to Rob Loxley in seventh period..."

I blushed, recognizing the name as the guy Juliette said had a crush on me. Vivian didn't notice. Her concentration was solely focused on the project in front of her.

"Really nice guy," she said. "Cute, too. Quiet, though. He hasn't said much to me all year and then, suddenly, out of the blue, yesterday and today he became Mr. Chatty."

My face was really heating up now. "Hmm, weird."

Vivian glanced up at me for a second, then went straight back to work cutting and gluing. "I tried to think what could possibly have happened in the last two days that he would suddenly take an interest in me, but nothing has changed. Nothing, except that I've become friends with *you*."

She finally stopped what she was doing and gave me a look that said we both knew what she meant. There was no point in denying it. "Juliette said he likes me. She offered to give him my number. I told her I'd think about it."

"You'd *think* about it? Why?"

"I don't know."

"He's a decent guy, Ella. He wouldn't care about the scars or the cane. Especially after I make it look so cute."

"Maybe, but that's not the only problem. I'm not in the best place mentally right now. I don't know that a relationship would be a good idea."

Vivian frowned. "That sounds suspiciously like an excuse. Are you sure you're not just scared?"

"I'm terrified," I admitted.

Vivian considered this and then shook her head. "Well, who says you'd have to get into a relationship? Maybe you could just be friends. You're the one who told me you're under doctor's orders to make more friends."

"Yeah. I guess. Maybe."

"You could invite him over here for a movie night this Friday along with some of the kids from your dance studio," Glen suggested. My face turned an even deeper scarlet as I realized he was trying to help play matchmaker. "It would force your father and me to have to finally clean up around here."

Vivian jumped up as if she could snatch the idea out of the air and make it happen. "Ooh! I like it!" I wasn't sure if she was more excited at setting me up with Rob or the idea of her dads cleaning up a bit. "What do you think?" she asked me.

I was saved from having to give an immediate answer—even though I knew she would eventually get her way—because my phone rang.

"I'll get it!" Vivian chirped, happily reaching for my backpack.

"That's okay; I'm sure it's just Cinder. He can leave a message."

"Cinder? That's the guy who's *not* your boyfriend, but texts you like a twelve-year-old girl experiencing her first crush?"

I laughed. It was a fair comparison. "I've recommended he seek help for his phone addiction many times, but he never listens to me about anything."

"Well, we can't let him go to voicemail, then, because he'll just keep calling back until you answer."

"Vivian!" I warned, but she'd already scooped up my phone.

"Relax. I'll put it on speaker. You can cut me off at any time." She answered the phone, doing her best imitation of a perky secretary. "Thank you for calling Ellamara's phone. I'm afraid the priestess is currently busy lending her body to a couple of ruggedly handsome men right now, and is unable to take your call. Would you care to leave a message with her ever-so-helpful assistant slash best friend?"

I choked back a laugh, but Cinder didn't miss a beat. "Great voice inflection and enunciation, but there were two things very wrong with that little speech. First of all, *I* am Ellamara's best friend. *Me*. Not you, whoever you are. Me, me, me."

Vivian glanced up at me with a questioning look, amused at the hint of the temper tantrum in Cinder's voice. I rolled my eyes, but I was grinning like an idiot.

"And seeing as how I am Cinder, kick ass prince of the Realm," Cinder continued on like a dork, "it is my right to discipline anyone who tries to steal her from me. I warn you now, the punishment for such a heinous crime is death by flesh-eating worms."

I cracked up, but Cinder didn't hear me because Vivian barked out a louder laugh. *"Flesh-eating worms?"*

Cinder remained one hundred percent serious. "Hell yes, flesh-eating worms. It's a very slow, painful, and grotesque way to die. Highly undignified. I wouldn't recommend it. If I were you, I would just stick with the assistant title, and maybe, if you prove to be worthy, you can be Ellamara's second best friend." He paused a second, then added, *"Distant second."*

Vivian laughed again. "Gee, thanks. Are you finished?"

"Not even close. There's still the issue of the two soon-to-be-dead men you mentioned manhandling my woman."

Vivian's eyebrows shot up and her smile turned wicked. "What's the matter, Prince Cinder? Are you jealous?"

"Of course I am. Princes don't share. But besides that,

whoever they are, they aren't good enough for Ella."

"How do you know?" I called out, unable to hold back any longer.

"Ah, *there's* my girl."

Cinder's voice warmed in a way that had Vivian turning on me with wide eyes. I tried my best not to blush, but I knew I'd be having a long conversation with her as soon as this phone call ended.

"How do you know they aren't good enough for me?" I demanded again, just to get Vivian's attention off of me.

"Because no guy is worthy of you, Ella. All men are dogs. Absolutely no sharing your body with any of them. Ever. I forbid it. Well, except for Brian Oliver. You have my permission to let him ravish you in the most ungentlemanly ways imaginable."

Vivian gave me a strange look, and even Glen and Stefan were blinking up at me after that brilliant comment. All I could do was laugh and shake my head in shame. "Your man crush on Hollywood's Boy Wonder is disturbing, Cinder. It really is."

"You know you'd like it. Admit it."

"I know *you* would."

"*I* certainly would," Vivian offered.

"Me too!" Glen called out, winking over at Stefan.

"I fantasize about it regularly," Stefan added, and we all burst into laughter.

Oddly, Cinder didn't seem to appreciate the Brian Oliver lovefest. "Wait a minute. Who was *that?*" he demanded. "Are there really guys *manhandling* you right now?"

"Of course not." I laughed. Then, because I simply couldn't resist, I added, "They're being very gentle. Stefan hasn't even poked me yet."

"Ellamara!"

His horror was so genuine that I doubled over laughing until I had both Stefan and Glen yelling at me to hold still. "I'm sorry!" I called out, still lost in giggles. "I'll stop teasing. You know you're the only man in my life."

"As I should be."

"Actually, that's not entirely true," Vivian said. The sudden thoughtfulness in her voice made me nervous. "You say you're her best friend, right?"

"I *am*," Cinder promised vehemently.

"Then maybe you can help me convince her to go on a date with this guy from our school. He's really sweet and he's crushing on her pretty hard, but she's too scared to give him a chance."

I felt the blood drain from my face. I didn't want to hear his answer. It would kill me when he declared he was happy for me and encouraged me to go for it. Which was what I was sure he would do. And, of course, he did. Sort of. I think.

"Ella…" His voice softened in that way it does sometimes, as if he would be holding me tight in his arms right then if it were at all in his power to do so. "What could you possibly have to be afraid of? Any guy would have to be out of his mind not to fall head over heels for you."

Stefan sighed and Glen threw a hand over his heart. Vivian practically melted in her chair. Me? I did the most embarrassing thing ever—I cried. Not like noticeable sobs or anything, but my eyes misted over enough that Vivian brought me a tissue.

"You know, it doesn't have to be *Rob* she goes out with," Vivian said into the phone. My gut just about exploded from stress when I realized what she was about to do, but before I could stop her, she said, "Ella and I are having a movie night at my house this Friday. You could come in Rob's place."

My heart stopped. How did I not see that coming from the second Vivian answered the phone? How could I let it happen?

Cinder had never asked to meet in person. Not once. He'd never even hinted that he'd like to. The only time the topic ever came up was when he found out I moved to LA, and then he said how much he liked that we'd never met.

I know I said I didn't want to meet him, either, but of course I did. I loved him so much. I wished everyday that we would meet in person someday and fall madly in love. I was just afraid he wouldn't want me because my body was broken and scarred. That, or he'd start treating me the way my dad and Jennifer do: as if he thought *I* were broken and not just my body.

If Cinder ever started treating me as if I were made of glass, it would kill me. But then, Vivian didn't walk on eggshells around me, and if this Rob guy could have a crush on me the way I am, then maybe Cinder could, too. Granted, I wasn't one of Cinder's supermodels, but he cared about me. That had to count for something. Maybe this was a good thing. Maybe Vivian was giving us the push we both needed.

I held my breath as I waited for Cinder's answer. He didn't say anything for so long that Vivian checked the phone to make sure she hadn't dropped the call. "Hello?"

"I can't."

I shut my eyes to keep tears from sliding down my cheeks. He didn't want to meet me. Deep down, I'd already known it. We'd tiptoed around the subject before, but neither of us had come out and said it outright. I'd told myself he was just nervous like me and that we'd get there eventually, but his "I can't" sounded so final. I was sure he heard the quiver in my voice when I finally responded. "It's okay."

"I have to go out with the shrew on Friday," he explained, almost as an afterthought. "We're having dinner with her dad and some other people. I can't get out of it."

Vivian, trying to be helpful but completely missing what was really going on, said, "So we'll do Saturday instead. Are you busy then?"

"I—" Cinder's voice broke off and he let out a frustrated breath. "Shit! Ella...I...I *can't*."

He sounded downright tortured, and I was suddenly terrified. "It's okay," I said quickly. I didn't want this to make things awkward between us forever. "Don't worry about it. I totally get it."

"I'm sorry."

"It's okay."

A heavy silence settled on the room. Vivian and her dads didn't dare move. They had no idea what was happening, but they knew enough to wait it out in silence. Cinder was the first to speak. He cleared his throat and asked, "Is it okay if we read tonight?"

He sounded strange. Hesitant. It was a far cry from his usual confident self.

Even though I knew the answer, it took me a minute to say yes. I was far more upset than I wanted him to know. My heart was breaking, but I knew I'd never be able to give him up even if it was going to hurt every time I spoke to him from now on. "Of course."

He let out a breath of relief. "I found a new book that I think we'll like. That's why I called. I thought we could give it a try together."

"Sounds like fun."

"Good. Call me later?" He still sounded unsure.

"Wouldn't miss it."

I gestured for Vivian to hang up before my voice cracked. As soon as the phone was off, Vivian looked up at me in a panic. "I screwed up. I don't know how, but I know it was bad."

"It's a long story."

My body sagged so drastically that Stefan had to jump up and steady me. He helped me off the stool, declaring my work done for the day. Vivian offered to take me home after that. All of them could see that my conversation with Cinder—his official rejection—had exhausted me.

WHEN I GOT HOME FROM VIVIAN'S IT WAS ONLY A LITTLE AFTER four, so I was surprised to hear my dad's jovial voice coming from the kitchen. "That is not funny!" he declared, but he was laughing as he said it.

In response, I heard both Anastasia and Juliette fly into wild peals of laughter. The mood was light and cheerful. At first it made me smile—as it would anyone, because good moods are generally contagious—but the smile quickly faded as I realized I'd not heard any of them sound so natural since I arrived. They were enjoying themselves like a happy family would. It was obviously a familiar tone for them, too—playfully teasing each other and enjoying one another's presence. It was like that now because I hadn't been there. Juliette was right. I was ruining their family.

I stood frozen in the doorway, unable to walk into kitchen and make my presence known. I didn't want to be the thorn in everyone's side, didn't want to be the mood crusher. I didn't want to ruin this family. Anastasia aside, they weren't bad people. They deserved to be happy. The second they realized I was home, all the playfulness would stop. That thick, heavy blanket of awkwardness would return and settle over us all again like the inevitable, inescapable fate that it was.

I decided not to go in. I didn't have anywhere to go, but I figured I could at least do my homework on the front porch or something for a while and give them a little bit of a break from me. They obviously needed it.

Before I could make my escape, Jennifer came around the corner and spotted me. Her eyes flashed, and it took her a second too long to put a smile on her face. "Back from your friend's house already?"

"Something came up."

"Everything all right?"

"Yeah, it's fine."

She hesitated but didn't ask anything else.

"I can leave again if you want me to."

Jennifer flinched when my words registered. "What?"

I pointed a thumb over my shoulder at the front door. "If you want me to stay away for a while, give you guys some time, I can do my homework on the porch or something."

She actually looked conflicted for a moment before shaking her head. "Why would you say something so ridiculous?"

She sighed when I raised an eyebrow at her, calling her out. "I'm sorry, Ella. It's not you. I just hate to see Anastasia having such a hard time. She's been a different girl since you got here."

Jennifer sounded as if she was asking for my sympathy, but Ana was being a baby. Everyone in the house was struggling with this arrangement. Ana needed to suck it up just like the rest of us were doing. "I don't try to antagonize her."

Jennifer let out a breath and sat down on the bench by the front door. She surprised me when she patted the space next to her. Warily, I sat down beside her and waited for her to speak. "My ex was not a nice man. He was abusive to the girls and me. I met Rich when he was doing some pro-bono work in Boston for a battered women's shelter where I was living with the girls—hiding, actually, from their father."

This news was startling. All these years I'd never had a clue how my dad met Jennifer. The way my mother talked about her, I always figured she was his waitress at Hooters or something.

But the story did sound very much like my dad. He was always trying to be the hero, always saving someone. He was so smart and got the best grades at one of the top law schools in the country. He could have been an amazing, highly-paid corporate lawyer, but he always wanted to help people. He was a public defender before he got his job as a state-appointed district attorney. Hearing Jennifer's story, I could finally see why they were together. He was her heroic knight in shining armor, and she was his beautiful damsel in distress.

Dad was a modern-day Hercules, and it only made his abandonment hurt that much more. I'd always wondered how such a hero, who spent so much time helping others, could be the villain of my story. How could a man like that just walk away, leaving Mama and me on our own?

"Rich swooped into our lives like a guardian angel," Jennifer said, pulling me from my thoughts. "He saved us, and we all fell in love with him. Ana, especially, has really grown close to him. She's always been daddy's little girl. I think she's afraid you're going to take her dad away from her."

"I don't think she has to worry about that," I muttered, pulling myself to my feet. I didn't want to hear any more of this. It was salt in my wounds. He had chosen to play the hero and be the best dad in the whole world. He had just chosen to do it for someone else's family. I had to swallow back a sick feeling in my stomach.

Jennifer rose with me and set a hand on my arm. "No, she doesn't," she agreed. "Rich has room in his heart for you both, but Ana doesn't know that yet."

I doubted it, too.

"I'm sorry she's been mean to you, Ella, and we're putting a stop to that, but could you at least try to be nice to her, or talk to her sometimes?"

That made me angry and I pulled myself out of her grip. "I may defend myself when she forces me to, but I'm never just mean to her."

"You're never friendly, either." I froze, shocked by the directness. Jennifer's face softened into something desperate. "I know she doesn't deserve it, but one of you girls is going to have to be the bigger person and be kind first. I hate to admit it, but from what I've seen of you, you're the stronger one in that respect." She gave me a watery smile that was equally sad and proud, and possibly even a little jealous. "You're just like your father that way."

I had no idea what to say to that. I didn't even know how I felt about it. Did I like being compared to my father, or complimented by Jennifer, even if the compliments were given with a grain of grudging salt?

I sat back down again. This entire conversation blindsided me and I needed a minute to recover. I think Jennifer could see that because she patted my shoulder and went to join her family after saying, "When you're ready, everyone's in the kitchen trying to decide our dinner plans. Special night tonight, so we're celebrating. You'd better not wait too long if you'd like to have any say in the matter."

My heart sank. After that conversation, and what happened with Cinder earlier, I didn't think I had it in me to make it through another family dinner debacle like the last one. I was trying to figure out if the cramps excuse would work in this house when I reached the kitchen.

As expected, the girls' faces both fell and the laughter stopped immediately. My dad looked surprised, but seeing me didn't kill his mood. His voice stayed chipper, his eyes bright. "You're home early."

"So are you."

"Court adjourned. I decided to take the rest of the day off to celebrate."

"I take it your case ended well?"

My dad puffed out his chest, and his grin broke out into a wide smile. "We nailed the bastard."

I managed a smile for him. It was small, but at least it was sincere. "I'm glad."

My dad had been on this particular case since before my accident, and his team had struggled, thanks to my dad having to spend so much time in Boston with me. I was really relieved he'd won his case—and not just because he'd been prosecuting a man accused of kidnapping and killing three girls.

"So, sweetheart, we're going to dinner to celebrate, and we're having some trouble agreeing."

"Providence!" Juliette insisted.

"No," Anastasia groaned. I think it was the first time I'd ever agreed with her on anything. "We did sushi last time."

"How about Italian?" Dad suggested.

"No!" Jennifer cried, horrified. "Nowhere with breadsticks and white cream sauce the day before a shoot! You will *kill* me!"

My dad's snicker made me think he'd only suggested Jennifer's biggest food weakness just to rile her up.

"I want Mexican," Anastasia said. "We never get to eat Mexican."

"That's because there aren't any decent Mexican places around here," Juliette argued.

"Gloria's," Anastasia replied, as if everything was settled.

"I said *around here*. Gloria's is in Culver City. It would take us two hours to get there this time of day."

"Mexican does sound good," Dad chimed in, rubbing his belly. He smiled at me in a conspiratorial kind of way. "Though no restaurant will ever compare to your mother's cooking."

My blood froze in my veins at the mention of Mama. Dad didn't seem to notice that he'd given me a heart attack. He was smiling at Anastasia and Juliette. "Ella's mom was the most amazing cook in the world. If there was one thing I missed after we split, it was Lucinda's green chili enchiladas."

He may as well have shoved a butcher knife into my heart. Actually, that probably would have hurt less and healed faster. I sucked in a painful breath right about the same time Anastasia laughed and said, "Oh, burn!"

"Dad!" Juliette hissed.

It took him a minute to understand. I watched him go back over the conversation in his head, and then all the blood drained from his face. "Oh, no! Honey, no! That came out wrong. Of course I missed you, too."

That had to be a lie. He couldn't have thought of me all those years, because even now, with me standing right here, I'd still been nothing but an afterthought. Juliette had had to spell it out for him.

I was about to run for my room—Dr. Parish's rules be damned—but when I whirled around my eyes locked with Juliette's and I couldn't leave. Juliette wasn't making any kind of mean face—if anything, she felt bad for me—but just seeing her made me remember what she'd said. I couldn't run away.

After a deep breath, I turned back around and forced myself to speak. I couldn't say it was all right or that I was fine, because anyone would have heard the lies in my voice, so I chose to completely change the subject. "Would you like me to make enchiladas for you?"

The Easter Bunny could have come down the chimney armed with machine guns and opened fire on the house, and everyone would have been less surprised. Dad tugged at his ear as if it were playing tricks on him. "What?"

"I used to really enjoy cooking," I explained awkwardly. "Mama taught me how to make her enchiladas *suizas* when I was twelve. If you'd like to have them for dinner, I can make them."

The entire family was still so shocked that I felt stupid for making the offer. My face heated up from embarrassment and I quickly tried to backtrack. "I mean, if you guys want to go out for dinner, it's fine. Do whatever you want. We probably don't have everything we need to make them, anyway. I'm going to go change."

My retreat set my dad and Jennifer into motion again. "I can go to the store and pick up whatever you need," Jennifer blurted the second I moved to leave. Her whole body was shaking, as if she were having a hard time containing her excitement. "Trader Joe's is right down the hill."

I glanced at my dad, waiting for him to make the decision. He bit his lip and hesitated a second, but then quietly asked, "You would really make your mother's enchiladas for us?"

I nodded, but then looked down at my right hand and shrugged. "I mean, one of you would have to do most of the cooking—I won't be able to do much chopping or anything—but I can walk you through it."

My dad started to smile, then pulled back his emotions into a neutral mask. Maybe he was afraid to make a big deal out of this and have me change my mind. "I'd like that," he said, swallowing really hard. "I'd really like that a lot."

Twenty minutes later, my dad and I were standing in the kitchen wearing matching pink and white polka-dotted aprons. Dad had pulled all the different ingredients out of the grocery bags and spread them out on the countertop as if we were starring in our own show for the Food Network. He was holding up a soup spoon and a dessert spoon from the utensil drawer with a giant frown on his face when Jennifer held up her phone and said, "Smile!"

Dad stepped next to me, puffed out his apron-clad chest, and grinned proudly. I smiled too, but probably looked really nervous because this was the first picture we'd taken together in over nine years. I was surprised after Jennifer snapped the shot how badly I wanted a copy of it. I felt too shy to ask Jennifer to text it to me, though, and hoped she might do it without me saying anything.

The second we were done posing, my dad went right back to staring at his spoons. "How do you know which one of these is a teaspoon?"

I shot Jennifer a look and she laughed. "No. I'm afraid he's not kidding."

"The key to good enchiladas *suizas*," I said, taking the spoons from my father and placing an onion and knife in his hands instead, "is getting the sauce just right. It's a delicate balance of cream and kick, which is why *I* will be measuring the ingredients, and you will do the chopping. If I remember correctly, the only thing you ever cooked was Froot Loops."

Dad resigned himself to his place at the chopping board and sighed. "Yes, but you have to admit I had that dish mastered."

"He still does." Juliette plopped onto a barstool and checked out the scene in the kitchen with no small amount of curiosity. She smirked at my dad. "He just has to hide the evidence from Mom. She doesn't allow 'sugar' cereal in the house, so he stashed his Froot Loops and Lucky Charms in the cupboard above the dryer in the laundry room and only eats them when she's gone."

"What?" Dad gasped. "I do not! How did you know about that?"

Juliette and I met each other's eyes and both burst out laughing. Jennifer kissed the pout on my father's face. "We *all* know about that, honey," she teased, joining Juliette and me in our laughing fits. Soon, Dad was laughing, too. He laughed so hard the tears running down his cheeks might have been from crying and not just the onion he was chopping.

The mood stayed light as we continued to cook, and eventually Juliette asked what she could do to help. She freaked at the idea of cooking the chicken or frying up the tortillas—apparently as wary of the stove as my dad—so I put her to work grating the cheese.

Jennifer sat at the counter the whole time, but refused to lift a finger—something about having too many cooks in the kitchen. She was clearly enjoying having someone else do the cooking for once, though she eyed the butter, heavy cream, and cheese with a trepidation that made me laugh.

Dinner turned out to be a success. The food was great and the atmosphere was the lightest it had ever been since I'd come to the

Coleman house. Even Anastasia ate her dinner without slinging a single insult in my direction.

My father scraped the last bite of his plate, then leaned back in his chair and groaned. "Ellamara, you are amazing. I think those were even better than your mother's."

Something inside me warmed at the first genuine compliment I'd received from my dad. Still, I had to shake my head. "Not even close. But Abuela showed me the secret to her sopaipillas before she died, and those I did manage to cook better than Mama. Maybe this Christmas we could…" My voice trailed off as I was hit with a crippling pang of grief. I brought my napkin— an actual cloth one—up to my eyes and muttered an awkward apology.

"What's wrong with her?" Anastasia muttered.

Juliette tried to deflect Anastasia's question by asking, "What's a sopaipilla?"

Dad jumped on the life raft Juliette threw him. "The way her mother used to make them, they were like deep-fried pumpkin doughnuts dipped in maple syrup. They were delicious. We used to have them for breakfast every Christmas morning with hot chocolate. Ella was always more excited about the sopaipillas than she was about her presents."

"It was tradition," I whispered, falling into a lifetime of memories. "Last year was the first Christmas I ever missed them."

"Well, you'll just have to eat twice as many this Christmas to make up for it," Dad said.

My head snapped up and I felt ridiculous when my eyes pooled with tears. "Really? We could make them on Christmas? That would be okay?"

"Of course."

"Yeah, that definitely sounds like a tradition I could get behind," Juliette said. "Usually all we eat for breakfast on Christmas morning is whatever chocolate we find in our stockings."

The mood was saved, but still seemed fragile somehow. It probably had something to do with the way Anastasia was glowering into her lap. We all noticed, and were trying our best to ignore her, hoping she wouldn't explode.

Dad tried to move the conversation along. "Abuela really told you the secret?"

I grinned. "You have to use *chancaca* instead of regular brown sugar. It's hard to find, but makes all the difference in the world. I never did tell Mama what it was. Abuela made me pinkie swear. It was our secret. Drove Mama crazy."

Dad laughed, and I smiled, too. It was so surreal to be sitting here reminiscing with him about Mama. When she died, I felt as if I couldn't talk about her because I had no one to talk about her with. There was no one else in my life that knew her. But Dad had been married to her for over eight years. It'd been so long that I hardly ever made the mental connection that he was the man from my childhood memories.

"Abuela…," Juliette said, pulling me from my daydream. "That means *grandma*, right? She's your mom's mom?"

I nodded.

"Does she live in Boston?"

I released a heavy breath. "She died when I was fourteen. Granpapa died when I was eleven and Mama was an only child, so it was just the two of us after Abuela passed. I didn't have any other family."

"Yes, you did," Anastasia snapped. "You had a dad."

My dad had been reaching for his glass and missed, spilling wine all over the tablecloth. Anastasia was too busy glaring at me to notice. "You're not an orphan, Ella."

"I never said I was," I mumbled.

The good mood was officially gone. There would be no salvaging it. The only question was exactly how bad was the coming train wreck going to be? You never knew with Anastasia.

"How come you never told us about her?" Anastasia asked Dad suddenly. "We didn't even know she existed until the police called after her accident."

I hadn't known that. I looked up for some kind of

confirmation of this. My dad wouldn't meet my eyes, so I glanced at Juliette. Her grimace said all I needed to know. Anastasia was telling the truth. He never told them he had a daughter. I really had been nothing to him.

I didn't realize I was crying until I sniffled, and suddenly everyone's eyes were on me. "I knew about you," Jennifer whispered quietly. "He used to tell me stories about you when we first started dating."

"Did he tell you he was still married when you started dating?" I asked the question sincerely. Not because I wanted to hurt anyone's feelings, and not because I wanted to throw their mistakes in their faces, but because I needed to know.

Jennifer must have seen the desperation in my face, because she shut her eyes and nodded. "Yes."

"How come you never told us about her?" Anastasia demanded again. "If you loved her so much and have all these fun memories of her, you'd think you would have mentioned her every now and then, or kept a picture of her around here somewhere."

My dad couldn't come up with an answer to this, so Anastasia turned her anger on me. "Why didn't you ever call or send him your school pictures or anything?"

"Ana," Dad pleaded.

His plea didn't matter. Not to Anastasia, and not to me. I didn't need him to fight my battles for me. I was so sick and tired of Ana twisting the knife in a wound that was painful enough without her help. I sat up as straight as my body would allow, squared my shoulders, and looked her in the eyes.

"I sent pictures, drawings, cards, and letters telling him how much I loved him and missed him and *begged* him to visit me for *years*. He was the one who never wrote me back or called. For the first few years all I got was the random birthday card or Christmas card, but even those stopped coming after a while, so I gave up. There's only so much rejection a girl can handle before her pride takes over."

Anastasia glared at me, but didn't have a snarky reply. It was my dad who broke the silence. "I'm so sorry, baby."

His voice was barely audible. I pretended not to hear it and glanced at Jennifer. "May I please be excused?"

Tears spilled from Jennifer's eyes and rolled down her pale cheeks when she nodded.

The last thing I heard before I escaped to my room was Juliette shouting, "Are you happy now, Ana? You ruined every-thing!" and then stomping upstairs.

I broke Dr. Parish's rule and retreated to my bedroom to hide. There were several knocks on my door that night but when I didn't answer them, people took the hint and left me alone. Cinder was apparently denser than my stepfamily. He called, and when I didn't answer, he called again. And then again. Then he got online and made my computer start beeping at me with instant messages while my phone continued to ring.

> **EllaTheRealHero**: Sorry, Cinder. I'm not in the mood to read tonight.
> **Cinder458**: We don't have to read. We can just talk. Call me?
> **EllaTheRealHero**: I can't. Not tonight.
> **Cinder458**: Is this because of earlier?

I stared at the screen with my fingers poised over the keys to type a response, but I had no idea what to say. I was in no place to deal with Cinder at the moment. This day had completely wrecked me. I'd taken a huge step in trying to be part of my dad's family tonight. I'd offered up a piece of myself to them, and in turn it opened the lid on all the memories I'd been suppressing for years.

For a while, it had worked. For a few minutes I had my dad back—the dad I remembered from my past. Anastasia's question had taken him away again. She'd opened up those old wounds while I was in the middle of reliving the happy memories, so it hurt like a fresh cut. Normally I would let Cinder cheer me up, but I didn't even have him tonight. He'd rejected me this afternoon too, just like my dad had all those years ago.

Cinder458: Ella?

Cinder458: I'm so sorry.

Cinder458: Ella, please talk to me. Let me explain.

EllaTheRealHero: You don't need to explain yourself. I'm the one who should apologize. I'm sorry Vivian put you on the spot like that. I only met her a couple of days ago. We hadn't had the "Cinder" conversation yet. She didn't know what she was doing when she asked you to come Friday. If I'd known she was going to do it, I would have stopped her. I'm sorry.

Cinder458: You have nothing to be sorry for. It's me, Ella, not you. I know how that sounds, but it's true. You know how much I care about you, right? You have no idea how much I wanted to accept your friend's invite. I just...

My phone rang again, but I didn't pick it up. I didn't want him to hear me cry.

Cinder458: Can we please not do this over the Internet?

EllaTheRealHero: Do what?

Cinder458: Have this talk.

EllaTheRealHero: We don't have to talk about anything. I understand. It's okay.

He called me again, and I ignored it again.

Cinder458: No, you don't understand. It's not that I don't want to meet you; I just can't. My life is really complicated. I don't want you to get hurt because of it.

EllaTheRealHero: Are you saying that because you have a "sort of" girlfriend who you hate, but can't dump?

Cinder458: That's a big part of it.

EllaTheRealHero: But Cinder, I don't care about that. Well, I mean of course I care, and I want you to break up with her because she makes you miserable and you deserve better, and I want you to be happy. But I don't mind that you have a girlfriend. That wouldn't hurt me. I'm not asking to date you. I just think it might be nice to finally meet my best friend.

Cinder458: But that's just it. You're my best friend too, and if we met everything would change. It could ruin our relationship. I'm not ready to take that chance. My life is too crazy right now, and I need you too much. I need our friendship. You're the most important thing to me right now. The one thing that keeps me grounded. I can't lose you.

EllaTheRealHero: You're not going to lose me. Things would change between us a little, I'm sure, but it would only make us better friends. There's no way it could ruin our friendship. Nothing could do that.

Cinder458: I know you *think* that, but you don't understand. You're so sweet, Ella. You're still so young and naïve, and my lifestyle is so different from yours. You couldn't handle it.

Right then was a really bad time to have this conversation. I was already emotional thanks to Anastasia, and Cinder could be so infuriating. I lost my temper and dialed his number. He picked up almost instantly and sounded relieved. "Hey!"

"You're kidding me with this, right? You know how arrogant that makes you sound, don't you? You're what, twenty? Twenty-one?"

Okay, he'd sounded relieved until he realized I only called to yell at him. "It's not arrogance. It's just reality. And I'm twenty-two, FYI."

"Oh, twenty-two, *excuse me*. You're so old and wise. Those three-and-a-half years or whatever you have on me must be vital ones if I'm still so *young and naïve* compared to you."

"I didn't mean that as an insult," he said with a tired sigh. "You're not immature—hell, you're way more mature than I am by far—but you're so innocent in some ways. You'd be like a gold-fish in a shark tank in my world. You'd get eaten alive. People like my own damn girlfriend would rip you to shreds. *I* can barely handle the bitch, and I'm a master at the game."

"Screw you, Cinder! I'm not some kind of baby. I've been through more than you can possibly imagine and I've survived so far."

I was up now, barefoot and pacing my bedroom. It was making my toes hurt, so I braved the risk of earthquakes and stepped out onto my deck. I leaned against the railing, taking the majority of the weight off my feet, hoping the view and crisp air would calm me down.

The line was silent for a long time and then Cinder quietly said, "That's different, Ella. I know you've been through a lot. And you're right, I have no idea what that must have been like for you. I'm sure you're tougher than most people in some ways, but trust me, if I sucked you into my bullshit, it would crush you. And if we met in person, you *would* get sucked in. It would be unavoidable."

"Thanks for the faith, jerk."

Cinder sighed again. "I'm sorry. I know you're frustrated. I know I sound like an asshole, but I swear to you if there were any way I could make it work, I would. My life is too insane and I don't really have any control over it. You would get hurt, and you would end up hating me for it. Will you please just trust me on this? Can't you let what we have right now be enough? *Please?*"

Ugh. He sounded genuinely desperate. There was no way I'd be able to say no to him, but I couldn't just give in and let him have his way, either. "Fine. Whatever. I have to go."

I hung up on him.

He called me back.

I turned off my phone.

By the time I went back inside and climbed into bed, Cinder had gone back to instant messaging me.

Cinder458: Come on, Ella. Don't be like that.
Cinder458: I'm not trying to be a jerk.
Cinder458: Hello???
Cinder458: Ella!
Cinder458: Stop ignoring me, woman!!!

I should have signed off and put my laptop away. Instead, I responded.

EllaTheRealHero: I'm sorry, but I am just so pissed at you right now.
Cinder458: I know, and I'm sorry. I understand if you need some time. Just don't stay mad forever, okay? I'll miss you too much. I need you, Ellamara. I need this friendship.

I read his message and pulled my pillow over my face so I could scream into it.

EllaTheRealHero: Ugh! I hate how you do that!

Cinder458: Do what?

EllaTheRealHero: Make me love you even when I'm *so mad at you!!!!!*

Cinder458: I love you too, Ella. More than anyone in the whole world. I'm sorry you're mad at me.

EllaTheRealHero: I'm sure I'll get over it. Eventually.

Cinder458: I know. That's why I'm not worried. Go have your girly freak-out and call me when you love me again.

EllaTheRealHero: I hate you.

Cinder458: No, you don't. Goodnight, Ella.

EllaTheRealHero: Goodnight, Cinder.

I WAS DEVASTATED THAT CINDER DIDN'T WANT TO MEET, BUT IN A way I was also relieved after our talk. For one thing, I no longer had to stress about the What Ifs. It was nice to understand what he was thinking, why he'd never asked to meet.

His reasoning was stupid, but at least he wasn't rejecting me. Not really. He was afraid of losing me. Which, if you thought about it, was really sweet. It also happened to be exactly why I was scared of meeting him all this time. For me to not understand his hesitation would make me the biggest hypocrite in the world.

The other thing my conversation with Cinder did was free me from that small hope I'd had that someday we would have a happily ever after. I told myself all the time that Cinder and I would never be anything more than friends. I reminded myself every time I spoke to him that he dated other girls all the time. But of course, like any normal girl in my position would do, I *hoped* that he secretly loved me and held my breath waiting for the day he would finally admit it. Now I could stop waiting and start trying to get over him. At least, that's what I told myself I would do when I finally met Rob Loxley after school the next day.

Vivian had come home with me because she'd never had a friend who'd lived up in the hills before, and she wanted to see the house. She flipped when I showed her the remote control windows.

"Ridiculous, right? The view *is* pretty amazing, though."

"Whoa!" Vivian barged out onto my patio and spun around. "Is this for real?"

I laughed at her reaction. I couldn't blame her. My private balcony was big and had a view all the way to the ocean. It wasn't as large as the deck off the family room where the fire pit and the hot tub sat on the side of the cliff, but there was room for a round patio table with four chairs and a hammock.

"This is awesome! I'd live out here all the time."

"I don't go out there much," I admitted, laughing. "With my luck, we'd have an earthquake and I'd plummet down the cliff and *live* through it."

Vivian frowned at me as she plopped her bag down on the small patio table. "Criminal."

She lifted her face to the sun and sucked in a deep breath. The sight made me smile. If there was one thing I loved about Southern California, it was the weather. It may have been November, but it was still seventy degrees outside. It would be strange to have Christmas without snow, but I had no doubt I'd get used to it quickly and without complaint.

"Get your butt out here, Ella."

I sat down in the seat across from her, but I left the French doors hanging wide open so that I could dive for safety at the first sign of any trembling. We'd just pulled our homework out when Juliette barged into my room and threw herself down onto the hammock. "What's up?" she snapped, glaring with all her might into the house toward my open bedroom door.

Vivian and I followed her gaze. We couldn't see anything, but we could hear the laughs of several different people in the kitchen. As was quite common, a handful of the twins' groupies had followed them home today. Anastasia's grating voice stood out above the others. I couldn't understand what she was saying, but the anger in her tone was unmistakable.

"Did you just get us involved in some kind of sibling war that will no doubt eat us alive as collateral damage?" Vivian asked Juliette.

Juliette huffed. "I don't care. I am not hanging out with her while she's being such a jerk. She's pissed at me because she got chewed out after what happened at dinner last night. As if any of that was *my* fault!"

"Well," I said, turning back to my trig homework, "you are welcome to stay, so long as we don't have to listen to any of the drama."

Juliette glanced at me, surprised, and I managed a smile. "Vivian and I were just discussing the possibility of a Brian Oliver marathon this Friday night at her place. That new comedy came out on DVD last week, and the *V is for Virgin* movie is on Netflix now. I haven't seen it, but it's supposed to be fun."

"I'm in," Juliette said without hesitation just as Dylan Traxler, Juliette's latest fling, became our next surprise visitor.

Dylan was gorgeous and popular, but he didn't bat a single eyelash at whom Juliette had chosen to hang out with. He saw the empty space on the hammock next to her and landed like a fly on sticky paper. "What are we in for?" he asked as he laid back and pulled Juliette with him.

"Movie night at Vivian's this Friday." She glanced at Vivian for approval. "Or is this a girls-only thing?"

"Co-ed is fine," Vivian answered, doing a decent job of masking her shock. "But small. My place is tiny."

"Cool," Dylan said. I took that to mean he was "in" too.

Other than a shared glance, Vivian and I managed to act as if we had chill parties involving popular people all the time. Before either of us had to figure out what to say next, Dylan's friend Luke moseyed into my room.

"Switchin' it up, huh, Jules?" he asked, joining us on the

patio. "Personally I was hoping for a Coleman twins catfight, but I'll settle for a little love from the elusive stepsister."

He pulled out the chair to my right and straddled it. Grinning, he nodded at me in an extremely bro-dog kind of way. "Sup, Ella? Word on the street is you're secretly a pretty cool chick. What's up with the loner status?"

I decided to forget the fact that Luke used to tease me about my limp when I first got to school. "Well, you know, having a fan club is kind of a hassle so…"

Luke laughed, and then his eyes caught sight of something in the house behind me and he lifted his hand. "Yo, Rob! Party's out here today, bro."

I had just enough time to share another look with Vivian, who seemed every bit as bewildered by our hijacked study time as I was, before Rob Loxley walked out onto my patio, one hand in his pocket and the other holding an energy drink.

I didn't quite know what to make of Rob. He was no earth-shattering hottie like the guys Juliette and Anastasia dated, but he was decent-looking. He was a little short for a guy, only a couple inches taller than my five six. But since I'd never wear high heels again, I didn't see his height as a problem. He had really short brown hair, green eyes, and a clear complexion. He was still in his school uniform, but he'd loosened his tie and untucked his shirt. It looked good. He wore casual as if he'd invented the concept.

I'd heard him described as both *quiet* and *nice*, but there was something about him that suggested those two things didn't equate to shy. Maybe it was the nose that sat a little crooked on his face as if he'd broken it once, or the arms so lean his veins stuck out. The guy was little, but I bet he was ripped beneath his shirt. *Scrappy* seemed an accurate description. He also had an air of confidence that couldn't be faked. He was comfortable with himself. Quiet and nice, he might be, but he was very intimidating at the same time.

Rob sat down next to me and then went to work sipping on his energy drink. He let his eyes drift over the balcony railing to the city below us, clearly enjoying the view. He didn't speak, and it left me flustered. I had no idea what to do or say. When I looked to Vivian for help, Luke laughed. "My homeboy Rob is a man of few words, but the dude is seriously awesome. He's a superstar soccer player. Captain of our school's team, and he's being recruited by a ton of colleges."

Rob rolled his eyes at Luke's bragging, but the corners of his lips twitched as he fought back a smile. He was modest but still loved the attention. I liked that.

"So, what's up, Ella?" Luke continued when neither Rob nor I said anything. "Are you dating anyone? Jules said she thought there might be a guy."

I couldn't be sure, because I was too busy blushing, but I think Rob kicked Luke under the table.

"There's no guy." I didn't know if I was more embarrassed by the question, the answer to it, or the fact that my face was on fire and everyone could see it.

"What about Cinder?" Juliette asked suddenly.

I hadn't thought she was paying any attention to our conversation, but her eyes were on me now, along with everyone else's. *Thank you so much, Juliette.* If it had been Ana that asked, I'd have known she brought Cinder up to torture me, but Juliette looked honestly confused.

"Cinder's just a friend," I mumbled. "We've never even met in person. He's just someone who knows me from my blog."

Vivian, like an awesome friend, tried to get the attention off of me. "We're having a movie night at my place Friday night, Luke." I met her sympathetic smile with a grateful look. She winked at me and then smiled at Luke. "Nothing special, just a handful of people, some snacks, and the latest Brian Oliver movie. But if you and *Rob* want to come...?"

Now it was my turn to kick my friend under the table. I tried to take back my grateful look by glaring at her, and she winked again. I risked a glance at Rob, horrified that he might have seen her wink and think I'd asked her to say something. He met my gaze and slid me a wry grin. "Is it just me, or are we being set up?"

I wasn't sure if he'd asked to be set up, or if his friends had just picked up on his interest, but either way he was waiting for me to answer him. "It would seem so," I mumbled, feeling my face reach new levels of red.

Rob's eyes never left my face as he took another sip of his drink. After a moment, he said, "I'm okay with that."

Again, I had no idea how to respond...unless my eyes doubling in size counted as a response.

"Is it cool if I come to your party on Friday?"

I blushed again. "It's not really a party. Just a couple of us hanging out and watching movies."

"Those are my favorite kind of parties."

He wasn't going to let me off the hook. I took a deep breath, willing myself to keep it together. I tried to appear a lot more relaxed than I felt as I shrugged. "Then I guess you'd better come."

He smiled and it lit up his face, making me realize that he was cuter than I'd given him credit for. "Good. It's a date."

I HADN'T EXPECTED JULIETTE AND HER POPULAR BOY FAN CLUB TO suddenly become my best friends—and they didn't, of course—but Dylan and Luke both nodded and said hello when they passed me in the halls, and Rob even started sitting by me in the one class we shared and sometimes joined Vivian and me at lunch.

I was still mostly an outcast, but the animosity toward me seemed to be gone, with the exception of Anastasia and her most loyal friends. It made life at school a little more comfortable. Unfortunately, the tension at home got worse. Anastasia hated that Juliette and I were becoming friendlier with one another. The angrier she got, the less Juliette wanted to be around her, and suddenly Ana was the one hiding in her room all the time instead of me.

It was nice having Vivian and Juliette and even Rob to talk to, but I missed Cinder. By Friday night I still hadn't spoken to him. It had only been three days since our fight, but it felt like forever. I wasn't sure why I hadn't contacted him yet. Being stubborn, mostly. I wanted him to be the first to break. Even though he said he cared about me, him not wanting to meet me hurt.

I knew I needed to get over him, so I tried to forget about

him and enjoy myself at Vivian's house. Our movie night was a success. Everyone was relaxed and in a good mood. We stuck to our plan to rent a Brian Oliver flick. Since it was a teen comedy, the guys all liked it, too. There was a lot of laughter and popcorn throwing.

Everything was perfect, except for the fact that I couldn't make myself like Rob. He was a really nice guy. He was cute, interesting, smart—and I could tell that he really liked me—but there was nothing there for me. I liked him, and would love to have him as a friend, but there were no butterflies when I looked at him. He sat next to me during the movie with his hand resting on his thigh as if he was waiting for me to pick it up or give him any indication that I wanted him to take mine. I cradled the popcorn bowl and pretended to be oblivious.

I managed to hide my misery well enough, because even though I didn't flirt with Rob he seemed in good spirits when he left Vivian's house, and Juliette talked about how excited she was for me all the way home.

The following Friday I turned nineteen. I hadn't said a word to anyone about it, hoping the day would come and go with no one being the wiser. I was dreading it for several reasons. The first—and most obvious—was that it marked the anniversary of my mother's death. The morning of my eighteenth birthday Mama woke me up with an off-key serenade to the tune of "Happy Birthday," and announced that she was pulling me out of school for the last two days that week. She was taking me on a weekend ski trip to Vermont. She promised me an expensive dinner and a candle to blow out in the dessert of my choosing once we got to the resort, but I never got to make a wish.

Then, of course, I was also dreading the day this year because of the fact that my father had either forgotten or just ignored my birthdays for the last four or five years. The first time he forgot my birthday, I was eleven. The last time he remembered it I was fourteen. No matter how hard I tried, I never stopped being disappointed each year he forgot, so Mama became determined to help me forget about my father by making the day the most special one of the year for me—no matter what it took.

For years now my birthday had been a *big deal*. This year would be different. This year there was no one to make sure it was special. I wasn't even sure if my father knew when it was anymore, and I wasn't about to ask him. Things were awkward enough between us.

I told myself I could get through the day. I was determined to treat it like any other, but by the time I came out of my room dressed for school I was already so weighed down I felt as if I couldn't breathe. When I came out into the kitchen and found a bouquet of yellow roses so big it had its own center of gravity sitting on the counter with my name on it, I nearly burst into tears. As I stared at the flowers, a heavy arm fell around my shoulders. "How are you doing this morning?" my dad asked solemnly.

I couldn't have spoken even if I knew how to express myself. I shrugged beneath the weight of his arm.

My father suddenly crushed me to his chest in a hug that was as much for his sake as it was for mine. For a moment I stood frozen in shock, but I quickly melted against him and squeezed back with everything I had in me.

"Happy birthday, kiddo," he whispered, his voice thick with emotion.

"I didn't think you'd remember."

"I've missed enough of your birthdays."

My dad squeezed me even tighter, and I let him. The seconds began to pass. Neither of us spoke, and neither of us let go. The feel of his arms around me, his concern for me, and the warmth and love in his embrace completely did me in. I buried my face in his chest and let him hold me as I cried.

After a few minutes of ruining my dad's shirt, I finally pulled back enough to look up at him. His eyes shone with unshed tears as he forced a heartbreaking smile down at me. "I didn't think you'd want a lot of attention today, so we didn't plan a party. No surprises, I promise, but I hope you'll let us take you to a birthday dinner somewhere, at least. You could bring your friend Vivian along too, if you'd like."

"Can I get back to you on that? I'm not even sure I can make it through the day right now."

My dad swallowed back a lump in his throat and then nodded when he couldn't speak.

"Would you like to stay home from school today?"

I jumped at Jennifer's voice and pulled back from my father as if I'd been caught doing something I shouldn't. Pain flicked across my dad's face, but he buried it quickly. He looked at Jennifer and then back at me. "She's right. If you aren't up for classes today, you don't have to go."

I met my dad's eyes, then glanced around the kitchen. Jennifer and Juliette were both standing there with small, supportive smiles. I guess the secret was out. They clearly knew this wasn't just my birthday. Even Anastasia sat at the bar with a subdued expression. Wiping my cheeks dry, I shook my head in answer to my dad and Jennifer's suggestion. "I think moping around here alone will make it worse."

"I'm sorry we can't go visit your mom's grave. Maybe we could take a trip back to Boston over Thanksgiving break next week, if you'd like that. For now, I could take the day off from work and we could go do something, just the two of us."

"You don't have to do that. I think it'll help if I stay busy. School will be a good distraction."

My dad looked disappointed again, so I added, "It would be nice to go visit Mama and Abuela and Granpapa sometime, though. It doesn't have to be Thanksgiving, but whenever there's a good weekend."

"I'd like to come with you," Juliette said.

I looked at her, surprised and touched. She smiled back tentatively. "You could show me around Boston, maybe visit a few of your old friends." Her smile morphed into a mischievous grin. "I could get them to tell me their best stories about you. A sister needs blackmail material, you know. Even a step one."

That did it. I laughed. Juliette surprised me even more by giving me a light hug. "Happy birthday."

"Thanks." I said, and shyly retuned the hug. "A trip to Boston sounds fun. If we wait until the summer, we can go to Nantucket and I can show you how East Coasters do the beach. And I'll take you to a Red Sox game at Fenway Park."

Juliette grinned. "I'll be sure to wear my Dodgers jersey."

Dad's misty eyes bounced back and forth between Juliette and me. "I'll book a hotel today. We'll make a whole vacation out of it."

Anastasia broke up the moment with a sigh just before it could get awkward. I waited for whatever snide remark she had prepared, but all she said was, "Are you guys ready to go? I don't want to be late."

When we got to school, Rob was waiting for us in the student parking lot with a single red rose. As I accepted it, he planted a soft kiss on my cheek and whispered, "Happy birthday."

"Thanks."

I brought the bud to my nose, wishing it would hide my blush while Rob took my backpack and slung it over his shoulder with his own book bag. As we headed toward the school, he glanced at me. "You weren't going to tell anyone, were you?"

"I wasn't. How did you know?"

"I told him." Juliette rolled her eyes at my frown. "You can't let what happened last year take over your birthday for the rest of your life. You need some good to help balance out the bad."

I smelled my rose again and a smile crept over my face. I was surprised at how right Juliette was. "Thanks."

As the three of us stepped into the main breezeway and merged into the crowd of students, we could tell instantly that something wasn't normal. There was some kind of buzz in the air. It took me a minute to realize that I was the focus of the excitement. It was the oddest combination of emotions ranging from fascination, to confusion, to utter contempt. People were staring and whispering—some of them excited, others unable to hold in their disgust. As we neared my locker, I started to make out some of the whispers.

"It's her!"

"I can't believe she knows him."

"She's not *that* pretty."

"What does he see in her, anyway?"

I had no idea what was going on. I glanced at a group of younger girls who looked so excited they could barely contain their giddiness. One of them caught my gaze, and that energy finally burst. "Hi, Ella!"

Once the first greeting came, a chorus of others followed it.

"Hey, Ella!"

"Happy birthday, Ella!"

"You are so lucky, Ella!"

"Don't you just love Brian Oliver, Ella?"

"Happy birthday!"

I glanced at Rob first, but he was just as mystified as me, so I turned to Juliette for an explanation. She threw her hands up in surrender. "Don't look at me. I only told Rob and Vivian. I have no idea what's going on."

It was seriously like we'd left Los Angeles and landed in some alternate dimension. "Brian Oliver? Can I believe *what*? What's going on? What is everyone talking about?" I asked, though I knew neither Juliette nor Rob had any answers.

Mitchell Drayton, the most gorgeous guy in school, who also happened to be the snobbiest because he had an agent and had landed a few bit parts on a couple of TV shows, walked right up to us. "Hey, Jules," he said to Juliette and then turned his devastating smile on me. "Hi, Ella. Are you having a party or anything for your birthday? Need a date?"

Rob stepped a little closer to my side and glared at him. Mitchell glanced at the rose in my hand, and then gave Rob a once-over. He took a step back, chuckling to himself. "Sorry, bro. Didn't realize I was stepping on anyone's toes." To me, he said, "I'm having a party tomorrow night with some of my actor friends. You should come. Bring Rob and Jules too, if you'd like. Eight P.M. Jules knows where I live."

My mouth hung agape and my heart pounded as I watched him walk away. Every teen movie that was worth anything started out with a scene like this—everyone being unusually nice to the poor, unsuspecting outcast right before she gets publicly humiliated. "Do you think Ana is trying to play some kind of prank?" I whispered.

"No way." Juliette sounded confident, but I wasn't so sure. She noticed my skepticism and shook her head. "Seriously. Did you notice the lack of snottiness this morning? Mom read us both the riot act last night and told us that if either of us so much as frowned at you today, we would be grounded until we were thirty."

Great. Not that I didn't appreciate the gesture, but that had to have pissed Anastasia off more than anything. I was lucky she hadn't exploded already.

"It's not Ana," Juliette insisted.

"Well, it's definitely something," Rob muttered, frowning at a couple of guys who were staring at me.

"I'll figure it out," Juliette said as we reached her homeroom. "Lunch together today?"

"You know where to find me."

Juliette disappeared into her classroom, and Rob scowled at everyone we passed as he walked me to mine. He was as skeptical about my stepsister as I was, because he said, "It had to be Ana. Vivian wouldn't have said anything. I'll figure out what's going on."

He'd stopped us at the door to my classroom and grabbed my hand so that I couldn't walk away. A girl whose name I didn't remember accidentally bumped into my shoulder as she walked past us into the room. "Watch it!" she snapped. When she realized it was me in her way, her eyes narrowed. "You think you're so special now? Well, you're not."

Another girl walked in behind her, smiling viciously. "I bet she paid him to do it."

They walked to their seats, cackling.

More confused than ever, I looked at Rob again. "You going to be okay until lunch?" he asked.

The worry in his eyes made me smile. "I guess you don't remember what it was like for me when I first got here," I teased.

His face grew dark, a storm of emotion brewing in his eyes. I felt terrible when I realized he knew exactly what I'd been through these past months, and how much it upset him. "Hey." I gave his hand a squeeze. "It's all good. I'm fine. Thank you for my flower."

He finally smiled. "You're welcome."

Vivian was bubbling over with energy when she came into the cafeteria at lunch. "Brian Oliver wished you happy birthday on Twitter!" she squealed. "What the hell?"

"I know. Juliette told me in second period and 'What the hell?' was my thought exactly. I don't get it."

The looks and greetings all made sense after I heard the news. Brian Oliver had made me the center of attention when he publicly wished me happy birthday that morning. The excitement and jealousy, and even Mitchell's party invite, all made sense now. But that was about all I understood.

"How did he know it was my birthday? How does he know I even exist?"

"Because you're brilliant," Rob said, sitting down next to me.

"What?"

"He's a fan of your blog."

"No!" Vivian shrieked. "Let me! Please? I've been dying to show her all day!"

Rob laughed and waved his hand in a be-my-guest gesture, making Vivian's whole face light up. I was afraid she was going to pull a muscle when she smiled because her mouth stretched across her entire face. "It all started with this."

Vivian really had been waiting to tell me the story. She already had her phone cued up to a specific post on Brian Oliver's Facebook page. "'Happy birthday to my favorite blogger and number-one fan, Ellamara!'" Vivian read aloud. "'Your words of wisdom are unparalleled.' And look!" she squealed. "He posted a link to your review of some movie he was in."

I looked, and sure enough there was a link to my review of the movie *The Long Road Home*—the apology letter I'd written to Brian Oliver.

"That's not all," Vivian said. She began scrolling up Brian Oliver's Facebook page. There was post after post of him sharing *Ellamara's Words Of Wisdom* posts.

"He's been quoting me on Facebook?"

Vivian nodded so enthusiastically that she looked like a bobblehead doll. "All day! He's been doing it on Twitter too, and now other people are doing it. 'Ellamara's Words of Wisdom' is *trending* right now."

This I had to see. I pulled up my Twitter on my phone and nearly had a heart attack. "No way!"

"What?" Rob and Vivian both leaned in and read over my shoulder.

"Yesterday I had just over six thousand followers on Twitter. Today I have over twenty-five thousand!"

Rob laughed. "That's what happens when Hollywood's golden child tells the world to listen to you. I hope your personal information isn't attached to your blog anywhere."

"No. I have a separate e-mail, Twitter, and Facebook page for all my blog stuff, and a PO Box for publishers to send books to. I should be safe, but this is *insane!*"

"Right?" Juliette said as she finally joined us.

With Juliette there, we started over from the beginning. She'd brought an entourage with her to get the scoop—Dylan and Luke and a few other friends who were curious enough about the story to brave being seen talking to me at lunch—but there simply wasn't a story to tell. I didn't know Brian Oliver. I had no idea how he discovered my blog.

"I have a question," Rob said, finally joining the impromptu Q and A session. "How did Brian Oliver know it was your birthday? He could have come across your review on his own, but how did he know today was your birthday? I read your blog. I know you haven't mentioned it."

I'd wondered that myself. In fact, that was the most mind-boggling part of this whole ordeal. "I don't know. Honestly, I was surprised that *anyone* knew it was my birthday. I didn't even think my dad knew it was coming up. The only person I've talked to about it was…"

And suddenly, everything made perfect sense. The entire table fell quiet, waiting for me to reveal the big secret, but all I could do was smile. "Of course. I should have known."

"Was *who?*" Vivian demanded.

I sighed. "It was Cinder."

"The Internet guy?" Rob asked.

I nodded.

My heart sank and soared at the same time. Cinder and I hadn't spoken since I told him I was pissed and hung up on him, but I knew he still cared about me. He knew what today was. He'd been the one to bring it up a couple weeks ago.

He remembered the day because he'd been texting me at the time of the accident. He said he was dreading the day, and that as it got closer it felt as if it was haunting him. I was really surprised until he explained. For him, that was the day he lost me. When we talked about it, I confessed that it had been my birthday. He promised he would find a way to distract me today and make sure that I enjoyed my birthday and didn't just think about the accident.

"He kept his promise," I whispered to myself, fighting back sudden tears.

Vivian waved a hand in front of my face, trying to regain my attention. "What promise?"

"He knew what today was. I mean, what it is besides my birthday. He promised he'd distract me so that I wouldn't think about it. Even though I yelled at him and haven't spoken to him yet, he still kept his promise."

Vivian sighed. "That's so romantic. You have to forgive him, Ella." She'd been urging me to do that ever since I gave her the details of our argument. "You've got to call him back."

Rob didn't seem to agree. "How do you know *he* did this?"

"He's the only one who could have. He's the only one who knew it was my birthday, and his dad is some big shot in the film industry, so he could have managed to get in contact with Brian somehow. I've always known Cinder has connections in show biz. I should have figured it out sooner."

"How do you know? You've never even met him. The guy's probably a liar."

I shook my head. "He's been feeding me Hollywood insider information since we met. He always knows stuff before it hits the trades. He must have had his dad call in a favor or something."

"Maybe he knows Brian," Vivian said. "I mean, if they were friends, it would explain why he likes the guy so much."

"True," I agreed. "He's mentioned knowing a few celebrities, though he's not a name dropper, and I've never asked which ones. I guess they could be friends. Knowing Cinder, it wouldn't surprise me."

That made everyone around us whisper and giggle. One girl even said, "I can't believe you know someone who is friends with Brian Oliver!"

"I don't, really. I'm not sure how Cinder did it. He could know Brian, or his dad could just know a guy who knows a guy who knows him."

"That was a pretty cool thing to do, though," Rob said. It took me a minute to realize he meant Cinder making sure I was distracted today.

A smile crept across my face. "Yeah." I was going to have to call him later and apologize for not talking to him all week.

"Just how close are you with this guy?" Rob asked. The suspicion in his voice was embarrassing.

"He's my best friend."

"But you've never met in person, right? You're just, like, pen pals or whatever?"

I finally understood the reasoning behind Rob's line of questions, and my heart sank a little. I stared at my lunch, having no idea what to say to him. He seemed to understand because he said, "This is the part where you kick me to the curb, isn't it?"

I forced myself to look at Rob. He didn't seem crestfallen or anything, which I hoped meant his interest in me hadn't been as strong as everyone else believed it was. I didn't want to hurt him.

"I'm sorry. I'm in no position to be dating anyone right now. Technically, I am single. There is nothing going on between Cinder and me, and there never will be, but I love him anyway. I hate that I love him, and I try *not* to love him, but I fail miserably."

Rob studied me for a minute in that quiet, intense way of his and asked, "Are you sure there's nothing between you? You're sure he doesn't like you, too?"

I nodded. "He has a girlfriend and he specifically told me he doesn't want to meet in person. He likes that we don't know each other."

Rob's face pinched up slightly as if Cinder's request pissed him off, but he didn't say as much. "So we need to get you over him. Would it help if you had someone else—a boyfriend—to help take your mind off him?"

I blushed when I realized exactly what Rob was saying, what he was offering me, but I immediately shook my head. "That's really sweet, but I don't think it would be fair to you."

"Do you like me?" Rob asked.

I nodded reluctantly. "I do, but—"

Rob didn't let me finish my sentence. "Are you attracted to me?"

My face flamed at the question. I dropped my eyes to my lap and chewed my bottom lip so hard it hurt, but I managed a small nod.

"Then that's enough."

When I looked up confused, he smiled. "You don't have to be in love to date someone. We don't have to be serious. We don't even have to be exclusive if you don't want. You could just give it a try. Go out with me and see if something sparks."

I considered his offer. I *did* really like Rob. He seemed like a laid-back guy. Maybe he wasn't really looking for anything serious, either. It didn't seem fair, but I did need to try to get over Cinder, and the more people I could show Dr. Parish I had in my "support system" the sooner I'd earn my independence. Still… "I don't know. I think it would feel like I was using you."

Rob picked up a slice of pizza from his lunch tray and grinned at me. "Use away, Ella. Maybe it won't work out, maybe it will. Either way at least you tried, and we get to have some fun."

He bit into his pizza and his eyes twinkled with mischief as he chewed. Once his mouth was clear, he said, "You look like you could use a good rebound, and I just want to make it very clear, right now, that I am always down to be a pretty girl's rebound."

I finally managed a smile that reached my eyes. "Good to know."

"So what do you say?"

I'd be an idiot if I didn't at least try. "I guess we could give it a shot. My Dad wants to go out for my birthday tonight. He already asked me to invite Vivian." I glanced at Juliette. "Do you think he'd mind if Rob came, too?"

Juliette shook her head. "He'll be cool. It's my mom you have to worry about. She gets all crazy excited when Ana or I date anyone. She's going to freak that you have a boyfriend."

I blanched at the term and Rob laughed. "So no title, then."

Vivian snorted. "Other than Rebound Boy, anyway."

I grimaced, but Rob laughed again. "It has a nice ring to it."

· · · · ·

By the time I got home from school I was mentally exhausted. I wanted nothing more than to relax to the sound of Cinder's deep, rumbling voice. I knew I needed to call him. I missed him, and he deserved my thanks.

My dad had recently lifted the ban on my room, so I escaped to the sanctuary as soon as I got home from school. As I was shutting the door, I heard Anastasia speak for the first time all day. She'd been silent on the rides to and from school, obviously striving for the Thumper method of not getting in trouble—if you can't say anything nice, don't say anything at all.

As soon as I was out of sight, she pounced on Juliette like a starving lion. They were in the kitchen—Juliette rummaging through the fridge for her daily after-school snack—and their voices carried easily across the great-room style main floor to my bedroom.

"How did she do it?" Anastasia demanded.

Since she was talking about me, I left my bedroom door open a crack and shamelessly eavesdropped on the conversation.

"She didn't," Juliette answered. "She was just as surprised as the rest of us. Cinder did it. It was his birthday gift to her."

"Cinder?" Ana gasped. "The creepy Internet guy?"

I heard the fridge shut and the sound of a can opening. "He's not creepy," Juliette insisted. "He's actually kind of cool."

"How do you know? Have you talked to him?"

"No, but I hear Ella talk to him all the time and their conversations are completely normal. Plus, I read her IM feed once when she went to the bathroom and left her laptop open on the couch."

"Nah-uh! Did you read anything good?"

I was surprised by the confession, but I found it hard to be mad at the invasion of privacy because of the smile I heard in her voice. "It was highly entertaining. Those two banter back and forth like a romance novel heroine and her dastardly pirate captor."

There was silence for a minute, and then Juliette said, "She's witty, Ana—funny, smart, nice, and generally pretty cool. You'd probably like her if you'd just give her a chance."

I was shocked to be so defended. I knew Juliette didn't have a problem with me anymore, but right then she sounded as if she were truly my friend. Anastasia wasn't nearly as moved by her speech. "Why should I? She's never given me a chance."

"How could she? You've been horrible to her since the second she got here. If you ask me, she tolerates you a lot better than you deserve."

Anastasia's scoff sounded vicious. I didn't need to see her face to imagine the daggers she was throwing at Juliette with her eyes. I was also sure her claws were fully extended now. "I can't believe how far you've turned on me. She's not part of this family, and you're siding with her over your own twin! *I'm* your sister! Not *her!*"

"She *is* part of this family, Ana. You need to accept it."

"I'm not accepting anyone who's trying to take over my life!"

Juliette must have been just as confused as I was because there was no immediate reply. What did Anastasia mean? In what reality was I trying to take over her life? Because it surely wasn't this one.

"She's already taken my room, my sister, and the boy I like! She doesn't even want Rob, and he follows her around like a lovesick puppy! Mom and Dad fawn all over her, and now *Brian Freaking Oliver* is wishing her happy birthday!"

"None of that is Ella's fault!" Juliette shouted. "She couldn't have the upstairs bedroom because she's freaking handicapped. Would you want to have to gimp around the way she does? Have you ever seen her do her physical therapy? It hurts her so bad she cries. Making her walk up the stairs every day to get to her bedroom would be cruel."

"Fine, but Rob—"

"She can't help how Rob feels. She's been honest with him about her feelings for Cinder. He's the one who insists on trying to win her over anyway. I think she did the right thing agreeing to go out with him."

Ana scoffed again.

"She didn't steal *me* from you, either," Juliette continued. "I just can't stand to be around you anymore because all you do is whine about Ella. And Dad *should* be sucking up to her. He *abandoned* her. If anyone stole anything from anyone, we stole Dad from her. It's a miracle she can forgive any of us!"

Juliette paused, probably to take a breath. It was quiet for a minute. I wondered if Anastasia would respond, but she didn't. It was Juliette who broke the silence. Her voice was much calmer now, but I could still hear the intensity in it.

"Not everything has to be about *you* all the time. I'm glad Cinder managed to pull off the Brian Oliver thing because it gave Ella something to think about other than the fact that today is the one-year anniversary of the worst day of her life. Can't you just be happy with the fact that something good happened to someone who needed it?"

Again, Anastasia didn't say anything. Not that I expected her to. Juliette must have been finished unloading all of her frustration because I heard the TV downstairs click on and heard a door slam somewhere on the floor above me.

I couldn't help feeling a little sorry for Anastasia. She's a self-centered troll, but she still has feelings. I'd never even tried to see things from her perspective before. Juliette and Jennifer both mentioned that Anastasia felt threatened by me. I hadn't believed them, but obviously they were right.

I wasn't going to cow myself and put up with Anastasia's crap—our situation wasn't my fault, and I didn't deserve to be punished for it—but it was nice to understand where her animosity came from. I supposed I could try to be a little more sensitive to her feelings.

I finally shut my door and decided to soak in a hot bath.

19

Brian

FANTASYCON IS THE WORLD'S BIGGEST FANTASY CONVENTION—Comic-Con for *Lord Of The Rings* and *Dungeons and Dragons* fans. It's held annually at the Los Angeles Convention Center in November and was the first of many publicity appearances I would have to make to promote the release of *The Druid Prince*.

I loved FantasyCon. I'd come every year since I was sixteen, and this year I got to be involved as more than just a spectator. It was the only stop on *The Druid Prince* publicity tour I was looking forward to, but it turned out to be one of the worst days of my life.

Today was Ella's birthday and the one-year anniversary of her accident. All day long I had to smile and greet fans and play up my fake romance with Kaylee when all I could think about was Ella and what she must be going through right now. I couldn't even be there to comfort her because she still wasn't speaking to me.

I couldn't blame her for being mad. I hurt her deeply when I refused to meet her, but I didn't have any other choice. I figured she'd take a couple of days to cool off and then call and forgive me, but those couple of days turned into almost two weeks.

I checked my instant messenger for the millionth time. Ella still wasn't signed on so I did the only other thing I could think to do and sent another *Ellamara's Words of Wisdom* tweet out to my fans. This time I quoted something she'd said almost three years ago about the brilliance of Margaret Weis and Tracy Hickman's *Dragonlance* series.

I promised I'd keep Ella distracted today, but since she still wasn't speaking to me this was the only thing I could think of to do. Hopefully it was working better for her as a distraction, because all it was doing for me was reminding me how much she would love to be here. I hated that she was missing it.

"Would you put that damn thing away?" Kaylee muttered when she noticed the cell in my hands. "It's *rude*."

I pocketed the phone. Kaylee wasn't pissed that I was texting; she was just mad about *what* I was texting. Her anger made me smile. It was the little things in life that counted.

Suddenly in a slightly better mood, I greeted the young teenage girl and her mother that were now standing in front of me. "Kaylee's right. Forgive me. You have my undivided attention now."

"Oh, it's okay!" the girl promised as she handed me a photo to sign. "You were just posting another *Ellamara's Words of Wisdom* quote, right?"

I grinned. The last time I checked Ella's Twitter, there'd been a twenty-thousand strong jump in her followers so far today. She was going to *freak* when she saw it. "I was. Have you been reading them?"

"Oh, yes!" the girl cried. "Ella is so funny! I can totally see why she's your favorite blogger. I started following her this morning, too. I think it's so sweet what you're doing. I would *die* if I got a birthday present like that. I'm sure she loves it."

"I hope so." I chuckled again. "What's your name, sweetheart?"

"Nancy."

"Well, Nancy," I said as I signed her photo and handed it back, "would you like to help me wish her a happy birthday again?" I shifted my gaze to the girl's mom. "Would it be all right if I take a picture with Nancy and post it on my Instagram?"

"Oh!" Nancy turned to her mother and tugged on her sleeve. "Please, Mom! Can I? *Please, please, please?*"

When Nancy's mother laughed and nodded, I gestured for the girl to come around to my side of the table. My day got a little better again when I asked Nancy's mom to take the picture so that Kaylee could be in it, too. Kaylee had no choice but to smile pretty.

I sent Kaylee a wink and read the caption out loud as I uploaded it. "Kaylee, Nancy, and me wishing Ellamara the best birthday ever from FantasyCon! Join us in the fun! #HappyBirthdayElla!"

The look on Kaylee's face as I posted the picture to the Internet almost made my fake engagement worth it.

AFTER THE AUTOGRAPH SESSION WAS OVER, KAYLEE AND I WERE supposed to go straight to our next event. It was a celebrity knight's tournament. Myself and a bunch of other actors from other fantasy movies and TV shows were all dressing up as our characters and competing in a NERF sword fighting competition to win a kiss from the fair princess Ratana.

The event was the coolest idea ever, and I was going to rock it. I'd always kicked ass in my swordplay lessons before filming *The Druid Prince*. I just wished Ella could be there to enjoy it, too. She was the biggest *Merlin* fanatic, and I was competing against Prince Arthur in the first round.

After changing into my Cinder costume, I checked my phone again. I'd just dedicated my first match to Ella and linked her review called *Merlin and Arthur: The Best Bromance on TV*, when I finally got a text from her.

You kept your promise.

The message lifted a weight off my chest. Ella *did* know I was behind the Brian Oliver posts. She knew I was thinking of her, and she was finally talking to me again.

Glancing around the luxury hotel suite Kaylee and I had been put up in for the duration of the convention, I plopped down on the bed. I was already running a little late, but my duel wasn't up first and I couldn't go anywhere without talking to Ella.

I tried my best, I texted back. **Did it work?**

Yes.

I'm glad. Ella, I am so sorry. Please forgive me.

You're forgiven. You know I can never stay mad at you.

Good. So do I have permission to call and wish you a happy birthday?

Only if you sing to me.

I cracked a smile and immediately launched into a semi-decent rendition of "Happy Birthday" when Ella answered her phone. "You should definitely stick with reading," she teased when I was done, even though I stayed in tune the whole time.

I couldn't laugh with her. "Ella..." I cleared my throat. My voice was surprisingly strangled. "How are you today?"

Her reply was quiet, but not as weak as I feared it would be. "Surviving better than I expected." There was a pause and the sound of water, and then Ella let out a soft sigh. "The bath is helping," she said, effectively scrambling all thoughts in my brain.

"Did you say you're in the *bath?*"

"Mmhm. Soaking in lavender. My stepmom swears it's therapeutic, and I'll never admit it to her, but she is right. I am so relaxed right now."

I choked back a startled cough. "Damn it, Ellamara, what are you trying to do to me, woman?"

"What are you talking about—oh." Ella laughed. "You perv. How can you be turned on? You don't even know what I look like.

I could be four hundred pounds, hairy, and covered with warts, for all you know."

Yeah, right. "You aren't. I saw your picture on your blog back when you used to post about those trips with your mom. You're hot. You have that sexy half-Latina thing going on."

I hoped she'd respond to my flirting for once, but she just said, "You're so full of it. Those pictures of me in all my brace-face glory back then were hideous. I'm average at best. At least, I was before. Now there aren't many guys that would look twice at me—not for the right reasons."

I sat up. What did she mean by *before?* Before her accident? Had something happened to her that she'd never told me about? She was in the hospital for a long time, but she'd never explained her injuries to me. She always said she didn't want to talk about it. "Ella, what do you mean?"

"Nothing. It's not important."

The hell it wasn't. "Ella—"

"What I'm trying to say," she interrupted, "is stop fantasizing about me and let me enjoy my bath. I need it, after the day I had. Your little stunt made everyone who's been ignoring me for months suddenly either want to be my best friend or gouge my eyes out in an envious rage. I thought Rob was going to start hurting people on my behalf."

I forgot all about Ella's injuries. "Rob? Is that the guy your friend mentioned? Are you guys dating now?"

"Kind of, I guess. I mean we're not exclusive or official or anything, but he finally asked me out. He's coming to my birthday dinner tonight."

I squeezed my phone so hard I nearly cracked the screen. Some high school punk was taking her to dinner for her birthday and she didn't think that was serious? Bullshit. Birthdays were a big deal. Guys feared women's birthdays. Always. Whether Ella thought so or not, this Rob guy definitely had major intentions if he was willing to spend her birthday with her. But at least Ella hadn't sounded all that enthusiastic. "I can tell you're jumping for joy. Do you actually *want* to go out with this guy?"

Ella sighed. "I don't know. I haven't dated anyone since before my accident. I'm not sure I'm ready, but I've got to start living again sometime, right? At the very least, Rob deserves a chance."

It took all the acting skills I possessed to sound like a politely concerned friend instead of the jealous asshole I was. "Don't you dare settle for second best, Ella."

"It's not that. He's good-looking and really sweet. He's one of the most popular guys at school because he's some kind of super soccer player, but it doesn't bother him at all that I'm a social leper. I promise he's a good guy."

An athlete? My little fantasy-loving book nerd was going out with a *jock?* That was so wrong. "Good isn't great," I said, a bit of a growl escaping me. "You're not a B-list kind of girl."

Suddenly there was a pounding on the hotel room door and Kaylee shouted my name. When she started fiddling with the lock, I cursed her for having a key and bolted for the bathroom. I wasn't done with this conversation yet, and I sure as hell wasn't going to end it for Kaylee.

I hated that we had to share a room this week, but our management team was paranoid about the secret that our relationship was a sham would get out, so they'd insisted. I got the bathroom door shut and locked just as Kaylee walked into the suite. "I know you're in there!" she shouted, banging on the bathroom door. "What the hell are you doing?"

It was bad enough that I had to hear all about Mr. Fantastic Soccer Dude. Dealing with Kaylee on top of that news was asking too much of my temper. "What do you think I'm doing? I'm hiding from you!"

"Hilarious!" Kaylee jiggled the handle and pounded on the door again when it wouldn't open. "Get your ass out here now! We're late!"

"*You're* late! I don't have to be there for fifteen minutes."

"I am not showing up to this stupid thing *alone!* Get off the damn phone and get out here now!"

She'd never leave me alone. Muttering a string of curses, I sighed into the phone. "The cavalry finally found me. I've got to run. I'm at this crazy work thing this weekend. I'm actually locked in a bathroom at the moment because I'm supposed to be somewhere, but when I saw your text, I couldn't wait to talk to you."

"That's okay. You can call me later."

I was relieved to hear a smile in Ella's voice, and even more grateful that she was asking me to call her later. It meant she wasn't mad anymore. I really was forgiven. These last two weeks without her had been some of the longest of my life.

"Maybe we can read tonight for my birthday?" she suggested.

I groaned. I would have liked nothing more than to curl up in bed tonight and read with Ella for her birthday, but there were so many people in town for the convention that there was this huge party going down tonight and there was no chance in hell Kaylee would let me miss it. "That sounds like heaven, but I'm at this conference through Sunday, and the nights have been running really late. I don't think I'll be able to get away. Can we talk Monday?"

"Sure."

I heard Ella's disappointment and tried to swallow my own. "Good. I can't wait. I've really missed you, woman. You have no idea how much. After just one day I had to delete your number out of my phone so that I wouldn't lose all dignity by calling you a billion times to beg for forgiveness."

Ella laughed at the same time Kaylee pounded on the door again.

I yanked my hair in frustration. "I really have to go. Love you, Ella. No more silent treatment, okay? These last two weeks were hell. Happy birthday. I'll call you Monday."

"Thanks. Love you too, Cinder. I'll wait by the phone Monday, holding my breath for your call."

Her parting words warmed my heart. They would be enough

to help me survive the rest of the weekend. With my smile back, I went to face the shrew and hopefully kick Prince Arthur of Camelot's ass in a NERF sword fight.

AFTER TALKING TO CINDER, I FELT REJUVENATED ENOUGH TO GO out for my birthday dinner. My father had reservations at the Chart House, a steak house on the waterfront in Malibu. Steak isn't my favorite, but my dietician would be pleased because I'd lost a little weight recently from stress, and he'd demanded I start a higher calorie diet with more protein. In fact, he was probably responsible for my father's restaurant choice. Anyway, at least it wasn't sushi. Ick. On the plus side, the restaurant was beautiful. Seeing the sun set over the ocean was worth the drive in itself.

Dinner was pleasant, seeing as how my dad adored Vivian, was still thrilled by the new camaraderie between Juliette and me, and didn't ask Rob any horrible so-you're-dating-my-daughter questions. Even Anastasia hadn't pouted too much.

The only embarrassing moment was when Jennifer gushed over Rob because he'd pulled out my chair for me. Poor Rob had turned bright red. I was sure I looked the same. Both Juliette and Anastasia hissed at their mom, wearing frighteningly identical glares. Thankfully, Jennifer got the hint and tried not to act too mom-ish from then on.

After dinner everyone was stuffed, but Dad insisted we order a few of their signature hot lava cakes—this was a birthday party, after all. Not one to say no to fudgy goodness, I happily agreed. As we waited for the dessert to arrive, Juliette started bouncing in her chair. "Can we do gifts now?"

"There are presents?" My cheeks heated up again. I hadn't expected any gifts.

"Good ones," Juliette said. "You're going to love them. Can we give them to her now? Please, please, please?"

It was like watching a kindergartner on Christmas morning. We all laughed at her. "All right." My dad conceded and handed me a long envelope that he'd pulled from the inside breast pocket of his suit jacket. "This is from the family. It was Juliette's suggestion, so if you don't like it, blame her."

Juliette rolled her eyes but grinned so big she looked like she might burst. "Just open it!"

Her excitement was contagious, and I tore into the envelope as fast as my damaged fingers would let me. I nearly screamed with excitement when I saw what was waiting for me. As it was, I squealed a little, causing several other restaurant patrons to frown at our table. I was holding tickets to this year's FantasyCon in my hands. I seriously couldn't believe it.

"Are you kidding? I know this makes me a huge dork, but I have wanted to go to this every year since I was, like, twelve! Oh my gosh, I can't believe I finally get to go! Thank you! I love it!"

The convention runs for five days, but the best day was always the last day—Sunday. I had, in my hands, five Sunday passes.

The day after tomorrow I would get to spend all day immersed in the worlds of my favorite books and movies. I'd get to meet a ton of my favorite authors and actors, get sequels to books that still haven't come out yet, hear guest lectures, and get sneak peeks at a couple of upcoming movies. There was even a rumor that they were going to play ten whole minutes of *The Druid Prince!*

"Those aren't just FantasyCon tickets," Juliette said. "We got you seats for *The Druid Prince* discussion panel. I looked it up. The writer of the books and the director, producer, writer, and cast of the movie are all going to be there! They're having a private meet-and-greet for all panel attendees, so you're going to get to meet your BFF Brian Oliver! Can you believe it?"

Juliette was squealing now, enough that Dad told her to take a breath. I myself was in shock. As soon as my brain started functioning again, I realized just how many tickets I had. "You got me *five* tickets? Do you know how much these must have cost?"

Juliette waved dismissively. "Whatever. Dad owed you anyway."

I decided not to think about that and asked another question before things could get awkward. "But why so many?"

Juliette flashed a wicked smile. "Well, obviously you didn't want to go by yourself, and I thought it would be rude to get you only two tickets and make you have to choose between your friends."

"You mean you were afraid I might not pick you," I teased.

Juliette didn't deny it. "Hello! *Brian Oliver!*"

I laughed again. "Okay, but why five? Did you have a specific guest list in mind?"

"Well, obviously you, me, Vivian and Rob, and I thought…" Juliette hesitated, biting her lip nervously.

"Who?" I asked. I honestly had no idea who else she could mean.

"I thought you could invite Cinder." Juliette blushed, and hurried with the rest of her explanation. "I mean, *The Druid Prince* is totally your guys' thing. I thought it would be the perfect excuse for you two to finally meet."

I was shocked. Juliette wasn't just trying to indulge one of my biggest passions—or hers—with this gift; she was doing so much more than that. She was trying to give me my best friend. It was one of the most thoughtful things anyone had ever done for me. I was so overwhelmed by the gesture that I couldn't speak.

"What do you think?" Juliette asked nervously.

"This gift is amazing, Juliette. Thank you so much for thinking about Cinder. That means a lot to me. I'd love to be able to go to this with him, but he's out of town for the weekend at some work thing. He called to wish me happy birthday, and we could only speak for a couple minutes. He was so busy he said he wouldn't have time to talk until Monday."

"Bummer." Juliette's face fell into a pout for only a second before she perked back up. "Whatever. We'll get him when the movie comes out. I mean, there's no way you guys aren't going to watch it together."

My heart ached at the thought because I knew it was a hopeless cause. Cinder and I would never meet. I wouldn't get to watch the movie with him, even though there was no one else in the world I'd rather see it with.

I needed to change the subject before I started to cry. "Well, anyway, Cinder can't come." I looked at my other stepsister, who was studiously ignoring everyone by playing with her phone. "Why don't you come with us, Ana?"

Everyone at the table froze. Vivian, Rob, and Juliette gaped at me with incredulous, shocked faces. My dad and Jennifer were just as surprised, but they both watched Anastasia with held breaths and hopeful expressions. Anastasia was just as startled as everyone else. *"Me?"*

I ignored her unfriendliness and shrugged. "Sure. Why not?"

The glare she hit me with was impressive, even for her. "I don't need a pity invite. What makes you think I'd even want to go to some repulsive convention full of freaks with you and your friends, anyway?"

The looks of disappointment on both my dad's and Jennifer's faces angered me more than Anastasia's insult. I wanted to say something rude back but when I glanced around the table again at my new family, I didn't have the heart to make matters worse.

"It's not a pity invite," I said, forcing all the nonchalance I could manage into my voice. "Consider it more of a truce. A peace offering."

Anastasia's eyes narrowed as she waited for me to explain.

"Juliette and Rob are your friends too, and I know you like

Brian Oliver. Come with us and have a good time. I'm not asking you to like me, and I don't want you to come because I feel sorry for you. I'm inviting you as a way to apologize. I can't help that I've intruded on your life and I can't remove myself from it. What I can do is try to make up for it by giving you the chance to steal Brian Oliver from Kaylee Summers. As much as it pains me to say it, I think you're prettier than she is. If anyone could manage it, you could."

Dad and Jennifer were still frozen in place, unable to believe what was happening, but Juliette, Vivian, and Rob all laughed.

"She's definitely aggressive enough," Juliette agreed. She grinned at her sister and said, "You're like a barracuda."

Anastasia scoffed, but I could tell she was trying not to smile. "It doesn't matter. I'm grounded until Christmas."

"If you'd like to go with your sisters to the convention, I suppose I could unground you," Dad said. "Assuming you can behave yourself."

Ana looked as if she was grinding her teeth as much as I was at being referred to as sisters, but neither of us corrected him. Ana narrowed her eyes and asked, "Ungrounded for just the day?"

My dad and Jennifer shared a look. Dad shrugged and Jennifer nodded to Ana. "Ungrounded, as in early release. You can be done with your punishment as long as your behavior stays acceptable."

I got the feeling getting let off the hook wasn't something that happened often in this family because both Juliette's and Ana's eyes popped open in shock. Ana recovered faster than Juliette and shrugged in my direction, feigning indifference. "Fine, whatever. I'll go to your stupid thing."

The server came with our cake, and while everyone was distracted my dad reached over and squeezed my hand. "Thank you," he mouthed.

"Thank you for my gift," I said in return. "I love it."

We all dug into our dessert—thankfully, there was no singing involved—and after a few minutes of comfortable silence, Rob turned to me. "So you're not interested in winning Brian Oliver for yourself?" He was teasing, but there was true curiosity in his voice. "He's already a fan of yours. All you'd have to do is tell him it was your blog he's been quoting all day."

"Oh, no!" I laughed. "That is *not* happening. I already have one rich, arrogant, playboy twisting up my heart. I don't need another one. He's all yours, Anastasia—unless Juliette wants to fight you for him."

"Oh, I intend to," Juliette said, making us all laugh again.

"All right, all right, enough of this," Vivian interrupted. "It's my turn to give you your gift."

Vivian placed a large gift bag overflowing with colorful tissue paper in front of me.

"You got me a present? You didn't have to do that."

"Oh, yes I did. Hurry and open it before I tell you what it is."

When I pulled the tissue paper away and saw folds of beautiful white lace, I gasped. "Did your dads make me a dress?"

I pushed my chair back and stood up as I pulled the gown out of the bag and held it up to my body. It was beautiful! It was a floor-length gown made of chiffon and white lace. It was the most elegant dress I'd ever seen. More than that, though, I *recognized* it. "Wait. Is this…?"

Vivian nodded. "I am not good with secrets; ask anyone. I almost spilled the beans about Sunday so many times, but Juliette would have killed me. When she told me what your dad was getting you, I went straight to my dads to help me with your costume. They were excited to help."

"This is amazing!" I hoped my eyes conveyed my gratitude, even though I felt like panicking. The dress was gorgeous, but it was sleeveless and backless. It would show so much of my scars. I knew I'd felt beautiful when I'd tried on that gown at her house, but I didn't think I could show my scars off at the convention no matter how much I wanted to dress like my favorite character.

"Look in the bag," Vivian said, reading my thoughts.

I gasped again when I pulled out a gorgeous white cloak that matched the dress, and a pair of long, formal white satin gloves. "I know the gloves aren't an official part of Ellamara's costume," Vivian said, "but they match, and will cover your scars perfectly. And here!"

Suddenly a hostess stood behind me, though I'd never seen anyone flag her down. The girl was holding a beautiful walking stick. It was about six feet tall, made of wood, and carved to look like intertwined tree branches. On the top, a large, pale-blue crystal-like orb was encased in the branches. It was an exact replica of Ellamara's magic staff. I gingerly accepted the gift from the hostess, who wished me a happy birthday and then returned to her post. "It's beautiful."

Vivian pointed to the bottom of the staff. "It's also fully functional."

There was a thick rubber foot on the bottom, same as you'd find on crutches…or my cane. I gasped again and tested my weight against the staff. It would work perfectly.

"As much as I love Candy Cane," Vivian said—she'd named my cane Candy after giving it its facelift because I said it reminded me of the board game Candy Land, "this just goes so much better with the outfit."

I took a few steps to try it out and then whirled around to face a table full of smiling faces. "This is amazing, Vivian! Thank you! Thank your dads, too!"

"Sunday you won't just be Ellamara Rodriguez; you'll be Ellamara—the beautiful and mysterious mystic druid priestess."

"There's a costume competition," Juliette added, "and we are so winning."

"We?"

"Yeah. Vivian helped me with my costume, too. I'm going as the Princess Ratana."

"And I'll be going as the evil Queen Nesona," Vivian said. "My dress rocks. We're going to look fabulous!"

I squealed again. This was going to be so awesome. It was like a dream come true for a fantasy geek like me.

"I'll tell my dads about Ana when I get home tonight. They won't have any trouble finishing another Princess Ratana outfit by Sunday."

I snorted. "Yeah, shouldn't be too hard. There's not really much to that costume."

Juliette stuck her tongue out at me. "I think it's hot." She'd heard my rant on the stupid warrior-girl's lack of clothing before. "Twin Princess Ratanas will definitely catch the judges' attention. Not to mention, Brian Oliver's."

Rob laughed. "I get to hang out all day, just me and four amazingly hot girls dressed up like medieval princesses? Sweet."

Vivian looked at Rob with a mischievous glint in her eyes that made him sit up in his chair. "What?"

She grinned at him with a sweet smile that was all too innocent. "There is a price for the honor of escorting us to the convention."

Rob frowned. "What price?"

"Nothing too bad," Juliette chirped. "Just a tunic."

"A *what?*"

"And tights." She giggled.

Rob processed this and then his face paled. "Oh, no! No way!"

All of us laughed, even Anastasia.

"Yes, way," Vivian said. "You didn't think that the Mystic Priestess, the Fair Ladies Ratana, and Evil Mummy Dearest were going to show up without their champion druid prince, did you, dear Cinder?"

"Um, yes, I did."

I sort of felt bad for him, but not enough to let him get out of wearing a costume. "If it helps, you get to have a sword," I offered.

"You can't already have a costume for me," he argued. "How would you know what size to make it?"

Vivian laughed. "My dad has a gift for sizing people up. You met him the night you came over to watch movies. Not to mention there are so many helpful pictures of you on Facebook."

At Rob's confused frown, Vivian smirked. "All those after-school practices you do without wearing a shirt have proved too tempting for the girls in our school."

Wow. I was really going to have to friend some of the girls in our school. Or maybe start watching some soccer practices.

Vivian purred appreciatively, making Rob blush so fiercely I was sure his face would never be a normal shade again.

"Sorry," I whispered, offering him my hand under the table for support. He snatched it up as if it might make him invisible, and shot me a grateful smile.

"Just think of the outfit as a uniform, and you'll be fine," Juliette teased.

"The costume will fit," Vivian promised, "but you should come over to my place early in the morning Sunday, just in case they need to make any quick alterations. Actually, all of you need to come over early because my dads asked their friends from the show to come over and do our hair and makeup."

"No way!" Juliette, Anastasia, and I all shouted together.

Both my dad and Jennifer erupted with laughter. "Nothing like a makeover to get a girl excited, eh?" Dad teased, sending a sympathetic smile Rob's way.

Rob sighed and squeezed my hand again. "Fine. Because it's Ella's birthday, I will be her Prince Charming for the day."

"My Prince *Cinder*." I leaned over and kissed Rob's cheek. "You're the best."

He gave me a rueful smile with a look that said I owed him, then turned back to Vivian. "I draw the line at makeup."

FANTASYCON WAS EVERYTHING I'D EVER DREAMED IT WOULD BE, and my friends and I looked amazing for it. Vivian's dads were so good, we didn't look as if we'd stepped off the movie set— we looked as if we'd found a way to transcend worlds and come straight from the Realm itself.

None of my friends were actual fans of fantasy like me. They weren't familiar with the references, authors, and concept artists we met, like I was, and they didn't almost faint when they got to meet Richard and Kahlan from *Legend of the Seeker* the way I did, but that didn't matter. They got a kick out of all the other people in costume and took no small amount of pleasure in laughing at my geekiness. That was okay. It was still one of the most amazing days of my life.

The Druid Prince panel discussion was an experience all its own. It made me so excited for the movie I didn't think I'd be able to wait until its Christmas release. After it was over, the people with tickets for the meet-and-greet lined up to get their autographs from the panel members.

Vivian, Juliette, and Anastasia had scarcely breathed since we walked into the room and saw Brian Oliver sitting just a few feet from us, and poor Rob was reduced to a drooling mess at the sight of Kaylee Summers. My starstruck friends indulged me, though, and waited patiently for me to meet *The Druid Prince* author, L.P. Morgan, first.

He was paired at a table with the movie's screenwriter, Academy Award winner Jason Cohen, and I almost died when I got caught up in a discussion with them and a few other diehard *Cinder Chronicles* fans about the adaptation process and how they were handling the sequels. I got to take my picture with them both, and they even let me record our discussion on my phone for my blog. It was seriously a dream come true! I was on cloud nine when I was finally pulled away from them and carted off to meet Brian Oliver and Kaylee Summers.

"I can't believe you got all fangirly on those two skeezy old guys when *Brian Oliver* is standing right over there," Anastasia said as we waited in line for our turn to meet the guests of honor.

Not even *her* attitude could kill my mood today. "Brian Oliver is hot, but L.P. Morgan is my hero. The man is a genius." I hugged the hardback book I'd brought with me to have him sign. I wished it could have been my mother's copy of the book from when she was a girl, but I would still treasure this new book. I squeezed it again, releasing a dreamy sigh. "I can't believe I finally got to meet him."

Anastasia shook her head. "You are so weird."

Vivian threw her arm over my shoulder. "Yeah, but we like her anyway."

"So, Ella, are you going to thank Brian Oliver for your birthday present?" Juliette asked.

"No." I repeated myself when everyone looked at me as if I were crazy. "*No.* I don't want him to know who I am."

"Why not?"

Because he probably knows Cinder, and then he'd tell him he met me. "I just don't want to, okay? Please don't say anything."

"He probably knows Cinder," Vivian said, voicing my exact thoughts—except she made it sound like that was a good thing.

"You could get him to tell you Cinder's name, and then we could find him on Facebook and see if he's as hot as he sounds."

"I don't need to confirm that. Cinder doesn't want to meet me. Ever. I don't want to know how good-looking he is."

Vivian and Juliette both frowned at me, but Rob came to my rescue. "You guys, leave her alone. Cinder's a jerk anyway for not wanting to meet her. We should be helping her get over him, not encouraging her."

Anastasia scoffed, but I wasn't sure if she was annoyed by what he said, or miffed that he'd slipped his arm around my waist. She continued to glare at me until we finally reached the front of the line and came face to face with Brian Oliver.

Brian Oliver was hot on TV. In person, he was downright mesmerizing. Those eyes that somehow smoldered while they twinkled… and that smile…

"You five look incredible!" Brian said, breaking the silence for us when his physical presence had rendered us all speechless. "By far the best costumes I've seen this year. I hope you entered the competition." His eyes moved to Anastasia and Juliette and immediately traveled the lengths of their bodies. "Twins," he purred when he was done ogling. "You fair maidens are the most beautiful Ratanas I've seen since this convention started."

I couldn't stop the snort that escaped me. If he really was friends with Cinder, it was no wonder why. They were two peas in a pod.

I blushed when Brian glanced at me curiously, but I was more concerned with the hurt look on Juliette's face and the glare on Ana's. I quickly swallowed my laughter. "Sorry."

Juliette shot me a "what the hell" look and I cringed. I was having a fairly progressive day with Anastasia so far, but insulting her in front of Brian Oliver was not going to put me in her good graces. "I'm sorry," I said again, more repentant this time. "Of course he's right. You know you're both gorgeous. I was just laughing at the cheesy line."

"Cheesy line?" Brian asked. His voice suggested he was

offended, but his twitching lips and laughing eyes told a different story.

I hadn't meant to insult him, but it was too late to take it back, so I had to defend myself. "Yes. It was cheesy. And I'm sure you've probably said that exact same thing to every girl you've met this week. I find it amazing that you can still deliver it with a straight face."

Brian blinked at me in surprise. Next to him, Kaylee Summers laughed. "What do you know, baby?" Condescension dripped from her tone, thick as molasses. "Someone else who's not impressed with your bullshit."

I was afraid I'd offended him for real this time, but he smiled as if I presented a delicious challenge. "She wouldn't be dressed as Ellamara if she were easily susceptible to charm," he told Kaylee, while never taking his warm brown eyes off of me. "I meant the compliment, though. Your friends really are two of the most beautiful Princess Ratanas I've seen this weekend." He sent a quick wink at Ana and Juliette, causing them both to blush. "Just as you are the loveliest Ellamara I've met so far."

I snorted again. "I'm probably the *only* Ellamara you've met."

Brian's grin widened into a heart-stopping smile. "You're still enchanting. Those eyes..." He paused a moment, staring rather intently at my eyes, and frowned. "Have we met?"

"Ha! No. We haven't met."

"Are you sure? You look familiar. I swear I've seen those eyes before."

I gulped. It was possible he'd seen a picture of me on my blog. I hadn't posted one since the last time I went on a book trip with my mom. That was months before my accident. I looked a lot different now—older with no more braces—but my blue eyes with my brown skin and dark hair were unmistakable.

I forced myself to smirk. "I'm pretty sure I'd remember meeting a famous movie star." He still looked skeptical, so I added, "Especially one who uses such cheesy pick-up lines."

Finally, Brian laughed. He poised a Sharpie over a glossy

headshot, ready to sign an autograph for me. "All right, I give. What's your name, beautiful?"

My cheeks flamed despite my best efforts. I pointed at his picture and shook my head. "That's okay. I don't need one of those. I just wanted to bring you this."

I handed him a copy of *The Druid Prince*. Unlike the nice hardback I had L.P. Morgan sign, this one was one of the cheap mass-market paperback versions that had replaced the original cover with the cast of the movie. Brian happily accepted the book, then looked up at me. "And who am I making it out to?"

I suppressed an eye roll. "I don't want you to sign it. I want you to *read* it."

Brian squinted up at me. "Come again?"

I sighed. "You're playing one of the most cherished characters of all time. I don't care how many academy awards Jason Cohen has won for his writing; there's no way the screenplay could do the book justice. I know it's too late to help you with the first movie, but there are four more to go. I really, *really* want you to understand who Cinder is, so I'm begging. Please. Read the books. I swear, they're worth it."

Every stranger within earshot gaped at me like I was a total freak, except for the other diehard fans that clapped and cheered. Juliette and Anastasia wore matching horrified expressions. Even Rob and Vivian both looked a little taken aback.

Brian Oliver's expression was hard to describe. He appeared to be having the time of his life. His smile had somehow, impossibly, gotten bigger—but he also looked baffled, and he stared at me with something resembling suspicion in his eyes. "You think I haven't read the books?"

That's exactly what I thought. "You mean you have?"

He laughed. "Why do you think I demanded to play the role? I agree wholeheartedly that Cinder is one of the most cherished characters of all time. I couldn't let someone else play him. I can't wait to film *Reign of Glory*. That was my favorite book in the series."

I snapped my mouth shut, unsure when it had fallen open, and my lips quickly curved into a big smile. "*Reign of Glory* was good," I agreed, "but *The Druid Prince* is still my favorite. I'm a sucker for a good origin story. Cinder's is so tragic and moving, yet it brings such a sense of hope to a desperate kingdom. Not to mention the mystery of who he is was done masterfully in that book."

"No doubt," Brian agreed. "*The Druid Prince* is my second favorite. But I love it when Cinder finally gets to go back home, not as a useless farm boy, but as a kick-ass druid warrior. The dude lays the smack down like a master. The action in *Reign of Glory* is epic."

Now I did roll my eyes. "Battle scenes. You are such a guy. I bet you love what the movie producers have done with Princess Ratana's outfit, too."

Something changed in Brian then. Fire filled his eyes, a truly heated passion that I didn't quite know how to explain. His suspicion melted into a knowing smirk and he flicked his gaze back over Ana and Juliette before giving me a rakish grin. "I definitely didn't complain."

As I groaned, Brian sat back and folded his arms over his chest, appraising me with amusement. "Tell me something. Why did you dress as Ellamara? Was it because she's covered from head to toe? Are you some kind of prude?"

I scoffed and Juliette slapped her palm to her forehead. "Oh, great! Now you've done it. She'll be griping about this for *weeks*."

As Brian considered Juliette's words, I clenched my staff and resisted the urge to smack him upside the head with it. "I am *not* a prude. I just don't appreciate Hollywood sacrificing the integrity of something just to get perverted guys like *you* to buy tickets. In the books the Princess Ratana was a warrior, but she was still a *princess*. Your dad turned her character into some useless, slutty bimbo. It's so demeaning to women! We *can* be beautiful while fully clothed, you know."

"As I see," Brian teased, blatantly checking me out.

I swear I *felt* his eyes travel the length of me, like a caress. I fought back a shiver.

"So why Ellamara?" he asked again.

"Because she's the greatest character in the books."

Juliette recognized one of my rants coming on and tried to push me aside before I got started. "Okay, Ella, there are still other people waiting. We don't want to take up all of Brian's time."

"She's right, Brian," Kaylee said, not bothering to hide her annoyance. "Just sign the girl an autograph and send her on her way."

Brian ignored his girlfriend. "You think *Ellamara* is the greatest character in the books? What about Cinder? He's the hero. He saves the entire kingdom."

The question was clearly a taunt. He was riling me up on purpose. As much as I tried not to let him bait me, I couldn't resist arguing. "Sure he does—because he had *Ellamara* to guide him. Without her, he would have been nothing."

"Nothing?" Brian scoffed. "He had his magic. He still would have rocked it."

"Yeah, but he would have come into his power and become just another self-entitled, snobbish, idiot prince, drunk on his own power." *Not too unlike the guy sitting in front of me.*

From the look on his face, Brian knew what I was thinking. "As it was," I pressed on before he could call me on it, "he still chose to marry the hot chick when he was truly in love with Ellamara."

"But Ellamara became a priestess. She took a vow of celibacy."

I groaned. I'd had this very same argument with Cinder like a million times. In fact, it was the very first argument we'd ever had. The first time he left a comment on my blog, it had been to defend Cinder's decision to marry Ratana even when it was Ellamara he truly loved.

"She became a priestess because Cinder rejected her. He broke her heart!"

"He didn't have a choice!" Brian yelled back, getting as

passionate about our argument as I was—clearly a true fan. "He may have loved Ellamara, but she was a commoner. Ratana was Crown Princess of the Flatlands. Their union created peace between the two kingdoms. Cinder did the noble thing, putting his own feelings aside for the good of the kingdom."

"Noble?" I groaned again. "What he did wasn't noble at all. It was an act of cowardice. He did what was expected of him because it was easier. A *real* man would have fought to be with the woman he loved—social class be damned."

Brian reared back in his chair, stunned by what I said, but I wasn't going to take it back. His shock disappeared quickly, though, and that satisfied, knowing smirk settled back on his face. I didn't get the joke, but whatever it was, Brian Oliver was clearly enjoying it. He arched a brow at me and folded his arms stiffly over his chest. "I thought you just said Cinder was one of the greatest characters of all time."

I matched his stubbornness. "Every great character makes mistakes. Cinder was wise by the end and able to rule over his people only because *Ellamara* taught him how to think beyond himself. He was a great character, but—"

"I know, I know," Brian interrupted with an over-the-top sigh. "Ellamara was the real hero."

I froze. As I looked into Brian's eyes, he stared back at me with a knowing smile, waiting for me to catch up. Punch line delivered. The message came through loud and clear, and my heart stopped beating. There was no way! It couldn't be possible!

"What made you say that?" I was hardly able to speak loud enough to be heard.

Brian's face smoothed out and he shrugged his shoulders. "It was what you were going to say."

"Yes, but how did you know? Why did you say those particular words?"

We both knew I already knew the answer. Brian leaned forward in his chair, watching me with a new intensity. His grin turned positively wicked and he whispered, "Say *car* for me."

Next to me, someone gasped. I thought maybe it was Juliette, but I couldn't be sure. I was still in too much shock to think clearly.

Cinder! I was talking to Cinder! Cinder didn't *know* Brian Oliver. Cinder *was* Brian Oliver!

I felt as if lightning had struck me. The shock was so great that it knocked me back a few steps. I stumbled into Rob, who grabbed me when my knees tried to give out. He held me around the waist to steady me—which was good because I wasn't sure I could stand on my own.

Then, I stared, incredulously, as famous Hollywood heart-throb Brian Oliver jealously watched Rob's arms slip around my waist. The hint of malice in his expression was so subtle that I doubt anyone besides me noticed it. Well, and maybe Rob, because his grip on me tightened a tiny bit, and he practically growled as he said, "Are you okay, Ella?"

"I'm fine." Things were so very, very *not* fine. Brian was Cinder! I'd been talking to *Cinder! I* was *looking at* Cinder!

Cinder's eyes snapped back to mine. "Ella?"

To anyone else, I'm sure it sounded as if he were simply asking so that he could sign an autograph, but I heard his surprise. We'd never asked each other what our real names were. He probably assumed Ella was only a screen name, like Cinder was.

I nodded, dazed. "Ellamara," I whispered. My mouth had gone dry. "My mom really loved the books, too."

Brian's entire face sparkled with delight at learning my real name.

"Brian!" a shrill voice hissed in an angry whisper. "Baby, you're starting to cause a scene. Stop *flirting* with her and sign a damn autograph already."

I broke away from Brian's stare to find Kaylee Summers giving me a glare so nasty it could have brought *Anastasia* to tears. So many things clicked into place. Cinder complained so many times about his life being crazy, complicated, and out of his control because he was a *famous movie star*. And the girl he was being pressured to date—the shrew—was his co-star, Kaylee Summers.

His *fiancée.*

The realization stunned me all over again. "Congratulations on your engagement," I muttered to her, choking back bile. "I'm sure you'll make a beautiful bride."

I didn't realize I was shaking until Rob crushed me to his chest. "You okay?"

I buried my face in his shoulder and shook my head. I was definitely not okay. My heart was breaking. It had broken before—when my dad left, and again when I learned my mother was dead. It had even broken a third time when Cinder had refused to meet me. But it had never broken like this. "I need to get out of here."

Rob didn't ask questions.

As we turned to walk away, Cinder called out to me in a panic. I looked back and wished I hadn't. His eyes bore into me, begging for understanding. His pain and frustration were so plainly on display that I felt it all the way to my soul. Or maybe that was my own agony.

After a noticeable moment of the two of us staring at one another, Cinder pulled his eyes away from me to scribble his name on a photo. When he gave it to me, he didn't let go right away. He cast his eyes down to the picture we were both holding, as if he wanted me to look. My eyes dropped and I almost gasped again. Instead of an autograph, he'd written:

I can explain.
Meet me at the Dragon's Roost. Six P.M.
-Cinder

"It was *truly* a pleasure to meet you, Ella."

I jumped at the sound of his voice. When I looked back up, he mouthed the word *please* and let go of the photo.

"Thanks," I muttered, and then let Rob drag me out of the

way so that everyone else could have the chance to get Brian's and Kaylee's autographs.

Somehow, I felt as if I'd been run over by a train.

Brian

ELLAMARA WAS THE MOST INCREDIBLE WOMAN I'D EVER MET. SHE was witty and spirited and not the least bit intimidated by my fame. And she was so beautiful! I'd noticed her before the discussion panel even started. Aside from the fact that she and her friends really stood out among the crowd with their amazing costumes, I'd seen hundreds of Ratanas and Cinders over the past five days—and even a few Queen Nesonas—but Ella was the first person to dress as the infamous druid priestess.

She intrigued me immediately, and I kept an eye on her throughout the whole discussion panel. I could tell she was a diehard fan and found myself getting impatient for her to come talk to me after the panel, when she headed straight to L.P. Morgan first and then stood there for nearly twenty minutes having what was clearly the discussion of her life with him and Jason Cohen. It killed me not to be a part of that conversation.

Once she was finally standing in front of me, I saw for the first time how truly striking she was. The other girls with her were all pretty, but Ella was so different, with her soft brown skin and those big, bright eyes that just popped out at you beneath the hood of her cloak.

I didn't know why I never considered the possibility that *my* Ellamara would come to FantasyCon now that she lived in Los Angeles, or that this mysterious, exotic beauty could be her, but it didn't take long to figure it out. The thought crossed my mind when the first words out of her mouth were an insult. It was just so *Ella* to not be impressed with my harmless flirting. Then she dropped that damn book in my lap and insisted I *read* it. Only Ella! And, of course, her comment about Ratana's costume confirmed it.

She was brilliant, amazing, everything I ever dreamed she'd be…and she was in the arms of another guy. Now I understood why Kaylee was so crabby with me all the time. When that scrawny soccer bastard put his hands on Ella, I wanted to jump over the table and strangle him. Here I was, finally in the moment I'd dreamed of having for years, and all I could think about was the way that guy held Ella as if she belonged to him. And she was letting him! When Ella finally came out of her shock and realized that I was Cinder and that I was "engaged" to Kaylee, she'd thrown herself into that lucky jerk's arms and asked him to be her knight in shining armor. The asshole was even dressed up as Cinder.

I was supposed to be her Cinder! Ella was supposed to be *mine!*

I asked her to meet me, but I saw the look on her face—the horror in her eyes—and wasn't sure she would show. If she didn't, I was going to track her down, even if I had to break down every damn door to every damn house in LA.

Kaylee was all over my case the second we were back in our suite after the meet-and-greet was over. "Brian," she began in that sickly sweet voice that grated on my nerves until they were raw, "let me explain something to you about being in a relationship. When you're supposedly in love with someone, you don't flirt with *every damn pair of eyes that strikes your fancy!* What the hell was that in there?"

Stripping off my shirt, I headed into the bathroom to examine my face in the mirror. To shave again or not? I knew Ella found a five o'clock shadow sexy. She'd said as much many times when she went through her *Prison Break* phase. But if we ended up getting close—and I very much hoped we would—smooth would probably be better.

"That back there was the end of this publicity stunt," I said after Kaylee followed me into the bathroom, waiting for an explanation.

I briefly met Kaylee's eyes in the mirror, then picked up my razor and went to work making my face kissable. "I'm done, Kaylee." My mind had been made up the second I recognized Ella, and once I knew I was finished with this game, I was filled with serenity. "We can end it however you want. You can tell people it was you, or you can say I dumped you and play up the heartbroken angle—I don't care. Whatever you want, but it's over. I'm not doing it anymore."

"Excuse me?"

I rinsed my razor in the sink, and as I brought it back to my face I wondered if having sharp objects nearby while having this conversation was the best idea. "That wasn't just any woman back there; that was *Ella*."

Kaylee didn't say anything for a moment, but her eyes narrowed and her lips pursed together tightly. She was remembering the meet-and-greet and seeing my interaction with Ella through a new light.

"*That* was Ella? You can't be serious." She laughed a hard, humorless laugh. "That sarcastic little bitch is what you've been fussing about all this time?"

I put down my razor and whirled on Kaylee, backing her against the wall behind us. "Don't talk about her like that. I'm done with you, Kaylee, and I'm going after her. You can either make this easy or complicated, but if you try to pull any shit, I'll come clean about the relationship being a sham from the beginning. I'll tell everyone how the spoiled little princess threw a Lindsay Lohan-style tantrum and blackmailed me into a fake engagement. I'll tell everyone how you threatened to ruin my career, get my dad fired, and sabotage the film all because you're crazy and obsessed with me."

"Obsessed with you?" Kaylee scoffed. "You're not worth the drama. There are hundreds of guys out there better-looking and richer than you who would be grateful for the chance to be with me."

"Good. Go torture some of them."

Ignoring Kaylee's glare, I finished shaving my face, spritzed myself with a dash of cologne I hoped Ella would find irresistible, and went to find something fresh to wear.

"No one will believe you, you know," Kaylee argued, following me into the bedroom. "Not with your reputation for being such a player."

What a joke. "Trust me, Kay, everyone in town already knows you're a coldhearted bitch. *Mentally unstable diva* wouldn't be too far of a leap."

I rummaged through my things and found a dark gray V-neck sweater that women always seemed to like. Hopefully Ella would, too.

"What about the Zachary Goldberg film? The contracts are still in negotiations. Nothing's signed yet. I can still make my father back out."

"You're overestimating your importance, *baby*," I said as I slipped the sweater over my head. "You may have persuaded your father to hear the proposal, but I was at that meeting, too. He loved the script and has the most prestigious director and the hottest up-and-coming actor already attached. The project is gold."

I patted myself down and checked the mirror one last time. Satisfied with what I saw, I slipped my wallet and phone in my pocket. It was already six, so I called the restaurant to tell them I'd be a little late and not to let Ella go anywhere.

"I can still ruin your career," Kaylee said darkly. "I can drag your reputation through the mud. I can have the paparazzi so far up your ass you'll need surgery to have them removed."

Her anger rose as she became more desperate, but she no longer had any effect on me. I was beyond caring. "Do your worst. Whatever damage you do won't be permanent."

"You'll lose your Oscar."

A few months ago that might have bothered me, but what was a damn statue worth if it meant I'd lose Ella? I shrugged. "Maybe. But even if you ruin my chances this year, I've got time to prove to people I'm for real. I've got four more *Cinder Chronicles* movies and a project with Zachary Goldberg coming up that may as well be called *Brian Oliver is the Man*. I only needed you to make me look good in the first place because I was an immature asshole, but I'm not that guy anymore. I have Ella now, and she won't just make me *look* like I'm serious. With her, it's real."

Kaylee stood there, staring completely dumbfounded, as she finally realized she'd lost this argument. In one last desperate attempt to get what she wanted, she crossed the room and placed her hands delicately on my chest. "Brian..." She gazed up at me with lust-filled eyes as she slid her arms up over my shoulders and pressed her body against me. "Baby, please don't go."

As Kaylee brushed her lips over my freshly-shaven jaw, I wondered how I'd ever found her tempting. I grabbed her arms off my shoulders and untwined myself from her grip. "Sorry, Kay. There's only one woman for me now, and you aren't her. You don't even come close."

For the first time since I met her, Kaylee's true emotions cracked the surface and she was unable to hide the hurt my rejection caused. I felt bad for exactly two seconds. Then, a knock on the door made my stomach explode with butterflies. "That would be Scotty."

"Brian, you can't do this!"

Ignoring Kaylee, I opened the door, suddenly in the biggest hurry of my life. Scott stood there with an excited grin on his face, holding up the book I'd asked him to get and a large green cloak.

"I have the things you asked for."

"My hero!"

"Good luck, man."

"Brian!" Kaylee shouted again.

"Sorry, Kay, I gotta go." I wrapped the cloak around my shoulders and pulled the hood over my head. The cloak was more *Lord of the Rings* than *The Cinder Chronicles*, and hopefully the disguise would be enough to get me through the convention center to the restaurant, unnoticed. "Scotty's going to pack up my stuff for me and check me out of the room. Play nice and leave his man parts intact."

Kaylee glared for all she was worth and I blew her a kiss in return, giddy from my new freedom. "See you on the set of the sequel, *Princess*."

THE DRAGON'S ROOST WAS A RESTAURANT INSIDE THE CONVEN-tion center. I stood back across the aisle from the entrance, scoping out the scene. I wished I'd picked a more private place to meet, but I panicked when Ella started to walk away from me and the only place that came to mind was the café where I'd eaten lunch that afternoon.

Considering the event was packed, dining options were limited, and it was prime dinnertime, the restaurant was crowded. There was a line at the hostess stand twenty people long. At least I'd reserved a booth in the back ahead of time, and so far, my Elven cloak of invisibility had done its job. I blended right into the crowd of fantasy lovers. No one in the world besides Ella and Scott had any idea I was coming, so as long as Ella and I didn't cause a scene, we should be fine.

I was fifteen minutes late, but I wasn't the only one. Just as I was about to head inside, five people in amazing costumes

I instantly recognized walked up next to the hostess stand and stopped.

"I don't think I can do this," Ella said as she peered nervously into the restaurant.

My stomach flipped. She was standing just three feet from me. Too tempted to get a read on her feelings, I leaned against the front wall of the restaurant and pulled my hood just a little lower over my face. I kept my head down and pretended to be very interested in texting someone while stealing as many glances at her as I could.

"Of course you can," the redheaded girl in the Queen Nesona outfit said.

The blonde with the long hair just frowned at her. "Why not?"

It was a very good question.

A crazed laugh bubbled up from Ella's throat. "Why not? Because he's *Brian Oliver*. He's America's favorite bad boy. He's dating *Kaylee Summers*, for heaven's sake!"

The redhead snorted. "Yeah, because *that* was a healthy relationship."

I choked back a laugh. Apparently Kaylee and I weren't as good at acting as we thought.

"Guys like him do *not* hang out with girls like me, Vivian."

Ella's fierce declaration was startling. How could she think that?

"But he's *Cinder*. He's your best friend," the blonde argued.

I wanted to hug her for pointing that out, but Ella's response was frantic. "Because he doesn't really know me! It's different online. If I meet him now, everything changes. What if he's disappointed and I end up losing my best friend?"

Impossible. I found it ironic that now she was the one worried about losing me when it had been the other way around the day I refused to meet her.

"There's no way he'll be disappointed," the redhead, Vivian, promised, "but if he is, then I'll be your new best friend and we can feed *him* to the flesh-eating worms."

I smiled at that. It was easy to see why Ella liked Vivian.

The Ratana with the long hair put her arm around Ella. She had to be one of Ella's stepsisters—Ella had mentioned they were twins—and she was obviously the good one. The evil one was standing back from the others, wearing a very Kaylee-esque scowl.

"The guy's clearly nuts about you," the good sister said. "He was flirting like crazy with you even before he figured out who you were. In front of his fiancée!"

Well. At least *someone* appreciated my charm. Obviously not Ella, though, because she groaned and said, "He flirted with *everyone*. It's his *job* to be friendly with his fans."

Her annoyance was amusing, but my attention was drawn by a loud scoff from Mr. Fantastic. Thankfully, he wasn't glued to Ella's side anymore, but he was still standing close enough to make me crazy with jealousy.

"That was way beyond friendly, Ella. The guy was seconds away from jumping over the table and punching me in the face just for standing next to you."

Soccer Boy was really perceptive. I had been close to doing exactly that, but not because he was just *standing* next to her. The evil sister agreed with me. "You mean *hanging* on her," she muttered. "You may as well have peed on her."

It was funny—and completely true—but Ella blanched and her other stepsister was pissed. "Ana, don't be so mean!"

"It's Ella's fault," Ana argued. "She's been stringing Rob along for weeks because of her *precious Cinder*, and now she doesn't even want to meet him. What a tease!"

Before I had time to try and decipher what that meant, Ella snapped. "Of course I want to meet him!"

"Then what's your problem? Obviously he wants to meet you too, or he wouldn't have asked you to come."

"I hate to agree with Ana," Vivian said, "but he did ask you to meet him, and he didn't have to do that. If you don't talk to him, you know you'll regret it for the rest of your life."

"But he doesn't know about me," Ella blurted suddenly. "I've never gone into detail about my accident. He doesn't know I'm... I'm..."

I glanced up so sharply that I would have been discovered had not all of Ella's friends been too shocked by her confession to notice me. The looks on their faces ranged from pity, to sad, to sympathetic, and, of course, a very satisfied smirk from Kaylee Jr.

"You've never told him?" Vivian asked quietly. "Even after all this time?"

Ella looked as if she wanted to cry as she shook her head. I was going to go crazy if I didn't figure out what she was talking about. Ella needed to go inside already so I could talk to her myself.

"Cinder was the one person I never had to talk about my condition with, so I didn't. I didn't think it would matter. I didn't think I was ever going to meet him."

The nice sister shook her head. "It won't matter. He's going to love you anyway."

Well. And that was the truth.

Ana laughed and it came out as a cackle. "Sure, he is!" she cried. "He's going to give up *Kaylee Summers* for *you*. It'll be the real-life version of *Beauty and the Beast*, only backwards!"

I nearly dropped my phone because I was clenching it so hard. Ella wasn't joking when she said her stepsister had a lot in common with my girlfriend. I was damn near ready to break cover and give her a piece of my mind, but Rob beat me to it. "Shut up, Ana! I'm so sick of your attitude!"

Ana looked so shocked to be yelled at that I wondered if any guy had ever dared do it before. Probably not. Only, Rob didn't stop there. "You want to know why I didn't ask you to the dance? It's because it doesn't matter how hot you are; every time I look at you, all I see is a cruel, selfish bitch."

The entire group was stunned stupid by Rob's outburst. Even me. Damn the man for earning some of my respect.

Ana's eyes filled with tears and she stalked off without another word. I almost felt bad for her, but quickly forgot all about her because the second she left, Rob took Ella's face in his hands and plastered a passionate kiss on her. If he hadn't said what he said next, I would have decked him. "You are *beautiful*, Ellamara," he promised. "And I am jealous as hell right now because you are going to go in there and make Brian Oliver fall madly in love with you. I have no doubt."

Too late, I thought, smiling to myself. I decided I couldn't begrudge Rob the kiss since the guy really seemed to care for Ella, and it was the only one he was ever going to get.

"Go get him," Rob told her, and then gave her a gentle nudge toward the front door.

I tugged my hood down again and slipped away when the group took a step closer to me. I waited a few minutes because Ella looked like she might need a moment to compose herself after all the drama, but then I went inside, determined to finally claim my druid priestess.

I FELT SLIGHTLY SICK TO MY STOMACH AS I ENTERED THE RESTAU-
rant. I knew what my friends all believed, but the idea of someone like Brian Oliver wanting someone like me was too insane to
accept, even if I *could* make myself understand that he was the guy
I'd known for years.

I was so lost in thought that I didn't see anyone approach me
until a man said, "Miss Ella?"

I drew back a step, startled. "Yes. That's me."

"Welcome. Your table is ready for you." The guy flashed me a
brilliant smile. "Right this way, please."

I was a little baffled by the special treatment. Then again, it
made sense when the man said, "Mr. Oliver is running a few minutes late as well. He asked me to convey his sincerest apologies,
but he should be here in just a few minutes."

"Okay. Thanks."

The restaurant was all one big, open dining floor with tables
in the middle and booths lining the outside edges. It wasn't the
best place for privacy, but I could tell the manager had tried his
best because he led me to a booth in the far back corner. We
wouldn't be tucked away entirely, but we wouldn't be in the

middle of everything, either. I was grateful for the effort.

The manager fussed over me for a minute, lighting a small candle in the middle of the table. Before he left, I had to ask. "Excuse me, but how did you know who I was?"

The man smiled again. "When Mr. Oliver called ahead for a table, he described what you would be wearing. He also said I'd know for certain it was you by your 'stunning eyes.'" The man didn't move his hands, but the air quotes were definitely there in his tone.

"And was I not right?" a quiet voice asked. A voice that made me shiver.

Cinder slid gracefully into the booth across from me and smiled from beneath the hood of a heavy cloak—a cloak a lot like my gorgeous white one, except for its dark color. His face was shadowed, but the flicker of the candle on the table caused his eyes to gleam in the soft light. Those eyes never left my face as he thanked the manager for reserving us a table and ordered dinner. They burned into me like lasers.

The manager hurried off to give our orders to the kitchen, leaving me alone—well, as alone as two people can get in a crowded restaurant—with my best friend, who just happened to be a famous movie star. For a moment, all we could do was stare at one another.

"Ella."

He said my name with reverence and deep satisfaction. My response sounded nervous and unsure. "Cinder?"

"Call me Brian, Ella. Please."

He paused, waiting for me to respond.

"Okay… Brian."

He grinned, and the effect was devastating. "I've always wished I could tell you my name. Every time you called me Cinder, it felt like a lie. I hated that you didn't know me."

Finally, the shock cleared from my head. His words caused reality to crash down on me with vengeance. "Then why didn't you ever tell me?" I was unable to keep my spiraling emotions in check. "How could you not tell me this?"

His smile faded a little. "If I'd told you, you wouldn't have believed me."

"Maybe not three years ago, but two weeks ago when you said we could never meet? You could have just told me you were famous and way too busy with your big movie and your psycho fiancée to spend time with me."

Cinder flinched as if I'd slapped him. He seemed stunned by my anger, but what had he expected? His face crumpled with regret. "Ella, that wasn't it. You don't understand."

"No, I finally do." My head spun as everything fell into place with perfect clarity. "It all makes so much sense now. Everything. That's the last piece of the puzzle I've been missing this whole time. Your relationship with Kaylee is a scam. It's a publicity thing, isn't it?"

Brian grimaced. "I didn't want to have any part of it, but I was in a vulnerable position and everyone insisted it would solve my problem. Plus, there were a lot of people that had a lot to gain if Kaylee and I were together. At the time, I didn't have an excuse to say no. I didn't have you back yet."

His confession startled me. I wasn't sure what he meant, but it was very hard not to read into it and see things I wanted to see. Impossible things.

He reached both hands across the table, in a gesture asking for mine. When I didn't give him my hands, he pulled his back and started fiddling with his glass of ice water.

"When you and I first started talking, I'd done a few TV shows and a Disney movie. I was pretty unknown. When I made the jump to teen comedies, everything changed. The fame was crazy. Landing *The Druid Prince* took my star status from crazy to *insane*. I can't go anywhere without being mauled. I don't have any real friends. Nobody knows how to treat me like a regular person anymore, and I hate it."

He closed his eyes and took a deep breath before continuing. "You disappeared right as my life started to spin out of control.

I didn't handle it well. Suddenly I had a whole world of friends, but not a single relationship that mattered. I shut down. Stopped caring. By the time you contacted me again, my entire life was superficial. I was basically dead inside—the world's biggest asshole. That first night we talked again felt like waking up from a foggy dream. You took away the numbness. You made me remember how to feel, how to care about someone other than myself."

His speech took my breath away. The thought that I could mean so much to somebody, that I could affect someone in such a way, wasn't just shocking, but overwhelming. My heart pounded in my chest, and butterflies bounced around in my stomach like lottery balls. I had to look away from him before I could regain the ability to speak. "Are all actors so…passionate all the time?" I focused on my water glass as my face heated from embarrassment.

I expected him to laugh at me, but he didn't. His voice sounded as serious as ever. "When it comes to the things we love, we are."

Startled, I looked up into his eyes again. The emotion I saw there was indescribable.

"Aside from my mother, you are the only person in my life that matters to me," he insisted, attempting to penetrate my soul with his gaze. "When I found out you were still alive, I tried to call everything with Kaylee off. I told her I wasn't going to go through with it. I was going to fly to Boston and tell you who I really was."

"Seriously?"

Brian nodded. "But Kaylee already had the ring, and she caused this huge scene, acting like I just asked her to marry me. There were people everywhere, people I have to work with and reporters. I was stuck. After that, she blackmailed me into playing along. She threatened to ruin my career and get my father fired from the *Cinder Chronicles* sequels. She's evil, Ella, ruthless, and she especially hated the idea of *you*. I didn't want to get you involved, but I always planned on explaining everything as soon as I could. We were supposed to 'break up' after the awards season was over. I was just trying to wait until then to keep you out of the insanity and away from Kaylee. I didn't want you to get hurt."

"Um…" I didn't even bother to hide how flustered I was. "I suppose you're forgiven, then."

Cinder let out a breath. His entire body sagged as relief flooded him from head to toe. He reached his hands out to me again, curling his fingers in a clear "give me" gesture. There was something so vulnerable about him that I couldn't refuse this time. I gave him only my left hand, knowing I wouldn't be able to extend my right far enough to reach him. He didn't seem to notice. He simply took my one offered hand in both of his. His touch felt like fire, even through the satin of my glove.

"I *am* glad that we met," he promised. "I'm glad fate stepped in and did what I wasn't brave enough to do."

Again, I had no idea how to respond to him. Had it really been fate? Did he actually believe in fate? And the way he was looking at me…

He let go of my hand and sat back when he realized how much he was overwhelming me. In the blink of an eye, he reverted to his calm, casual, playful self. "I have something for you."

It took a minute for my brain to switch gears with him. By the time I caught up, he was pushing a book across the table to me. I gasped, recognizing it instantly even though I'd never seen it before. It was a first-edition copy of *The Druid Prince.*

Taking the book with caution, I reverently ran my hand over the cover. It was in good condition yet well worn at the same time, as if its previous owner had cherished it—read it over and over again while taking care not to damage it. I knew that if I opened the front cover I would find it signed to me by L.P. Morgan. It was perfect.

"As soon as I met you earlier, I had my assistant drive to my house to pick this up," Cinder said as I studied my new treasure. "That's why I was late. I was waiting for him to get back."

I pulled the open book to my face and breathed in its rich scent, not caring if the action made me look like a freak. I'd always loved the smell of books.

"Do you remember that day?" Cinder's voice, nothing more than a whisper now, sounded haunted.

I couldn't speak above a whisper, either. "Just bits and pieces, but I remember this."

I flipped to the inside cover and touched the inscription. Even though I'd just met L.P. Morgan for myself this afternoon and had another book with his signature in it, this was different. It was infinitely more special. I swallowed back the emotions that were suddenly threatening to explode from me.

"I was worried giving it to you would remind you of that day, but I really want you to have it."

I met his solemn gaze with glistening eyes. "I love it. Thank you."

The moment was broken between us when a young waitress appeared with our food. As she set our plates down, she noticed who was sitting there, hiding beneath his Elven cloak of invisibility. She gasped and nearly dropped Cinder's plate in his lap. It slipped to the table with a loud clang—embarrassing, but luckily harmless since nothing spilled. The girl was mortified. "I am so sorry, Mr. Oliver! Are you all right?"

Cinder didn't miss a beat. He flashed her a smile she was likely to dream about for the rest of her life and said, "Ah, no worries. If a girl as pretty as you had taken me by surprise, I'd have done the same thing."

I suppressed a groan for our waitress's sake. She ate up the attention like a starving child, and blushed an attractive pink. "Th-thank you, Mr. Oliver. Is there anything else I can get you?"

How strange would it be to have everyone know your name and reduce people to such clumsy, stuttering messes all the time? I could understand why he'd always liked the anonymity of our relationship so much if this was how everyone treated him. I'd only been with him for fifteen minutes, and I already knew I would hate fame.

Cinder glanced at the food on the table and started to shake his head, but then looked at me and changed his mind. "Actually, would you mind taking a picture for us?"

The way the girl's face lit up, you'd think he just offered to take her home in his Ferrari. "Sure!"

I tried not to smile at how the girl's hands shook as she accepted the phone. I must have failed to hide my amusement because Cinder gave me a subtle wink. It was no wonder the guy had an ego bigger than the moon.

The girl stepped back to get both Cinder and me in the shot, but before she could take the picture, Cinder got up from his seat and slid into the booth next to me. He threw his arm around me and tucked me snugly into his side.

I stopped breathing.

No, I came completely unglued.

Geez! I was worse than the waitress!

Everything about him flooded my senses. The smell of his cologne—a spicy, musky scent that was one hundred percent yummy, sexy, male—led the assault, followed by the feel of him. He was no longer just an Internet persona. He wasn't just a face from a movie anymore, either. He was real. He was warm, and strong, and very, very *touchable*. I clasped my hands together in my lap so that they couldn't betray me in any embarrassing way.

"Hang on." Cinder pulled the hood from his head, then eyed mine. "Do you mind if I just…" He didn't finish his sentence before reaching up to push the cloak off my head. "Don't want that beautiful face of yours hidden in the picture."

He fussed with my hair for a minute, smoothing it down. His fingertips grazed my cheek as he tucked a random lock of hair behind my ear. It took everything I had in me not to gasp. "There." I could hear the pride in his voice. "You're ready for your close-up, Miss DeMille."

The play on the famous Gloria Swanson line barely registered with me. My skin was still tingling where he'd touched me. I looked up at him in a daze.

He smiled arrogantly, as though he knew exactly what he was doing to me and liked the effect he had on me. "You didn't seem so scared of me earlier when you were busy making fun of my pick-up lines and calling my character a coward."

"You were just Brian Oliver then, and there was a table of space between us," I murmured, blinking over and over again as if doing so might magically clear the fog from my brain. No such luck.

"I was *just* Brian Oliver?" With a shake of his head, Cinder laughed—a deep, throaty chuckle that promised trouble. "Only you, Ella."

Suddenly he ducked his head and put his lips to my ear. When he spoke, his breath blanketed my neck, warm and sensual. It sent a chill through me that raised goose bumps on my arms. "Smile for the camera, Ellamara," he whispered. "I promise I won't bite." But even as he promised this, his teeth gently nipped my ear.

Now I did gasp, and he laughed again. "Not hard, anyway," he amended.

He leaned back up and winked at me before turning his glowing smile to the girl waiting to take our picture. Her eyes were as big as saucers. I'm not sure whose face was a deeper red—hers or mine.

"Um, are you guys ready, then?"

"Smile pretty, Ella," Cinder chirped, giving me a gentle squeeze. "This is going to be my new desktop for my computer."

The waitress kindly waited to take our photo until I broke from my stupor enough to manage a smile. Then she handed the phone back to Cinder and hurried off to the kitchen to relay the story to the rest of the restaurant staff. Her cheeks were still flushed as she disappeared from our sight.

As soon as our waitress was gone, I elbowed Cinder. Hard. "You jerk! I can't believe you just did that!"

He doubled over, but only because he was laughing so hard.

"I'm not one of your little playthings, you perv! Quit invading my personal space and go back to your side of the table. Your dinner's getting cold."

I shoved him and he laughed even harder. He reached across the table and pulled his plate to him—not going anywhere. If anything, his grip on me tightened.

"I didn't peg you for shy, but I like it. You're absolutely irresistible when you blush. See?" Grinning, he held his phone up so that we could study the picture. Sure enough, I resembled a tomato. "Look how adorable we are together. It's the perfect picture for your first Cinder and Ella feature."

"My what?"

"On your blog." Cinder took a big, sobering breath. "Remember how you used to do those 'Up Close and Personal' posts on your blog whenever you and your mom met a new author?"

For a brief moment my lungs seized up at the memories, but Cinder pulled me tightly into him, and I found I could breathe.

His voice turned soft, shifting with our moods. "I had an idea a while ago. I thought that if we ever did meet in person, we could start a new feature on your blog. It would sort of be like your old one, except instead of collecting authors' autographs in books, we could collect photographs of us with different celebrities."

Shocked by the thoughtfulness of his idea, I stared up at him. He met my gaze with a sad smile. "I know it wouldn't replace all the books you lost—nothing could replace those, and I wouldn't want to try—but I thought maybe you could start a new collection." He swallowed nervously and added, "With me."

I didn't know what to say.

"I could whisk you off to different events or movie sets all over the world and introduce you to the actors of the movies you review. We could call it 'The Adventures of Cinder & Ella.' We could even get an artist to draw us as characters for it, like our own comic. That would be so awesome."

When I didn't respond, he shifted in his seat and ran his hand through his dark locks. I felt bad for making him nervous, but I was so shocked all I could do was gape at him.

"What do you think?"

"You're serious?"

"Of course."

I let out a nervous bark of laughter. "Don't be ridiculous. That sounds amazing, but I couldn't let you do all that for me."

For some reason, his nerves disappeared. His expression softened into something that made my heart flip in my chest. The smile on his face wasn't one of amusement or even happiness; it was so much more than that. It was as if somehow, by saying no, I'd just made all of his dreams come true. "But that's just it," he said. "You *can* let me do that for you. Any other girl would let me. Hell, most of them would *expect* me to. But for you, I *want* to."

He released his hold on me so that he could turn and face me fully. He took both of my hands in his. "Do you have any idea how much I care for you?"

My stomach lurched up into my chest as he pulled my hands

to his lips and kissed my gloved knuckles. "I would take you any-where, Ella, give you anything you wanted. All you'd have to do is let me."

It was my wildest fantasy come true. No, it was every girl in the world's wildest fantasy. Except it was too good to be real. I knew it was. He made it sound so easy, but nothing about either of our lives was that simple.

I pulled my hands from his grip and put a few precious inches of space between us. "What about Kaylee? Need I remind you that, real or not, you have a *fiancée* right now?"

He shook his head. "That's done. I ended it the second the meet-and-greet was over. I mean, the media doesn't know yet, but Kaylee definitely does." He smirked at a memory. "She was DEF-CON 1 level pissed."

I couldn't believe it. He'd dumped his supermodel girlfriend for *me*. My heart was ready to give in, but my brain was screaming all kinds of warnings at me. Talk about DEFCON 1. I was on such high alert the hairs on the back of my neck were standing at attention. I had to keep this logical. "What about your career? You said Kaylee threatened to ruin you."

Cinder shrugged. "She'll try her best. She might do a little damage, but nothing I can't recover from. Nothing that wouldn't be worth being with you."

My heart fluttered again. It was winning the wrestling match against my head at the moment. My resolve was crumbling to bits. "And the bosses you talked about?"

"Agents, managers, publicists, lawyers… There's a whole list of people who control my life."

That's what I thought. "You think all those people are going to be happy about you breaking up with your co-star for *me?*"

Cinder hesitated long enough for me to see the truth he was trying to deny. He glared down at his plate. "We'd be fine." He sounded as if he were trying to convince himself. "They only wanted Kaylee and me to hook up because it would generate some free press for us and douse some of the flames on my reputation."

I raised a brow at Cinder and he grinned sheepishly. "In my defense, I only went through so many girls because none of them ever came anywhere close to the only one I really wanted." He kissed my hand again. "As the world will soon discover."

Talk about needing to douse some flames, I was tempted to dump my ice water on my face to cool the heat rising from it.

Brian chuckled. "The breakup will be bad news because Kaylee won't be classy about it, but the public will like the idea of me dating a normal, non-famous girl. The fans will go crazy over it. Our story would get a ton of press. My management team will have to be okay with it."

Aside from the panic the idea of "getting a ton of press" gave me, I knew his team of people—the ominous They—would never approve of me. The kind of press I'd give Cinder would only hurt him. I didn't want to harm his career any more than I wanted to expose myself to the world. I was the last person that should ever be in the spotlight.

Cinder started to look excited, but I couldn't share his optimism. "I don't think so, Cinder—er, Brian. I'm the last person your people—especially your fans—would ever accept."

He opened his mouth to argue, but I didn't let him get a word out. I had to say this before I lost the nerve, because he needed to know. He *deserved* to know. "There are things you don't know about me, too. Things I never told you, because, like you with your fame, I was afraid of you treating me differently."

Wariness and determination battled it out on his face as he waited for me to elaborate. I really, really didn't want to. After having him this close, saying all the things I always dreamed he'd tell me, it was going to kill me when he decided he didn't want me anymore. And I was under no illusion that he would. How could he—at least, not in the kissing-my-knuckles-and-nibbling-my-ear kind of way?

"Ever since my accident, everyone treats me differently, too. Suddenly I'm *that* girl. The one everyone stares at and whispers about. I'm the girl with all the baggage. The one whose mom died.

The crippled girl with the scars."

"Crippled?" Cinder jerked in surprise. His eyes swept the length of me and he frowned. He couldn't see anything wrong.

"Didn't you notice when I walked away from you after we met at the meet-and-greet?"

His brows scrunched up on his forehead as he tried to remember our earlier encounter. "Things were a little hectic then. I was thrown from having met you at all, and I was trying to pay attention to you and my fans at the same time. Besides, how was I supposed to notice anything except how that guy you were with was *all over you?*"

I almost snorted. If I weren't in the middle of something as painful as revealing the truth about myself, I'd have lectured him on the idiocy of jealous, testosterone-filled guys. Instead, I shut my eyes and took a deep breath. "My staff isn't just a costume prop. Today, it's doubling as my cane. My friend had it specially made so that I could leave my regular cane at home."

"You use a cane when you walk?"

I nodded. "The doctors told me it was a miracle when I learned to walk again after my accident. I'm grateful that I can do it, but the action isn't pretty. My limp is very pronounced and causes me a fair amount of pain. And I'm slow. That's why I was almost as late as you tonight. It took me that long to walk here from the meet-and-greet. I'm handicapped, Brian."

His face fell as my news started to sink in. His eyes raked me over again, focusing on my lap, but of course there was nothing to see. Yet. "You said you were hurt, but you never mentioned..." His voice trailed off as he was overcome with emotion.

I figured my condition would upset him, but I hadn't expected the amount of devastation he displayed right then. He didn't even know the worst of it yet. "Brian..." I gulped, hating to see his sadness. "If you can't deal with that, then there's no way you can handle the rest."

His head snapped up. "The rest?" he asked, horrified. "There's *more?*"

Despite my best efforts, tears finally pooled in my eyes. "There's so much more."

I closed my eyes again because I couldn't stand the look on Cinder's face, and I felt a thumb wipe a tear from my cheek. The gentle action, so sincere and caring, only made more tears fall.

"What else is there?" Cinder asked in a voice as soft as his touch.

I shook my head, refusing to open my eyes. "I don't want to tell you."

Cinder wrapped me up in the safety of his arms. Hugging me tightly, he rested his head on top of mine. "Whatever it is, Ella, it won't make a difference to me. I won't think any less of you."

His promise hurt my heart. I knew he meant it, but he had no idea what he was facing. "Yes, you will."

Unable to stand it any longer, I carefully pulled the long white glove off my burnt arm. "Looks are important to you," I said as I worked the material off my fingers. "You always date the most beautiful girls in the world."

With one final tug, the glove slipped off and I held out my exposed hand for him to see. Brian tried to hold in his gasp, but his sharp intake of breath was unmistakable.

"I'm not beautiful," I said, pulling away, preempting his rejection. "Maybe I was once, but I'm not anymore."

"Ella," he choked out in a strangled attempt to speak.

Gently, he took my damaged fingers and caressed the scarred skin. I stiffened when he picked up my hand, but I didn't pull away. He was the first person other than my doctors I'd ever let touch my scars. I didn't know how to feel about it. The moment was torture—both good and bad. The sensation was amazing, but my heart ached.

He kept my hand loosely in one of his while his other hand drifted up my arm, realizing that the scars kept going. When he finally spoke, his voice trembled. "What happened to you?"

"The car caught fire. Over seventy percent of my body was burned."

"Seventy percent…"

Our eyes met and suddenly I was desperate to do something I'd never done before. I wanted to show Cinder my scars—as much as I could, anyway. Now that I knew his true identity, I wanted him to know everything about me, too. I didn't want any more secrets between us.

We were tucked in the booth in the back of the restaurant, and since he'd scooted in beside me he was blocking me from the rest of the room. I was pretty sheltered and no one was paying us any attention, so I reached for the tie at the base of my throat that kept my cloak in place. With shaking hands and my eyes glued to my lap, I pulled the cloak off my bare shoulders and let it fall to the seat behind me.

Cinder said nothing. I wondered what he was thinking, but I refused to look at his face. He was a very dramatic guy, and everything he couldn't say would be written in his expression. I wasn't ready to see that. I was too raw.

I lifted my hair and turned so that he could see my back, knowing the low cut of my dress would allow him to get an idea of the kind of damage I'd suffered. "It goes all the way down my right side and covers everything from the waist down. My feet are so burned that my toes are deformed."

"Ella." His voice did more than tremble now. I knew that if I looked, I'd see him crying.

I turned back around, but still, I couldn't look up. I couldn't face him. "I've never shown anybody this besides my doctors and Vivian," I mumbled. "I always keep my scars covered. People are cruel to me. They stare, laugh, and say awful things. I'm bullied at school, and those kids have never even seen anything but my hand and the way I walk. And what's worse…?"

I took a breath and turned my arms over, exposing my wrists and the different set of scars there. Cinder choked on another gasp and took my wrists into his shaking hands.

"Are you—" He swallowed. "Are you okay?"

There was no point in being dishonest. He knew the answer

already. Still, I reassured him as best I could. "I'm not suicidal anymore. I promised you that, and I meant it. I'm not in danger of hurting myself, but I'm not always okay, either."

I finally looked up and was unraveled by the pain I saw in Cinder's face. Tears streamed unabashedly down his cheeks. My own eyes welled up to match his. "I can't hide this. Your fans—and all those people in charge of your career—they would find out, and they would never accept this. They would never accept *me*. Even if they did, I'm not sure I could handle all of the attention. I couldn't deal with the entire world knowing everything I've been through—everything I've *done*."

Brian shut his eyes and lightly squeezed my wrists as he took a deep breath. "No one could blame you for this. You went through something horrific. You lost everything dear to you, including your own body." He brushed his thumbs slowly over my scars. "This is nothing to be ashamed of. What matters is that you survived and got better. Look how far you've come."

I pulled my hands out of his, unable to take any more of his touch—it was all too overwhelming. Brian watched me closely as I used my napkin to wipe away the tears that had escaped down my face. There was something different about him now, something in the way he looked at me. His innocence was gone. He knew the truth, and now saw me the way everyone else did—as if he expected me to break any moment. He finally saw me as a damaged, frail creature that he would have to handle with caution.

I'd just changed everything. I knew from the look in his eyes that things would never be the same between us again.

Cinder pushed his plate away, his appetite gone. We'd been eating in silence for a good ten minutes, but neither of us managed to take more than a couple of bites. He looked at me, trying to figure out something to say. His pity ripped my soul to pieces. "Please don't look at me like that."

"I can't help it. How am I supposed to react to this? I can't believe you've never explained all this to me. Didn't you trust me? Didn't you think I'd want to help you though this? You'd rather have done it *alone?*"

The hurt in his voice made me feel ashamed. My panic rose with my need to make him feel better. "Of course I trust you. You've helped me more than anyone else."

"That's not the same." Anger clouded his voice as he struggled to keep hold of his spiraling emotions. I knew exactly how he felt.

"Please understand," I begged him. "I didn't want you to treat me differently. I know you know what that's like." Brian frowned down at his plate. "I didn't have anyone, Brian—no family, no friends. All I had was a man who'd abandoned me ten years earlier, and his family who resented me because I was his deep, dark secret. The only thing that's kept me going these past few months was *you*. You didn't treat me like I was crazy or fragile. You weren't afraid to joke with me and make me laugh. I couldn't lose that."

I looked into his eyes again and completely lost it. His horror and pity made me angry. "I knew if I told you the truth it would change everything! I knew you'd look at me exactly the way you are now!"

"It's a lot to take in, Ella! You have to give me time to process it. My heart is *breaking* right now."

My eyes started to burn again. "I didn't mean to hurt you."

Cinder placed his hands on my shoulders. His grip was featherlight though he looked as if he wanted to shake me. "No, Ella, it's breaking *for* you. I knew losing your mom had to be hard, but this…I can't even imagine…"

"Please don't." I turned my face away from him. "I don't want your pity."

Cinder released my shoulders and placed a hand under my chin. He turned my face back to his, and I was startled by how close he suddenly was. "It's not pity," he promised with all the fierceness of the powerful druid prince he played in the movie.

He brushed my hair back and wiped away my tears again. "I don't know how I feel right now," he said. "I'm overwhelmed."

He took my hands and lifted them up between us. So slowly it felt as if time had crept to a standstill, he brushed his lips over the back of my good hand and then my bad.

I gasped at the feel of his lips on my scars. The touch was more intimate than anything I'd ever experienced. My eyes fluttered shut, causing my tears to get tangled in my lashes.

"I wish there were some way I could take all of this away for you."

He pressed his lips firmly against each of my knuckles, one at a time, as if he were attempting to kiss them better. A violent sob racked my chest and escaped me in the form of a whimper.

"Ella." As Cinder whispered my name with a new kind of

desperation, his hands came up to my face. I knew he was going to kiss me, and even though I was in emotional agony, I wasn't about to stop him. This was Cinder—my best friend in the whole world, the guy I'd been in love with for years. I wanted this kiss more than I'd ever wanted anything in my life.

His lips came down on mine gently, as if he were savoring every second of this moment, taking in every sensation and filing it away in his brain for safekeeping. His mouth brushed back and forth over mine—exploring and seeking permission. I gave it, opening up to him with a soft sigh that robbed him of all restraint.

Passion overwhelmed him and he crashed our mouths together in a kiss worthy of the silver screen. His fingers dug into my hair as his tongue became intimate with my own in a heated dance. My hands, resting lightly on his chest, rose up and down with his wild breathing. His heart pounded beneath my palms, and mine beat just as hard.

The moment was magical. A fairy tale. And just like a fairy tale, it ended too soon. The clock on our bliss struck twelve as a bright flash went off in our faces. It was followed by an endless succession of flashes and shrieks.

Brian and I pulled apart to find our booth surrounded by several men with cameras. Behind them a crowd of fans gathered, creating an impenetrable wall of bodies. The restaurant was in mayhem. Girls shrieked, and people filmed us with their cell phones. The men blocking our booth, filming us and snapping endless photos, were shouting all kinds of questions at Cinder.

No. Not Cinder. Brian Oliver.

It was in that moment that "Cinder" vanished and I finally saw the guy I'd been kissing as Hollywood heartthrob Brian Oliver. The heat that had so fully enveloped me only moments before turned to ice. I broke out into a cold sweat as I took in our audience.

Brian must have been used to this kind of thing because he didn't freak out until he read the panic on my face. Then he finally glanced up at the chaos. His eyes flickered back and forth several times from my frightened expression to the crowd of people, and the blood drained from his face. "Ella, I am so sorry. I shouldn't have kissed you here… I wasn't thinking."

With another look out at the crowd, he cursed under his breath and pulled out his phone. "Scott," he said urgently into the phone, "are you still hanging out around here? Good. Can you get convention center security over to The Dragon's Roost? Ella and I are going to need an escort. Yes. And hurry, it's going to get ugly. Thanks, man."

I couldn't breathe and started to shake. I knew I was beginning to hyperventilate as anxiety took over, but I didn't realize just how panicked I was until Brian grabbed me by the shoulders and bore his eyes into mine. "Everything's going to be okay, Ella," he cooed in that that low, soothing vibrato he usually reserved for our reading sessions.

My eyes drifted back to the crowd and he took my chin in his hand, forcing my gaze back to him. "Hey, look at me. Right here. Right into my eyes."

I tried to do as he said. I tried to concentrate on nothing but those beautiful, dark eyes, but I couldn't push the sounds out of my ears.

"Who's the girl, Brian?"

"What about Kaylee?"

"Have you been cheating?"

"Tell us her name!"

"Are you in love?"

"How do you know her?"

"Brian!"

"Brian!"

Brian ignored them all. His attention was for me alone. "You're okay, Ella. This is normal. I've been through it a hundred times. We're going to be fine, all right?"

His hands slid from my shoulders down the length of my arms and he took my hands in his again.

"You, girl! Where'd you get those scars?"

"What happened to you?"

"Brian, what's wrong with your new girlfriend?"

At the mention of my scars, a new horror surfaced in my mind. I wasn't wearing my cloak or my gloves. I yanked my cloak back up over my shoulders, but it did nothing to make me feel better. It was far too late. Right this minute, images of me were being recorded and would be all over the news before I even got home. My worst nightmare had come true.

Brian had to tie my cloak for me because my hands were shaking too badly. After that, he pulled me into his arms as if shielding me from the vultures currently ripping apart my soul.

I buried my face in his chest and sobbed until I heard the angry shouts of people trying to push the crowd back. I started to lift my head, but Brian held me to him and stroked my hair. "Hang on, Ella. It's almost over. It's going to be okay in just a minute."

I knew what he meant, but his words sounded like a lie to my ears. This was not going to be okay in a minute. I wasn't sure it would ever be okay again.

I tried to make myself stop crying as I listened to the commotion. Most of the uproar was now coming from the restaurant manager who'd helped me when I first arrived, but I could hear several other deep voices shouting for people to vacate the premises.

"Brian!"

"Scott!" Brian blew out a breath. "Thanks for getting them here so fast. Would you stick around and speak to the manager? Clear up the bill and tell them I'll call later to make sure everything's been taken care of."

"You got it. I'll even give them your apologies."

"How did I ever live without you?"

"Very disorganized."

Brian laughed, and then a deep voice said, "Mr. Oliver? We'll take you to the security office, but I'm afraid it's all the way across the main hall."

Brian sighed and pulled my face out of his chest. "You ready to make a run for it?"

I was definitely not ready, but I nodded anyway.

"We'll be fine, Ella."

Brian climbed to his feet and held out a hand to me. I slowly pulled myself up. Reaching for my staff, I took one step in the direction the towering giant of a security guard was ushering me and froze. The convention center security had forced all dinner patrons back to their tables and managed to clear the restaurant of everyone else, but a large crowd was gathered outside, waiting for us.

"Brian," I whispered in horror, "I can't do that. What if just you leave? I could wait here and call Juliette after the chaos dies down."

"Not a chance."

"But—"

"I am not leaving you to deal with this *alone*." Brian glared at me, but his anger really had nothing to do with me. He glanced out at the cameras that were still flashing and shook his head bitterly. "It wouldn't work, anyway. I'm supposedly an engaged man. You and I just created one of the biggest scandals Hollywood has seen in a while."

He tried to smile for me, but it fell flat. "At a convention with this many celebrities, every paparazzi in LA is here. Those photographers want to know who you are. If I leave, some of them will follow me, but the rest would wait for you. They'd wait as long as it takes, and then they'd follow you. They'd follow you to your car, and then they'd follow you all the way home and camp out on your front lawn."

My eyes grew wide as the reality of what was happening hit me. Whether I liked it or not, my life would never be the same again.

"Welcome to fame, Ella," Brian mumbled, regret heavy in his voice. "I'm sorry it happened like this, but we'll get through it together, okay?"

He held out his hand to me, but I couldn't take it. I looked out at the crowd that seemed to have doubled since I stood up.

"Mr. Oliver," the security guard interrupted, "the longer we wait the larger the crowd will gather. There are *thousands* of people in this convention center today."

Brian held out his hand to me again.

I shook my head, trying not to panic. "I can't."

"Ella, I really am sorry, but you don't have a choice. We've got to go."

"You don't understand!" I snapped. "I mean I *physically* can't. I can barely walk. I'll never be able to push my way through that crowd."

Brian blinked as if he were only now remembering there was anything wrong with me. He looked at the way I was holding my weight on my staff and his face paled. That pain-filled, heartbroken expression reappeared. I couldn't stand to see it, so I turned away from him and realized that I'd gained the attention of everyone in the restaurant. My outburst had them all frozen with their dinner forks halfway to their faces.

Glancing around, I saw a hundred different pairs of eyes all focused on me, already judging. I closed my eyes and took a deep breath, willing myself not to cry again, but my tears returned anyway. "I can't fully extend my arm, either," I muttered, face flaming with embarrassment. "If I fall or someone grabs me, I could tear my skin grafts. It happened recently. I'm scheduled for another surgery in January because of it."

I didn't open my eyes until I felt Brian's tender touch as he wiped the wet streaks from my cheeks. "I'm so sorry, Ella. I don't know how they knew we were here. I should never have kissed you in public. This is my fault. I just didn't think."

"It doesn't matter now. Let's just get out of here." I couldn't meet his eyes as I added, "Someone is going to have to carry me."

It was so humiliating. Brian was a man so perfect, so loved and adored by so many, that there were literally hundreds of people gathering outside to see who he was with, and I couldn't even walk out of here by his side.

"That's not a problem, Miss, I can—"

Brian growled at the security guard who'd spoken. "*I* can do it." He scooped me into his arms as if I weighed almost nothing and cradled me tightly against his chest.

Two men who both looked like they could easily play defense for Brian's beloved Green Bay Packers huddled up on either side of us. "Ready, Mr. Oliver?"

"My things?" I asked.

"Scott?" Brian called.

"Already got 'em."

Brian gave me a small grin. "He really is awesome."

When I couldn't return his smile, he dipped his head toward me and kissed my temple. "I'm so sorry, Ella."

He nodded to the security guys and then headed out into the convention hall. A crowd of people with cameras swarmed us the second we walked out the door. They shouted and flashed their cameras as they all jockeyed for better positions with clearer shots. I buried my face in Brian's shoulder trying to shut them out, but a strangled shriek caught my attention. "Ella!" Juliette screamed. "Ella! Let me through, you big oaf! That is my *sister!* Ella!"

"Juliette?"

I couldn't see her, but Brian nodded to one of the escorts next to him and said, "Those four."

Seconds later Juliette, Vivian, Rob, and Anastasia were pulled into the huddle behind me. "Are you all right?" Rob hollered above the noise.

"This is crazy!" Juliette shouted.

I nodded in answer to both of them and then buried my face in Brian's shoulder again. I didn't look up until I was safely tucked away in the convention center security office.

THE SECOND BRIAN SET ME DOWN ON A SOFA IN THE SECURITY office, Juliette threw her arms around me in a fierce hug. "Are you okay?"

"No." My tears returned with her hug. "I want to go home. How are we ever supposed to get out of here?"

A man who introduced himself as the building's head of security stepped in front of us. "Did you drive here?"

Juliette nodded. "We left our car with the valet."

"We'll have them drive your car around to the back entrance where the delivery trucks unload. It's not far from here and that whole area is blocked off to the public. You should be able to leave unnoticed, but we'll send a police cruiser with you just to be safe."

I breathed a sigh of relief. If we could leave today without being followed, then it might not be too late to retain some semblance of privacy. Nobody knew who I was. Even Brian didn't know my last name or where I lived.

Rob handed our valet ticket to the man and he read the number into a handheld radio. After a quick reply, he smiled at us again. "It'll be here in about ten minutes."

I sank back into the sofa as far as the cushions would give, exhausted now that the adrenaline had left my system. My nerves were so frazzled I wasn't sure I'd ever recover.

Brian sat down next to me and pulled my hand into his. He said nothing, but he leaned over and kissed my cheek. A few minutes later his assistant Scott arrived. "Everything at the Dragon's Roost is taken care of," he informed Brian as he set down my gloves, book, and walking staff that I'd left behind in the restaurant. "The manager was pretty mortified that you guys were disrupted like that and refused to let you pay for your meal. *He* sends his sincerest apologies."

Brian nodded. He looked as tired as I felt when he pulled himself to a stand and handed Scott a set of keys. "One last favor, and then I demand you take a few days off. Would you mind getting Precious home safe?"

I loved the astonishment that washed over Scott's face. I imagine I'd look much the same way if Brian ever asked me that.

"Precious?" Vivian asked, confused.

She glanced at me to see if I knew what he meant, and I smiled my first smile in what felt like hours. "His Ferrari. He named her Precious." I sighed when no one got it. "As in 'my precious'... Gollum... The One Ring...?"

Still nothing. I threw my head back and groaned. "How can I be friends with so many people who don't understand that reference?"

Brian laughed.

"He's a huge *Lord of the Rings* nerd," I explained to my Tolkien-challenged friends.

"Fan," Brian corrected, his grin dissolving into a pout. "Not *nerd*. And like you can talk, Miss I-saw-the-movie-twelve-times-in-the-theater."

Everyone chuckled and Brian winked at me before turning his attention back to Scott. "Would you switch cars with me? Drive Precious home and hang out for a bit until I can bring your car back? There's a bonus in it for you."

"Sure."

"Of course, get one scratch on her and you're totally fired."

Scott gulped as he stared down at the keys in his palm. "Right. No problem."

Brian laughed and punched Scott's shoulder lightly. "I'm messing with you, man. You know I'd never be able to function without you. Just take care of my baby. I won't be too long. I only want to drive Ella home and make sure she's all right, but the paparazzi are too familiar with my car."

When I realized what he said, my heart lurched and my playful mood vanished. "I'd rather you didn't," I croaked in a shaky voice.

Everyone in the room froze, and then both Vivian and Juliette came to my side while Brian frowned at me, confused. I gulped, hoping I'd be able to do what needed to be done without hurting him too much. "I'm sorry, Brian." The statement was heavy and everyone in the room understood its full meaning.

"Are you sure about this?" Juliette whispered.

It wasn't what I wanted, but I was sure it was what needed to happen. What would people say when reporters splashed pictures of my hideous scars all over the media for the entire world to see? What would happen when they discovered my identity? My pain and suffering, my accident, losing my mother, and my suicide attempt would all be showcased to the whole world as nothing more than gossip and cheap entertainment. I didn't think I could live with that.

"I'm sure." I took a few breaths and then forced myself to meet Brian's gaze. He deserved that much at least. "I could have dealt with almost anything, but this..." I shook my head. "You were right when you said I couldn't handle your world. I can't. I'm sorry, Brian. I'm not the right girl for you."

Brian's eyes flew wide open. He crossed the room to me in two long strides, and both Juliette and Vivian scrambled up so he could sit down beside me. He took my hand again and pleaded "Don't do this" with all the passion that made him famous.

His emotion twisted my insides. I understood exactly why

he'd become an actor. His eyes said so much more than words ever could. Right now they were telling me how confused, hurt, and even scared he was. I couldn't stand it. Somewhere underneath the Brian Oliver exterior was my best friend—the single most important person in my life. I never wanted to cause him worry, and I especially never wanted to hurt him.

The dam behind my eyes threatened to break again. "Two weeks ago it was you begging for what we had to be enough," I said. "Now I have to ask the same."

Brian shook his head furiously. "You think there's any way we can go back after today? We can't, Ella. We belong together, and you know it."

He wasn't making this easy, but I squared my shoulders, determined. "It wouldn't be that simple."

Brian raked his hand through his hair so violently I feared it would leave a bald spot in its wake. "I know fame is a lot to deal with—I know it's asking a lot of you—but I swear I would make it worth it for you."

I believed he would try, but I knew he wouldn't really have control of the situation. He complained all the time about not having any control over his life. I knew for a fact that who he dated mattered—hence the reason he'd been with Kaylee Summers.

Dating a girl like me would completely ruin his image. It already had. I'd just destroyed everything he was trying to accomplish with his fake relationship when I'd "cheated" with him in public. People were not going to forgive me for that. His world would never approve of me. I was a nobody. I was *worse* than a nobody. I was crippled and deformed, scarred and ugly.

We really were Cinder and Ella. I was the commoner, and he a prince. Even if he loved me, eventually he would make the choice expected of him—the *noble* choice, as he so often told me. He would choose Ratana. Maybe it wouldn't be Kaylee Summers, but it would be someone famous. Someone beautiful. Someone worthy of him.

"I can't do it. People tear apart even the most beautiful

Hollywood starlets for having a less-than-perfect nose, or an extra ounce of fat. Even if you can overlook my flaws, the rest of the world never will. I can't handle the things they'll say about me. I'm not like you. I'm too self-conscious. Too vain. Too *weak*."

"Ellamara, you are *not* weak. It might not be easy, but we'll deal with it together. Give us a chance. *Please*."

I closed my eyes again and fought against more tears. What I needed to say would be the hardest words I'd ever speak, but they had to be said. "You are still my best friend. You know I love you more than anything. I will always be there for Cinder, but I can't be a part of Brian Oliver's life. I'm sorry."

I gulped back my emotions and looked to my other friends. "Vivian?"

Vivian knew what I wanted. She brought me my walking staff and helped me stand up. Brian stopped me before I got to the door. "I know you're a little freaked out about the fame thing, but—"

"I'm not a *little* freaked out, Brian." My last shred of control finally broke and I screamed at him. "I'm *terrified!* I'm on *probation* with my therapist right now. I'm one anxiety attack away from being locked up in a mental hospital. One bully attack away from being kicked out of school, and I'm already a full year behind from spending eight months in the hospital."

"Eight *months?*" Brian whispered in horrified surprise.

I stopped yelling and the hopelessness I felt seeped into my voice. "Yes. And I still have years of recovery ahead of me. I have my *thirty-seventh* surgery scheduled for January. I'm still grieving over the loss of my mother, still struggling to accept everything that's happened to me. I'm *barely surviving*. I don't think I can handle the kind of pressure you're asking me to take on."

When Brian replied, his voice was small. It was the first time I'd ever heard him sound insecure. "It's not always like that. What happened today was unfortunate, but—"

"Unfortunate?" I choked on a sob that caught me by surprise.

"Today was so much more than unfortunate. Only my family and Vivian have ever seen my scars like that, and *no one* besides my doctors has ever touched them. Do you know how huge of an emotional step that was for me? Do you have any idea how vulnerable I was with you today? You shattered every emotional defense I had. You broke me wide open so that I was more exposed than I've ever been."

"I didn't mean to…" Brian scrambled for words. "I was just so overwhelmed by everything. I didn't realize—" He paused a minute to steady his voice. "Ella, I am *so* sorry."

I felt awful for making him feel guilty. "Please don't apologize, Brian. Tonight you made me feel beautiful, special, and loved when I didn't think I'd ever feel like that again. I'm grateful to you for that.

"I'm only upset because right when I felt the first real ray of hope since my accident, those camera guys came and stole it away. The first thing they asked was why you were with me, and what was *wrong* with me. That moment between us was one of the most beautiful and special moments of my entire life."

Brian stepped up and wrapped his arms around me. "Mine too, Ella."

I finally broke down into a bawling mess. "But that moment is about to be broadcast to the whole world for people to mock and judge and gossip about. My pain and suffering is about to become the nation's entertainment. I can't handle that, Brian. I don't know how to deal with it. I'm sorry."

I broke free from his grip and looked at the security guy. "Is our car ready?"

The man glanced nervously back and forth between Brian and me, and then nodded.

"Ella, wait. Please."

Brian tried to argue, but I quit listening. I couldn't bear it. Juliette seemed to understand my need to get away. "Not here, okay?" she said to Brian. "You guys can figure this out, but not now. Let her call you after she's settled down."

"But—"

"Let her go," she said sternly and gestured for the security man to show us to our car.

I EVENTUALLY MANAGED TO QUIT CRYING, BUT I STILL SNIFFLED all the way home. It was the only sound made in the car the entire drive. When we pulled up into my driveway, Anastasia was out of the car and slamming the front door shut before the rest of us even had our seat belts off. I hadn't heard her say a word since Rob told her off. I wasn't sure if she was still mad about that, or just really hated Brian's don't-leave-me-we-belong-together speech. I assumed it was all of the above and doubted she'd ever speak to me again.

Before either Vivian or Juliette could hand me my walking staff from the trunk, Rob scooped me up into his arms and carried me up the front walk. I was so heartbroken and exhausted that I didn't argue. By the time we got to the front door, my dad and Jennifer were standing there, clinging to one another in a worried embrace.

"What happened?" Jennifer gasped.

I didn't have it in me to explain.

Rob looked at Juliette. "Why don't you two tell them. I'm going to take Ella to her room."

Rob nudged the door shut behind him as he carried me into

my room and set me on my bed—which I thought was breaking a house rule, but I didn't mention it. He sat down next to me and didn't say anything. The silence was comfortable, but I still broke it. "Thank you."

Rob reached for my hand. He hesitated a second when he realized the closest one was my scarred hand, but then he picked it up anyway. "Are you okay?" he asked as he started running his fingertips over the back of my hand and then my palm, exploring the feel of my skin.

For some reason, I was relieved by his actions. There was no repulsion from him, and now there was no more fear of him touching me. It was as if we'd reached a new level of trust and acceptance. If we could share this moment with no awkwardness between us, then he was truly my friend.

I sat there a minute, watching his fingers on my skin and enjoying the peace in the atmosphere. "You're a good friend to me, Rob. I don't deserve it."

Rob laced his fingers in mine and smiled. "Yes, you do."

His answer came so easily and was so sincere it hurt my heart. "Rob...I really appreciate you trying to help me move past Cinder, and maybe someday I'll be ready to do that, but I don't think I can date you right now. I'm sorry."

"Don't be." Rob sighed, but he still smiled at me. "It's not your fault. I didn't get it, Ella. I thought you just had some infatuation with the guy because the mystery was exciting. I thought you'd eventually decide that a real flesh-and-blood boyfriend was better than a phone buddy, but what I saw today was *not* infatuation. Not for either of you."

Rob placed his other hand over the top of our intertwined fingers. "It won't matter how long I wait for you. I could wait forever and it wouldn't do me any good. You belong to him."

I blushed and choked out another apology. He chuckled this time. "It's okay, Ella. I can be just your friend. And as a friend, I think I have to tell you not to give him up."

I looked up, startled, and he smiled at me. "You guys are in love. Don't give that up because you're scared. It'll be hard, but anything worth it always is, and you'll have your friends to help you."

"He's right, you know." Vivian smiled from the entrance to my bedroom. I hadn't heard the door open. "You'll always have us."

Juliette stood next to her, face beaming with a bright smile. "You'll have your family, too." She grabbed the remote for the TV, and she and Vivian climbed up on the bed. "Come on; we'll all check out the damage together."

It took ten minutes of watching the news before the story came up. An anchorman and woman sat behind a desk and the picture displayed on the screen behind them was one of Brian and me kissing. Besides making me blush in front of my friends, seeing that picture hurt. It teased me with the memory of Brian's kiss. It made me remember how wonderful everything had been for a moment, and at the same time reminded me that I could never have him.

"In entertainment news," the young, sharp-looking woman said, "*The Druid Prince* star Brian Oliver caused a bit of an uproar at FantasyCon this evening when he was seen kissing a woman who was *not* his fiancée, *The Druid Prince* co-star Kaylee Summers."

As if a picture weren't bad enough, the screen cut to some-one's video footage of my kiss with Brian. Beside me on the bed, both Juliette and Vivian sighed. Rob sighed in response to their sighs.

On the TV, Brian and I snapped apart. My panicked face blinked up into the camera, like a frightened child. I seemed so young and pathetic, freaking out while Brian tried to comfort me. The image became even sadder when I scrambled to cover my scars with my cloak and then started sobbing into Brian's chest.

The image on the screen changed to one of us leaving the restaurant—me in Brian's arms—under the protection of our hulking security guards.

"The lovebirds had no comment for the cameras," the anchor-woman said, "but later Brian's management team issued a statement saying, 'It wasn't what it seemed. Brian was working with a charity organization that grants wishes. The girl was a fan who'd nearly burned to death in a terrible accident and had been granted a wish—a kiss from Brian Oliver. Miss Summers was aware of the situation and fully supportive. The two, though they still have not set a date for their wedding, are as happy as ever and excited for the upcoming premiere of *The Druid Prince* next month.'"

All the air left my lungs, and my eyes burned. They told people I was a *charity case?*

"What?" Juliette gasped.

She stared at the TV with wide eyes. Vivian was gaping at the screen too, shaking her head in disbelief. "There has to be an explanation."

"There is," I muttered. "Damage control."

"But we saw you guys together. Ella, the way he looked at you... I don't think he would have—"

I cut her off before she could defend him. "I'm sure he didn't want to, but he does whatever he's told. He was only dating Kaylee in the first place because his management team made him. His people obviously thought leaving Kaylee for an ugly nobody was bad for his career."

"Ella." Rob frowned.

I shook my head, not wanting to let Rob contradict me. "Just turn it off."

Juliette reached for the remote, but paused when the anchor-woman said, "Brian may have been a little camera shy, but we managed to catch up with Kaylee and she had plenty to say on the subject."

"I'm sure she did," the older man next to her joked with a chuckle that set my blood boiling.

"This can't be good," Vivian muttered.

The screen changed to a picture of a woman holding a micro-phone out to Kaylee. Kaylee stood poised and perfect for the cameras. "Oh, please," she said when asked about Brian kissing me. "Do you really think Brian would cheat on me for some little girl like that?" She waved a dismissive hand. "He met her for one of those make-a-wish-come-true charity things. The girl's a really big fan of his. He agreed to it because she has some blog he likes. He spent the whole day Friday tweeting about it."

"So you were okay with him kissing her?" the reporter asked.

Kaylee's responding glare made the reporter take a step back. As soon as she could bury her annoyance, she plastered a smile on her face. "Obviously I wasn't very happy about that," she said, "but I forgive him. I'm sure he just felt sorry for her. I mean, you saw what she looked like, with all those scars. And she can't even walk. That's why he had to carry her out of there. Trust me, I'm not worried."

"She did not!" Vivian shouted, outraged.

"She's evil!" Juliette agreed.

Rob's fingers slipped into mine as Kaylee Summers' face flashed on the screen with a smug smile. I squeezed the offered hand for all it was worth.

On screen, Kaylee continued her phony gush-fest. "Brian's just such a nice guy. He has a hard time saying no, especially to his fans. He's always trying to please everyone." She sighed as if she thought Brian were a silly boy. "He's always trying to be the hero."

"It sounds as if he was the perfect choice to play the heroic Price Cinder, then," the reporter said.

"It's true," Kaylee agreed. Then, suddenly, the easy smile slipped from her face and she stared hard at the reporter. "And if that *stalker* ever tries to come anywhere near my fiancé again, she'll learn why I was the perfect woman to play the fierce warrior princess Ratana. Brian is *mine*."

Juliette finally turned the TV off.

Rob, Vivian, and Juliette immersed me in a group hug. I was grateful to them, but when they tried to console me with words I asked them to leave. I'd had a long day, and I just wanted it to be over.

. . . . .

BRIAN'S LIE MAY HAVE SAVED HIS REPUTATION, BUT IT DESTROYED my life. I woke up the next morning to an e-mail inbox full of hate mail. Brian and Kaylee fans alike didn't take kindly to the psycho stalker who almost broke up the "perfect" couple. My blog, Twitter, and Facebook were littered with profane, hurtful comments.

At school it was worse because I wasn't just a stalker. To my classmates, I was a pathetic liar. Everyone accused me of lying about being friends with him. Never mind the fact that I never claimed to know him at all.

Rob and Vivian were both waiting for Juliette and me in the parking lot when we got to school. Their grim faces told me everything I needed to know about how this day was going to go—not that I hadn't guessed. All three of them walked with me through the breezeway, glaring and yelling at anyone who approached me. Their presence didn't stop the bravest people from laughing and shouting horrible things, but at least they kept their distance.

Juliette was the first to reach my locker and, with a startled gasp, she whirled around and threw her back against it, covering the front from my view. "Why don't we just go to class? Who needs books?"

"I appreciate the gesture, Juliette, but I have to get in there, so I'm going to see whatever it is, anyway."

Juliette shook her head.

"Jules, whatever it is I'm going to hear about it sometime today."

When Juliette finally stepped aside, Vivian echoed her gasp and Rob made a noise that sounded an awful lot like a growl. My lovely classmates had been so kind as to decorate my locker permanent marker-style with words like *psycho*, *stalker*, *whore*, *loser*, *ugly*, *freak*, and *cripple*.

I told myself they were just words and that they weren't true. I told myself my classmates were jealous and that they didn't know the truth. I told myself that I had three friends standing with me who supported me, and that was all that really mattered. Still, no matter what I told myself, seeing my locker like that hurt.

When I closed my eyes against the sting of tears and sucked in a deep breath through my nose, a hand came down on my shoulder. "Let's call Mom and Dad," Juliette said. "They'll let you go home today."

"What would be the point?" I asked. My voice shook as I fought to keep control of my emotions. I opened my locker and swapped out the books I needed for my first class. "If I'm not here today, they'll just wait until tomorrow to harass me, or the next day, or the day after that."

As I slammed the locker closed, Rob's arm came around me. I leaned into him, letting his presence comfort me. He kissed my forehead and then began escorting me to my first class. "We're here with you, Ella."

I squeezed him back and took another breath. "Thanks."

If only the three of them could have been with me the entire day. Juliette was in my second class, but none of them were in my first class. I was on my own for the walk from first to second period.

I kept my head down to avoid the nasty looks as I walked down the hall. I didn't see the group of guys trailing me with trouble in their intent until it was too late. "Hey, freak," one of them greeted me. That was the only warning I got before he kicked my cane out from under me.

I crashed to the ground amidst a roar of laughter. Luckily, I broke my fall with my good arm, managing at least not to do any more damage to my skin grafts. My reconstructed hip that caused most of my limp slammed against the floor, sending a shooting pain through me so intense that my eyes welled up with tears.

A girl from my first hour class who'd been particularly mean all year draped herself against the guy who'd just kicked my cane and laughed. "Where's Brian Oliver to carry you to safety now, Ella? Oh, that's right—he's with his real girlfriend, because he doesn't really care about you. You're just a pathetic stalker."

I reached for my cane so I could pull myself up and some other jerk kicked it across the walkway out of my reach. "Oops, sorry!"

I couldn't get to my feet from the ground without something to pull myself up on, so I was literally stuck there until someone decided to take pity on me. It was completely degrading, and the meanest thing that had ever happened to me in my entire life.

With the exception of when Jason tore my skin graft, I never cried in school and I didn't want to start now. That's what these people wanted—to reduce me to tears. I didn't want to give them the pleasure, but I was so humiliated that I couldn't stop my eyes from welling up.

"Oh, no," Mean Girl taunted. "Is poor little Ella going to cry again like she did on TV last night?"

Unable to take it any longer, I finally gave them what they were waiting for. I buried my face in my hands and began to sob.

A girl standing by who'd witnessed the scene picked up my cane and tried to hand it to me, but some other random jerk plucked it out of her hands and began to play keep-away. "You guys, cut it out!" The girl bent down, and after asking if I was okay, informed me that her friend went to get the principal. It was nice of her to stand up for me, but I still couldn't stop crying.

"What the hell is going on?"

Relief washed over me at the sound of Rob's voice. He dropped to the ground and wrapped his arms around me. "Ella, what happened?"

"I don't know why you're bothering with her, Rob." I didn't look to see which guy was talking. I figured it was better if I didn't know. "Did you see her scars, dude? Nasty. I heard they cover her whole body. Do you seriously want to hit that?"

The arms around me disappeared and seconds later there was a loud crack and a ton of shouting. The commotion only lasted thirty seconds at best before several teachers broke up the fight, but it was long enough for Rob to bloody the nose and lip of the guy who'd kicked my cane out from under me.

Instead of trying to figure out what happened right there, the teachers sent everyone present—eleven of us in all—to the principal's office.

The girl who stood up for me and two other people tried to help me up, but Rob shooed them away and wouldn't let anyone near me. He helped me to my feet and handed me my cane, but my hip hurt so badly I couldn't put any weight on my leg. For the second time in as many days, I had to be carried away.

THE FOUR GUYS INVOLVED IN PLAYING KEEP-AWAY WITH MY CANE and the three girls who egged them on, laughed, and said rude things were all suspended for three days. Rob and the guy who'd kicked my cane out from under me both got a week's suspension for fighting, and they were discussing the possibility of expulsion for my "assailant," since his intentions had been malicious and resulted in me getting hurt. My fate had yet to be determined.

When my father showed up in the office—Jennifer, Daniel, Cody, and Dr. Parish in tow—I threw myself into his arms and soaked his shirt with tears. "Dad, take me out of this school. I don't even care if I ever graduate. I'm done."

My dad hugged me tightly and ran a hand over my head. "Okay, kiddo. We'll find another way for you to finish."

He barked at someone over my head, probably Principal Johnson. "I'm removing my daughter from this school. I expect a full refund for her tuition, and I'm having this place put under review."

"Mr. Coleman, what happened today was inexcusable," Principal Johnson said, "but don't you think that is a little extreme?"

My dad let go of me and whirled on the man. "*Extreme?* This is the *second* time my daughter has been assaulted on this campus during school hours! Where the hell was your staff, and why can't you keep your students under control?"

Principal Johnson sputtered and stepped toward Dad with red cheeks. "I beg your pardon, Mr. Coleman, but this is an excellent school and my staff is extremely capable. Until your daughter came here, our track record for student altercations was almost spotless."

"Are you saying this was *Ella's* fault?"

"I'm saying trouble seems to find your daughter. You can't blame that on this institution."

"The hell I can't! You are responsible for what happens here, and I'm going to make sure you're held accountable for this."

While the two of them continued to argue about this, Cody and Daniel bombarded me with questions and made me do all kinds of movements and stretches. After their brief examination, they decided I had a bruised hipbone and would have some extra stiffness that I'd have to work out with Daniel in physical therapy. Otherwise, I was okay.

Physically, anyway. Mentally, I was broken, and it didn't take Dr. Parish much effort to get that bit of truth from me. "Ella, talk to me. How are you feeling right now?"

That one simple question made me explode into another round of sobs. "How am I supposed to feel right now? How can people be so cruel? And why? Why would anyone treat me this way? What have I done to any of these people to deserve this?"

"Nothing, Ella. You didn't deserve this. No one would deserve this."

Dr. Reassurance didn't help. I felt as if my chest had burst open and spilled all the pieces of my broken heart on the floor. "Things were getting better here but the second they had some new material to tease me with, the torture started all over again— only *worse*! Is this going to be my life from now on? Am I always going to be tortured because I'm different?"

My question quieted the entire room. Everyone watched in silence as I broke down. And I didn't just fall apart a little: I broke completely. Whatever was left of me—of my heart, my mind, my soul—shattered. I was swallowed by an ocean of hopelessness.

"I can't do this anymore," I sobbed. "Why even keep trying when there's no point? I'm so tired of hurting. I'm tired of fighting. Tired of trying. None of it ever does any good. I wish I died in that accident with Mama."

My father was at my side again, and pulled me back into his arms. "Ella, don't say that."

"But it's the truth."

The room fell quiet again, with nothing but the sound of my sobs to break the silence. When Dr. Parish recommended I be hospitalized a few minutes later, I was so heartbroken I didn't put up a fight. Anything had to be better than this.

28

Brian

THERE WAS A LOUD POUNDING THAT JUST WOULD NOT STOP. I
rolled onto my back with a groan. After wiping at the drool on
my face, I risked opening my eyes. It was dark. Dark was good.
Now if I could only get rid of the noise.

"Brian!"

I frowned. Since when did my inner monologue sound like
my assistant?

"Brian! Don't make me get the hotel staff to open this door!"

I blinked again and looked around. I was alone in a dark
hotel room in…Las Vegas? My brain started to wake up and con-
nect the dots. After Ella rejected me, I'd driven to Vegas and gotten hammered. How long ago was that? A few hours? A day?

"Brian!"

Well. However long I'd been here, it was long enough for
Scotty to come looking for me. Damn my overzealous assistant. "I
thought I told you to take a few days off!"

With another groan, I rolled out of bed and stumbled my

way to the door. I immediately shut my eyes against the violent stream of light that poured in the room from the hallway. "Why don't you just come in and beat me to death with a sledgehammer? Enough with the damn pounding."

Throwing the door open for Scott to enter, I grumbled my way back to bed.

"Here." Scott chucked a bottle of aspirin at me as I crashed back onto the bed. "That ought to help."

"It will if I chase it with a bottle of Scotch. You don't have any of that in that magical man purse of yours, do you?"

"Someone's a grumpy drunk." Scott pulled a bottle from his messenger bag and tossed it to me. Water. Damn.

I chugged the water, along with a handful of painkillers, and then frowned at Scott. "I am a very lovable drunk, thank you very much. I'm just a lousy morning-after."

"Try two mornings after."

Two days? I tried to think and it made my head hurt. "Has it been that long?" I rolled over and snuggled up with my blessed pillow. "What have I been doing for two whole days?"

"Not answering your phone."

"I don't even think I've left this suite since I got here."

"I'm sure," Scott replied. "If you had, you'd have seen the news, and I doubt if you knew what was going on you'd be living your own personal *The Hangover* sequel."

"That sounds ominous." I pulled the covers all the way up over my head. Maybe if I couldn't see Scott anymore, Wonder Assistant would disappear and let me go back to sleep. "So Kaylee's on the rampage, then? Is my life ruined yet? Am I the most-hated person in America now?"

Scott yanked my covers all the way to the floor. "Not *you*." There was enough irritation in his voice that I finally noticed the sense of urgency. "Ella."

I sat up so fast my head spun. "What do you mean? What happened?"

Not waiting for Scott's answer, I swiped my phone off the

night table and dialed Ella's number. "That's not going to work," Scott said, just as the operator informed me that Ella's number was no longer in service.

Fear caused adrenaline to pump through my body, instantly pushing the last of the fog from my brain. "What's going on? Why isn't Ella's phone working? Is she okay?"

"I don't know. I haven't been able to get ahold of her. I tried the phone number, e-mail, and instant messenger you have listed in your contacts, and they're all out of service."

I was ready to wring the answers from Scott if he didn't explain everything right this damn second. I was so upset over Ella refusing to be a part of my life that I forgot I'd made her an overnight celebrity. Had her identity been discovered? Was she being harassed? Had Kaylee done something?

"Talk to me, Scotty. I know it's bad if you followed me all the way to Las Vegas in your POS Toyota."

"Actually, I flew here. I thought you'd want to go straight home and wasn't sure you'd be in any condition to drive."

Judging from the look Scott gave me as he assessed my rumpled state, he was probably right. "Good thinking."

Scott smirked. "I thought so. I also used your credit card to book the flight and upgraded myself to first class."

Even in the midst of my panic I had to smile at that. "You're really starting to get the hang of this job."

Scott pulled out his laptop and patted the table space next to him. "I learn fast. Pull up a chair. You're going to want to sit down for this."

I HAD BEEN PACING THE HOTEL SUITE FOR TEN MINUTES, STILL too enraged to speak. This was a nightmare.

I knew there was going to be a media frenzy over the incident on Sunday, but I thought Ella would be safe. No one knew her real identity. *I* didn't even know her identity. But I knew that *something* was going to happen. How could I just take off and not wait around to see what the fallout would be?

Ella's personal identity hadn't been leaked, but, thanks to Kaylee, her online one had. Her Facebook and Twitter had been deleted and her e-mail address was no longer valid. Her blog was still there—thank the Lord for some miracles. I would have been heartbroken if all of her posts for the last three years had been erased forever—but the comments feature had been disabled and she hadn't posted anything since Saturday.

I didn't have to imagine the kinds of things people posted on her social media for her to delete everything, because there were plenty of other places on the Internet for me to read it. A charity case? An obsessed fan? A psycho stalker? And those were just the nicer things. I wouldn't repeat the nastier stuff.

And it was my own damned people who started the rumors. Ella must hate me. In fact, I knew she did, because even if she had to delete her online persona, the public didn't know her cell phone number and instant messenger ID. She didn't have to get rid of those, but she did. She'd made it impossible for me to contact her.

She didn't just delete her online presence—she deleted *me* from her life. It was unacceptable. I had to do something. I couldn't let her write me off without giving me the chance to explain. I needed a plan, but I wouldn't be making that plan with the people who usually helped me.

I stopped pacing and turned to Scott, who still sat at the table in front of his laptop, waiting for me to come back from my internal rant. "I have a lawyer, right? I've got to. I probably have a whole team of lawyers, right?"

Scott nodded. "Candice Regan and Associates."

"Candice Regan." I committed the name to memory. "Get me Candice Regan on the phone."

Scott tapped on his iPad for a minute, then dialed my cell

phone. "Yes, I have Brian Oliver on the line for Candice Regan. Then I suggest you interrupt it. I really don't think Mr. Oliver is in the mood to wait. Yes, I'll stay on the line, thank you."

Scott handed the phone over just as an older woman's cheerful voice came on the line. "Brian! What a pleasant surprise. I haven't spoken to you directly in ages. What can I do for you?"

"My entire management team," I said slowly, trying to control the anger still raging inside me. "I want them all fired by the end of the day, and I don't want to be sued for it."

"Fired! Well!" Candice sputtered a second and then said, "But they're all under contract, Brian."

"Which is exactly why I called *you*. Are you aware of the story they ran with Sunday evening?"

"The charity case with the wish for a kiss?"

I gritted my teeth. It wasn't this woman's fault. I shouldn't yell at her. Still, when I spoke, I sounded downright dangerous. "It was bullshit. All of it. Ella is *not* a fan. I was not working with any charity, and I wasn't even still engaged to Kaylee when I kissed Ella. My so-called team made up the story with Kaylee in a meeting I wasn't present for. They ran it without my knowledge or approval, against the protests of my personal assistant, who told them I'd never allow it."

Candice was too flustered to speak.

"There has to be a breech of contract in there somewhere."

"I'm certain we can find something, but if not?"

"They're all still fired," I said firmly. "It'll just cost me more."

"If they really acted without your permission, it shouldn't be a problem."

"I've been unavailable. The first I heard of any of it was fifteen minutes ago."

"In that case, give me a couple hours and I'll let you know what I find."

"I appreciate it. I'll wait to drop the news until I hear from you."

I hung up and Scott smiled. "That had to feel good."

"Not as good as firing them will."

"So what's next?"

I thought for a minute. "I've been with my agency since I first started out. My career's come a long way since then. I think I'm due for an upgrade, wouldn't you say?"

"Definitely. Am I calling CAA, ICM, or WME?"

"All three." I started pacing again, trying to stay focused, even though my thoughts kept drifting to Ella. "Inform them of the situation—the *whole* situation—and tell them if they want me, they've got until tomorrow morning to come up with a plan as to how they would approach this mess. Tell them I'll sign with whoever has the best idea. And Scotty?" Scott looked up at my pause. "Do make sure they understand that Ella is my top priority here, and not my own damn career."

Scott absorbed that statement and shook his head as if he thought I had lost my mind. "This should be interesting," he murmured as he began tapping away on his tablet again. "I'll have it all set up by the time you're out of the shower."

I looked down at the pajama pants I'd been wearing for apparently *two* nights and ran a hand through my messy hair. "I take it that's supposed to be a hint?"

"More like a friendly request," Scott said, never lifting his eyes from the glowing screen in front of him. "You stink, boss."

I laughed all the way to the bathroom.

My rehab center in Beverly Hills was quiet, luxurious, and surprisingly peaceful. There were only a handful of "guests," as they called us, including someone whose music I had stored in my iPod. If it weren't for the mandatory therapy sessions, I would have thought they'd sent me to a spa resort for vacation.

I had daily visits from Dr. Parish and joined the other patients for a group therapy session every other day. My dietician came once after I'd arrived and had a meeting with the clinic's kitchen staff about my diet, and my nurse, Cody, came on his regular weekly visits.

Delicious Daniel came to work with me every day like Dr. Parish. Even though I'd banged up my hip, this wasn't necessary— we'd been on a three-days-a-week schedule before—but I think he felt sorry for me and wanted to keep me company. He's awesome like that. Of course, I think it also had a little to do with that beautiful popstar I mentioned who was staying at the center as well, who liked to hang out in gym where Daniel and I did our therapy sessions. Daniel denied this accusation, but always blushed when I pointed out that he was staring again.

I was glad for Daniel's company, because other than my

doctors I wasn't allowed any outside contact with anyone. The point of being there, Dr. Parish informed me, was to get some rest and relaxation in a stress-free environment. The No Visitors rule was because my family was a major stress point for me, and the No Friends, No Phone, No TV, and No Internet rules were meant to be a shield from the whole Brian Oliver debacle. While I missed my friends and was bored out of my mind, I can't say I hated missing all the media attention.

The total seclusion had to end at some point, though, and that point was about a week after I'd checked in. Dr. Parish allowed my father and Jennifer to visit under the condition that our time together be supervised. The visit was basically family counseling—which Dr. Parish recommended my father and I start doing regularly. I was shocked that my father agreed without hesitation.

"If that's what we need to fix things between us, then of course I will," he said when he saw my surprise. "I *do* love you, Ella. I've loved having you back in my life this past year. I know an apology isn't nearly enough, but I *am* sorry for leaving you."

"I understand people get divorced," I whispered, "but you never even said good-bye. You never called. You never came to visit. Why did you just abandon me?"

I'd been really good about not crying since I'd arrived at the clinic, but my eyes started to burn.

My dad sighed his defeat, then began his explanation with a warning. "I wish I had some really good excuse that would make what I did okay, but I just don't. The truth isn't pretty, honey. I don't want to hurt you any more than I already have."

I could hear the desperate, unspoken plea to let it drop, but I needed to know. "Not understanding is what hurts the most."

"Without understanding, Ella won't be able to forgive you, Mr. Coleman," Dr. Parish said gently. "It's what keeps her from being able to move on. If you can't be honest with your daughter, you will never be able to build a true relationship with her."

My dad's body seemed to cave in on itself. If Jennifer hadn't been sitting with him, holding him so tightly, he might have collapsed from despair. "I've made a lot of mistakes in my life, Ella, and they all started when I met your mother. I should never have married her."

I swayed in my chair. Dr. Parish had to get me a glass of water before I could speak. My hands shook so hard I spilled a little as I drank. "W-hat?" I stammered once I could finally think again. "How can you say that? Did you even love her?"

"I grew to love her in some ways, but not in the way you're asking, and I don't think she ever loved me, either."

I started gulping my water and my father turned to Dr. Parish with a look of stark fear. "Are you sure this is a good idea? Are you sure she can handle this right now? Her mother was her hero, her best friend. This won't be easy for her."

"Just *tell* me." If he didn't explain it soon, I would lose my mind.

Dr. Parish regarded us both calmly and then met my father's look with a gentle sternness that only doctors and mothers were capable of. "Whatever it is, Mr. Coleman, you and I are both here to help her cope."

My dad swallowed and then turned back to me. His whole body sagged the second he looked at me. "I was in my last year of school at one of the top law schools in the country. It was a brutal and competitive program. I studied nearly every second I wasn't in class. My life was so stressful. Meeting your mother was like a breath of fresh air. She was so fun and exotic. We went out every now and then when I could find the time, and we had a great time together, but things were never serious between us. We were never in love. We were never even a couple."

My dad winced when my eyes bulged, but he pressed on. "I was shocked when your mom told me she was pregnant. The last thing I'd wanted at that time was a child. I was getting ready to take the bar. If I passed, I had a job lined up that I knew from my internships would be really demanding on my time."

My stomach rolled with sudden queasiness. "Did you ask her to get an abortion?"

My father looked at his lap. I heard his swallow from the opposite side of the room. After a minute, he met my eyes and whispered, "Yes."

I felt the blood in my veins freeze and had to remind myself to breathe. It wasn't easy to do. My heart was hammering in my chest and the water I'd sipped felt like it wasn't going to stay put in my stomach. He'd never wanted me. Not ever.

"Your mother was raised religious. She absolutely refused to terminate the pregnancy and asked me to marry her instead. I offered to pay for everything, and help however I could, but I didn't want to get married. Your mom and I weren't a good fit. We were too different. We weren't in love. But your mom insisted.

"Your Abuela and Granpapa were religious fanatics. They were outraged by the whole baby-out-of-wedlock thing. They said if we didn't get married they would disown your mother. You know how close she was with her parents. She was hysterical. Plus, she would have been on her own, and she was going to have a baby. My baby. I may not have been raised with religion, but I *was* taught to take responsibility for my actions."

"So you married her."

My dad let out a breath and nodded. "So I married her."

I was an unwanted pregnancy and a shotgun wedding. My parents never even loved each other.

My dad read the look on my face and grimaced. "It was bad right from the start. I resented her for trapping me, she resented me for feeling trapped, and I blamed the baby—" Dad swallowed again and corrected himself. "I blamed *you* for my unhappiness."

I closed my eyes against my tears, but they escaped down my cheeks anyway.

"I was wrong to feel that way, Ella. Your mother and I were to blame for what happened, not you. I'm sorry it took me so long to realize that."

My father and Dr. Parish gave me a minute to compose myself. Once I could speak I asked a question I wasn't sure I wanted an answer to, but had to know nonetheless. "Did you *ever* love me, Dad? I know I was little, but I don't remember things being that bad. I remember you laughing and playing with me sometimes. Was all that just a lie?"

"Honey, life isn't black and white," Dad replied. "I did love you, but I couldn't ever get past my issues, and neither could your mother. She held the abortion thing over my head the entire time we were married. She never forgave me for not wanting you, and she would never let me forget it. It always made her angry whenever you and I got close. She said I didn't deserve you. She drove a wedge between you and me on purpose, and with her making it difficult, it was easier for me to distance myself. I worked as much as I could, and I let you and your mother do your own thing. I stayed out of your way."

"What kind of wedge?" I asked, completely unable to picture my mother doing something so mean.

"She raised you as if you were all Chilean. She completely ignored the fact that you were half white—half *my* child. She immersed you in a culture I didn't understand, taught you a language I didn't know. She practically raised you with your grandparents, and ignored all of the family traditions I was accustomed to. We only visited my family twice the entire time we were married. It was hard because they lived out West, but your mother didn't exactly make any effort to see them, either. Most of the time I went to visit them by myself. She didn't want you to be a part of my family. You haven't seen them since you were three."

"Your family?" I asked, confused.

My father sighed. "You have living grandparents, Ella, *my* parents. And an aunt and uncle and three cousins."

I gasped. This was news to me. "I *do?*"

It all made sense, of course—my dad having parents and a sibling and all that—but in all the years I could remember, I couldn't recall ever hearing about them. My mother definitely never mentioned them. After my father left, she barely ever said two words about him except to blame things on him or curse him in Spanish.

"I guess I should have thought to tell you this before now, but yes. My parents and my younger brother Jack all live up in the Bay Area outside of San Francisco. They were down to visit not that long ago, while you were still in the rehab center in Boston. Whenever you're ready, I can take you to visit them, or have them come down to LA. They're curious and excited to meet you— same as I was when the hospital called me."

I flinched at that confession, unsure how I felt about it. "You were excited to meet me when the hospital called?"

The disbelief in my voice made my dad's shoulders hunch, weighed down by guilt. "Yes, Ella. You're my daughter. We might not have had the greatest relationship, but I raised you for eight years. That's not something a person just forgets. I *have* thought about you over the years. I knew you were probably happy, because I knew how much your mother loved you, but I have wondered what you looked like and how you turned out.

"When I came to Boston, I was very curious to see what kind of young woman you'd grown into, and I was terrified that you weren't going to survive and I'd never get to find out. This is going to sound terrible, but I was excited for the opportunity to spend some time with you without your mother around to poison you against me. When I took you in, I hoped it could be a chance to start over."

Some start we'd had.

"I would still like that," my dad said quietly, "if you'll give me a chance."

At that moment his words hit me hard. I heard the plea in his voice and realized that the rocky relationship I had with my father was mostly my fault. I knew he was trying, but I wasn't giving him a chance to get close to me. It was strange. I wanted him to love me, to want me and know me, but I'd never let him in.

"I'd like that too," I admitted. "I'll try to be better, but I think it's going to take me time."

Dad nodded. "I understand."

"Do you?" I asked, unable to keep all of the antagonism out

of my voice. "I'm so angry, Dad. And I'm *hurt*. You *left* me. I grew up without a *father*. When I came here and saw how happy you were with Jennifer and Juliette and Anastasia, it ripped me apart. They call you *Dad* while I feel like I should call you *Mr. Coleman*. Do you have any idea how that makes me feel? I want to build a relationship with you, but I hate living in your home because I am so jealous of your family."

Dr. Parish got up and walked the infamous Box of Tissues to me. I grabbed one and then took three more for good measure. I was about to snatch the entire box, but then Dr. Parish turned and held it out to my father and Jennifer.

I was shocked to see my dad's eyes glistening. I'd never seen him cry before. "I'm sorry, Ella. I can't help loving my family. When I met Jennifer—" His voice gave out and he took a minute to compose himself. "When I met Jennifer, I fell in love for the first time in my life. I hadn't known what I was missing—how unhappy I really was—until Jennifer filled the hole in my heart."

Jennifer blinked a few tears free from her eyes and squeezed my dad's hand. I wanted to be mad at her. I wanted to hate her— to hate them both—but any idiot could see how in love they were. How could I begrudge them that? How could I not want my father to be happy? He didn't deserve to be miserable for life any more than I did.

"My years in Boston were a bunch of painful memories," Dad said. "Jennifer and the girls were so happy to have me in their lives. It felt so nice to be needed and loved for a change that I just decided it was best if I started over with my life. Your mother hadn't wanted me to be a part of your life even when we were married. There was no way she was going to let me be a part of it after the divorce. I know it was wrong, but after that, it was so easy for me to leave and put the two of you behind me. I'm sorry, Ella. I made a mistake. I made a lot of mistakes. It's too late to take any of them back, but I want to make them up to you, so tell me how I can do that. What do you need from me?"

I took a deep breath. If we were being honest with each other, then there was only one thing I needed from him. "I need you to let me go."

Dad's face pulled into a frown, and Dr. Parish started taking notes again. "Can you explain what you mean, Ella?" she asked.

"I mean I need my freedom. When I'm ready to leave here, release me from my dad's custody. I'm an adult, but I'm not allowed to make my own decisions. Instead, someone who is practically a stranger to me is making them for me. I know he's trying his best, but what might be best for him and his family isn't necessarily what's best for me. I need people to trust me."

Dr. Parish encouraged me with a smile to go on, but she nodded toward my dad. She already knew how I felt. She wanted me to say this to him.

My dad didn't look away when I met his gaze. He even tried to mirror Dr. Parish's encouraging smile, but I could see that this was hard for him. I saw his disappointment.

"I'm trying to get better," I told him, "but being with your family is holding me back. I feel like I can't breathe in your house. I feel like an outsider, an intruder. I feel like I'm only causing you all trouble, and that I'm not wanted there."

"Ella, of course it's been an adjustment, but I do want you."

"You do," I agreed. "But does Anastasia? Does Jennifer?"

Dad looked startled when I said Jennifer's name, and he turned to his wife. She didn't automatically say yes, and it stunned my dad. "I'm trying," she promised me. "It's not that I don't like you. I think you're a wonderful girl. I just wasn't expecting…it's been so hard on my girls…" She reached for the tissues. The box was going to be gone before the hour session was up. "I'm sorry, Ella. I never meant to make you feel unwelcome."

"It's okay," I told her. "I understand. I do. Honestly, I don't blame you. None of us asked for this to happen. That's why I think it would be best if I moved out. Vivian said I could come stay with her until I find my own place, and Juliette has mentioned rooming together next year if I'm allowed to leave your house for college."

"Honey…"

I looked at my dad again and tried to give him an encouraging smile of my own. "If you really want to build a relationship with me, that's great. Let's get to know one another. Let's go to dinner sometimes or the movies. Let's talk. But please don't do to me what Mama did to you. Don't trap me. Don't force me to be part of a family that, let's face it, isn't mine. If you want me to love you, then don't make me resent you."

Everyone was quiet for a minute. Even Dr. Parish's ever-scribbling pen was still. Then my dad let out a breath so big I watched his body deflate with it. "Are you sure that's really what you need?" he asked.

I didn't hesitate. I didn't need to. I knew. "Yes. It's what I need. It's what Ana needs, too."

I held my breath and let it out when I saw my father's decision in his eyes. "All right. Let's just focus on getting you better while you're here, and when you're ready to leave, we'll work something out. Is it too much to ask to let me help you come up with a plan? I'd feel more comfortable if you'd let me at least be a part of the decision-making process."

I felt a huge weight lift off my chest. This time when I smiled for my dad, I felt it reach my eyes. "I think that sounds like a reasonable compromise."

I'D ALWAYS DONE MY BEST TO HATE MY APPOINTMENTS WITH DR. Parish, but I had a smile on my face today. After an entire month, I was facing Dr. Parish for my last session in the rehab center. I was being released this afternoon.

"The smile looks nice on you, Ella," Dr. Parish said when I sat down across from her.

The comment made me smile wider. "It feels nice."

Dr. Parish matched my grin. "You're excited, then? No anxiety about leaving the center?"

I'd be lying if I said no, so I didn't. I'd learned over the last four weeks that I got a lot further with Dr. Parish when I didn't fight her. Her questions and thoughts were never meant as accusations. She really did want to help me, but she couldn't when I would never be completely honest with her about how I felt.

It took being honest with my dad for me to learn that. After our first therapy session together, something shifted between us. He and I still have a long way to go, and it hasn't been easy, but we're cooperating now to try and make things work. It's changed our entire relationship.

I was working with Dr. Parish, too, and making progress. A

lot of progress. I'm a stronger person now than I was.

"Of course I'm nervous about having to go back out into the real world. My accident, my scars, losing my mother, and my shaky relationship with my father are all still there. I know it's going to be harder to deal with them once I leave, but I think I'm able to face those things now. I'm *ready* to face them."

For once, Dr. Parish's pen didn't move after I spoke. Instead, she smiled again. "And you're sure you want to leave your father's house? You can't run from your problems, Ella, I know you know that. I just want to make sure that moving in with Vivian isn't an attempt to escape a hard situation."

I pulled my shoulders back and met her eyes. "It's not." I was sure of myself. "I'm not running from anything; I'm running *to* something. You said I need a support system. Vivian and her dads want to be that for me. I want to be there, and they're *excited* for me to come. I'm not running from my dad or his family; I'm just giving each of us our much-needed space."

Dr. Parish gave me a look that I had to roll my eyes at. "Okay, maybe I'm running from Anastasia a little, but I'm still going to have counseling sessions with my dad, and Juliette is one of my closest friends. I'm still going to be a part of their family. I've agreed to stay through Christmas, and I'm going to meet my relatives. My grandparents and my uncle and his family are coming to LA for the holidays so that we can get to know one another."

Dr. Parish's face brightened. "That's good. I think that will be a very good thing for you." She took a moment to appraise me and then set her notepad down and sat back in her chair. "Well, Ella, it sounds like you've got a pretty good support system built and a solid plan—at least for the immediate future."

"I do. I promise, I am ready."

"I believe you are. There's just one last issue I want to address today."

I cringed. Whenever she said that, it was never happy news.

"Let's talk about Brian." My heart sank. "That is a problem you're still running from."

I didn't try to deny it. I was running as far and as fast as I could from Brian. I hadn't spoken to him since FantasyCon. After my father dropped me off here, he'd gone on a deleting rampage. My Facebook, e-mail, instant messenger, Twitter, and even my PO box for my blog were all gone. I couldn't bear to let him delete my blog, so he'd left it up, but he'd deleted all the horrible comments and changed the settings to not allow any future comments. He'd even changed my cell phone number because he'd been worried about the kids at school leaking it as a cruel prank.

Juliette told me he'd gone to the school and spoken to the entire student body in an assembly, explaining what would happen to anyone who decided to leak my identity to the media. He'd brought one of his good friends from the FBI to explain how they would be able to find out who did it if it happened, and what kind of legal action would be taken. Knowing how Big-Bad-Prosecuting-Attorney-Scary my dad can be, he probably had half the school peeing in their pants.

So far, my identity had not been leaked.

Whether he'd intended to or not, my father had made it so that Brian had no way to ever contact me again. I still knew Brian's e-mail, phone number, and IM screen name, so I could find him if I wanted to, but I wasn't sure that was the best idea.

"Have you figured out what you plan to do about him yet?" Dr. Parish asked. "Are you planning to get in touch with him?"

My heart hurt just thinking about him. How would I ever be able to keep up a friendship with him? "I don't think I can."

"He is your closest friend, Ella, and the strongest link in your new support system. You need him."

"But now that I've met him in person, I don't think I can go back to the relationship we had before."

"So don't," Dr. Parish said simply. "Let it evolve."

"But I can't have a real relationship with him."

Dr. Parish frowned for the first time all day. I couldn't complain, though; we'd never made it this far into a session without a frown before. "You *can* have a relationship with him. You're just afraid to."

"Is it so wrong to want to protect myself? Brian warned me that his world would hurt me, and he was right. I was with him for an hour, and look at what happened. I became the nation's biggest laughingstock. People hated me so much that Brian had to lie about our relationship in order to salvage his career. He had to pretend I meant nothing to him—that he didn't even know me. That's not going to change. I don't want to ruin his career any more than I want to have to hear how ugly and pathetic people think I am for the rest of my life."

Dr. Parish pursed her lips together as she thought. Eventually, she sighed. "No, you're right. That would be a very unhealthy and stressful situation for you. But what if that wasn't the case? What if your relationship with Brian could be a positive thing? What if you could be good for his image instead of bad for it? Would you consider it then?"

I snorted, which caused Dr. Parish to frown at me again. "Fine," I groaned. "*If* by some miracle people accepted me and I could be with Brian, then I would forgive him in an instant and I'd run straight into his arms and never let him go."

"The fame wouldn't bother you?"

I snorted again. "Are you kidding? It would be a nightmare. I would hate it. But I would find a way to cope with it because Brian would be worth it." I scoffed and added, "That's assuming he would even still want me, which he probably doesn't. He saw my scars, found out the truth about me, and then *I* was the one who couldn't accept him for who he was. *I* was the one who ran away. I can't even blame him for letting his managers make up that story about me. I mean, it was just like with his engagement to Kaylee—I rejected him, so he didn't have a good enough reason to say no."

I got another no-nonsense look from Dr. Parish. "Do you honestly believe that? That he wouldn't love you anymore because you got scared after going through a very traumatic ordeal the first time you guys met? Do you really believe he didn't understand that you were overwhelmed?"

In truth, I didn't know what I believed. But I was afraid of that enough that I was too scared to call him. I completely freaked out on him. He asked me to give him a chance, and I told him I could never be a part of his life. He probably hated me now.

I was beginning to think that Dr. Parish was a bit of a mind reader, because she always saw right through me. This moment was no exception. She sighed and stood up. "Will you come with me, Ella?"

I was a little surprised when she walked to the door and opened it for me. We'd only been talking for fifteen minutes and she *never* let me out of a session early. "Where are we going?"

"There's something that I think you need to see. We've kept you away from all media this month, and after today you won't be able to hide from it anymore. I think it's best you get a heads up about what you're going to be facing before you leave the center."

I swallowed down some chunks that tried to come up from my stomach. I knew it was going to be bad, but if it was bad enough that Dr. Parish wanted to show it to me before I left, that meant it was bad enough that she was worried it might cause me to relapse.

I didn't want to do this, but she was right. Better to get it out of the way now. I followed her out of the small visitor's room we used for our sessions and down the hallway toward the recreation room. When we got there, I was shocked to see the room packed full of everyone I cared about—my dad, Jennifer, Juliette, Rob, Vivian, both of her dads, and even the rest of my rehabilitation team.

I nearly cried. My dad and Jennifer had come weekly for our counseling sessions, and Vivian and her fathers had been allowed to visit me once with my dad when we discussed the possibility of me staying with them. But other than that, I hadn't seen any of them in a month.

I glanced up at Dr. Parish with a questioning look, and her frown turned back into a smile. "They're your support system,

Ella. They wanted to be here for you through this."

Great. This was going to be worse than I thought. I pushed back my anxiety because if I lost it before I even saw anything, Dr. Parish was likely to send me back to my room and lock me in for another few weeks.

We walked into the room and Juliette was the first to see me. She pounced like a crazed kitten, squealing and crying and hugging and laughing until Cody pulled her off me, claiming she was going to break me.

First, there was a round of hugs and catching up. We talked, we laughed, we cried. Daniel tried to make me do a few stretches—to which I told him he could take his stretches and shove them someplace very inappropriate until my next PT session—and then, finally, we sat down in front of the television and Dr. Parish pulled up a DVR menu.

As I sat down on the couch I could sense everyone's anticipation, but it didn't match my own. There was an undercurrent of excitement in the room that I couldn't explain. "What's going on?" I asked, unable to help the nerves that were starting to flutter in my stomach like a net full of butterflies. "What kind of video is this?"

Juliette flashed me a cryptic smile as she claimed the spot on the couch next to me. "You'll see."

Vivian beat Rob to the open space on the other side of me, but she pulled her feet up underneath her so that Rob could sit on the floor next to me with his back against the couch. He sat next to my legs and draped his arm up over my lap while Vivian and Juliette both rested their heads on my shoulders.

I smiled at my three closest friends' obvious needs to touch me. They were as comforted to have me back as I was to have them. After everything that had happened, the four of us had formed a special bond. We were as close as friends could be, and I knew we would be for the rest of our lives. It seemed like a miracle that I could have my father back and luck out with two amazing friends, and the very best stepsister anyone could ever ask for.

My good mood evaporated when Dr. Parish searched through the DVR menu on the TV and selected a prerecorded episode of a primetime talk show with popular comedian Kenneth Long. The summary read: special guest Brian Oliver. The second I saw his name, my heart began to pound and my breath became shallow.

Dr. Parish gave me one last supportive smile and then hit PLAY. Immediately, Brian's beautiful face came up on the screen. It was the first I'd seen of him since FantasyCon, and I was filled with so much more emotion than I'd expected. My heart literally throbbed with longing.

I must have started trembling or something because Vivian squeezed my arm and said, "It's okay." Juliette followed her, saying, "Trust us." Even Rob squeezed my leg and smiled up at me, asking me in his usual quiet way to just go with it.

I took a deep breath and held it as I watched Brian walk onto the stage and shake Kenneth Long's hand. After waiting out the screams of the audience, they fell into easy discussion about Brian's upcoming movie, *The Druid Prince*.

Watching this interview tore at my heart. I couldn't figure out why everyone was so determined to put me through this torture until the conversation turned to me. "I hear you demanded to play the role of Cinder as soon as the movie was announced," Kenneth said to Brian.

Not one to ever act humbly, Brian raised his chin and puffed out his chest. "You bet I did. I was born to play that role. Cinder is one of my all-time favorite characters."

"So it's true that you're the book's biggest fan?"

Brian's attention faded out for a moment. His smile turned sad and distant. "I think there's only one other person who loves the book more than I do."

The way Kenneth jumped on the statement, I was sure that he'd been instructed not to bring up the subject of me. But since Brian opened the can of worms first, it was fair game. "Would this be the fan that you met last month at FantasyCon? The one whose wish was a kiss from Brian Oliver?"

My throat went dry, but I felt Rob's hand give my leg another reassuring squeeze.

Brian pulled himself out of his own head and forced a smile. "That's exactly who I meant. Actually, if you don't mind, I'd like to talk about her for a minute. Is it all right if I set the story straight?"

Brian had obviously veered off script. A shocked Kenneth Long fumbled his reply. "Uh...o-of course! I think the viewers would love to know what really happened. We're all very curious after seeing that kiss, and then hearing of your breakup with Kaylee and the abrupt replacement of your management team. It was quite the scandal, Brian—even for you."

No matter how much I didn't want it to, my heart responded to the news. "Breakup? What breakup? He's not with Kaylee anymore?"

Both Vivian and Juliette shushed me and pointed at the TV. "Just watch!"

On screen, Brian pulled out his beloved phone and handed it to Kenneth.

Kenneth held it up. "Can we get this put up on the screen?"

A stage tech grabbed the phone and a few seconds later the picture of Brian and me in the restaurant was plastered on a giant screen. The audience cooed at the picture's adorableness and my face turned as red as it was in the picture on the TV.

"She's beautiful," Kenneth said.

Brian nodded, staring up at my face on the screen behind him. "Very beautiful." His voice growled the slightest bit as he said, "She is *not* a fan I met through a charity organization. Her name is Ella, and she's my best friend."

31

It felt as if time had stopped. At the very least, my heart had. Brian had just announced to the entire world that I was his best friend. He'd told the world the truth. Part of it, anyway. I was shocked and instantly filled with hope. Could this have been the base behind Dr. Parish's strange questions about Brian? About me helping his reputation instead of hurting it?

I felt everyone's eyes on me, but I couldn't look away from the screen. Brian's confession was obviously the first the world had heard of this story because the audience gasped, and Kenneth was at another loss for words.

Brian's energy was high when he finally fell into the story. "I met Ella through her blog over three years ago, after I came across a post she'd written about my favorite book series." He flashed the audience a devastating smile. "You guys might have heard of it—*The Cinder Chronicles* by L.P. Morgan."

Cheers erupted, and after the noise died down Brian continued on. "She had this insane theory that Prince Cinder should have chosen Ellamara instead of Princess Ratana, which of course I absolutely *had* to argue with. I wrote a very nice and polite Letter

To The Editor explaining how completely misguided her theory was."

Brian chuckled, but I scoffed. "*Nice and polite?* He called me a pig-headed, naïve feminist romanticist!"

Everyone in the room laughed, and even I had to smile because a secretive smirk crept over Brian's face. No doubt he was thinking about the exact same thing I was.

"When she wrote me back, it was love at first fight," he said, earning another gasp from the crowd.

My gasp was louder, and everyone in the room with me snickered again. My face had barely recovered from its last blush, but that didn't stop me from turning bright red again.

"Love!" Kenneth exclaimed.

Brian laughed and nodded. "It was for me. We started e-mailing back and forth and she quickly became my best friend, even though we'd never met in person. She knew everything about me except for my true identity."

Kenneth leaned so far over his desk toward Brian that I was afraid he might fall out of his chair. "So, you knew this girl for three years and you'd never met?" he asked, incredulous. "She had no idea you were a famous movie star?"

Brian shook his head. "We only knew each other by our screen names." He smiled to himself again. "Cinder and Ella."

The way the audience crooned over that made me want to die so that I could be spared this embarrassment.

"Ella—being the huge fan of the books she is—came to *The Druid Prince* discussion panel at FantasyCon. There was a meet-and-greet after the panel. Ella and I had no idea we were both going to be there. When we met, she thought she was talking to Brian Oliver, and I thought I was meeting a random fan. We each realized who the other was when we started discussing the book and fell into our age-old argument." He shook his head as he laughed this time. "We only got to talk for about a minute, but I was done for. I broke up with Kaylee right after the meet-and-greet. It wasn't fair to Kaylee, and I'm sorry that I hurt her, but I didn't have any other choice. I couldn't stay with her when I was in love with someone else."

Brian's smile vanished and was replaced with barely concealed anger. "*I'm* the one who asked Ella to go to dinner with me that night. I kissed her because I couldn't help myself. I'd been in love with her for *years*. I was trying to convince her to date me when the cameras interrupted us. Kaylee lied about us still being together because she was mad at me. She wanted to hurt Ella. I fired my management team because the statement they issued about Ella being a fan with a wish was a complete lie, and they issued it without my permission."

There was another round of gasps from Brian's audience and even a few cries of outrage. Kenneth Long's mouth dropped open. I knew how they all felt. I was as shocked as they were. "He didn't know?" It seemed impossible. "All this time, I thought he'd let them do it. All this time, I was so hurt." I couldn't believe it. "I was so stupid! If I'd just talked to him, let him explain."

"Ella, you never had a chance," Vivian said. "You went to bed after the news report and came straight here the next day."

She was right, but I still felt horrible. "I need to call him. I'm being released today; that means I can use my phone now, right? I need to talk to him."

"Wait!" Juliette said. "Watch the rest first."

"I miss her like crazy," Brian was saying. "Between Kaylee and my old management team, they turned Ella into a joke. People have been so cruel to her. They've said awful things. There are entire hate websites dedicated to her. There've been death threats."

"Death threats!" I gasped.

"It's okay, Ella," my dad promised. "They were all unwarranted—just people ranting. Your identity was never leaked."

"Ella's blog was important to her and it was ruined. She hasn't posted on it since that statement was issued. She's also changed her phone number, e-mail address, and instant messenger screen name. She's deleted her Facebook and Twitter accounts. She had to disappear." He raked a hand through his hair and shifted in his seat as he murmured, "I've lost her again."

The entire audience fell into silence.

"What do you mean, you've lost her again?" Kenneth asked.

Brian, now unable to sit still, reached for the infamous coffee mug that guests are always given on all those talk shows. The way he chugged it, I wondered if it was filled with whiskey.

"Just over a year ago, Ella was in a terrible car accident," Brian explained. "I was actually instant messaging with her at the time of the accident—and no, she wasn't driving. Never text and drive, people. We were talking, and she was there one minute and gone the next. At first I thought her phone died, but then she never contacted me again. She just…disappeared."

My chest constricted as I watched Brian drift off into a memory and shudder. When he spoke again his voice was so soft, but it didn't matter because the audience was silent. They were completely enraptured by his story. "I never knew what happened to her. I assumed she was dead."

The audience murmured at this, and Kenneth finally rejoined the conversation. "You *assumed?* You never found out?"

Brian shook his head. "I had no idea who she was. I didn't know her real name. I didn't have any idea how to find her. It was almost ten months before I learned about the accident. She'd been in a coma and spent over eight months in the hospital recovering from her injuries."

Brian waited out the gasps of the crowd before he continued. "When she wrote me that first e-mail, it was like she'd come back from the dead. I completely freaked out. I should have broken it off with Kaylee right then. I knew I would never care for Kaylee the way I felt about Ella, but I wasn't sure how Ella felt about me. We'd never talked about meeting in person.

"Plus, there was the whole issue of my true identity. I didn't know how to bring it up when she'd just been through such a horrible tragedy. She lost her mother in that accident and received permanent injuries and scars. I wasn't sure she would want a relationship, especially not one that would be as complicated as dating a movie star. But when we came face to face that day at FantasyCon…"

Brian clenched his hand into a fist and pounded his chest as if he'd been shot through the heart. The audience swooned over the playful gesture. *I* swooned over the gesture.

"There are only two kinds of women in the world for me now, Kenneth: Ella and Not Ella. I'll never be able to settle for anyone but her, and now I've lost her again."

Another murmur swept the audience and Kenneth asked the obvious question. "What do you mean? Why have you lost her *again?*"

Brian reached for his mug again. The stupid thing had to be empty by now. He took a sip of the mystery drink and whispered, "She thinks I did it." He cleared his voice and spoke up. "Why wouldn't she? It was *my* management team who told that lie about her being a fan with a wish. *My* people who said I'd been working with a charity. *My* fiancée who confirmed it and said we were still together. Ella's life was ruined, and she believes I did it to save my own reputation."

My chest caved in on itself. I had thought that, but after hearing it come from his mouth, I realized how absurd it was. How big of a jerk I was for even thinking it. "You guys, I have to call him!"

"Shh!"

The shush came from everyone in the room.

"Couldn't you just call her and explain?" Kenneth asked.

Brian sighed. "I was upset because had Ella rejected me. I'd shut off my phone and driven to Las Vegas because I needed to clear my head. It took me two days to realize what had happened, and by the time I found out, it was too late. She'd already disappeared."

Kenneth digested this while Brian went for his mug again. This time when he brought it to his mouth it really was empty. He held it upside down and shook it as if that might make more coffee or water—or whatever was in it—appear. As he set it on the table, Kenneth yelled off screen for someone to bring Brian another one.

While Brian gulped his second cup, Kenneth brought them back on topic. "Can we go back a second," he asked, "to the part where you said Ella *rejected* you?"

My heart started thumping so hard I wondered if everyone in the room could hear it. "It's okay, Ella," Vivian whispered. "I promise."

"My fame was an issue for her," Brian explained. "She was afraid people wouldn't accept her because of her handicap and her scars. People have been so awful to her since her accident that she doesn't believe she's beautiful anymore. She didn't realize that her scars make her even more beautiful to me. They show her strength.

"She's been through so much, survived so much, lost so much, and yet when I asked her out she was worried about *me*. She didn't think people would accept her. She was worried she would hurt my image—be bad for my career. She was afraid she's not good enough for me, but really, it's the other way around. I don't deserve her. She's the strongest, most amazing woman I've ever known."

Rob's hand found mine and squeezed. "I second that," he muttered.

"Me too," Vivian whispered.

Juliette nodded and smiled at me with glossy eyes.

My throat clamped up, and I'm not sure if it was because of Brian, or my friends, or both. Someone reached over my shoulder to hand me a tissue. It was Jennifer. She and my dad had been standing behind the couch with their arms wrapped around each other. They both smiled down at me with moist eyes.

"Wow," Kenneth said after a moment. "You really weren't kidding before. This is love with a capital L."

Brian fidgeted as if he were trying very hard not to get up and start pacing. He sat forward on the very edge of the couch and shook his head firmly. "It's more than love, Kenneth. I think she's my soul mate."

I was glad this comment sent the audience into a frenzy,

because their shrieks and cheers covered most of my startled cry.

"I *need* her," Brian said, "but I can't find her. I still don't know her last name. I don't know where she lives. We were interrupted before we got that far."

Vivian nudged me with her elbow and said, "Only because you skipped the introductions and went straight to the making out."

"Vivian!" I gasped, and everyone laughed at me.

"*Not* that we blame you," Juliette added with a dreamy sigh.

When I looked back at the screen, Brian was raking his fingers through his hair again. The guy looked like a nervous wreck. "She's taken herself out of my life, and I can't accept that. Ella belongs with me."

Brian turned his attention from Kenneth and looked directly into the camera. I recognized the passion that filled him. He looked the same way he had at the convention center when he'd pleaded with me to give us a chance. "Ella, wherever you are, if you're out there listening, I love you. You are my entire world. You've always said you thought Cinder was a coward for doing what the people expected of him instead of following his heart. Well, I'm not a coward. This Prince Cinder chooses his Ellamara. I choose *you*, Ella, and I'm not going to let you be a coward, either. I'm not going to let my fame scare you away. We're *Cinder and Ella*, woman! We're supposed to get our fairy-tale ending!"

The audience erupted into wild cheers.

As my mind raced and my heart began to beat erratically, Brian pulled something out of the inside pocket of his blazer. I couldn't believe it when he held up the long white gloves I'd taken off for him that day. I hadn't even realized I'd left them.

"These aren't glass slippers," Brian said, dangling the gloves in the air, "but if I have to try them on every girl in LA to find my princess, I will."

The crowd went so crazy it took a very, very long time to settle them down. Kenneth even had to stand up and whistle loudly. Of course, once it was quiet enough, he was still laughing so hard it took a few more seconds before he regained his composure. "I think you have your first group of willing candidates right here," he teased, gesturing to the audience, which made the women shriek again. "Shall I line them up for you?"

Brian smiled again and shook his head. "Hopefully it won't come to that. I have a plan."

Kenneth rubbed his hands together eagerly. "This sounds exciting."

Brian took a deep breath. I instinctively took one with him and held it in my lungs as I waited to hear whatever crazy scheme Brian was going to attempt on my behalf. "I still need a date to the premiere of *The Druid Prince*," he said, pausing to let his fans get the squealing out of their systems. "I want to go with Ella. This is *our* movie, our story. I took the role for her as much as I did for myself. *The Druid Prince* is the entire reason we met. It would be a crime to go see this movie with anyone other than her."

Brian began to fidget again, but this time his restlessness was from excitement instead of stress. "Even if Ella won't come with me I still need to find her, so I will accept anyone as my date that can tell me how to get in touch with her."

"How can you do that?" Kenneth asked over the excited murmurs of the audience. "You'll get a million people claiming they know her."

Brian shook his head. "Ella left something at the café that night besides her gloves. Something very important to both of us. Something I gave her. I'm positive that anyone who knows what that gift is would know how to get in touch with Ella. Even if Ella doesn't want to come herself—even if she doesn't want to have anything to do with me ever again—I want to make sure she gets this gift back."

"My book," I whispered. My first-edition autographed copy of *The Druid Prince*. "I can't believe I left my book."

"I knew it was a book!" Juliette squealed. "What are the two details? I've been dying to know!"

"Details?" I asked, confused.

Vivian shushed us. "Shut up, Juliette. She'll tell us in a minute. Let her watch."

Brian pulled something else out of his pocket and held it toward the camera. "This is a ticket for the seat next to mine at the premiere of *The Druid Prince*. I'm going to leave it with the reception desk at the studio's main office for the first person that can tell me exactly what item Ella left behind the night we met. You have to be specific. You need to know two very important details in order to receive this ticket."

He sent a pointed gaze at the camera again, and I knew that the look was for me even before he spoke. "Or you could stop being stubborn and call me, woman. My e-mail, IM, and phone number are still the same as they've always been." One side of his mouth curved up into an infuriating, irresistible smirk. "Forgive me, Ellamara, oh wise, mystic priestess of the Realm, and let me give you the ending you've always wanted."

The audience lost it again and the show cut to commercial. That must have been the end of the interview—or at least the exciting part of it—because Dr. Parish clicked off the TV and suddenly it was over.

The room fell into silence as everyone waited for my reaction, but I couldn't give them one. I needed time to convince myself that it wasn't a dream. He hadn't lied. He said my scars made me even more beautiful. He called me his soul mate!

My heart was bursting.

"You're going to that premiere!" Juliette demanded, mistaking my silence for hesitancy.

Before I could get a single word out, everyone in the room chimed in their encouragement. Even Dr. Parish nodded. She pointed at the dark TV where Brian had just publicly confessed his love to me. "That man will cherish you and love you. He'll do more for your self-esteem than I ever could." She sighed then, very uncharacteristically, and said, "Besides, he's too gorgeous to refuse."

I was shocked. That was the most unprofessional thing I'd

ever heard Dr. Parish say. "Ha!" she squealed suddenly, pointing at me. "A smile! I finally made her smile!"

The rest of my rehab team burst into laughter. "I don't know if it counts," Daniel teased her. "I think it was the thought of Brian Oliver that made her smile, not you."

Now I wasn't smiling; I was blushing again.

"You're going to go, right?" Vivian asked.

Of course I was going to go. I was terrified of sharing his fame, but he was right—running from it would make me a coward. After what he did on that show in front of the whole world for me—and as many times as I had called Cinder a coward—I had to date Brian if for no other reason than he would never let me live it down otherwise. He'd never let me win another argument ever again, and *that* was so not happening.

"When did that air? It's almost Christmas. Did I miss it?"

"It aired two weeks ago. The premiere is in three days."

"Two weeks?" I asked, horrified. "He did that two weeks ago and thinks I've just ignored him all this time? He must hate me!"

Juliette rolled her eyes. "That man could never hate you and you know it. Here." She handed me my phone. Brian's number was already up on the screen.

When she started to hit the CALL button, I shrieked and snatched it from her. "No, don't!"

Everyone looked startled. Juliette and Vivian exchanged a glance and then Juliette's expression became desperate. "But Ella, you *have* to go with him!"

"Oh, I'm definitely going." I laughed. "But it will be so much more fun to *surprise* him at the premiere, don't you think?"

"That's cruel," Rob said.

"No, that's dramatic. Brian's an actor. He lives for drama."

"It's definitely more romantic," Juliette agreed. "So what are the two things?"

"It was a first-edition hardback of *The Druid Prince,* and it was signed to me by the author."

"Aww, that's so sweet." Juliette giggled. "Geeky, but sweet.

And perfect. We can send Dad to go pick up the ticket tomorrow while we go shopping for a dress."

Stefan cried out in horror. "*Shop* for a dress? Ellamara, don't you dare!"

"Ooh! Ooh! Yeah!" Vivian leapt off the couch and started bouncing up and down. "Let my dads make your dress!"

If I weren't handicapped, I would have joined Vivian in her giddy dancing at the thought of having another dress made by her dads. I loved my Ellamara costume, but I thrilled at the thought of seeing what they would come up with having *me* in mind.

I glanced at Stefan and Glen hopefully. "Do you think you would have time?"

Stefan and Glen looked offended by the question, but before they could answer, Jennifer said, "They don't need time." When she gained the entire room's attention, she smiled at me and said, "You already have the perfect dress."

There was only one dress she could possibly mean, but surely she wasn't talking about my mother's dress.

"It looks beautiful on you," she said, knowing I understood her. "And on a night that's so important to you, what would be more appropriate than to wear something that belonged to your mother?"

I wasn't surprised by the way Juliette and my father nodded their approval, but I didn't understand why Jennifer would suggest it. "*You* want me to wear my mother's dress? In front of hundreds of people, and TV cameras?" I asked. "It's revealing, remember? People would see my scars."

Jennifer's smile turned pained. "Ella, I've never been embarrassed of you. I'm sorry that you misunderstood my concern. I've only ever been worried about your feelings. I know how cruel people are. I'm a model. I've been to hundreds of auditions where I was criticized for my imperfections—my thighs and butt weren't firm enough, my nose was too big, my boobs were too small, eyes too far apart, I needed to lose a few more pounds…there was always something."

The world was truly unjust if Jennifer didn't look good enough for it. She had to be the most gorgeous woman I'd ever seen. I couldn't imagine people criticizing her for the way she looked. I couldn't see a single flaw.

"When I first started out, it was hard not to take every single comment to heart. I obsessed about everything everyone said about me. I got depressed. I developed an eating disorder. I self-destructed because I was insecure about my looks."

Her eyes misted over. "I just didn't want you to feel that way. I didn't want people to be cruel to you. You were dealing with so much already, losing your mom and having to adjust to a new family. I didn't want you to be hurt if people stared or said mean things. I was trying to protect you. I'm sorry I hurt your feelings."

"It's all right." I looked her over again and wondered if she looked any different now than she had when she first started modeling. Obviously the "boobs too small" comment had driven her to the unnaturally perfect chest she had now, but I wondered how much else she'd changed. I didn't think it was much. "You still model," I said, "but you're perfectly confident now."

"People still criticize me sometimes, but I don't need to listen anymore." Jennifer smiled at my dad with more love and sincerity than I'd ever seen anyone accomplish. "Your father makes me feel beautiful, and that's enough." She turned her smile back to me. "Maybe Brian Oliver will be the one who does that for you."

What Jennifer said made sense. I thought back to the night Brian and I met, how he stole my breath away when he kissed my scarred knuckles. He'd told me I was beautiful then, and I'd believed him.

"If he makes you smile like that," Rob said suddenly, "then he's worthy of you."

I hadn't realized I was smiling, but my cheeks heated again under everyone's stares.

"Okay, fine," Vivian said. "Since I can't help with the dress, then at least let me do your hair."

"And I'll take you for a manicure," Juliette offered. "If you aren't comfortable going to a salon, I'll give you one myself. I'm pretty handy with a bottle of nail polish."

My entire body shook as I stood in front of the full-length mirror in my bedroom. My nerves hadn't given me a single moment's reprieve in three days. Sometimes I was so excited I thought the wait might kill me, and other times I was sure it was the fear of what was coming that would do me in.

I'd caught a little of the news over the last few days. The city of Los Angeles was anticipating tonight's premiere. Everyone was speculating about whether or not Prince Cinder's Ella would show. Local news anchors, talk-show hosts, radio DJs—everyone.

The craziest part is that they were all excited. They *wanted* me to show up. Brian's interview had been a stroke of genius. He turned the two of us into a modern-day fairy tale—the ultimate romance. I'd gone from the most-hated woman in America to being a national sensation overnight. I was no longer a crazy obsessed stalker, but a beautiful, smart, funny, strong survivor. The public loved me now.

Of course, it was also genius on Brian's part because it guaranteed him he'd get what he wanted. If I didn't make it to the premiere, the nation would hate me all over again a million times worse than they'd hated me before. So fickle, the American people were. And enthusiastic. Such a large crowd had gathered outside the theater in Westwood where the premiere was being held that the police shut down traffic on two city blocks. All those people were waiting for *me*.

"I think I'm going to throw up."

"And mess up my lipstick?" Vivian asked from where she was sprawled on my bed, flipping through a magazine. "I will kill you."

Juliette smirked as she tucked the new silver and pearl comb my father had given me into my hair. "Brian's going to ruin her lipstick the minute he sees her, anyway."

Vivian snorted and I blushed. For, like, the twentieth time that day. You'd think after the hundreds of jokes that had been made at my expense over the last three days, I'd be desensitized to them by now, but no. Any reference to Brian at all and I still went completely middle-school shy.

Vivian smiled at Juliette in the mirror, a wicked gleam in her eyes. "Brian is allowed to mess up the lipstick. She's not." She studied my face again for a moment, then frowned. "I totally hate you for looking so good in that shade of red. I would kill for your tan."

I looked at my lips. The bright red she'd painted on me was killer against my caramel skin and looked even better coupled with the bright yellow of my dress. Add to that the way my blue eyes popped, and I looked exotic. Mysterious. Perfect for a mystic priestess.

My hair softened the picture. Juliette decided to leave my hair down and just give my natural curls some "umph." *Umph* turned out to be, like, thirty gallons of product. My chocolate-brown curls fell around my shoulders and down my bare back with one tiny section pulled delicately away from my face by my comb.

My new hair comb was beautiful and very elegantly matched my mother's pearl necklace. My father surprised me with it this morning saying that he wanted to be there in spirit with me tonight too, like Mama would be. I cried like a baby and both Juliette and Vivian flipped out—screeching about puffy eyes.

You'd have thought it was my wedding day and not just a first date.

Granted, it was a *really big* first date.

"You know?" Vivian said thoughtfully as she looked me over. "The strangest part of this is how perfectly Candy Cane completes the ensemble."

I smiled. "I told you it would work."

After I agreed to go to the premiere the other day, the first thing Vivian did was demand to see my dress. She offered to give Candy Cane another facelift and turn it yellow, but I wouldn't let her. I liked the way the rainbow of color added to the personality of the dress. My spirited mama would have loved it.

"Girls!" Dad bellowed from across the house. "The car's here!"

Sheer terror had my knees locked up in an instant. I stopped breathing, too.

"You're going to be fine," Vivian said. "It's just *Cinder*. You're just going to see a movie with your best friend. That's all."

"Yeah." Juliette snickered and turned my head so that I was looking at the huge poster of a shirtless Brian she'd tacked to the back of my bedroom door. "And Cinder looks like *that* and wants to father your babies."

"Not helping," I breathed.

Anastasia appeared in the doorway and sighed. "Brian Oliver is so wasted on you."

Both Juliette and Vivian glared, but I refused to get angry. Anastasia was not going to ruin this night for me. "That's probably true," I agreed, surprising her with my playfulness. "Still, I'm not going to look a gift horse in the mouth."

It could have been my imagination, but I swear Ana's lips twitched once. She ran her eyes up and down my body and I waited for the nasty, snarky comment, but this time she surprised me. Shrugging, she leaned against the doorframe, hovering at the threshold to my room as if she didn't want to leave and yet didn't want to come in at the same time. The silence got awkward pretty fast.

I was actually surprised to see her. She hadn't said a word to me since I got home. She'd done a good job of never being in the same room as me. She didn't look happy right now, but for the first time since I'd met her there was no hostility. She was actually trying to make an effort for once. It was probably Dr. Parish's doing. My dad and Jennifer had been making Ana see my psychologist for a few weeks now. About time, if you asked me. The girl had as many issues as I did, if not more.

"You look good," Ana said suddenly.

I tried to play it cool and failed miserably. I'd never had a decent poker face, though. "Um, thanks?"

"You know," she added, "for a freak."

I knew she was teasing, but neither Vivian nor Juliette appreciated the humor. "Did you need something?" Juliette snapped.

Ana glared at her sister, but then met my eyes and a look of determination swept over her face. I couldn't tell what the look meant, but it wasn't anger. Her determination wasn't defiance. It was something else. Resolve.

"It was me who gave up your location that day," she said. "I took a picture of you guys with my phone at dinner and sent it to a couple of celebrity gossip sites. It's my fault you guys got ambushed."

I wasn't surprised she'd been the one—I'd always had my suspicions. What surprised me was the confession. She wasn't throwing the info in my face; she was *apologizing*. She looked as comfortable in her skin at the moment as I felt in mine. It was as if feeling remorse and admitting wrongdoing was a brand new experience for her.

I was glad no one jumped down her throat. If anyone had, I'm pretty sure she would have become defensive and the moment would have been ruined. She and I needed to get past our issues with one another.

"I didn't mean for everything that happened," she said.

I shrugged with what I hoped was nonchalance. "The lie Brian's people told wasn't your fault."

She shook her head. "But they wouldn't have told it if those paparazzi hadn't shown up at dinner."

"Maybe not that night," I agreed, "but it would have happened eventually if I kept hanging out with Brian."

Vivian snorted. "Uh, you guys weren't hanging out, you were *making* out."

Juliette burst out laughing. "Good one!"

I smacked them both and looked back at Anastasia, shocked to see that she was smiling. "Anyway, I'm sorry," she said, trying to wipe the grin from her face.

"Thanks."

She turned to leave and I stopped her. "Are you going to ride with us to the theater tonight?"

She shrugged again, managing to keep a bored look on her face, but I could tell she was touched by the invite. "I may as well. I've got nothing better to do tonight."

I smiled and said thanks again.

"Whatever," she replied. She started to saunter away but then stopped and said, "When you guys come up for air tonight, ask Brian if he can hook me up with Logan Lerman."

"You mean *if* they come up for air," Juliette teased.

"You guys! Shut up already! Seriously!"

I wasn't kidding, but for some reason all three of them laughed at me.

We came out of my room to find Dad and Jennifer waiting in the kitchen. To my surprise, Rob was sitting at the bar. His eyes fell on me and he jerked upright so fast he nearly fell off his stool. The way his Adam's apple bobbed, it looked as if he'd just attempted to swallow a baseball. "You look amazing," he rasped.

Chalk up another blush for the day. "Thanks." I came over and gave him a hug. It took him a little longer than normal to let go. "What are you doing here?"

"I had to come see you off. Couldn't let you leave for your big date without wishing you luck."

I hugged him again, this time with much more feeling. Rob

had a way of calming my nerves. It was all his cool confidence and calmness about everything. I'd been worried things would get awkward between us, but Rob was always so easygoing. He'd settled into the role of "just friends" with ease after he realized how much Brian and I really meant to each other. I was so grateful I got to keep him as a friend. I was going to have to find him a girl of his own sometime.

"You want to come in the car with us?" Juliette asked. "Dad rented a limo so we could all drive her over there."

"There's some concern that she'll hijack the car and make a run for it if we let her go alone," Vivian added.

I rolled my eyes at her, but she might have had a small point.

Rob's only response was a smile and an offered arm. I accepted it and did my best not to hyperventilate as we all piled into the limo.

It took us over an hour to get through traffic since we had to wait in the long line of cars arriving at the premiere. Then, suddenly—too suddenly—the car stopped and the door opened to a roar of noise and endless flashing lights. I looked outside and the first thing I saw was red.

"It's the red carpet!" Juliette squealed, bouncing with excitement after noticing the same thing I had. "You're about to walk the red carpet!"

There was a man in a suit waiting to help me out of the car. It was now or never. I gave a quick round of hugs, saving my dad for last. "Good luck, kiddo," he whispered in a voice clouded with emotion. He cleared it and then projected in a macho tone, "Remember, young lady, home by one."

Juliette groaned. "A *curfew?* Seriously? Dad, may I remind you that she's nineteen and as of yesterday legally no longer in your custody?"

I hadn't cared, but I loved that Juliette felt the need to argue on my behalf.

Dad sighed. "Cut me a break this once, huh? I haven't gotten to play the big scary dad for Ella yet, and I'm not even getting to meet her date."

Laughing, I gave his shoulder a pat. "You'll have a chance to threaten him soon enough, I'm sure." I grinned at the girls. "I plan on asking him to come help me haul boxes on moving day."

Vivian, Juliette, Ana, and even Jennifer all swooned a bit.

"See if you can get him to do it without his shirt on," Juliette said.

"Juliette!" My dad made a strangled noise in his throat and then let out a breath. "This Brian Oliver thing is going to turn me prematurely gray."

I laughed and gave my dad a hug, surprising us both when I kissed his cheek. "You'll love him," I promised. "And I'll be home by one."

My dad hugged me again and had to clear his throat before he replied. "I love you, kiddo. Go knock 'em dead."

With that, I took a deep breath and then climbed out of the car. The man waiting to help me ran his eyes over me, pausing for a moment on my scars and cane. His face lit up in a wide grin when understanding hit him. "I hope you're ready for this," he whispered, waving his hand in the direction I was supposed to walk.

"Not in the least," I assured him as I took my first step toward a brand new life.

The red carpet extended the entire block leading up to the theater's entrance. It was lined the entire way with bright lights, thick velvet ropes, and heat lamps. I smiled to myself when I saw the lamps. I'd tried to get out of the limo with my coat on—it was the week before Christmas, after all—but Ana threw a hissy. She snatched the coat, insisting that no one walked the red carpet hiding their outfits. It turned out she was right.

Photographers and reporters with video cameras and microphones stood along the outside of the velvet ropes, and behind them was a crowd of people so big I felt as if I were standing on the pitcher's mound at Fenway Park.

There were a number of people walking up the carpet ahead

of me. I recognized a few of them, and others were unfamiliar. Kaylee Summers was smiling pretty for the crowd, clinging obnoxiously to an actor I recognized from a popular movie about vampires. Somehow, it seemed fitting.

I didn't see Brian anywhere.

My stomach churned at the idea of having to get from where I was standing to the doors of the theater that seemed miles away. I wasn't sure I could do it, but I no longer had a choice. The people closest to me had already taken notice and were starting to whisper.

I took one step, and then, slowly, another. My joints weren't thrilled with the cold weather, so my gait was off a little more than normal. My limp caught people's attention and the murmurs turned into cheers. "It's her!" someone cried. "It's Ella! She came!"

At once, a wave of deafening noise erupted and worked its way from my end of the block to the entrance of the theater and back across the street until it was loud enough it could have been heard in Boston.

People screamed and shouted. They reached out as if to touch me. Cameras flashed in my face, blinding me. The frenzy was so much more than I could have imagined. Overwhelmed, I stumbled back from the ropes. A man twice the size of my father, wearing an expensive suit and some kind of earpiece, caught me. "Are you all right, Miss?"

I gazed at the crowd, unable to think. "This is crazy."

The man chuckled and set me back on my feet. "No one will cross to this side of the ropes. You'll be safe."

The people on the carpet ahead of me all stopped to see what the commotion was. They watched me with curious eyes. Some of them smiled while others didn't seem to appreciate my having stolen the attention from them. Kaylee looked as if she wanted to shred me to pieces with her bare hands.

"You'd better get moving, Miss," the security guard said, giving me a gentle nudge. "The show starts in fifteen minutes."

I nodded and started to walk again, but when I did the cheers grew impossibly louder and I felt as if the chaos had swallowed me up. I was afraid I was going to panic, but then I saw a commotion on the carpet ahead of me that made everything around me fade away.

Brian pushed his way through the crowd of celebrities toward me. I could tell he was calling my name, though I couldn't hear him over the noise. His movements were frantic; they matched the feeling inside my chest. I thought I would burst if I didn't have my arms around him in the next five seconds. And then he was there, coming to a stop a few feet in front of me. I didn't understand the distance he kept between us. I wanted to close it. *Needed* to close it. I needed to feel him, and smell him, and get lost in his eyes.

"You came," he breathed. When he spoke, a hush fell over the crowd. People were desperate to hear what we were saying. My focus drifted toward the audience for a moment but then snapped back to Brian when he said, "After the show, when you didn't call me, I thought…"

He thought he'd never hear from me again.

He couldn't say the words, and I didn't make him. "I…went away…for a while…after what happened."

I wasn't sure if Brian knew exactly what I meant, but the look of guilt and devastation on his face suggested his thoughts were on the right track, if not exactly correct. I hoped my smile would reassure him that I was okay. I'd have that conversation with him, but not right now.

"I only got home three days ago," I said. My smile turned wry. "My therapist played your interview in front of everyone I know. I was the only one who hadn't seen it. I had no idea what was going on and everyone stared at me the whole time. I had to watch that interview with my *father* standing over my shoulder. It was so embarrassing."

Brian crossed his arms over his chest and raised an eyebrow. "My love for you is embarrassing?"

Miracle of miracles, I managed to keep a straight face. "There's such a thing as subtlety, Brian. You could benefit from a few lessons on the subject."

I'd been doing well, but when Brian's face fell into a pout I burst into laughter. "I loved it."

Brian finally stepped forward and pulled me into his arms. "You're such a brat. I can't believe you made me sweat it out until the last possible second."

I shrugged. "After seeing that interview, I figured we were striving for dramatic. Surprising you seemed like the way to go."

Brian chuckled and scanned the near-riot my arrival had caused. "It was definitely that. You managed to cause quite the scene." He grinned at me then in a way that melted my heart. "I bet I can do better."

I smirked. "Of course you do."

The wicked glint in his eyes was the only warning he gave me before he dipped me back into a deep kiss.

Our first kiss had been tender. It had been a kiss to get to know one another. This kiss was entirely different. This kiss was hungry. Brian kissed me as if he were trying to fuse our souls together for eternity. He wasn't doing this for show. It had nothing to do with the hundreds of people watching and going crazy around us. It wasn't possessive, either. He wasn't staking a claim on me. He wasn't even trying to prove his feelings to me. He was simply taking what he needed.

I could feel his yearning, his ache for me, and it turned me into a puddle of mush. Whatever he needed, he could have it. I would gladly give it. He could have all of me. In fact, by the time he brought me back up and ended the kiss, he did have all of me.

"I love you so much, Ella," he whispered.

I didn't know what was cuter: his smitten expression or the bright red lipstick smeared all over his face. "I love you too, Cinder."

He gave me another quick kiss and then slipped his arm around my waist and led me toward the theater doors. When we got there, he stopped and turned us toward the crowd. "Say 'cheese', Ella," he teased.

I stood there and smiled until my face hurt, but it wasn't hard to do since I was so deliriously happy. Brian could totally tell too, because every time I looked up at him he chuckled as if I were the most amusing thing in the world.

I must have missed the signal, but eventually Brian decided it was time to move on. As we turned to leave, a man on the other side of the velvet ropes thrust a microphone at us. "Brian! Brian! Won't you give us a statement before you go inside?"

Brian stopped walking.

A hush fell over the crowd. The atmosphere turned almost reverent as the world waited to hear what Brian Oliver would say. I hoped, for his sake, whatever he came up with was good. I had a feeling this moment of ours was going to go down in Hollywood history.

Brian looked at the man and then back at me. His grin spread the entire length of his face and he said, "How about, 'And they lived happily ever after'?"

ACKNOWLEDGEMENTS

Thank you so much, as always, to Josh for your endless support, feedback, your beautiful covers, indulging me when I ask you to make me book graphics, for taking over a lot of the "mom" duties so I can have time to write, and especially for loving me despite my crazy writer quirks.

And thanks to Josh Jr., Jackie, Matthew, & Daniel for actually preferring foods like cold cereal, frozen waffles, yogurt, and pizza over home-cooked meals that I don't have the time, energy, or skill to make. You're the best kids a mom could ever ask for! (Yes, even though you fight so much.)

To Jen (Literally Jen), and Lisa (A Life Bound By Books) for your invaluable feedback and excitement for this project, and to Heather for always being willing to sit and listen to me talk plot issues out. (And for eating my extra donuts when I end up with too many!) You all help me to make my books the best they can be.

Thank you to all my friends and family for your love and support over the years, I couldn't do it without you. And I'm especially thankful to my Father in Heaven, for blessing me with a little talent and creativity, a healthy dose of patience, and the insane amount of personal drive it takes to be a writer! Through Him, all things are possible.

CPSIA information can be obtained
at www.ICGtesting.com
Printed in the USA
LVOW11s0544020317
525879LV00001B/33/P